M.N. LASH

Royally Divine

Book One in the Divine Providence Series

First edition

This book was professionally typeset on Reedsy.
Find out more at reedsy.com

Contents

Content Warning

Hi there! So, listen, this page is important. If anything on this list may be triggering to you, please do not read! Your mental health is important! I have listed all of the warnings I know of, but don't read this book if you have any doubts.

-Graphic/explicit violence and death

-Mental/emotional/physical abuse

-Mentions of death of a parent

-Animal cruelty (not described explicitly)

-Sexual activities (including a few not consensual kisses)

-Discrimination

For the Divine lovers. May you go as far as the goddesses will take you.

The Beginning of the End

And so I die.

The darkness is comforting. I like the warm embrace, like an old friend or a lost lover come to claim me at last. It is better than any feeling I have ever had. Calms me like nothing else ever will.

I think I want to stay in this dark place as long as I can.

Chapter 1
Celeste of the Lunar Court

My feet slide from the hard turn I make, my aching fingers grasping at the corner of the building I am using for momentum. My feet thunder on, unhindered by the slick grime coating the alleyway. I can hear her voice in my head already, berating me for my tardiness. It is enough encouragement for me to gain speed. If I didn't really, truly need this job, I would have never left my bed this morning.

I curse at myself for getting into this situation. *Again.* I pray to the goddesses (who I am fairly sure do not exist) that I make it in time. I can feel the wind pulling at my hair, a few loose curls tumbling down in response. I grumble to myself, frustrated with my flimsy updo. I slow down upon approaching the back of the castle, desperately smoothing down my wrinkled dress. I cringe at the thought of my appearance. We are supposed to be clean and perfect. The Divine love to look at pretty things. I am most definitely *not* that today. I didn't even clean my face, too hurried to bother.

I rarely see the Divine, anyway. Servants aren't meant to be *seen*. Nevertheless, my employers won't take the chance of a guest seeing anything but perfection. Not when they embody the word. The usual hires tend to be small, pretty, female Undivine. We mostly work inside the house, as maids and cooks and such. I have seen a few men in the kitchens, but they are also remarkably good-looking for Undivine. If you want a good-paying job in this Court? Be pretty. Soldiers, though? If you are of age, and you can at least *hold* a sword, you're hired. It doesn't matter what the men who have been hired to protect you look like, so long as they do their job. Any man who became decent at fighting could work their way up the ranks, but the Low Divines do have advantages with their magic and tend to make rank faster. Someone in my position couldn't dream of being promoted so quickly. Not that I want to be promoted. I am perfectly fine being held to low standards and having people expect very little of me.

I slide through the small worker's door, wincing at the thought of Ryleigh, the head maid, waiting on me. Sometimes, I imagine smoke coming out of her ears to ease the blows. How can such a sweet, innocent-looking woman suddenly start spitting venom? Truly, it is miraculous. And yet, somehow, I am always forgiven for my transgressions. She will sigh, her face will shift, and she will begin the work to clean me up. Whisper that she understands and she just wants me to do better. She's just...a soft core in a hard shell. Maybe we have that in common.

Sometimes, it isn't up to her when it comes to punishment. If someone rats on me, nothing can be done. I can lose my wages anywhere from a few days to a few weeks, maybe even receive a few lashes. Or, worst of all, fired. I shudder at the thought, grateful I have not yet received that particular punishment.

Ryleigh and I have been friends ever since she hired me.

Well, not exactly ever since. She saw me passing by in the city market one day, fingers reaching down into a Divine pocket, and slapped me so hard I cried. She told me to be at the castle just after dawn or she would see to it that my sticky fingers were cut off. I hated her at first. I thought she was cruel and selfish. Now I realize she is definitely cruel, but she was never selfish. She saw a scared, desperate girl and swept in before I got myself killed. I owe her my life. Over the years, I have developed a trust in her that cannot be put into words. She is like a mother to me, nurturing and caring in a way my own never was. We may snarl and spit at each other often, but we always forgive and forget. That's what family does.

I never took to any of the other maids. Ryleigh has always been enough for me. I don't *need* friends. I *need* to survive. Ryleigh and Irissa are the only exceptions to that. I don't have the time or energy for anyone else. Those two are handfuls by themselves. Besides, most of these girls know me as Ryleigh's second. That means they expect me to be cruel and mean, too. And I usually am fairly harsh on them. Who would want to be friends with someone like that, anyway?

I keep my head down as I finally enter the kitchen, feeling gazes hot against my skin. I gulp down the congested air, desperate to catch my breath. Maybe today will be the day she finally gives up on me, the day she turns me loose. Ryleigh knows about my little sister, Irissa. She knows we will be on the streets in a matter of days if I am fired. That is what I fear more than anything. Already we are in a small house with small clothes. Already we are underfed and underpaid. Already we suffer from sickness and the near-deaths that follow. What more can we take? My only hope is the kind heart that Ryleigh hides from a world that will take advantage of it.

"Celeste"

I freeze at the sound of her voice, cringing. I slowly turn my head, tilting it back with a cocky grin. She makes a small huffing sound, crossing her arms. Quietly she asks, "Irissa?"

"Yes." I clear my throat with the word, trying to avoid her eyes. "She had another episode. I could barely contain it."

She knows it isn't a lie, even if it is an excuse at its core. She's seen the aftermath of Irissa's fits before. She saw me weeping on the ground, begging her to help me clean the blood up between desperate gasps of precious air.

"We need to clean you up immediately. There is no time for scolding, no matter how badly I wish to. You can consider yourself lucky. Hurry along." The scowl appeared and left, replaced by something I had never seen in her before: fear.

She turns sharply, heading down the long hallway to my right. I rush to follow, practically running to keep up. Ryleigh is one of the tallest servants at nearly six feet; a near-impossible feat for an Undivine. I stand a whole foot beneath her, another reason to fear her wrath. She can stomp me beneath her stiletto and move along with her day. Some days I would gladly let her.

"Why?" The question escapes before I can stop it. Ryleigh only shoots me a glare in response. I watch as she kicks the bathroom door open, not bothering to answer. A cook stands at the sink, washing her hands. She freezes up immediately, glancing between us with worried eyes.

"Out." Ryleigh commands. She doesn't lift a finger, doesn't make a gesture. All it takes is her voice to make the cook flee. Within seconds, she is on me with a rag in hand. I wince as she scrapes my face, the harsh fabric digging into my skin.

"Why?" I question again. Typically, the castle is peaceful. There is no need for this *nonsense*. I clean rooms no one has stepped in for months. I follow other maids around, waiting to be called on by a High Divine. I am not unfortunate enough to be near a Royal Divine. There is *never* a reason for Ryleigh to be scared.

"We have guests." She sniffs impatiently, moving her hands into my hair. I cry out as she yanks on it, pulling it down and attacking it with a brush. The tangled mess is barely manageable for someone as unskilled as me, but she somehow gets through the nest of curls in a matter of minutes. She chooses to ignore my cries of pain. "When was the last time you washed?"

"Not sure." I shift awkwardly, eyes falling to my feet. "This week? They turned the water off for a few days because I was behind on the payments. I dipped in the creek yesterday, but I didn't bathe. Irissa has been..."

"Difficult? I know. The full moon is tomorrow night. You know what that means for her. I'm sure she's already feeling its effects."

"As am I." I huff, thinking of the broken home I will have to return to. Her fingers work tirelessly, pulling every blond curl into perfect formation. Not a single curl slips out of place, as if they, too, are scared to anger the woman.

"A quick steam." She hums, waving a small, magic-infused machine around my body. I shift uncomfortably, hating the heat.

My black dress clings tightly to my body since it is a size too small and five years old. My eighteen-year-old body and my twenty-three-year-old body had little change, but it was enough. My height hasn't changed, but the bust and hips of

5

the dress need an adjustment. My collar is a shimmering silver, the mark of the Royal family I belong to clear on the side. The same mark has been burned into my left ankle as a permanent reminder to whom I owe allegiance. The symbol is an intricate M, a crescent moon hanging around it, curling into it like two lovers who can't stand to be apart. A silver drop sits at the tip, so close to freedom but never able to fall. This mark is supposed to be a symbol for the Royals who are known to do great things underneath the light of a moon hung high. Once a month they draw power from the full moon, something only a Lunar Royal can accomplish. It not only replenishes their vast powers but also the powers of the Divine as well. Those of us without a semblance of power get nothing out of the whole ordeal. Sucks to be us, right?

"What's happened?" I ask shakily, closing my eyes tightly. This *can't* be good.

"I need to do your makeup."

"Makeup!" I cry out, spinning around to face her. "What do you mean? That stuff is *not* meant for us-"

"Do *not* argue with me, girl." I swallow, my breathing heavy. There is the venom that brings grown men down to their knees. I can only nod, left to stew in my thoughts. Maybe Ryleigh is a Low Divine and doesn't know it. Surely that quality can't be *natural*.

I can't help but wince when the powder hits my face, coughing as it flies in the air and down my lungs. I listen to Ryleigh mumble about how pale I am, telling me I am *ghostly*. She makes my cheeks glow, extenuates my eyes, and lengthens my lashes. I heave a sigh of relief when I see she didn't attempt to cover my freckles: they are the one thing I like about myself.

"Brown eyes." She clicks, shaking her head. "They usually

prefer blue or green, but it'll have to do. Can't do much about that. Cute nose. The dress helps show off that figure. What little you have of one, anyway. They always like that."

"Hey!" I snap, embarrassed. "Can you refrain from making rude remarks about my body?"

"I think you will do just fine. You're pretty and a good worker. They will have to love you."

"Who, Ryleigh? What is this all about? Don't you think I should be aware?"

"The Games are beginning." Her words are fast and quiet, her back turned to me.

I let out a small noise of shock, eyes wide. The Games aren't supposed to start for another year! And I certainly am not supposed to be participating in any way, shape, or form. I do *not* want to follow some High around, catering to their every need.

"Why? What's the rush?"

"There's been trouble at the northern borders. A few attacks, a couple of deaths. The people want a resolution. So, our wise king wants to form alliances. In my opinion, anyways. Maybe he just wants to keep the enemy close. Trade has also gotten more difficult and our people struggle for it. I don't understand much about that, to be honest. Just a few whispers from some of the girls. The Lunar Court has some of the only eligible bachelors for the Games, so the king has decided this is how we will promote change. We must abide by his wishes."

"The twins are only twenty-four." My mind races with arguments, this one the most obvious. The Games are a series of challenges that occur over the course of a few months, starting when a prince turns twenty-five. The Game of Impressions, the Game of Skill, and the Game of Power. Then,

7

at the end of the three challenges, The Choosing occurs. Some rulers choose to change the contents of the Games, others keep challenges the same in the name of 'tradition'. We aren't told much information leading up to the event. Undivines don't even get to watch, typically.

"Do not question the decisions of the Royals, Celeste." There is that tone again. It makes me flinch involuntarily. "I know they are breaking tradition. But right now, gaining alliances is more important than tradition."

"How many?" My voice comes out flat, sad, almost.

"I do not know. At least six from the Solar Court. I'm unsure of the numbers from the Light or Shadow Courts. Since the Light and Shadow Kingdoms became Courts, they haven't been very...forward with information. Trade with them has also been more difficult than usual. I'm sure you are aware of that, though. The Solar Court has been insisting we host the Games first, seeing as their prince is only twenty-three."

At one time, the Light and Shadow Courts were the Light and Shadow Kingdoms. They sit to the north of us, while the Solar Court sits to our east. The Light and Shadow Courts sit on each other's heels, similarly to the Lunar and Solar Courts. But they are small compared to us. We have never seen them as a threat until recent years as they began posting soldiers at the bridge. Now, no one is allowed to pass in or out unless given strict permission from their rulers. To our west sits a large ocean known as 'The Dead Sea' because most people don't make it far across without coming to an untimely death. Officially, it's named 'The Divine Abyss'. The Light Kingdom gained its name because it was meant to be an extension of us, a reflection of the moon. The Shadow Court belonged to the Solars, named after the creations of the sun. All together, our lands are known as the Divine Providence.

The story as I have heard it is that the Light and Shadow Kingdoms became restless. They wanted freedom and decided to separate from the Courts about a century ago. They allied together to make it happen. It didn't take long for a war to start, a war that lasted approximately six months with tens of thousands of deaths on all sides. They have been independent Courts since then, but never forgave the Solar and Lunar Courts for their violent and vindictive actions against them. They are on friendly terms and have no qualms with each other, but they are separated from us by a small amount of ocean. This stretch is connected by a large bridge right in the middle of the territories, but it makes it easy for them to be less friendly to us as, technically, the bridge belongs to their side of the continent. They have complete control of the bridge and they often remind their enemy Courts of it. Their Courts are full of brightly colored fabrics, and their lands are much more fertile with a wider variety of foods. They have magic infused in their goods, a type of power we have never mastered. The list can go on and on of the things they *do* have and we don't, and it seems that our goods are becoming scarcer by the minute. The land is dying, which means less food. More and more hangings happen in the villages, which means fewer hands to work. Overall, that means we have nothing to offer anyone in a trade, anyway. Trade and communication barely started after the war, and it definitely won't be improving anytime soon.

Our Court is the largest of the four and has the most villages: Everrock, Mightmond, Silkdale, Mossview, Slyvein, Darkgarde, and Newstall. Then, of course, there is Lunar City which is where the castle is located. It sits at the very edge of the town, just in front of a large forest. Most of the trees there are dying and decaying, and the animals with even an ounce of self-preservation are long gone. This has resulted in the city and closest villages having no meat to hunt, making the farther village markets ripe with buyers looking for meat and skins. That doesn't mean they have an abundance, though. Truthfully, some of the vendors are purchasing food from other Courts to resell at a higher price, typically from the Shadow and Light Courts. The Solar Court might just be worse off than us in the food market.

The Solar Court is the second largest Court with five villages: Sunmoor, Mythview, Sunshear, Goldspell, and Dryford. They also have a city named after their Court where their castle presides. The Sunmoor and Mythview villages are larger than any of our villages, but I've heard Undivines are packed into tighter quarters there despite the size. They, too, have woods nearby, but their trees are past the point of death. Not a single one lives on in those dying lands near the Whispering Rise Mountains. However, we do have a small set of trees serving as our border. It is not as large as a forest but still dense. Those are much more effective for hunting if you dare go where the wildly savage beasts roam. We don't trade much with them because of their barrenness, even though they are our closest allies.

Once you cross Brighlow Bridge you will be in the Shadow Court. They have Shadow City and only three villages: Edgemoor, Nightmond, and Rockborough. Though, they do have an impressive set of mountains called Deadsummit. It is rumored that they have a hidden tunnel system inside the caves where they hide the majority of their population. I think the rumors are a little outlandish, but who knows? I've heard it's colder over there, and that they even get snow at some points during the year. Their surroundings mean they have a completely different set of resources available to them. With the bonus of fertile lands, of course.

Lastly, there is the Light Court. Their four villages are larger than ours (Evervalley, Springshade, Oakenshore, and Lightgrove), but Light City is very similar to our own. They, too, are located in front of a large forest. The difference? Theirs is ripe and ready for the picking. Any animal you can imagine lives on their land. Furthermore, they can grow any crop you can dream of. Though they are a great distance from us, we benefit the most from their products. Our large Court needing aid from their small, rebellious one? Yeah, that doesn't cause any tension between the Royals.

"Who?" I finally ask. I know of many participants from our Court, many of whom won't be allowed to move on past the first Game. We want an alliance and it won't look good for our princes to marry one of their own. Those girls don't stand a chance.

"Silvi Merkelly of the Solar Court. Her father works directly under the Solar king as his advisor." The Solar King, Horace Zorander. "As it stands, she would be a great match for one of our princes. She is well-educated, very involved politically, and has a great deal of magic. I've heard she is beautiful, too." Of course she is beautiful. She's High Divine, after all.

"And you want *me* to be *her* maid? Why would you want that?"

I don't like High Divine. I don't like *any* Divine. They are snobby and demanding. They don't understand the Undivine or how we suffer. They are blessed with magic we can only dream of; magic that we *will* never and *can* never have. Some

11

say there were once three goddesses who blessed them as some favor or something. I don't know the lore and I don't care to know it. Fuck the goddesses. We are trapped in these magic-less bodies and are then punished for it as if we *chose* to be Undivine. The Divine consider themselves above us. So, we are mistreated, sometimes downright abused, for their pleasure. Most of us are forced to work for practically nothing. We can only find low-paying jobs, jobs no Divine would ever stoop so low to have. Some Undivines are trapped in a single Divine household their whole lives, never to see the light of day. They spit on us every chance they get, all because of a title and a little power.

We Undivine have practically no chance of advancing in the world. Every once in a while an Undivine couple will give birth to a Divine child. It's extremely rare, though. The child would be considered a Low Divine, which is still better than Undivine. The Low Divine can do simple things, mostly party tricks. Levitate objects, read minds and create mild storms. They can't down armies with their minds, can't destroy cities with a snap of their fingers. They aren't feared. Low Divine are known as half-bloods. Their parents have little magic, or maybe one parent is Undivine. High Divine are seen as pure-bloods. Their parents are born in the High Divine society, rarely venturing out of their Divine status. They are the ones who can destroy cities and break minds. And the Royals...well, they are something else entirely. They are born above even the High Divine, granted an unbelievable amount of power. They have practically no limitations and no one to keep them in check. They have absolute control over us all. The only way you can become a Royal is to be born one or marry into the family. The marriage ceremony makes them equals and gives the lesser half enough power to continue a strong family line. That's why there are so few of them. The ones that exist exist only to rule.

Powers aren't genetic or based off of your Court. They just *are*. Some are more common than others, of course, but you can't rely on your child having the same magic as you. A Low can have the same type of magic as a High, but their skill level will be much lower. It's all up to the goddesses as far as any of us know. No skill, no strength, no worthiness. All chance.

"You are one of my best. Disciplined and trained, you know when to stay quiet, and when to acknowledge your superiors. And you know when to report back to me."

"And what will I be hearing that I should report back? 'Oh, you wouldn't believe it! I forgot to put little berries on her pillow, so Miss Silvi decided to kill my family and friends!'"

"Don't be foolish." She practically growls, getting in my face. "The Divine talk around low-lives like us. They don't see us as people. Shit, they hardly see us at all. They will spill secrets like they're talking about the weather and not even realize how dangerous it is. How dangerous *you* are. Listen carefully. *Everything is useful.*"

"Well, can I at least know what this information is being used for?" I hope my raised eyebrow and crossed arms display this danger inside me.

"No time for that." I guess they don't.

Ryleigh starts waving her hands at me, pushing me out of the bathroom. I huff and roll my eyes, letting her push me down a hall to the left and steer me away from the prying question I am dying to ask.

"I'm not good at this," I admit quietly, frustrated.

"You will learn to be."

13

I'm not sure if that is true.

True or not, I follow her underneath the castle using the long hallways only we servants have access to. By the time we reached our destination, my head had begun to ache in frustration. We step towards a door, pushing it open gently. Ryleigh pokes her head out, glancing around briefly. I watch for the signal, a bob of the head, and follow her lead. The door is concealed by a painting, a beautiful and majestic white horse, to protect the servant's quarters entrance. We must always be quiet and alert when using this entrance.

Our pace doesn't slow as we speed through the halls, eventually entering a spacious, extravagant room. Luckily, I know this castle and will not get lost. Never again would I allow myself to be so careless.

"Oh! Your Highness!" I slam into Ryleigh from behind, stumbling as she falls into a curtsy. She yanks me down with her, cursing under her breath. I lower my eyes, my breath hitched, making sure to follow proper etiquette. Who is in front of me? I shake, unsure of which Royal I am about to face.

"Please, no need for that." The smooth voice gives me a chill that races through my bones. It is almost as if I recognize it, almost as if I have heard it before in a dream. My whole body gravitates towards it. Rising slowly, we still avoid the Royal's eyes. I shake under the strange feeling of familiarity that is weighing me down.

"What may I help you with?" Ryleigh puts on a placating smile, wringing her hands together. He laughs lightly and I can almost feel the way his body shakes. It is so unlike anything I've ever felt before. To not look at him and still *know* the way his body is reacting. And then I feel the heat. It almost pulses off of him, coming in waves. Ah. This is why I can feel the way his body is moving. I know instantly that this has to be Kyelin, one of the twins.

I have never met either of the princes before. I have glanced at their portraits, of course, but never seen them so much as roaming the castle. I sneak a peek, taking in his appearance. He is taller than Ryleigh by a foot, typical of a Royal. His crimson hair is tied back with a ribbon, the stray strands in the front hitting his shoulders. Those strands frame a chiseled face, bringing out beautiful emerald eyes. He has a full beard, curling around his lips and across his cheeks. He is muscular, but in a lean way. I can see those muscles beneath tan skin, a hint of orange hiding just underneath the surface. His lips curl up into a mischievous grin, eyes darkening by the second. I know they can reflect the flames that live within him if he demands them to. It's one of the Royal's favorite ways to scare their subjects.

"I wanted to ensure our arrivals have only the best of our servants, especially this guest in particular. Who have you chosen for Silvi?" Those piercing eyes meet my own and I can't help but stand up straighter. I can hardly breathe looking at him. He is just so...*beautiful.* My eyes can't seem to take him all in, and my brain is slowly turning to mush. I can't focus, can't see, can't breathe around this man. He is slowly taking away my life force and I am happily letting him.

"Celeste." I manage to choke out after an elbow to the rib. "My name is Celeste, Your Highness." I try not to show a hint of fear. From my experience, Divine men like that far too much.

"Celeste." The sound of my name on his lips is almost too much. I feel it reverberate right through me and straight to

15

my core. Do all Royal Divine have this quality to them? This ability to make someone fall to their knees with a lingering look and a single word? "Have you been a handmaiden before?"

"No." I can't stop myself from shrugging casually, earning a sly slap from Ryleigh. She hisses under her breath at me, keeping her beautiful smile.

"Celeste is one of my best, aren't you darling?"

"Oh, yes. For sure." I try to match her smile, but I can't find it in me to be genuine. This feeling swirling inside me is too unsettling.

"I have no doubts." He assures us gently as if we are scared pets. But I can see the look in his eyes as he stares at me. He does, indeed, doubt.

"Silvi is one of our most special guests. So, I obtained one of my most special girls. She will not disappoint." It is as much of a threat as it is a promise. It seems she recognizes that look, too.

"Of course." He agrees too quickly. "It's just...well...you don't look—"

"I am small." I interrupt. "But I am not incapable." That's what everyone uses against me. My *height*. I have been told by many a Divine that I am at a disadvantage due to my height. And looked at by many more like a *snack* because of it.

"Mmm." I receive one last, lingering glance before he whisks away.

"Wow. Oh, wow. This must be important for the princes to be involved. I wonder where Zaeden is?"

"Who knows? Who cares?"

Though I know little of either prince, I know Zaeden is the darker companion to Kyelin. His midnight hair is the same

16

length as Kyelin's, but his eyes are said to be much darker. They say no artist can capture their true depth. That his eyes are beyond gray, sullied by the darkness that lives underneath his skin. I have only once heard of his dark poison escaping from his control. It did not end well.

"'Who cares?' Mind your tongue, girl, before I mind it for you!"

"They are Royals." I spit venomously. "You know how I feel about the Divine, especially when it comes to our incapable leaders." Even if they *are* incredibly attractive and addicting.

"You will show more respect than this to Miss Silvi. Or should I tell you what the consequences will be if you disobey?"

"Of course I won't disobey. I don't have a death wish." I scoff with a roll of my eyes.

"I would think otherwise, the way you speak to me." She spits, staring me down. I finally sigh, looking away first in a sign of submission.

"You won't regret this. I promise."

"I better not. Or the extra money that comes with this job will be mine." Before I can ask how *much* extra money, she is gone and I am left to worry.

Chapter 2

I take two shots, one after the other. I always keep a small vial of liquid in my pocket, an alcohol nicknamed the 'nerve tonic' because of its fast-acting calming effects. The second vial came from Ryleigh, waiting along with a note. She doesn't know I keep one on hand. Nevertheless, I happily take them both. But as panicked and flighty as I feel, neither one does a thing to help soothe my nerves.

I have already heard the whispers, another maid floating in just minutes before. She whispered that Miss Silvi had arrived and to prepare myself, along with a few worried words about this twist in fate. I didn't bother trying to ease her fear; she should be scared of the Divine. It overwhelms me to think about my new responsibilities: the hair, the makeup, the apparel, the cleaning. A buzz is growing in my head and I wish I had another nerve tonic to take. Or even a whole bottle.

Designs flash in my head, ideas to give to the seamstresses. I can see the colors, the jewels, the *spectacles* I can create. Sometimes, these outfits mean more than the Games themselves. Everything is about appearance and who can pull off what. Who is brave and who is ready to blend in? It's a lot of pressure and I'm not sure if I can handle it all. I know the fashions in our Court; we tend to wear shinier clothes with dull hues. Sleeves hang low, dresses are long. The Divines here like to pretend they have a sense of modesty. But the Solar Court? I know nothing of their fashion.

In my panic, I have cleaned and cleaned again in a desperate attempt to escape my mind. There isn't a speck of dirt or dust to be found. I even picked out a few courtesy dresses in our styles, ones that will leave a good impression on the princes. The carpet is now too clean to pace on, and the lights are too bright to look at. I bite my lip, closing my eyes tightly as I wait impatiently on the High Divine. She does not keep me waiting long.

I hear the light voice before the door is ever open. A soldier's voice follows behind her, laughter ringing out in the dull air. It is so perfect and yet so *fake*. Her laugh is so...contradicting. It sounds like it belongs and yet it doesn't. It is like bells ringing, like the wind itself blows right through her mouth to bless us with its sound. And yet...and yet...something is *off*. Something is wrong, something is wrong, *something is wrong*.

I had been told Silvi was beautiful, and yet, I didn't expect her beauty to hit me so hard and fast. When she walks through the door, I know she is the most beautiful woman I have ever met. My throat dries out, my mind emptying. And even though I can't speak, I feel like drool is on the verge of pooling out of my mouth. Her presence overwhelms me in a completely different way than Kyelin's.

While she smiles at the soldier, promising to see him soon, I take in every inch of her. She is stunning. Her body is only curves, covered in a skin-tight, honey-yellow dress. The material is almost sheer, just invisible enough that I can see the perky breasts underneath. They push together in a way that results in some impressive cleavage. Her dark skin is glowing and smooth, with a hint of silver underneath. She is a beacon underneath the lights, her very presence lighting up the room. Her silver hair swoops down past her waist, a popular style among the Divine. Even her wave to the soldier is practically perfect, full of grace. Her long legs shift beneath her as the door shuts, that beautiful and dangerous body turning towards me. Her eyes glow like crystal waters, meeting my own with ease. That light and shiny look is reflected on her pink lips, glossy and plump like the rest of her. Everything about her screams perfection; if I didn't know better, I would think she was already a Royal. And yet...and yet...

I can't hold in the gasp when I see it.

A long scar stretches across her face, curving down from her left eyebrow into her cheek and cutting straight through the eye. It is hideous. As I look closer, I can see that the beautiful blue eye on the left is made of glass. It had been stolen from her. When she glances down at me, I tear my gaze down to her straight white teeth. I suck on my yellowing teeth, embarrassed.

"Hello." *That voice.* So soft and sweet, like a doll come to life. It takes everything in me not to tremble under her searing gaze.

"Hello, Miss Silvi." I finally get out, inclining my head in a show of respect that is expected for someone of the High Divine status. I watch her glance around, watch the nod of approval.

"What's your name?" The tone is soft and delicate. I am butter in her hands. And yet...and yet...

"Celeste," I say quietly, hoping to please her.

"I hope to be good friends, Celeste."

"Of course, miss. I would be honored." She smiles and my heart stops. That beautifully cruel face will haunt my dreams tonight.

"Let me see the dresses you chose. I am so excited to be in your Court, I truly hope the style and colors here are well suited for me." I can only nod, nervous. Straight to business, then.

"Yes, miss. They are in the closet. I will get them for you."

This is so important. She will be meeting the Royals tonight and the name of the game is to impress them. But how can she not? I mean...*damn.*

"Call me Silvi." She demands, that tinkling laugh sounding softly. "Or Sil if you prefer. Bring your favorite to me. I need something with a 'wow' factor, yeah? I have been praying to the goddesses every day to impress your Court and I need an insider's help to do it." My heart flutters at the wink she sends my way. I don't much believe in the goddesses that everyone haphazardly prays to, but I know I will get down on my knees and pray to this beautiful woman if she asks me to.

I throw the closet doors open, not needing to look to know what dress I want to pick first. I pull it out, not leaving room for doubt or second guesses. I beam when she gasps in delight, pleased with myself. The dress is midnight blue, the color of our Court. It is mostly sheer, similar to the fabric she has on now. The darker parts cover what they need to, though. The dress will hug her curves and fall free at the knees. A small train will follow behind her, just enough to cause a scene. Silver stars splatter across the dress, a perfect representation of the nights at the Lunar Court. Some glow contently while others almost burst out like shooting stars. It's strapless with a plunging neckline, dangerous and seductive. Something that will stand out against the typical fashion in our Court. I would do anything to wear a dress like this.

"It's perfect, Celeste! Oh, my Divine! It's to die for! We must get you something to die for, too! I would be one lucky girl to have you by my side tonight, yeah? Oh, how wonderful it is to know I will have you to help me on this journey." A blush fills my cheeks, my head bobbing cheerfully. I know she is just being nice about the dress, but the way she looks at me with that genuine smile and twinkling eye makes me feel *seen*. But that voice in the back of my head keeps coming back. She is so perfect...

And yet...*and yet*...

My foggy brain clears the moment I leave Silvi to settle, a wave of shame and revulsion crashing into me as a result. I *hate* High Divine. Why am I acting like such a fool around her? It isn't just me being nice to keep my job. It is like my *thoughts* are trying to please her! As if she will ever know what I am thinking! I revel in the clarity I feel upon leaving her quarters, brewing in my newfound anger. I need to keep this anger. Without it, I will be a bowl of mush for her to devour at her leisure.

Silvi won't *let* me move past my thoughts of her, though. Each time I finally make it down to the servant's quarters, I hear the soft ringing of a bell in my ear. It is the signal that Silvi needs me to return. So just like that, I turn and make my way back up the castle. She never *truly* needs anything. Just small, unimportant pieces of information she could have asked me all at once. Do these shoes match her dress? What's the best way to say hello? Is the food worthwhile? It is *exhausting*. Each time I approach her, that same, thrilling, utterly smothering, intoxicating feeling invades my senses. I can only breathe properly when I am distanced from her. She is a toxin invading my system, but my body is desperate to have more.

By the time nightfall approaches and it is time to meet the Royals officially, Silvi is practically burning a hole in the ground from how hard she paces the room. I give her a nerve tonic, hoping it helps her more than it had helped me. I force her into a stool, giving her a firm look when she tries to jerk back up. She sighs, dropping her head into her hands.

"I know I am losing precious time. Please, go ahead. Do whatever it is you need to do. Make me beautiful."

"You are already beautiful. I am only here to make sure everyone notices." A blush fills my cheeks and I can't meet her eyes, even through the mirror. Her fingertips graze over my hand and I tense, my breath stopping completely. When I finally find the courage to look at her, brush in hand, I hesitate.

"What? Is something wrong?" Her kind gaze falls on me, tenderness and love the only thing lurking behind those eyes. I swallow, shaking my head. What is it about her that makes me feel so...*powerless*?

"Well...nothing *wrong*...just...I am unsure of..."

"Ah, my scar. That's what you're wondering about, yeah? I understand. Just be blunt about it. I appreciate honesty."

"Yes, Silvi. I was wondering if you wanted me to try and cover it. I'm not sure if I can, but I-"

"No." I flinch at the delivery of that one word, regretting the question already. Suddenly, I remember why I am supposed

23

to be weary of her. "Leave it."

"Of course. I'm sorry, I shouldn't have even asked. Besides, it makes for a wonderful attention grabber. It certainly turned my eye. I'm sure it makes for a wonderful story, too." I scramble to find a positive to this, hoping beyond hope it isn't an offense as I blab.

"You have no idea, Celeste." She whispers, a ghost of a smile stretching her lips. The sound of my name on her lips leaves me numb, an excitement rushing through my body. What is it about this Divine that makes me experience so many new and wonderful feelings? I've always been attracted to both sexes, so it isn't an awakening by any means. It isn't like it matters, though. She is a High Divine preparing to compete for a marriage alliance with a Royal. I am an Undivine. Any and all thoughts I have about being attracted to Silvi must vacate the premises, especially when I am this close to her face.

I have been trained to use makeup, of course, but it is a luxury and not used often. That's why I was so shocked when Ryleigh used some on *me*. Even Low Divines struggle to get their hands on this stuff. For someone like Silvi, though? I barely know where to start. She doesn't *need* it. So, I keep it simple. In her case, less is more.

"I love it." She purrs at me, passing me another wink. "Much better than what they give me at home. Sometimes it looks like I have a black eye when they get done." She laughs lightly, running her fingers down her scar. I was careful to avoid it, tracing around the edges as best as I could. Suddenly, an idea strikes, and I can't help but to speak.

"Can I make it shine? Your scar, I mean." Her body freezes, eyes meeting mine through the mirror. Slowly, unsure, she

24

nods. I try to pass her a gentle smile, unsure of myself. I don't know exactly what made me think of it, much less say it. I'm not sure why I'm being so kind to a High Divine, either. I am just...*doing* it.

I dip my brush over and over that stretch of skin, not stopping until it shines brighter than the stars on her dress. Until it glitters in the light like diamonds. It's breathtaking. I see the moment she realizes it, too.

"Thank you." It is barely a whisper. "Most people see my scar as ugly but you have just made it beautiful. I don't think I have ever had anyone *not* want to cover it, much less enhance it." Something about that sentence seems more genuine than anything I heard from her today. More raw. I watch as her head tilts, the scar dancing in the light.

"Our princes will be lucky to have you. I am glad you were chosen to compete for your Court." For some reason, I *meant* it. Before today, I would have never thought of the Royals finding a match as a *good* thing. I can see how good Silvi will be for her partner. Her face, her skin, her body; how could someone not love her? How could someone not choose her? And yet...*and yet*...

Something is still itching at the back of my head, desperate to get through the fog. But I look at Silvi again and her smile pushes every thought away. I preen underneath her gaze, grateful for the attention she bestows upon me.

"They might fight over me." She smiles, eyes wide.

"I would get in a fight over you. I'd wrestle a Royal down into a headlock if it meant there was a chance of you falling in love with me." I agree with a blush. Silvi only laughs, shaking her head at the image I've given her.

"I can't picture you being so violent, little Undivine. Do you

25

think I can get them both to fall in love with me? I'm not good at choosing so I need to keep my options open here."

"Oh, I'm sure they will have a difficult time *not* falling in love with you. You're perfect. I'm sure you know that already, though."

"Oh? You think? You know, you don't look like an Undivine. You're much too pretty. Truly, where did they manage to find you? Your parents *must* have had Divine lineage."

"Oh? Really? I'm not sure about being that pretty. I am nowhere near Divine levels." Is she…flirting with me?

"Oh, I am. Have you ever looked in a mirror, Celeste? I am serious! You are gorgeous."

"Well, it's too bad you have two princes in line ahead of me as suitors. I don't stand a chance," I deflect.

"Never say never." She purrs with a grin.

"You are competing to be married, Silvi." I laugh awkwardly. "You can't be courting an Undivine."

"I wouldn't mind having a little variety in my life. I don't want to be with only one person. So boring. At least one of the brothers will have to be good in bed, right? And when I get tired of one I will always have a backup. Maybe I will find you sometimes, too. Yes, I don't see them both being in love with me an issue at all." I let out a surprised laugh, my face hot all over.

"Yes, I suppose I can see the benefits of not choosing one over the other."

"No, I won't choose. I will do whatever it takes to make them happy. I must, for the sake of my Court. For the sake of my people. We need this alliance. And so do you." I can only nod.

"Fix my hair?" Her tiny smile sends shivers down my spine

and I nod eagerly.

I use the top half of her hair to make a braided crown, adoring it with a few jewels and trinkets. The bottom half hangs down in loose waves, the kind most Undivine would die for. Maybe some Low Divine, too.

Natural beauty is a trait all Divine possess. The higher in status you are, the more beautiful you will be. Some of us Undivine can pass as a Low, those are the ones who are usually hired here in the castle, like me. But most are not so lucky. The unnatural beauty of the Divine is enough to cause most Undivine to fall to their knees and pray, enough for them to be willing to do anything for just a glimpse of that life. It's the reason many Undivines have fallen into such unfortunate circumstances. They just can't stop themselves from falling under the Divine spell. I'm starting to think I'm more like those Undivines than I originally believed. Some carry delusions that a Divine will marry them, but it's very rare to increase your level of divinity. It can only be done through marriage. A Low might marry an Undivine, but a High or Royal would never stoop so low. They may fool around with us, but they would never pursue something serious. And Highs rarely married Lows. Royals only marry Highs because they don't want to marry their family members. Plus, it is a good way to introduce new powers into their bloodline.

"Beautiful." I manage to get out, trying not to be jealous.

"Thank you, friend. You will be there tonight, won't you?"

"No, I-"

"Nonsense." She waves, the decision made. "I only want the best escorting me around. And you, Celeste, are beautiful, intelligent, and my only friend in this castle. If I didn't know any better, I would think you are Divine."

"I'm not sure-" I barely have time to process her compliment, to understand the implications and her insistence.

"It will be done. You are coming." There is no room left for questioning. I want to argue, but my tongue is stuck to the roof of my mouth. And I know my place. You don't tell the Divine 'no'.

"As you wish, Silvi."

"Is there something...nicer for you to wear? I meant it earlier when I said we should find a dress for you. Yours is a little drab. I want you to stand out, like me. If you are to be by my side, you need to look the part. And, please, let your hair escape that dreadful cage you've locked it in. It looks ready to burst. You're strangling it." Her laugh rushes through me again, convincing me that this *is* a good idea. What is it about her that makes me so submissive? I'm not gullible. I haven't forgotten what she is. So why do I keep giving in so easily to this woman I barely know?

"T-this is my only dress." I stumble over the words, stumped by the strange request. I thought she was being kind earlier, not that she was serious about wanting me to go!

"Go down and find one you can have altered by tonight. Something simple and elegant. Be back before dinner." With a wave, I am dismissed. I can hardly breathe as I stumble back, watching her nimble fingers dig through a box of jewelry. I manage to get a hand on the door handle behind me, wrenching it open in a hurry. I find myself tumbling out, panicking. Dinner is starting soon, and I don't have very much time. *Fuck*.

I make my way to the servant's quarters in a haze, my mind in a panic. Can I just sit around with a bunch of Divine and masquerade as one of them? How can I bring myself to be okay with it? Will they even *allow* me to do such a thing?

A woman appears in front of me, on her way out with a handful of white rags. My hands find her shoulders, fingers digging in to pull her to a stop. I watch with guilt as the rags slip from her hands, unfolding as they crash to the floor.

"Where is Ryleigh?" My voice comes out more breathless than demanding, and I quickly clear my throat.

"How should I know, Celeste? Go torture someone else with your presence." She easily bats me away, bending down for the lost rags. What is her name? Ah, what does it matter now, anyway?

"You!" I dive for a much younger servant, her pretty green eyes widening as my glare turns to her.

"Me?" Her squeak is barely audible. I manage to force out a little smile. She looks barely of age, maybe I should be a little nicer.

"Where is Ryleigh?" I try not to be so mean, but it still comes out harsh. Being mean is the only way to get things done around here, though. The only way you get any type of power in this position. Or respect. Though, I don't feel the need to be snippy with Silvi. At least, when I am with her, anyway. Right now I have lots of things running through my head that wouldn't be polite to say to her face.

"She is on her way here." She breathes out, eyes dancing around my face. I grin, enjoying the blush that spreads across her cheeks. She is too young for me, but I get the same look from lots of people. I am used to being ogled at by Undivine. "I think she is dropping someone off with another Solar Court

29

arrival." She offers up at the sight of my grin.

"Thanks." I send her another smile, eyes lifting just in time to see Ryleigh strutting in.

"Celeste? Unhand her this instance! Run along now, Barley." My hands slipped off Barley, her feet moving as fast as my hands did. She is gone in seconds, her barely-brown hair whipping around the corner after her.

"I need your help." I am not harsh with Ryleigh, that doesn't work with her. But I know the break in my voice *does* work because her shoulders slump instantaneously. She pushes a few gray hairs out of her face, the wrinkles in her forehead scrunching up with her eyebrows. Those scary hazel eyes meet mine and I know she is going to drop everything for me.

"What are you doing here, Celeste? What do you need help with?"

"She wants me to get a dress and escort her to dinner. And she wants me to let my hair down!" The last part comes out as a whine. My hair is what one may describe as *wild*. It has a mind of its own.

"She *what?*" The shock is evident. We are servants and Undivine, the lowest of the low. We aren't supposed to attend dinner with Divine, much less Royals.

"I know. I don't know why I said yes. But I couldn't say no! She's Divine for goddess's sake! What am I going to do? *Fuck!*" I scrub my face in frustration, pouting up at the ceiling.

"*We* are going to find a dress and fast."

Ryleigh grabs my arm and tugs me down the hall, leading me to a pair of double doors I know well. She throws them open, and our eyes are ambushed with a wave of colors. This is the sewing room, the place where we store and create dresses. It is fuller than usual, every wall lined with dresses of all shapes, sizes, and colors. A few sewing machines are set up on tables, and several Undivines are sitting in chairs attempting to work on various projects. Extra scraps have been thrown in a large pile in the middle of the room.

"She wants simple and elegant." I breathe, eyes darting around the room. Most of these can't be described as anything *close* to simple.

"What is she wearing?"

"The star dress."

"That does make things a bit more complicated." I turn to her with pleading eyes. "Please, Ryleigh. I know this is stupid. But I don't want to be punished by the Divine for being insubordinate. Isn't there something we can do?"

"I have some leftover material from that dress. Some that I didn't put stars on. It'll probably be big on you. It was a design fail. I scrapped it almost immediately after I finished sewing." I sigh in relief.

"That's perfect. Where is it?" She digs around in the discard pile, letting out a noise of triumph after a few minutes as she rises with the faulty dress. It it is very simple, something that looks more like a slip than a dress, really. Ryleigh shrugs in apology upon seeing the disappointment in my eyes.

"I got the measurements all wrong but it was too late. Too small for Silvi, too large for you."

"It can swallow me for all I care. Maybe you can pin it some, though?"

Her only reply is, "Strip." I slip my old dress off with a struggle, letting her replace it with the new, shiny fabric. It attempts to cling to me in the same way Silvi's does, but it is much too large. I hold it up at the top, slipping the band on my breasts off discreetly. The dress falls to my ankles, loosening around my thin thighs where it would have clung to Silvi's. My mark is still clearly visible, so Ryleigh won't have to alter the length.

"Can you make some straps, please? And maybe clamp it in the back?"

"Already on it." Sure enough, she is holding two thin strips of material in one hand and a needle in the other. It doesn't take her skilled hands long to attach them and already I feel confident enough to let go of the front.

"You can't even tell I have boobs in this dress. Or an ass." I laugh.

"That's 'cause you hardly have them to begin with." She grins back playfully, already working on pulling the fabric tighter in the back. "Better?"

"Yes, now you can't see down my dress unless you are trying *really* hard."

"Don't do anything crazy in this, there aren't many stitches holding you in. I wouldn't want to test that theory about not having to try too hard to see down it. I'm not sure you would win that bet."

"No dancing. Got it." I start pulling at my hair, grunting in pain until it is finally free from the ribbon. It falls down my back, the bouncy curls tickling my ears and face. "Ready to tame my hair?"

"Let me comb it a little, I don't want to brush it. It will get too frizzy. Besides, your curls are beautiful. No need for taming." She combs gently, patting a little water in to help with the tangles. It isn't enough to fully get rid of the knots, but it is enough to get rid of some of the wildness. I don't bother to look at myself in the mirror or touch up the makeup that Ryleigh had applied so long ago. This isn't about me, anyway. It doesn't matter how I look. Besides, I'm not sure I am capable of truly feeling beautiful. This is probably the closest I will ever feel to it. That is the life I am meant to have as an Undivine.

"Thank you," I whisper, turning before she can see the emotions battling in me. I leave before she has the chance to reply, whisking out of the room and away.

I'm not sure what Silvi is going to get out of this. There has to be some kind of angle, right? Divines don't just walk around with Undivine like they're friends. Maybe I should be grateful. Most Undivine would be. But I can't get past the *wrongness* of it all.

"Miss Silvi." I knock after approaching the door, waiting for that hypnotizing voice. Once I have permission to enter, I quickly open and shut the door. I hardly leave room for myself to squeeze through. It's bad luck for any of the Royals to see her before the first official meeting and I don't want to risk it.

"Oh, don't you look wonderful? I knew you would! And we match! How exciting! Oh, but look at those shoes. You can't wear those old things." I glance down at my worn and rugged pair of slippers, scratching the back of my neck sheepishly.

"I don't have another pair," I admit. We also don't keep extras in the sewing room. These aren't made, they are imported from the other Courts. Sometimes a few shops downtown have them in stock, but it's rare.

"What size are you? Rather small, yes? I, too, have small feet. I know, surprising for someone of my size. Let's see how they fit." Before I can stop her, she has shoved a small pair of golden slippers into my hands. She gestures impatiently for me to put them on, and I hesitantly do so. They are almost a perfect fit. Maybe a half size too big.

"Wow. I guess you were right, Silvi."

"Of course I was. I have a great intuition. I'm rarely wrong about these things." She beams. Something about the smile throws me off and makes me second-guess her kindness. It's sneaky, almost conniving. But that thought is pushed away instantly. She is a friend. Obviously. But *why*—? No. A friend.

"Are you ready?" I interrupt my internal debate with the question.

"Oh, yes. Most definitely."

I nod, turning to escort her away. I blush when she grabs my hand, smiling kindly. It feels illegal, forbidden. But she makes me feel relaxed, makes me trust her. It's an unusual feeling, one that sweeps over my entire being. Yet, something still feels wrong. I still have this inkling in the back of my head, one that won't go away. It's like a siren going off, warning me. But of what? It is so unfamiliar and foreign. So, I do what seems to be the most logical thing to do in this situation: I ignore it.

"You look beautiful," I say in an attempt at small talk. The walk to the dining room is long, and the quiet suffocates me.

"Thank you." She breathes, the bells tingling. "As do you. Keep the dress and shoes. You were meant for them." She doesn't so much as glance at me. I feel nonexistent while standing next to her. I *am* nonexistent standing next to her.

After what seems to be an eternity of silence, one I so desperately wish she would fill just so I can hear her voice, we reach a pair of golden doors. Two soldiers are standing guard, only moving to grab the handles. They pull the doors open, giving us a view of the room inside. There is a long wooden table, already set for dinner. At the head of the table sits the king, the queen sitting comfortably next to him. The two princes are across from her, staring intently at us as we walk in.

No, not at us.

At her.

I feel that tingle in the back of my head when she speaks next.

"Your Majesties." She curtsies with me, going low to the ground. Her voice is so sweet, so soft, but it is thick with confidence and power. She knows what she is and she flaunts it confidently.

"Rise." The king insists, unsmiling.

"You are our first arrival." Zaeden smiles, his handsome face as hardly bearable as his brothers.

"And you brought a guest," Kyelin adds, his eyes meeting mine, "You look familiar. Have I met you, miss…?"

"Celeste." Silvi smiles softly. "My handmaiden. She has been very kind and has made me feel very comfortable in your home. I consider her a friend. I offered an invitation to escort me here tonight rather than a soldier I am not familiar with. I did not want a man by my side when I met you both tonight." I can feel the subtle tension in the air, the surprise. She smiles, almost wickedly, and gestures for me to leave. Ah. *That* was the angle. To do the unexpected, to stand out in a way that means more than just being kind to an Undivine.

"No, Celeste. Stay. I remember you now. I would love to speak with you more." Kyelin stops me after my first step. I meet his eyes in surprise. The last thing I want to do is dine with the Royals. Silvi I can tolerate, but them? If it means I can see her longer, though…

"I can't, Your Highness. Really. I appreciate your kindness.

35

I truly do. However, I must respectfully decline." I can feel my heartbeat in my ears, pounding and pounding and pounding. You don't tell Divine *no*.

"Nonsense." Zaeden shakes his head, glancing at his brother with a colluding grin. "Stay. If not as Silvi's special guest, then as ours. We insist." I open my mouth in an attempt to decline again, but Silvi is pulling me to a seat already. She sits me between her and Kyelin. I glance her way, panicked, but she ignores me. Suddenly, I'm not feeling so grateful to be in her presence.

They make small talk around me as they wait for two more girls, but I look down into my lap for the duration. I do not belong here. I do not want to be here. This feels wrong. So, so wrong.

"Silvi," I whisper into her ear, "Please. I need to leave."

"Relax. You're doing fine. Just stay quiet and you won't bring attention to yourself." She laughs, little bells tingling. Immediately, my body begins to unwind. I feel the nerves as they leave my body, the panic dissipating. Something seems wrong about that, too, but I am too relieved to notice.

"Celeste, right?" I look up at the sound of a voice, nodding in response. Kyelin is towering over me in his seat, the heat radiating off his body causing sweat to drip down my skin.

"Yes, Your Highness." I look away quickly, not wanting to be sucked into those endless eyes.

"How long have you worked for us?"

"Five years." Five very long, very frightful years.

"And we never noticed you, hmm? A beauty like yours is hard to ignore. I don't know how I didn't recognize you before. I am an idiot for not noticing you sooner." I scoff inwardly, still avoiding his gaze. It doesn't matter how beautiful I am,

I'm Undivine. That is all that matters to his kind.

"Idiot indeed." I agree, giving a breathy laugh. I am trying to keep my words short and sweet, heeding Silvi's advice about being quiet. It isn't working.

"Not interested?" Zaeden teases from beside his brother, not as quiet as Kyelin.

"Not really." I shrug before I can stop myself, dragging up the courage to be bold. "I'm not interested in a Divine." Kyelin stares at me with those piercing eyes, and I feel the heat rising higher and hotter. I don't flinch away at the subtle abuse of power. I won't let him see that from me.

"I see." That is all he says, but it feels like so much more. I sigh slightly, standing. I no longer feel that overwhelming pull from either Divine. Mostly, I just feel annoyed.

"I'm sorry, Your Highness's, Your Majesties. I must insist I stay no longer. My sister is ill and I must go home to take care of her. It's getting late and I'm sure she is missing me. I'm sorry to leave so suddenly."

"But, Celeste." Silvi gapes, turning her attention to me at last. "We haven't eaten yet!" I can feel my will bending at her words, and it is suddenly hard to resist the offer. She makes me want to stick around, makes me want to forget about Irissa. I can't, though. I have to leave.

"I'm sorry, Miss Silvi. I must go home." With that, I take my leave. I don't look behind me as I walk out, trying to look more confident than I feel. It doesn't stop me from hearing the whispers, though.

"Silvi is much too kind. I would never be seen with an Undivine!"

"She let the filth into the room."

"How rude. Doesn't she appreciate this? She will never get

an opportunity like this again. She shouldn't have had the opportunity in the first place."

And the worst one, whispered by the king himself. "Thank the goddesses she is gone."

Chapter 3

I t takes a lot of courage to walk into my small, broken home after the day I had at work. The luxurious castle comes straight from an Undivine's dreams; our home is nothing compared to it. I don't mind the house itself. It's isolated, half a mile away from town with no neighbors. It resembles a cabin in size and appearance. It's one bed, one bath, but it's all the two of us need. Sure, it's old and creaky. But I don't need golden doors or a roof that has no leaks. I don't need indoor plumbing that always works or heated floors. I have a working fireplace and a decent-sized kitchen with working appliances. Though we don't have much, we do have each other. That's what happens when you run away, I suppose. You get to start from nothing and gain everything.

"Irissa," I call as I enter the house. One glance at the disaster in our living room and I know it's been a very bad day for us both. A selfish part of me hopes she doesn't answer. I want her to be asleep so I can fall into bed myself. It's later than usual and I know that messes with her routine. She doesn't like for her routine to be disrupted.

"Les." Her deep, rough voice answers. I sigh, rubbing my temples.

"I'm here. Have you eaten anything?" I shrug off my dress,

kicking the shoes off with it. I was beginning to feel mentally and physically drained. I felt like two different people all day long: the real me and the fool who took her place. There is something *off* about Silvi, and now that I am home I am beginning to feel a large amount of self-hatred. I don't want that fancy dress. I hate myself for even speaking to the Divine. I hate myself even more for being a pawn in Silvi's little mind games with the Royals. *Using* me to make herself look better. I should have taken these nice slippers and—

"Yes." Irissa interrupts my soon-to-be-violent thoughts. "I ate some leftover stew. I'm getting sick of that stuff." I force up a smile as she rounds the corner, grabbing a large shirt from the couch and pulling it over my head.

"I'm so glad, Iris. How do you feel today?" I am soft and gentle with my questions, trying not to irritate her. Irissa is sick. *Always* sick. And she hates it when I coddle her.

"Great." She lies cheerfully.

"What's with the mess, Irissa?" I look away, not wanting to meet those shifting eyes. Sometimes they are coal black, sometimes they are ice blue, and sometimes they are a mix of the two. Usually, they shift with her mood.

She says simply, "I was upset. You took too long. I flew out for a second to check on you I was so worried."

"No one saw you, right?"

"Why do I care? It's not like we get many visitors out here, anyways." She looks down at her dirty nails, taking one into her mouth.

"Irissa, we have discussed this." I clench my teeth. She can't just *not* care. They'd take her away and lock her up if they found out she existed.

"Blah, blah. Don't spew your whole 'they will take you away' shit. I'm not in the mood."

"Clearly." It's hard sometimes, to see her act like a normal, defiant teenager. When she regresses, she is anything but normal.

"Where did you get the dress." She questions, looking at the crumpled fabric on the ground.

"Some High Divine who came to win the heart of a prince. I think she was being nice to me to make herself look good, honestly. She was nice and made me feel like she was going to be my friend, but now that I'm away from her I'm realizing how idiotic that sounds. You can have the dress. It's meant for someone taller than me."

"Thanks." She chirps happily, scooping it up. "Maybe she *was* nice, Les. You never trust anyone, especially not the Divine."

"I trust you, don't I?"

"I suppose. But I'm only one person. A girl. Your sister. You need friends. Maybe a relationship, too." I run my hands over my face, exasperated. I start to pick up shredded pieces of wallpaper, still avoiding her eyes.

"No, I don't. You are enough for me, Iris. Besides, I'm really busy. I work all day and take care of you all night. My one off day a week I have to be with you. I don't have time for commitment. Besides, the last relationship I had didn't work out so well." I pile all of the paper into a corner, hoping I will remember to throw it all out tomorrow morning before work. She watches me silently, not bothered that I am cleaning up her unnecessary mess.

"Don't forget to grab the stuffing from the couch. I ripped some more of that out, too."

"Irissa!" I shout, exasperated. "I can see what you did! You

41

broke a glass cup, too! What if you had stepped on that, huh? You have one hour left. One hour! I was supposed to have been at work longer! What would you have done if you stepped on it while you were here, alone? Who would have taken care of you? Washed the blood out? Cleaned it? Bandaged it? I already have to do so much. When you lose yourself, I have to pick up the pieces until you find yourself again. You are nineteen years old! Act like it!"

"You aren't my mother." She snarls, eyes dripping into coal. "I can't control the change! You know that! Besides, I'm in control right now. Doesn't that count for something? I'm tired of having this same argument all the time!"

"You're in control, huh? Then stop acting crazy when you are back to normal! You chose to get your talons out and tear at the walls way past midday. Don't say you are in control. You need to get a hold of these anger issues before they get you in trouble. If a Divine finds out that you have these powers, they will take you away. Undivine don't get powers, you know that. You would be an experiment to them, and once they've gotten all the information they need, they will kill you. And no one would be able to save you. No one will ever know. It will be covered up, just like that girl from Mightmond."

A few years back, there were some whispers about an Undivine child being kidnapped. The mother swore it was the Divine. According to her, the child had been born with powers. Both of her parents had been Undivine. It is rare, but it does happen. The mother said the Divine were scared, that they saw her daughter as a threat because she had more power than a Low should. No one has seen her since.

"Please. The girl from Mightmond doesn't exist." She scoffs, flipping her straight, blond hair behind a shoulder. "Parents made that up to scare their children. I'm not scared, Celeste. I'm bored. Let them come and take me. I don't care. Anything would be better than the miserable life I live now, locked up and not allowed to leave my own yard!" She starts to storm off, but I leap forward and grab her wrist. She spins around, eyes meeting mine. I struggle to resist the power in those eyes, the power demanding I release her. She can't fully control someone by staring into their eyes, but she can get damn close.

"I care," I whisper harshly, "You are all I have. I am all you have. If we are separated, you will be dysfunctional. You can't live without me, Irissa. Your second personality is attached, too attached. I don't know how far you will go to get back to me. I don't want to know. I don't want you to go into a fit, and then come back to yourself just to find out you've murdered innocent people. Because that is what will happen, Irissa. I know I would do the same if someone tried to take you from me, even without powers like yours. Think about that, Irissa. You aren't just sacrificing yourself in this scenario. You could be sacrificing countless innocent people."

"I have no freedom." She finally releases me from the hold of her stare. "I have no friends. No one and nothing to keep me company. I can't even work to pass the time. All I can do is hunt measly rabbits and tend to my garden. I can't even catch deer. What kind of hobby is that? Killing and pruning for survival? At least you get to leave this village, this house, this grass. I will never know that freedom. *Never.*"

"I'm saving up money. Ryleigh says I should be making a little extra during the games," I admit, guilt, shame, and sorrow overwhelming me, "I am going to take you to one of the Followers since they worship the goddesses and not the Divine. They are much better healers. They will fix you."

43

"That's thousands of silver coins, hundreds of gold ones. You get two silver coins a week! We can barely live off of that! You can put back, what, one silver coin a month? And you almost always have to dip into those savings. This house is busted, I need medicine, you need shoes. We don't have anything to trade. Nothing we are willing to give, anyway. How can you expect to do that, Celeste? It's never going to happen. I might as well die and save us both the trouble!" Her face is red with rage, her voice rising louder and louder. I don't flinch away from her, don't back down. Instead, I growl. I pull out that growl from a deep place in my throat, trying to communicate with that beast inside of her. Trying to warn it to stop teasing the beast that is inside me, too.

"Don't ever say that again." I cry, shaking her roughly. She jerks away from me, taking two steps back. I can see the fight in her eyes, and the need to argue her point. But I can also see her strength waning. She only has thirty minutes left.

I bark out, "Go lay down. And don't leave that room!"

She flees the room, slamming the door to the bedroom behind her. I fall to the ground, face in my hands as the tears begin to fall. I don't want her to feel like an animal trapped in a cage, but how else am I supposed to take care of her? The powers she possesses…they are detrimental to her health. The transformations are normal enough, as is the strength. But the personality change? After midnight, she is no longer the sister I currently know. She becomes the sister I knew at age four, maybe five. A *child*. A child with no knowledge of where we are now, where her mother is, why I'm so old, or who I know her to be. She has no control over her powers, has no control over her anger. We have worked for years to manage it, to get her in control again. But once midnight hits she goes twelve hours without that control, without any idea what she did while she was gone. That's why I lock her up in this house. She is dangerous. Maybe not to me, but she is to others. What I wouldn't give to let her see the world, to have friends, to meet someone and fall in love. But I can't endanger other people, and I can't endanger her. Why doesn't she understand? Why does it have to be like this?

If there are real goddesses who blessed the Divine, then they have a cruel sense of humor.

I toss and turn all night, as usual. I can hear Irissa screaming and the torturous pain she is enduring. I've listened to this so often that I can tell when the talons come out, retract, come out, retract. The more she does it, the less painful it is. When she is back to normal, it doesn't hurt at all. But it isn't always like that. They bleed, at first. Tearing through layers of muscle and skin isn't painless or bloodless, especially when your mind and body feel like it's the first time all over again. I can hear her crying, the screams lessening. I can hear the skin tear off her back as it rips open, allowing an enormous pair of wings to sprout from between her shoulder blades. Then I hear her fall to her knees, her tiny, child-like voice crying out. It's horrible to listen to. It gives me nightmares constantly, though I know I have it better than her. I used to try and sit with her when it happened, to hold her hand through the pain. But she always hurt me, scratched me deep enough to need stitches, or gave me concussions after a good toss across the room. I didn't give up, though. She is the one who gave up for me. She refuses to let me in her room, refuses to let me see her like that anymore. Not until morning when the transformations have finally settled underneath her skin.

The full moon is a hard time for her. For most Lunar Court Divine, the moon is helpful. The Royals boost their powers, which usually means big parties and even bigger shows of power. But as a child with no control over her powers, the full moon does nothing for Irissa. Mostly, it makes it worse. All that power being enhanced in what her brain believes to be a small body? It is too much. It makes the transformations more frequent and more extreme.

I cry as I listen to her. It's hardly bearable. The voice of a child calling out, screaming my name. It is torturous and heartbreaking knowing there isn't anything I can do. I try not to make any noise, try not to call out her name. If she knows I'm here, it gets worse. Some days she tears down the door. Others she tears into me. By the time the sun rises, I've only managed a few hours of sleep total. Irissa didn't sleep any. She usually naps after breakfast once I've left for work. I hate leaving her like this. I feel like I'm leaving a child. But she always falls asleep fast and doesn't wake until past midday. And who could I get to watch her, anyway? No one who wouldn't turn her in for a bit of coin, that's for sure.

I groan against the hard floor, pushing myself up. The couch is torn to pieces so I can't sleep on it any longer. Besides, sleeping on the floor feels like a punishment and that's what I need. How can I be nice and pain-free while my sister screeches in the next room? No, I need this hard floor. I need to feel like she is getting revenge even though I know she wouldn't want that. I need to be *punished*.

Standing slowly, I tip-toe into the bathroom. I ease the water on, hoping it will be warm today. It isn't. I undress as the small tub fills, grabbing a rag and soap. Ryleigh was right yesterday about me needing to bathe. I step in quietly, sinking down and letting myself be doused in cold water. I keep telling myself I deserve it, that this tub could be filled with ice and it still wouldn't be enough. I sit like that for ten minutes before moving, scrubbing harsher than necessary to get the grime off. And when I am done and have patted myself dry, I attack my hair with a brush. It hurts, but I ignore it. Then I put the usual tiny uniform on, staring down at my scarred ankle. I am grateful Irissa doesn't have a matching one.

I open the door slowly, glancing out. Irissa had been quiet for over an hour, so I assume she finally fell asleep. I make my way to the kitchen, warming up a bowl of stew. It is the same thing I've eaten every meal for the past three days. I eat it anyway, though. It is all we have. I was docked a silver coin last week because someone reported me for being late three days in a row. Divine-loving bitch. If I find out which one of those mangy maids ratted on me, I will-

"Les? Les, where you go?"

"I am about to go to work." I smile as Irissa walks into the room, watching me put my bowl and spoon in the sink. "I will be back soon. I promise." I turn to look at her, frowning. Her wings are at full attention, the feathers glistening in the sunlight that streams through the window. They are the color of snow, and their touch is soft, warm, and sensitive. The muscle that controls them flexes upon my gaze, a sign of her annoyance. When she lifts her hand to point at me, her talons are elongated and blood drips from her fingertips. Her blue eyes turn dark, and I flinch before she even begins speaking.

"Work? No work! You stay! You stay with Irissa!"

"We have talked about this, Iris. I have to work, okay? I'm going to be late." I sit in a chair to pull my slippers on, avoiding the glare she is sending my way.

"We no talk! You no listen! You stay." Each word is a threat, each sound a hiss. She spits in my direction. The signs point to a tantrum on the horizon.

"No." I stand, hands on hips.

"Yes." She cries, and I duck as a bowl shatters against the wall behind me. I hear another bang as I crouch low, the sound of something shattering following. I sigh, standing upright.

"Come, Iris. Let's lay down together, hmm? You seem tired." Irissa nods, wiping tears off her cheeks. I gently take her hand, leading her to the sink first. Her talons sink in and I wash the blood from her hands, then run a wet rag across her back once the wings are gone.

We make our way to her broken bedroom and I gently lay her on the torn mattress. She slinks down with a sigh, eyes closing. She reaches for my hand, holding me tightly. I wait and watch as her chest rises and falls, the time slowly ticking away. Luckily, it doesn't take much for her to be in a deep sleep. I cover her with a blanket, one of the last ones still intact. I kiss her head softly, pulling my hand away. Once I reach her doorway, I send one last, lingering look before shutting the door behind me and leaving for work.

To make it to work, I have to ride on a cart full of food and other goods heading for the castle. Every day he takes a shipment, and every day he waits for me before leaving. Goddess what a blessing that is on days like this.

"Ho, Darius." I smile once I reach the cart, patting the old man on the back upon my approach.

"Late." He grunts, gesturing at the seat beside him.

"I've been later." I crawl up next to him.

"Mmm." As grumpy as he seems, he still hands me an apple.

"My favorite." I grin, not hesitating. "Thanks, old man."

"Mmm."

I knock on the door gently, shifting my weight from one foot to the other. I slip in discreetly once her voice calls out, barely making a noise. I have become well-practiced in that art.

"Miss Silvi." I smile, a feeling of comfort instantly washing over me. The tingle in my brain appears, too.

"Oh, Celeste! My friend! Am I glad to see you!" She leaps from the bed, her right palm against her forehead.

"Oh?" I try to sound casual, not too intrigued.

"I need advice, Les. Real advice."

"Oh, I'm not sure I'm the best person to seek out for advice. I'm just a servant, Silvi." What advice could I possibly offer her?

"Shush." She waves a hand dismissively. "I'm nervous about the full moon tonight. I don't know what to expect. I'm in a new place with new people. My people are the most powerful when the sun is high, but we don't have a ritual with a specific day or time like the Lunar Court. I just…am I going to be caught up in all that power? Will I be in any danger?" The way she asks it doesn't make it seem like she is worried at all.

"Oh, no! Of course not, Silvi. When the Lunar Divines have their powers at full strength, it means much more than just using power. They feel it in their whole bodies, they resonate with others from our Court. A lot of weddings take place on the full moon because it is believed the bond will be stronger.

49

It's not about power, you see. It's more about the feeling, the control, the intensity. You aren't in harm's way. Unless you are allergic to parties, then I might stay away."

"Can't you tell me more, Les? What do the princes do on this day? If not abuse the power, then what?" I hesitate at the questions, unsure of what I should divulge. It's no secret that our Royals perform a ritual on the full moon, but it isn't common knowledge as to what happens there. It's an invite-only ordeal.

"Oh, nothing, really." I decide on. Her eyes squint, a long index finger curling. I barely registered the finger curl, along with the sudden sharp look in her eye. I am distracted by the overwhelming feelings stirring to life inside me. Everything in me wants to tell her. She is my best friend, one of my only friends. I can trust her. Why would I want to hide anything from her? She would never do anything to hurt me. The feeling is so powerful, so overwhelming, I *have* to give in.

"Tell me." She begs in a voice laced with sweetness and innocence. So, I spill.

"They always have a huge party at midnight, and put on a good show for the ritual. I don't know where. I've never seen it, just heard the rumors. A lot of the soldiers and the trainees attend to demonstrate loyalty. One female is invited every month to be a part of the ritual. Anyone else is just there for the after party. I've heard they have drinks that will make you laugh until you pee yourself and food that will never fill you. Everyone dances and searches for a partner. No one can resist the draw of the moon pulling them to a specific partner for the night. That's how some people find their true love." It is beautiful to think about the moon helping you find your life partner. Helping you not only have a good night but a wonderful life. And the powerful magic that fills the air...

"I can find out the location," she says excitedly, "Hold on." She walks to the door, popping it open. She waves a hand down the hall, a beautiful smile plastered onto her face. I hear footsteps, accompanied by hard boots slapping down onto the tile. I freeze, panicked. Which soldier has she called?

"Hello, darling. I just had a quick question. You can help me, right?"

"Of course." His voice is robotic, but I don't recognize it. I take a step back, frightened. Why does he sound like that? "Where are the princes having their little party tonight? I would love to take part in the ritual!"

"On the other side of the lake, by the boat dock. But you can't be a part of the ritual, miss. They already have a female participant for tonight."

"Thank you. You may return to your post." He walks away at her dismissal, his retreating footsteps echoing down the hall. Part of me knows this is cause for alarm, the other part is relaxed and trusting. The two sides fight inside my mind, my head pounding at the effort. My eyes twitch a few times, my head shaking as I try to concentrate on a singular thought.

"Isn't that wonderful, Celeste! Now we can go! Maybe we can see it from one of the balconies on the upper floor, though, if not? You have to come with me! As my only friend, I insist." She smiles, white teeth sparkling. I find the courage to shake my head furiously. There is no way I am going to an event crawling with Divine. Not even for her.

"No, Silvi. I have something to do tonight. I can't go. I'm sorry, really. Thank you for the offer." I feel that overwhelming trust crashing into my body, alarms blaring in my head. I fight against the feeling. It doesn't matter how much I trust her, or how badly she wants me to go. I have to be home with Irissa. This is her worst night of the month. If I am not there…

"Oh, why not? We would have so much fun together." Her tone is sultry, her hand reaching out to touch my arm softly. I gasp at the touch, a rush of…of…*giddiness* running through me. I laugh, suddenly beyond happy. She laughs along with me, nodding as if to say *See? I told you!*

"Oh, I can't." I giggle. "Honestly, Silvi!" She squints her eyes, and my rush is gone. Suddenly, I am terrified.

"What are you doing tonight? You may be in trouble if you don't tell me. Your sister may be in trouble." I tremble, shaking my head. No. That can't be true. She is my friend, though. I trust her. For some, unbelievable reason, I trust her. She must be right. She would never lie to me.

"Irissa." I gasp out, clawing at my treacherous throat. I can tell I am leaving scratches, but I can't seem to stop myself.

"Who's Irissa? A lover?" Why does she sound so…jealous?

"No." I claw at my throat more, hissing in pain. "My sister. She needs me. Every night she changes. Full moons are awful. The wings and the talons hurt her. It's so painful. She screams all night. I wish I could hold her. My scars, so many scars. She is alone and needs my help. I have to be with her. Must go to her." I scream at the end, the words too painful to admit. My hands wrap around my throat. Why did I say that? How could I betray Irissa like that? For so long I have hidden her and now I've ruined everything for a Divine I barely know. Now she will be taken from me. "Take her, take her, take her!" The words are ripped from my throat, each one more painful than the last.

"Interesting. How very interesting. A Low, maybe? And yet,

you are Undivine. Half-sister is possible. But those powers seem a little strong, not typical of a Low. They can never make changes like that. Hmm. How very strange indeed." She pauses, gripping my arm suddenly. I jerk back, trying to pull free. I can feel the flashbacks approaching, my heart rate accelerating. I close my eyes, feeling another Divine's disgusting hands on me instead. I hear the laughter, the sound of a belt hitting skin, and the sound of my screams for help that never came.

Silvi reaches out for me again, desperate to make contact. I can see it in her eyes; she is scared to let me go. I take one step back, and she takes another forward. How can I try to escape a Divine? I'm not sure, but I am going to try. I can see the moment it clicks in her mind, can see the wheels turning. She knows I'm ready to flee. So, before I can, she is going to make sure I stay.

My body begins to spin, but she is faster. Her body makes contact with mine, practically a tackle. We both fall to the ground, her hair flying wildly around us. Her hand cups the back of my head, and we go down, down, down. The hand prevents me from getting hurt, softening the blow. A soft gasp leaves my lips, my eyes widening in surprise. And slowly, she meets my gaze.

Everything changes.

How could I have not seen it before? She is so *beautiful*. She is beyond words. Why was I ever scared of her? And her *hair*. Oh, her hair. It glistens like a drop of rain on a blade of glass. It is *iridescent*. I can't help myself, reaching out to twist a strand around my fingers. It is so, so soft. And she is so…so…*perfect*.

My fingers graze her cheeks, a blush forming across my

own. I'm just an Undivine maid. She can never feel the same way about me. But those eyes…the way she looks at me…it makes me feel hopeful. I definitely shouldn't leave. Why did I want to leave anyway? She is all I will ever need.

Her lips are coming closer, and I can imagine the kiss now. I can practically feel it. And with that imaginary kiss comes this certainty, something deep within me shouting out about my stupidity for ever doubting her. She would *never* hurt me.

It's so overwhelming. My feelings are too much. My heart is on fire. It hurts, it hurts, it hurts. *She* hurts.

It's as if Silvi can hear my thoughts, though, and is ready to prove me wrong. I barely notice as her hand comes out, slapping down. I barely feel it. No, the pain I feel comes from her words.

"Snap out of it, Celeste. Goddess, I'm so sorry. I used too much. *Snap out of it!*"

Something inside me rumbles, like a wave rolling and preparing to crash. That same something does, indeed, snap. It snaps like a vicious dog who has been let off her leash. It roars to life in me, ready to bite. And I can feel this small tendril inside me, like a rope, being gnawed in half. And when it finally comes undone, my mind becomes my own again. It feels like the wave has finally crested, washing anything and everything in my mind away. Clearing all of these crazy thoughts out of my mind.

"No." I screech, kicking away. I kick out as hard as I can, desperate to get away. She tightens her grip, face hardening.

"Relax, Celeste! Relax!" Silvi is much calmer than I am, a panic attack rising. Tears run down my face, fear all over my features. I know what High Divines are capable of. I know I am her prey. So, I fight. I fight with body and mind, hands scratching at every surface as I beg my unconscious not to give in. Beg it to not let her win. I have someone waiting for me at home. Someone who needs me. *A Divine will not kill me* I vow.

Silvi's beautiful eyes widen as I fight. And just like that, I know. She knows I know. She has a very unique power, one I should've considered yesterday when I first began questioning these intense feelings. Mind powers. They are rare among the Divine and she is strong. She has been inserting emotions into my mind, placing thoughts there. She has been making me feel relaxed, making me think I trust her. That's why I have felt so at war with myself the past two days. She is controlling me. She can force me into submission with a flick of her slender finger. She has been doing so since yesterday. Her powers are strong against the Lows and the Undivine, probably against Highs, too. They won't work on the Royals, but if she becomes one...well, I can't let myself think that far. I have to keep fighting now or die trying.

"How are you resisting me." She snarls, the sweet demeanor falling. I spit at her, but I miss and not a drop of saliva lands on her. She cries out, jerking back. It is just enough to distract her, her hold loosening. I jerk away, stumbling back and using the wall to pull myself up. Fumbling around for the door.

"No! No, Celeste, I'm sorry! Look, this is the only way I know how to do things. Please, don't be scared. I could tell you didn't like me the moment I laid eyes on you. I just wanted you to be my friend. Maybe...maybe more. Genuinely. Please."

"You just forced me to tell my deepest secret." I spit out, amazed at the audacity she has to say *this is the only way she knows how to make friends*. "One that I have kept for a long time.

55

That's not something *friends* do. You can't make someone like you. Trust you. That's just cruel to use your powers on an Undivine like that. Did you ever stop and think that that might be why I don't like your kind?"

"Please." She begs, head falling into her hands. "I just...I don't know anyone here. And you're an Undivine so I thought at least I would have someone around me who would be nice. But I could feel it. You would have been nice, but it wouldn't have been real. And if it already wasn't going to be real then why couldn't I just make you act the way I wanted you to? Feel the things I wanted you to feel? Goddess, look at yourself, Celeste. You're beautiful and sweet and so helpful. I know it wasn't right. I'm sorry. Everyone in my Court is scared of me. I thought I could start over here with someone who wasn't my competition. *I'm sorry.* Please, let me make it up to you. Let me help with your sister."

"How am I supposed to trust a word you say? How am I supposed to believe anything that comes from you after what you just did? The answer is *no.*"

"But-"

"I said no, Silvi. I don't want you anywhere near my sister. I don't want you talking *to* her or talking *about* her. End of discussion." My chest heaves as I try to keep my panting hidden. I shouldn't have talked to a Divine like that. Especially not a High. They can hang me for it. But it's my *sister.*

"Will you accept my apology, at least? Please?" I don't feel that push of her power, the rush that keeps overtaking my body. The feeling of something foreign inside me that does not belong. I can see a hardness in her eyes, though. A decision being made. I take a shaky breath, thinking it through. No matter what, I am stuck with her. No way would Ryleigh

56

let me exchange her for another High. Plus, since she has introduced me to the Royals, it will be suspicious of me to change things up. They would investigate. They would find out about Irissa. And do I want another poor Undivine stuck with her, not knowing and not able to keep her out?

"I accept." I breathe finally, glancing her up and down dismissively. Then, I twist the handle and flee. Already, I am forming a plan. I will pretend to understand her motives, pretend to be her friend, even. But I will keep fighting. If the scratches up and down my arms prove anything, they prove I can put up a fight. I will not let her in my mind anymore. I will not let a Divine have control over me. Not ever again.

I run as fast as my feet can take me. I will not be dragged back to that room. I will not sit there any longer as she force-feeds her sweet lies down my throat. Instead, I will make myself useful. I will do what Ryleigh asked of me. I am going to report to her. I am grateful no soldiers heard our altercation and stopped me. Or maybe they did and Silvi sweet-talked them, too. Convinced them it was all in their heads. Maybe it was a sign of goodwill, her calling off the dogs. Maybe she meant the apology. Either way, she will not be gaining my trust. Not that she had it in the first place.

"Ryleigh." I pant as I enter the sewing room, relief flooding me.

"Yes? Is this important," she says angrily, "I need to finish this dress, and the details are just-"

"She's an Empath," I reply breathlessly. "A crazy powerful version of one, anyways." She drops the dress, the needle and thread following. Her expression changes, curiosity settling in.

"What do you mean?"

"Her powers. They are crazy, Ryleigh. I've never heard of anything like it. She feels what we feel, sure, but she can change it, too. Can make you feel happy, make you feel sad. She made me trust her. Made me think I was her friend and she was mine. I watched her whisper to a soldier and he just *told* her everything she wanted to know! It's in her voice, her touch, her body. It's...effortless. She has a ton of control over it. She knows exactly what she is doing. I was terrified once I realized, Ryleigh." I admit shakily, shivering at the memory. "When she spoke to that soldier...I realized. It didn't take long for me to break free, then. I just fought and fought. Body and mind. And I'm free. I don't know how long, but I'm free." I hold up my arms, brandishing the scratch marks as proof.

"How?" She seems just as surprised as Silvi had been, suspicious even.

"I don't know. I just...pushed back. Maybe she isn't as powerful as she thought she was. Maybe I just got lucky." I shrug uneasily. I haven't thought much about the how.

"You said she used it on you?"

"Yes. She manipulated me. I'm sure she was using me to help herself seem like a better choice. That's why she brought me to dinner and made me wear a nice dress. I don't know where the plan is going or how far she is going to take it, but I have no doubt she plans to use me some more. I told her, Ryleigh. Told her about Irissa. She forced it out of me. I'm scared she might follow me. Or that she might report it. I need help. Please help me. I can't let her be taken away. I can't!" If Ryleigh can't help, no one can. Even then, I'm not sure how much she can do against a Divine.

"Don't worry. I'll get a few off-duty Undivine soldiers to help out. The ones I trust, anyway. I know a few Lows, too, who are much more accepting of us than the others. I can promise you this, Celeste: you won't be attacked again. I will personally see to it."

"If someone attacks me, I don't think it will be Silvi herself. She begged me for forgiveness. She is playing a game, and she has made me a part of it."

"Whatever it is, it's bad news for you. Don't let her back in your head. Do you understand?"

"I understand. Thank you, Ryleigh." We stare into each other's eyes for a moment, an agreement falling between us. We trust each other completely, and I am beginning to understand just how much love she has for me. She will take care of this. I know she will.

"You can go home, Les. Go take care of your sister. You two have a long night ahead. Go take a nap." With that, she turns back to her work. Her gentle, nimble fingers beginning to sew once more. I can only nod, grateful. I've never been sent home early in the five years I've worked in this castle.

I slip away, unsure about how I am going to get home. Darius doesn't leave until the afternoon since he has business in the city. I'll find a way, though. A pretty smile can go a long way around here. Besides, she is right. We *will* be having a long night. A night full of screaming, crying, and torture. A night where I hunker in the corner and beg for the moon to leave and never return.

Chapter 4

We have to wait two weeks for every girl to arrive. The castle fills up quickly with participant after participant arriving. A whole wing is now occupied. All but five maids are assigned to be handmaidens, leaving them with the brunt of the work we left behind. I am sure at least thirty women have appeared. I don't know all of their names because I rarely see anyone other than Silvi. I don't mind too much, though. I don't want to partake in introductions and idle talk. I barely know any of the other maids, and I don't want to start. Not like I would have remembered all of the participants and their maid's names, anyway.

Silvi has become docile. She hasn't tried to use her powers on me again. It is a trust tactic, I suppose. Things have been very awkward from my perspective. She makes small talk with me, occasionally bringing up my sister. I hardly reply, ignoring the weight of the hidden threats. She doesn't have to say she will destroy me and my sister outright. I already know.

On my only day off, I decided to go back to Lunar City. I am typically glad to escape that world for one day, but I can't stand by and let us go without essentials. I need to find new bowls and cups since Irissa destroyed them all during the previous full moon. Our village doesn't sell items like that. Not decent ones, anyway. I have to replace them often, another thing holding me back from saving coins for Irissa's treatment.

I am familiar with the city. The castle sits on the outskirts, a thriving market in the middle, and residency fills the outer layer. I live in Slyvein, which is only barely considered the second farthest from the castle. That's why I hitch rides into town; the walk is a killer on the feet. I have enough blisters as is. Beyond the castle are trees upon trees upon trees. No one ventures that way unless they are collecting wood, meat, or both. But since the trees are dying out and animals are fleeing, there won't be any value to those woods much longer. There is that small band of trees between us and the Solar Court giving us hope, though. Plus a few mountains on our borders have some delectable beasts. Most don't want to venture there, though. There are too many rumors about the danger of traveling between the Courts. Dangerous beasts and thieves hunt the line, making it difficult for anyone to leave or just pass through. Even more dangerous to go to the Light and Shadow Courts.

Low and High Divine alike live in the city. Undivine are given the villages, which is why there are so many. Our Court has the largest population of all four Courts, and most are Undivine. No Divine would be caught living in a village. Our villages have names but are also numbered officially as one through seven. The number that aligns with your village is burned into you. Easier to keep track of us that way. Plus, it's an easy way to tell where they need to hang us so our friends and family can watch. Mine is located between my shoulder blades. Irissa's is on the inside of her right wrist. We don't get to choose the location, unfortunately. We belong to village number three. And, since three isn't our original village, we have a second number burned into our skin. Our first numbers were healed by a Low Divine I paid off with my life savings long ago, but the faint scars are still there. A permanent reminder of where we come from.

If we break the law, our village is held responsible. For small things, we are lashed in public. For bigger ones, we are hanged. Some are lucky enough to sit in a prison cell. It's usually only captured spies who get the luxury of staying alive, though. They are tortured until they don't know where they come from or what their names are. No matter the crime, the village suffers the same. Sometimes they take away the water supply. Other times they take the horses for a week or two. Maybe turn the electricity off for a few days. Whatever decision they make about punishment, they always follow through. I've seen the Divine laugh about the punishments, treating us like dirt between their toes. It angers me. If I had any sort of power myself, they would all be dead. Maybe that's why I don't let Irissa leave the house. She doesn't need to act out on that bloodthirstiness.

I lower my dirty, ivy-colored hood as I approach the first stand. The vendor is busy with someone else, discussing prices in hushed whispers. I pick up a mug and inspect it, shaking my head. The red will enrage Irissa. No, it won't work. So I move along. I visit five of my regular stands, unhappy with the product or the value of the product. I only have four silver coins, four coins that have taken me half a year to save. Four coins that I can't use for Irissa's treatment.

I know the Followers don't do charity work. They need

money just like the rest of us. They are known Court-wide for their supposed work with the goddesses. We all know they worship them over the Divine, but not much other than that. They are secretive about their practices. Secrets keep you safe, after all. They don't share their knowledge about the goddesses, either. We know to pray to them, to fear them. But we know that about the Divine, too. We see the Divine every day, though. No one has ever seen a goddess. No one knows what they stand for; are they on our side or not? If they exist, will they intervene on our behalf at some point? But the Followers cherish them. Supposedly, the goddesses repay their loyalty with anything and everything they might need. That includes cures for any and every disease. I might not believe it, but I am willing to try anything. Willing to push aside my thoughts and what I want so I can do what is right for my sister. So, I keep telling myself that one day...one day I will get that cure.

I pass an old house on my way to the next stand. I tense as I pass it, glancing into a broken window. I've seen Divine in there before, partying and drinking. I've had a few members try to get me to join, but I know better than to put myself in a situation like that. Sometimes thieves hang out here, too. Waiting on a passerby to attack. Usually, they stick to the Divine. But I am a small female walking on my own. I am easy prey for anyone paying attention.

I clutch the hilt of an old dagger in my pocket, my only form of protection. Unfortunately, it isn't very sharp. Just something I've held onto for years, something that makes me feel a semblance of protection. I don't know how to fight properly, but I will swing this thing until it strikes true. No one will take my life without a fight.

I glance slowly around the corner of the house, looking left and right for any sign of life. I see a flash of movement and my heart stops, but it is only a rat scuttling away. I'm hesitant to move forward, an uneasiness settling in me. I can *feel* a presence nearby, I know something or someone is waiting in the shadows. I push that aside though, standing straighter. I may be a small, unattended female but I won't make myself look weaker than I already do. I have been hurt and preyed on by Divine my whole life, and that alone gives me the courage to move on. I don't have to continue to be their victim. I stride forward with feigned confidence, glaring into the alley daringly.

When the hand shoots out of the shadows and covers my mouth, I don't hesitate. I lash out, screaming and stomping down on the foot behind me as I pull the dagger free. I hear a hiss after I send my elbow back, the hand releasing me. I can hear groaning that signals I hit exactly where I had been aiming. The hand reaches out again, mumbled grunts following. So I slash at it without aim, heart pounding out of my chest. There is this primal urge arising, one telling me to turn around and end it. But they are already down. I don't want to kill. So, instead, I do the only other thing left to do.

I run.

I run as fast as I can. Unfortunately, the fight pulled me deeper into the alleyways than I realized. I am deep in the shadows now. This is a secluded section of the city, one many avoid. One I should have avoided, too. But it was a shortcut to my next destination so I rushed. It was stupid of me. Idiotic. But nothing has ever happened to me here before, so why would it now? I have my dagger and my wits, but I'm starting to realize that may not be enough.

I don't make it far. I'm in decent shape, but I have short legs. So, I lash out with the dagger again, slicing frantically as the hand slips over my mouth again. I try to bite down, but they use their index finger and thumb to hold my jaw shut. I can't make a noise, their grip is too tight. The other hand snatches my wrist, attempting to pry the dagger from my fingers. They slam me into the wall, pushing against my back. I still struggle, trying not to cry. I feel the heat of skin on my wrist, but it feels more like fire than normal body heat. I am forced to drop the dagger or continue to be burned.

"Stop fighting me." The voice hisses, annoyance dripping from his tongue. I feel the heat against my ear as he speaks. I freeze at the familiar feeling, petrified.

No. No, no, no. This can't be right. It can't be *him*.

"Thank you. Goddesses, Celeste. I didn't even get one word out before you cut me!" He releases me from his hold, but I can still feel his touch searing into my skin, my memory. I spin around quickly, breathing ragged.

"I'm so sorry, Your Highness." I blurt, panicked. I did *not* just cut Kyelin. A prince. A Royal. No, no, no. My life is officially forfeit.

"You should be." He scoffs. "You tore my shirt." He fingers at a hole in the sleeve, lips curling unhappily. *Spoiled brat.*

"And your skin." I let out a sharp laugh, unsure of what to do now. "I am *really* sorry. Please forgive me! I didn't know it was you. If I had, Your Highness, I would have never—" I lie through my teeth. Because, yes, even if I had known a prince was attacking me, I would have still fought.

"I snuck up on you." He says gently.

"Yes, you did. And you covered my mouth." I say quietly, absentmindedly touching my chin.

"I shouldn't have done that. I just...I'm kind of sneaking around the city right now. I didn't want anyone to see me, and I didn't want you screaming anything that could get me recognized."

We stare at each other for a long moment, not breaking contact until I blink. Then I realized what he said. He remembered my name. He recognized me. But why did he pull me away? And what is this nervousness balling in my stomach, threatening to rip through my skin the way my dagger ripped through his shirt?

"You do not need to be sorry. You do not need to apologize to me. There is nothing to forgive. I snuck up on you, you defended yourself. Very well, might I add. Though, you need a new blade. That one is extremely dull and rusted. And please, call me Kyelin." He laughs while patting my shoulder lightly. I imagine it looks like a cat petting a mouse.

"Okay...Kyelin." I'm not sure I agree about defending myself well. But what could I have done against him, anyway? I never had a chance. At least I scratched him.

"I saw you and wanted to apologize for my behavior a couple of weeks ago. I act a certain way in front of my family, you see. I don't want them to think I'm kind because, to them, that makes me an easy target. Kindness is a weakness as a Royal. Please, don't be angry with me." Why does he care what I think of him?

"I accept the apology." I finally say, hesitant. "Though I'm not sure it is necessary. You weren't *that* bad. And that apology was certainly not worth your life." He laughs louder than I expected, throwing his head back. His crimson hair sways with him, brushing against his back. I try not to stare too hard.

"Well, I had hoped to discuss other matters with you. Would you be open to a discussion right now?"

"I suppose so. I kind of owe you after the whole cutting incident." *He wants to use me for something, too. How typical of a Divine.*

"I need you to keep an eye on Silvi." *Of course this is about* her, *the evil beauty no one can resist.*

"Oh?" I try to act confident, but his hand comes to rest on my shoulder again. I try not to think about the heat, about how handsome he is.

"You must understand. I do not say this out of fear for my safety. My family ranks her highly among the candidates. Her family is well-connected, and her beauty is renowned. When compared to the other Solar Court participants, she is the best choice. As long as she performs well, I have no doubts she will be wedded to me or my brother. I just want to ensure that all is as it seems. That there aren't any surprises waiting for us. I want to know that she is truly suited for such a position and that she can handle it mentally. Not all of these girls are ready to have a kingdom on their shoulders. It's cutthroat being a Royal, and it's never rainbows and sunshine. Sure, we have enough power to destroy the world if we wish it. But sometimes, you don't need that power to be a threat. I just…she seems too soft. I'm not sure she is as capable of this world as we believe her to be. Even if she did grow up in it, I'm not sure she knows exactly what goes on behind the scenes." *I can't help but laugh, shaking my head. She has them* fooled.

"I can assure you, she embodies cutthroat. I have experienced it firsthand. Is that all you need? Because I can guarantee she isn't too soft, as you so kindly put it. Does she deserve to be a Royal? I won't give my opinion on that. If

67

you don't mind, I would like to leave now. You Divine make me nervous. And I just want to find what I was looking for and go." I try to push past him, done with this conversation.

"I will pay you." He uses that hard body to keep me in place. "You will be well compensated. I can swear on that." I freeze, eyes shooting up to meet his. Is he serious right now? If he is...

"Talk."

"I want to form an alliance, a deal of sorts. You give me information on Silvi. Anything and everything, relevant or not. I want to know what she plans, what she does, and what she thinks. From your reaction, I'm going to presume I am right to be nervous about her. Something is off, and I want to know what it is. When she waltzed you into my dining room like a shiny trophy, I knew something was up. In return-"

"First and foremost, I want you to promise safety for both me and my sister. She has already threatened us both, which I don't take kindly to. I'm not risking our lives to be your little spy just because you want to know her dirty secrets. Can you promise me this?" I shock myself, sometimes. Talking to a Royal in such a manner? A death sentence. And for some reason, I keep doing it. I should learn to keep my mouth shut.

"Of course." He doesn't seem surprised by the request, eyes still meeting my own with increasing intrigue.

"And you *are* going to pay me. Enough money that I can quit and live the rest of my life without ever wanting." For some reason, he sought me out. He wants *me* to be his eyes and ears. I might as well take advantage of it, right?

"Done. Happily so. Anything else?" I know that the Royals are drowning in money, but it still shocks me that he doesn't argue. Not that an Undivine's worth is anywhere near what a pair of those golden doors in the castle costs.

"Umm…well….this may seem odd and I'm not sure how to say this—" I pause at the gentle squeeze of his hand, my heart stopping.

"Just tell me. I won't judge." His whole face softens, eyes searching my own. He can sense my fear, I'm sure of it. Divine always can. They are drawn to fear like the moon is drawn to the night sky.

"The soldiers. Keep the soldiers away from me. They can protect me, but I don't want to see them. I don't want to know they are there. I don't want them to touch me. Ever. I can't accept this offer without this guarantee. It's hard enough walking through the castle on my own, but with the increase of them lately…let's just say I want to feel more secure." I can't believe I just told a Royal I don't trust his guards.

"Of course." His voice is soft and gentle. I know it's a strange request. But I try to never be in a room alone with one of them. There are a few specifically I never want to see again, their voices are the ones that haunt my dreams. It may be a big place, but I will run out of luck eventually. "If you give me specific names, I can take them down for questioning and—" He sounds worried at the idea of his men scaring me enough to make such a strange request. Good. Maybe now the soldiers will be the ones on edge for once.

"No." I screech, shaking my head furiously. "No. No need for that." I try to calm myself. If they find out I ratted on them…

"Okay. Okay. Let me know if you change your mind. We have a deal?"

"We have a deal." We shake hands, and I shiver at the feeling of his bare skin on mine. A burning fire lives under his skin, and I find myself wondering how it feels to have a power like that. What it would feel like to have those powerful hands on *me*.

"Anything you have for me now? You've been with her for a couple of weeks already. I'm sure you have gathered some information." I nod, the words spilling out of me. I tell him how I felt this instant connection, how I trusted her implicitly even though I trusted hardly anyone, how she forced herself into my mind, and how she made me her friend. I don't mention the attraction I felt for her, but that's because I'm not sure how much of that was real, either. I told him how she was easily able to get me to spill secrets, ones I guarded with my life.

"It was like she ripped the words from my throat." My voice cracks as I turn away. It was a *violation* and I am still not sure how I am ever going to get over it.

"Okay. Okay, thank you. I knew she was powerful, but that kind of influence…well that can be dangerous in the wrong hands. If the rebels got her onto their side…well, no matter. You don't need to worry your pretty head about that." I scoff, shaking my head. He gives me a sad glance, as if he feels sorry for me. Is that what this is really about? Do they think Silvi could be persuaded into an alliance with the rebels? As if!

"I thought the rebels weren't a threat? That's what you guys said before the participants started arriving. Remember? We all gathered below the castle and listened to your dad blabber on for an hour."

"Well, as I said, nothing for you to worry about."

The rebels aren't a new thing. They've always been around, typically Undivine who are unhappy with the system. It makes sense because the system is inherently wrong. But they can't just peacefully protest. They will be executed by the next morning. So they get creative. They get destructive. Bombs here and there. A few well-placed spies release information that is supposed to be hush-hush. About a month ago, though, they attacked Lunar City. Bombs all around the Divine quarters, murders in the castle. About twenty Divine died. A few Undivine were injured, but not killed. It has the whole Court shaken up and nervous. Because if they aren't safe in their homes or the castle, then where *are* they safe? Honestly, I don't care much. Undivines feel like that all the time, so I believe it is a little deserved. Even if I don't think it is ethical to murder people.

"Mm-hmm."

"Listen, I swore I would protect you and I meant it. I will check on you every day. If I can't, then Zaeden will."

"Good." I don't say thanks. I'm glad they are protecting me, don't get me wrong. But I don't want to feel grateful to a Divine who is only protecting me for his own purposes. I will accept the benefits of it though, even if it puts me in danger. For Irissa, I will do this.

"I saw you looking at dinnerware. Maybe you could use some silverware, too?" It's a distraction, but I allow it.

"I can only afford the dinnerware." I scoff dismissively. I can't buy everything I want just because I want it, not like a spoiled Royal can.

"Come." He laughs lightly. "I will find you the finest sets. And don't object. You've already done an excellent job, so consider it an advance."

"You want to buy them for me?" I ask, astounded. This Royal doesn't quite fit the box I put him in.

"Of course."

71

We walk together, hoods drawn to hide our faces. Because I don't want to be seen with him and he doesn't want to be seen at all. True to his word, Kyelin does buy me the fancy dinnerware. He finds ones with magic embedded inside, making them unbreakable. I am giddy when he buys them, even more so when he carries them for me as we talk. I am surprised at how easy it is to talk to him. How natural. He is generous, too. He buys bread for some children and surprises a pregnant woman with a bassinet. On and on it goes. I can't imagine having this kind of money. Even more, I wouldn't have ever imagined a man of his status ever looking at me the way he is right now, with wonder and excitement dancing across those enchanting emerald eyes. It makes me feel like I matter. Like he thinks I am beautiful. Like he cares. Yet, here he is, doing exactly that. Standing next to me, laughing like we have known each other for years.

What am I doing?

Chapter 5

"I won't tell you again," I grind out, my patience wearing thin. The sun has barely risen and Irissa is *already* being difficult. She has been restless, as usual, and has now become angered from lack of sleep. Typical behavior of a toddler. Except this toddler has the powers and body of a Divine. Bad days for her are worse days for me.

"No!" She screeches, throwing a shiny new fork with deadly accuracy. I duck, feeling a strand of hair being stripped from my head. I growl, taking a step forward.

"I mean it, Iris! That is good silverware! Expensive! If you ruin it—" I take another step, face hot all over.

"Stay back," she says with venom, "Stay away from me!" I duck again as a spoon flies above me, bouncing off the wall harmlessly. It lands with a clatter, the sound barely heard over the roaring in my head.

"What is your problem? Are you ill?" I ask, exasperated. This type of behavior doesn't happen often. Usually, she's just mad about the cold stew or stale bread. She flips her plate and stomps off. Maybe she'll leave a little claw mark on the table. She doesn't throw extreme fits like this unless something else is going on.

"My wings!" She admits as she flings another spoon at me.

"They hurt so bad. Hurt, Les. It not stop! It makes me so angry!" This time, a knife flies next to me. I barely manage to slide away, the sharp tip grazing my arm. I pay no attention to the small cut it leaves, nor to the little droplets of blood rising to the surface.

"Thank you for telling me. I have a soothing tonic. Let me help. *Please*, Iris. Just let me help. I won't hurt you, I swear it on my Undivine life." Pain is a sensitive topic with Irissa. Like most children, she doesn't like to take medication. Even if it helps.

"No! Don't touch me! Don't touch! Don't need help!" I scream out in frustration as a second knife flies. I know she isn't intentionally trying to harm me, much less kill me. She is just throwing what she has available, not realizing the consequences. That's why I can't let anyone else watch her. They won't understand. They will get mad, maybe hurt her. As horrible as she acts, I would never hurt her. Even if I want to some days. I have to remind myself that, right now, she is a young, impressionable child. If I do something violent, she will learn from that behavior and these little fits *will* have intent to harm.

A knock sounds on the door. We both stop screaming, heads whipping in that direction. She drops the silverware, the rattling noise echoing around the room. Slowly, I stand. No one comes to our house. I know I rag on Irissa about someone hearing her or seeing her little fits while I'm gone, but I don't expect that to happen. It's mostly a scare tactic. So why is someone here now? And who?

"Go to your room and don't leave until I say so." I hiss under my breath. Miraculously, she listens.

I don't have a peephole and I can't see anything out of the

cracked window. So, I grab my trusty, rusty dagger and approach the door. Once I know Irissa is safely hidden, I crack the door open. A hooded man waits on the doorstep, standing at a slight angle. He is tall, too tall to be an Undivine. Maybe it is a Follower? They come door to door sometimes to try and convert us and they have a few Divine members.

"No, thanks. I'm not interested in your bullshit." I don't turn my back, attempting to shut the door quickly. Even if it is just a Follower, I'm not taking any chances.

I hear a deep laugh just as a foot juts out to wedge itself between the door and the frame. I try to push harder, but I can't get it fully closed. My heart freezes, my mind racing. What did he hear? Does he know who I have hidden in this house? Or is he a thief? But thieves don't knock. They invite themselves in. Besides, anyone who gives my house more than a second glance can tell there is nothing worth stealing here.

"What a mouth." He purrs confidently, arrogantly. "You dare turn away a prince?" I groan inwardly, angry. Why is he *here*? They aren't supposed to come to my home. They did say they would be checking in on me. I didn't realize that meant they would meet me anywhere outside the castle. I suppose Kyelin didn't specify the location though, did he?

"I'm so sorry, Your Highness," I say, trying to mean it, "I shouldn't say such foul words around a prince. Your Royal ears are much too sensitive for such crude language."

"Oh, I like that you say foul words. The ladies of the Court would never. It's refreshing. And call me Zaeden, yeah? No need for the formalities." He laughs again, staring at my closed lips. I lick them before I realize what I'm doing.

"Okay, Zaeden. Thanks for stopping by to check on us. We

are good, so you can leave now." I move to shut the door again, but his foot doesn't budge.

"Can I come in?" I blink up at him, unsure. I was just trying to get him to leave and now he wants to come in?

"Oh, I don't know. My house isn't meant for visitors, certainly not ones who are used to such lavish and privileged lifestyles. It's old and ugly and a mess. Maybe another time."

"Or maybe now?" He makes it sound like a question, but it isn't. Begrudgingly, I move aside and open the door wider. It's not like I can stop him.

"Yes, of course. Just don't mind the mess. I don't have the time or money to fix this place up. You weren't standing there long, were you?" I glance at him as I ask, hoping beyond hope he didn't hear Irissa shouting. But it's not like these walls are soundproof. I'm sure he heard *something*.

"No, not long," he says quietly, stepping inside. He glances around, shifting something in his hands. I didn't notice before, but he was holding a small basket. The smell of warm bread wafts up to my nose, my mouth watering at the thought of such a delicious gift. This isn't the stale stuff the bakery sells me for cheap. This is *fresh*.

"You must have had a long trip." I try to start a conversation after a pregnant pause. I wish he would tell me what he wants and get out of here. I shut the door gently, embarrassment flooding my body. A prince is standing in my broken, messy home. This place looks like a wild beast visited and didn't like its stay. No wonder he doesn't know what to say.

"Ah, yes, well. It was well worth the walk. I like to have a little time to myself now and then. Walking gives me a little freedom, doesn't it? Plus, I get the pleasure of visiting a lovely lady like you. It's a win all around."

"Shit." I snort. "I wouldn't refer to myself as a lovely lady." I flinch, forgetting my mouth again.

"Ah, not one for flattery, hmm?"

"No need to be insincere. I know what I am. Who I am. You are here to do as promised, nothing more. No need for... whatever this is you are doing." I regret saying it instantly, but he doesn't even blink at my accusation. Just shakes his head.

"Who were you arguing with?" It's a very obvious topic change, but I think I would have preferred talking about his pretty words over talking about Irissa.

"No one." I shrug, flopping ungracefully into a chair at the dining table. He follows suit, placing his basket on the table. I watch his eyes fall to the silverware on the floor, following the path to the wall across the small room.

"Don't lie to me, Celeste. Who's here?" I swallow hard at the angry growl, flinching as his eyes snap to mine. I can see dark tendrils rising with his anger, that darkness feasting on my fear.

"Does it matter," I say, dodging the question.

"Are you in any danger here?"

"Of course not. This is my home! If I were in any danger, I wouldn't be here. Maybe your home is full of bloodthirsty aristocrats, but mine isn't. I have no one to fear here except *you*."

"Yeah? So you aren't hiding a lover back there? Someone who beats you then tells you how sorry they are. Who gives you flowers and begs for forgiveness? Then they repeat the cycle all over again? I heard you yelling. I heard your little sister, too. She sounds young. You going to let her stay with someone like that around?"

"No, and I resent your accusations." I spit, standing. "I

would never put my sister in a situation like that! We aren't in any danger here! Do you think I have time for a lover with the way you Divine work me? I hardly have time to sleep in my bed, much less do anything else in it!"

"Oh, don't tease me about what you do in your bed, Celeste. Besides, I heard screaming. I came in here to see silverware scattered across the ground in very distinct patterns. I heard them hitting the wall as I approached. I see the blood dripping down your arm. And now you are hiding the perpetrator's identity. You don't call that danger? I'm supposed to be protecting you and I find you hurt in your own home. So tell me who I need to be protecting you from before I go search the place myself."

"Well—I—umm—" I can't seem to form a sentence, can't sputter out a good excuse. How can I tell the truth? And why does he care so much anyway?

I don't have long to think. I hear the door as it creaks open, feet tapping on the ground. I scream out a panicked 'no', racing for the bedroom. I pray to make it in time, pray she won't come expose herself to this Divine.

Those prayers aren't answered.

Irissa stands there, wings out, talons extended. I jump in front of her, holding my arms out as a shield. *Please, please don't look* I beg in my mind like it will change anything. I watch Zaeden closely, expecting to see the realization dawning there. But his face doesn't change. His eyes flicker, and I know he knows. I can't tell if he is surprised or angry. But now he knows exactly why I didn't want him coming in, and it wasn't because of an ugly house or an uncouth domestic situation. This is very, very bad. If I had thought they would come here, that they would ever have a chance to see her, I wouldn't have-

"Won't you join us?" He questions softly, as though trying not to scare a timid deer. "I brought breakfast. Fresh loaves from the castle. I only brought two, but you can have mine. I'm not feeling hungry this morning. I may have slipped a few sweets in there, too." It shocks me how calm he is, how nice he is. I watch as he stands and pulls out a chair, gesturing for her to sit.

"Sweets?" Irissa pushes me aside, practically purring in happiness. I stumble, watching with wide eyes.

"For breakfast?" I question with a squint, trying to take back control of the situation. "She doesn't need sweets for breakfast. I told you not to leave your room, Irissa. You should have listened to me for once."

"I don't want time out, Les." She cries, that childish voice begging Zaeden more than me.

"You won't get time out." He reassures, smoothing a hand over her hair. I gape, fuming.

"Get your hands off of her, first of all. Second of all, she is *my* sister. You get no say in whether-"

"She will not be punished." He says firmly, staring hard into my eyes. A purple smoke rises just above the surface of his skin, those tendrils dancing in the iris' of his eyes. I flinch at the subtle abuse of power, backing down. It's not like I am *actually* going to punish her. She is a curious child and doesn't deserve punishment for something so natural. I just don't want a Divine coming in here telling me what to do and how to take care of *my* sister!

"Look what I do," Irissa states proudly, her wings flexing as I sit. She winces as they lift high then lower once more. She wiggles her long talons, pulling them in and struggling to extend them back out. A little blood trickles from her fingers, dripping onto the table. Zaeden glances down at it, chuckling at her display.

"Does it hurt?" She nods, biting her lip shyly. He reaches out and touches the soft wing, the dark poison sinking underneath his skin once more. "My advice? Work on building up muscle in your back. Some good exercise will go a long way in helping you control these massive things. You have to be strong to hold up your wings. Start working out, and lift heavy things. Pull them back. Like this." He shows her with his arms, his back muscles flexing. "Maybe even do some push-ups and sit-ups, too. Those build your core muscles. It will help, I promise. They won't be as sore." He gets down on the floor and demonstrates for her, mine and Irissa's mouths opening in surprise. I try not to gawk but, honestly, how can I not? This man is *hot*, and I am shamelessly ogling him.

"Promise?" She repeats, surprised. Most Divine don't make promises, or swear by anything. They can be binding under the right circumstances, which is why I took Kyelin's word so easily when we made our deal.

"Yes, of course. I'm a prince. Princes don't lie. And also? Maybe you can take it a little easier on your sister. Work on those anger problems, okay? She is just trying to take care of you. You should listen to her. Maybe when you get those angry feelings, you can go outside? Hit a tree? I could even get you some throwing knives. It will be much more satisfying than this silverware."

"Throwing knives? She is only—" I stop myself abruptly. Because she isn't only four like I was about to protest, she is nineteen and looks her age. That is something I struggle with often. How do I decide where to draw the line? When to treat her like a toddler and when to treat her like an adult? Because even though she doesn't necessarily understand everything the prince is telling her, she likes to throw and has the strength of a grown woman. It's not the same as letting an actual toddler have a knife. So how do I decide if that's a line to draw? I teeter on the edge of this cliff and I know my decisions can send us both tumbling down.

"Ignore her. I know you are a big girl." Zaeden shoots a glare my way. "I can tell you have good aim, and that you are strong, too. Give that tree a few punches in the meantime, okay? Be nice to your sister." Irissa's face falls, tears pooling into her eyes. She sniffles, trying to hide them as her head dips down. But there is no hiding from an observant Divine. "Ah, don't be upset. I'm not disappointed. What you feel is normal for a Divine. It's hard to have powers like ours. It's hard to control yourself. I understand. It is a lot of pressure you are under, and you are doing your very best. I'm proud of you."

"Okay." She brightens up in agreement, glancing over at me expectantly. "Will you be nice to me, too, Les?"

"I'm always nice to you." I roll my eyes. "But yes. Maybe I can try harder not to argue with you, too."

"Perfect, we are in agreement then." Zaeden boasts, smiling at my sister.

"Why don't you go back to your room to eat, Iris? Let the adults talk for a minute. It's very important." I let her take a piece of bread with her, along with a cookie. She runs off with eagerness, giggling. When I hear the door shut, I relax back into my seat. At least she is out of his sight now. Even if he is being strangely kind to her.

"How old is she?" He looks lost in thought as he stares off at her door.

"As her normal self? Nineteen. How old does she think she is right now? Four. Her days are split like that, twelve hours as herself and twelve as...not herself."

"That must be exhausting. For both of you." He finally turns to me, gentle, unassuming eyes meeting mine. I can hardly understand this man. He is being *way* too kind, and I can still feel dark energy radiating from him. Is that just how he feels? Like Kyelin with his heat, is Zaeden just surrounded by this *wrongness*?

"It is."

"Her name...was it meant to be a joke?"

"Yes. Mother thought it was funny to name her Irissa. Her little joke. Used to call her the 'iris in my eyes'. They turn completely black, as I'm sure you noticed. She thought it was funny, but instead, it's a constant reminder of what she is. I've tried to turn it into a term of endearment so she doesn't feel so...*wrong*."

"And what is she?"

"I don't know. Maybe a type of shape-shifter? But that doesn't explain the change in personalities. I've never dared to find out. Anyone who could have helped would have turned her in for dinner and a silver coin. Whatever it is, I plan on curing it."

"How long has she been that way? With the wings and talons? She was supposed to be Undivine, I assume?"

I pause, unsure how much I should admit. Though, does it matter now? We have been sworn protection. Whatever my sister may be, they have to abide by those rules. It isn't my fault they didn't ask any of the right questions beforehand. "Yes. She sprouted wings at birth, minutes after she left the womb. She was born with the talons. She made sure my mother would never have children again, almost killed her."

"I see." Those dark eyes stare into my own, detached and uninterested. My anger flares up at his nonchalance, my words harsh and spitting.

"Do you? Do you see? Because I have spent my whole life hiding her, and you came waltzing in and ruined everything I have worked so hard for. I swear, if you take her away from me, I will burn this Court down until she is returned to me. I will kill anyone and everyone you hold dear. Your family's blood will stain the hands that wrap around your neck and suck the life out of you. Your-"

"No need for the threats." He snaps impatiently. "Need I remind you of who and what I am?"

"I know exactly what you are. What, do you want me to get on my knees and beg? That will not happen. I will not cower like a dog beneath you. I won't kiss your ass like everyone else likes to."

"Not yet, I don't. But don't worry. We can get to the begging and ass-kissing later." The way he says it sends a shiver down my spine and has me sitting straighter than I thought possible.

"Don't play around with me, fuckwad. I'm serious."

"So am I." I jump back at the sight of purple leaking from his fingers onto the table. "I just want you to treat me like an ally. Not like some Divine scum who wants to use you and your sister."

"But you are. Using me, I mean. And now that there are two Divine who know my secret, how many more are going to find out? I'm going to have to leave this Court and start over somewhere new. I'm going to-"

"You aren't going anywhere. You are going to stay and finish the job we are paying you to do. And I am not going to tell anyone what I saw here today. Your sister is sweet. I'm not going to punish you or her for something that is out of your control."

"Really? Just like that? And you want nothing in return?"

"Yes, just like that. I do want something in return, actually. I want you to quit calling me such mean names. It pains me to hear you call me a fuckwad." He pouts playfully, jutting out a bottom lip. I scowl in return, sending him a middle finger.

"I'm not sure I can believe you. Is it my turn to remind you now of who and what I am? Do you really think I am going to believe you will treat me like an equal? An Undivine like me? I'm not gullible."

"You are very defensive when it comes to your sister." He remarks, not partaking in the argument I am trying to start.

"Yes, I am. I will do anything for her. I cannot and will not lose her. And if you have her taken away from me...well, I won't need powers for the things I will do to you." I try to make myself look like a vicious animal. Deadly, like his poison.

"Ha! Kyelin was right. I do like you. Relax, Celeste. I understand. Your secret is mine and I will take it to my grave, if needed. I'm not interested in your sister. I have much bigger things to worry about right now. Bigger things than your rudeness to the crown prince, which I could have you punished for."

"Good." I lean back in my chair, trying to relax. I shouldn't have threatened him. Or flipped him off. He has a right to be angry. First, I almost cut open one prince, then I threatened to kill the other. What is it about these two that makes me lose common sense?

"I do want you to understand that just because I don't plan

on telling anyone, it won't stop me from putting your sister in danger. I know your secret, now. I can spread rumors of a beast running around here. Of a crazy woman on the hunt. I can send special visitors at inopportune times. Do you understand?" Rage boils inside me, running down my throat and into my stomach like lava. If I had any power within me, I would have killed him, consequences be damned. I want to take that poison and shove it down his throat until it is pouring out of his ears.

"I understand." I grind out, eyes flashing in anger.

"Good. Now, for the real reason I came."

"Yes, please hurry it along. Your presence is very much unneeded. If any Undivine knew you were in my house...well, let's just say they aren't all fans of Divine sympathizers."

"Yes, because it is so horrible to be friends with me. Maybe if you had a little more patience, you would think otherwise." He scoffs, leaning onto his elbows. "The first Game begins in a few days. The Game of Impressions."

"Oh." Of course, I knew that they were starting soon. I just haven't put much thought behind it. I have been too busy preparing a new dress all week for Silvi for the special event.

"This Game is a show. A show of powers, of skill, of personality. It is a very important event. Half of the contestants are voted out on this alone. If they aren't beautiful enough, their skills mediocre, their attitude poor, they leave. They may not do anything particularly *wrong* and still have to leave. If my parents give the say-so, they are out. They have the final decision."

"You get no say?" I gape, surprised. "I thought you two were going to pick the girls you like."

"Of course not. It isn't about love. It's about finding the

best possible match to unite us all. And to produce the most powerful heirs, of course." He says it with no emotion, almost like it truly does not matter that he is about to be tied to a woman he barely knows for the rest of his life just because she is *pretty*.

"So what do you require of me? I'm not sure there is much for me to do right now."

"I require you to tell me her plan. If she even has one, if she waits until the last minute. I want to know who she talked to before or if anyone helped her. I want to know if she is prepared or if she has someone telling her what to do. I want to know of her arrogance: does she think she has it in the bag?" He hesitates, as if unsure of what else he can tell me. What has she done to get on everyone's radar? From what I have seen of her, there is nothing to worry about. She seems like a typical Divine: rude with a sense of self-entitlement. "I—we are worried about what she might be planning. She is cunning and manipulative, and we want to know exactly what to expect out of her display of power. I have this…feeling that it won't be something any of us expect."

I nod complacently. "Of course. I'll let you know what I find out." I watch as his eyes dart to mine, my unease growing. What plan do they think she has concocted? Maybe this isn't completely about Silvi. Maybe this is about *me*. My stomach rolls over and over, flipping and tossing the more I think about it. Before I can ask, he stands abruptly. A flicker of uncertainty crosses his face, his body stiff. I stand, too, unsure what to do. I grasp onto the table, keeping myself stable and rooted to this spot. I try not to stare, but his very presence is singing to me. *Royals must have that hypnotizing quality* I use the thought to convince myself.

"Celeste…are you Divine, too?"

"What?" I gape in shock. What makes him think that? I mean, come on! It's so painfully *obvious* that I am Undivine.

"Are you Divine? There's something about you…"

"I'm not Divine. Why would you ever think that? You can take one look at me and tell that I am Undivine." I deny breathlessly as I repeat my thoughts.

"I disagree. You are stunning. Divine stunning, Celeste. I've never seen an Undivine look like you. It…confuses me."

"Well—I—no—I'm not—" I sputter, trying to figure out what to say. Is he trying to imply that he is attracted to me? More attracted to an Undivine than he ought to be?

"Goodbye, Celeste. Thank you for letting me come into your home. And for providing me with such juicy secrets." He sends a wink my way, stepping towards the door.

"Wait! You're leaving already?"

"Didn't you want me to?" His eyes sparkle in amusement, laughing quietly as I gape up at him. He slips out before I can say another word.

Chapter 6
The Game of Impressions

I watch Silvi wearily in the mirror, her scar shimmering in the light. I pack on extra glitter, knowing the theater lights will shine bright tonight. I lift a golden brush in my hands, stroking it down her silky silver hair. I clear my throat, looking down to avoid her eyes before I speak.

"Are you nervous? You haven't talked much about the first Game at all. No preparations, no plan. I would be terrified." I have had no information to pass out and I am becoming desperate. I need the money and I need Zaeden to keep his mouth shut. I am going to pry something out of her, but I need to tread carefully while doing so.

"Oh, I have a plan." She laughs. I can't help but wince at the sound. Her voice has started giving me awful headaches. I suspect it is because her power laces every noise, every word that slides off her tongue. I don't think she is trying to use it on me, but that it is part of her. My body and mind resist, though. I haven't forgotten what it feels like to be under her control.

"Oh, really? That's a relief. I was getting worried. I don't want you leaving us too soon." I laugh, the lie passing over my tongue smoothly. I want nothing more than for Silvi to go home and for this deal to be over. Silvi is helping me become a very good liar, though. She has also helped me learn how to mask my emotions, and how to clear my mind. Nothing is safe around her. My emotions, my thoughts, my body language. She catches onto everything. But I am a quick learner.

"I know exactly what to expect. My mother participated years ago when King Mourner was looking for his wife-to-be. She told me exactly what happened. The Lunar Court loves its traditions and rituals. They won't change a thing."

"Oh, I don't know much about the traditions and rituals of Royals."

"I wouldn't expect you to. You are still Undivine, after all. You guys aren't privy to Divine rituals. You're too busy worshiping us for some coin." She is trying to get under my skin, but the comments don't affect me. I am not bothered by my poverty. Besides, things won't be like this much longer. Not since I have a deal with the princes.

"What do you expect to happen?" I ask instead, trying to get *something*. I need a little information at least. Otherwise, the twins might go back on our deal. And I will do anything to make sure that doesn't happen.

"Hasn't anyone told you? It's the Game of Impressions. A display of beauty, of talent, of heritage. It's a get-to-know-you where they don't care about who you are as a person but who you are as an asset. If you aren't pretty enough, you're out. If your family isn't highly connected, you're out. While we may be the best in our Courts, some of us are still not going to be good enough. For example, a servant like you could never make it. Even if you have remarkably good looks and a few mind tricks. You have no real family, no real heritage. You would be laughed right off the stage." She smirks at me in the mirror, waiting for the comment to hit home. I only laugh, unbothered. My mouth stays in check, surprisingly. I am becoming such a well-behaved Undivine pet.

"Well, you are blessed in all of those departments. You would make a good princess, in my opinion." Other than the suspicions of her willingness to become a traitor to the crown, anyway. Though, the more I think about it, the more I know it *has* to be something else. Just listen to her talk!

"A good queen, I hope."

"Yes, and Kyelin will be a wonderful king. He needs a strong partner like you by his side." I want to gag at the false flattery I must coat her with, not wanting to imagine her and Kyelin together. Kyelin is two minutes and thirty-seven seconds older than Zaeden. Unfortunately for Zaeden, that makes Kyelin the heir. Though, from the rumors I've heard, he cares not for the title.

"I will obviously be the most beautiful, don't you agree? Especially standing next to something as plain as you." She had foregone the whole 'I want to be friends' act a week ago when I slipped up and called her a Divine-loving bitch. Now, she has begun sending these petty insults my way in attempts to agitate me. Whoops.

"Of course, Silvi. Your scar makes you stand out. Truly, a one-of-a-kind feature." I mutter with a saccharine sweetness. Looks like my mouth has failed me again. I flinch as she snaps up to look at me, not able to hold it back. I don't take back the words or apologize, though. She will know it isn't sincere.

"You know of my talents, too. No one is going to show me up." She moves on, deciding not to take things further. I glance from her eyebrow to her cheekbone as I take in that long stretch of ruined skin, wondering if bringing up something so painful is taking things too far.

"No. They definitely won't."

"I know exactly what to do to show them off, of course. People underestimate me at first. They think my powers are just offensive. But I am going to show them how wrong they are with just a thought." *Finally*, I'm starting to get somewhere.

"What's your plan, then?" I ask airily, trying not to sound too curious.

"My secrets are mine alone, unlike yours." She laughs, an unbecoming smirk grazing her lips. The words make my heart stop. Nothing can happen to me or Irissa. I have protection from the princes. Logically, I know that. But can they protect me from every threat? Especially one as large as this?

"You really don't trust me? After everything, you still won't tell me something as unimportant as this?" I let out a painful giggle, pulling extra hard on a knot in her hair.

"Why do you want to know so bad?" She stands quickly, turning to glare down at me with squinted eyes. I take a step back, brush still in hand. I smile and shake my head softly, trying to appease her.

"I am sheltered. Serving you has been the most entertaining thing to happen to me in my whole life." I sigh dramatically, attempting to play on her ego.

"Of course I am. You have a pitiful, meaningless existence. Honestly, I think I would rather kill myself than trade lives with you. I don't know how you do it. Unfortunate, truly." I grit my teeth, trying to produce a smile. Instead, I nod. She only smirks again, knowing that, this time, she managed to get under my skin.

I spit out bitterly, "I may do it yet. But I do wish to take my enemies to the deep abyss of darkness that is death with me."

She glares, trying to decide if I am threatening her or not.

"Yeah? How do you plan on doing that?"

"My secrets are mine alone." I taunt. "What's got your undergarments in a twist? You've been awful to me all week. What did I do to you?"

"I've seen you hanging around the princes. Seen the way they look at you. Especially Kyelin." Was she…jealous?

"You introduced me." I shrug innocently. "Turns out we have a lot in common."

"Like what?"

"Just certain…interests," I say coyly, playing on her jealousy. I can tell her mind instantly goes to a sexual image, her face heating up in anger as a scowl turns up her plump lips.

"I don't think they would stoop so low to be involved sexually with an Undivine like you."

"Ah, maybe so. Maybe so." She doesn't like that answer, doesn't like the nonchalance or the way I brush her off.

"You must escort me tonight. I require it." The subject change has me spinning, my mind struggling to form a reply.

"Oh?"

"Yes. I have a special role I saved just for you."

"Role?"

"Yes, as my escort. Obviously." She backtracks. Maybe she said too much?

"But you said-"

"Just do your job and escort me." She snaps, baring those pearly white teeth.

"Of course, Miss Silvi. Anything for you. I will take my leave now so I can prepare." I bow before I leave, letting her believe she has won once more. Little does she know, I'm running to my masters like the good little bitch I am.

By the time I reach the princes suite, I am panting. I ran like my life depended on it because, really, it does. The guards let me pass without a second glance, only needing to look at my ankles. They just need to see that scar that will always mark me as someone's property. I knock on the door loudly, anxiety running through me until I start to tremble. I hope I'm not too late, the information too little. Before I can debate the possibilities of what will happen behind this door, it swings open. I freeze, stiffening up. The image I am greeted with sends a spark right down to my core, a throbbing in my heart that begins and doesn't stop.

Kyelin stands before me, his crimson hair soaked and dripping with water. His shirt is non-existent. I can see every inch of that tanned chest, the flex of each muscle. I jump back, mortified. I shouldn't be seeing the prince like this, no matter how good he looks. I close my eyes tightly, ignoring his laugh as I will myself not to peak.

"I'm sorry for the intrusion, Your Highness. I wanted to update you on my assignment."

"Of course." He continues to laugh at me, stepping aside. "Please, come in. Don't worry, you are not the first woman to see me this way and you won't be the last. I'm surprised someone like you is embarrassed by skin."

"Someone like me?" I ask with a roll of my eyes, stepping through anyways.

"My apologies. You are just so beautiful, I assumed—never mind. I'm digging myself deeper into a hole, aren't I?" I just laugh, taking a look around in an attempt not to blush from embarrassment.

The first thing I set my eyes on is a massive couch, its royal blue velvet alluring. Zaeden lies across it gracefully, his legs hanging over the end. They are crossed at the ankles, his head hanging off the side at an odd angle. Even with the odd angle, he looks every bit the prince he is supposed to be. Something about it pulls at my chest, and I can't help but find him incredibly attractive. I shut that thought down quickly. I can't think of a Divine in that way, especially not a Royal. That will only end in heartbreak for me.

I look down to meet his dark eyes, though, unable to look away. It feels too intense, feels like there is a secret passing through us. I don't look away until Kyelin speaks again.

"What information do you have for us, Celeste?" He's much calmer than I am as he takes a ribbon into his hands. A shiver runs through me at the intimacy he uses when my name leaves his lips. I watch as he slowly pulls his hair up, gathering it at the base of his head. A few rebellious strands fall forward, framing his face.

"Well, Silvi told me a couple of things. Not a lot, and not much willingly. I think she was becoming a bit suspicious of me." I'm able to control my emotions relatively well around Silvi but with these two? It's extremely difficult and I'm not sure why; probably another Royal thing.

"I'm worried that she is going to involve me in some way. She said that she had a special role for me, then backtracked and said it was just as her escort. I don't…I don't want to escort her. I'm not sure what she is going to do to me. I know I'm just an Undivine servant, and it's my job, but…"

"I agree," Zaeden says, sitting up from his lounging position, "Something is amiss. But you do not need to worry, Celeste. As per our agreement, nothing is going to happen to you."

"Yes, most certainly." Kyelin agrees. "She may be up to something. And if it does involve you—well, I am only sorry we did not find out sooner. We may have been able to prevent it."

"You can't prevent it now?" I try to avoid sending lustful looks his way, try to avoid staring at that delicious show of skin.

"I'm sorry, but we are going to insist you do what she asks. The Game is about to begin, it will look suspicious if you suddenly disappear. If we were the reason why. We don't want anyone questioning you or us."

"I'm sorry, too." I glance at Zaeden, letting the hurt flash across my face. I don't want to be in harm's way. I don't want anything to do with these plans Silvi has. Irissa needs me. I can't do anything to help her if I am dead. With his next words, he almost reads my thoughts in the way they are so eerily similar.

"Of course, we know you don't want to be in harm's way. And you won't be. We won't let that happen. We most certainly won't let you die. We swear not to let things go that far. And if they do? Well, you can feel assured that your sister will be well cared for."

"Thanks, that's *so* reassuring. 'Go let Silvi play with your life, Celeste. We don't want anyone associating us with you, an Undivine, so we won't help.'"

"It's not like that—"

"I think it is." I send a glare to both men, trembling. I turn to leave, but I stop when Kyelin puts his hand on my back. I freeze, flinching away from his touch. I take two quick steps to the left, putting distance between us. I expect to see a look of hurt on his face, but amusement dances in his eyes, instead.

"I must admit, women don't usually react to my touch in such a way."

"I'm sure they don't," I say shakily, "But they aren't Undivine, are they?"

"It's not such a big deal. Not to me."

"I think I've heard enough pretty lies today, Your Highness."

Before he can say anything else, I slip out of the door and away from the suffocating room. My world is spinning and my vision is fading. I can feel myself hyperventilating, my breathing heavy. This is different from being grabbed in the streets. There, I didn't feel trapped. There, I became a beast. One who fights back against her attacker and wins. Here, the beast has been placed in a cage. And very quickly that beast is becoming prey.

I'm not sure how, but I make it to the servant's quarters before throwing up. Over and over and over until nothing's left. My stomach is already fairly empty, but now everything is gone. I try to tell myself this is a rational response. That I am allowed to have reactions to trauma. But it's hard to truly rationalize things like this. A hot prince, a hot *half-naked* prince, put a hand on my back. It wasn't even on bare skin! It wasn't menacing. He didn't have impure motives. It was just a reflex, a kindness he was trying to show me. And yet, here I am, having a panic attack over it. How fucked up is that?

My mind replays that awful night. I see three men, staring viciously into my soul. Those eyes and their voices are the only things I will ever recognize if I see them again. I remember the bruises their belts left, and the ringing in my head after being slammed over and over again into the wall. The prince isn't like that. Neither of them are. And I should be ecstatic to have an attractive Divine giving me such attention, even if it isn't sexual. But I'm not. And it's hard for me to be rational about that.

I stumble into the sewing room, running out of time. I'm about to be presented in front of the king and queen. Again. I need to look decent for that. I sit down on a small stool, combing my hair quickly and efficiently. I sigh at the wildness. Most of the time, I hate my curls. And right now? Well, they make me feel exactly the way I am trying to avoid: decent. My vomiting leaves no time for a touch-up on my makeup, but I don't mind. I'm not used to wearing the stuff and I won't be allowed to once this is all over, anyway. Ryleigh puts it on me every morning now. She says it is necessary. I have to *look* impressive to *be* impressive, which is what will allow me to keep my job. Little does she know, I plan to retire very early.

"Delivery!" Someone shouts with a bang on the door. I jump, glancing over in confusion. Usually, other maids bring in the material deliveries. And that voice sounds distinctly male.

"Bring it in!" I shout back in response.

"You Celeste?" I nod at the small boy, glancing at the big box in his hands. It is a beautiful shade of dark blue, typical of our Court. Stars dance across it, shining like they are real. It is eerily similar to the dress Silvi wore on her first day here. He shoves the box into my hands, leaving abruptly. I gape at his back, trying to object. He never turns back.

I set the box onto my makeshift desk, curiosity overwhelming me. I gently lift the lid, holding my face away just to be safe. Part of me is fearful of what I will find inside. When nothing jumps out, I inch closer. What I see takes my breath away. It is a dress. And even folded up, I know it is beautiful. Beautiful and expensive. On top sits a small sheet of paper, intricate writing spelling out my name. I flip it over, reading the message.

We're sorry.

It isn't hard to guess who it was from.

I pull the dress from its cage, gasping. I have never seen a dress like this. It is the color of lavender, its length flowing to the floor. The fabric is soft and voluptuous, yet elegant and suave. It is mostly sheer, like most of the materials we have been working with lately. Much like the dress Silvi wore on arrival, you would see the outline of my breasts but nothing more. The layers from the waist down prevent anything else from being visible. Its purpose is to tease, most certainly picked out by the princes themselves. It is something made with a man's view in mind. The sleeves look like bells, the neckline dipping dangerously low. I can see how the top will hug me, but the bottom won't. It flows like water, the different fabrics drifting away from each other. If I dare put this on, I'll look like a Divine.

So, of course, I put it on.

It is made to my exact measurements, the length and fit perfect for my frame. I'm not sure how they knew what size to get, since this had obviously been made in advance. I'm not sure why though, either. I hadn't been upset with them until recently. At least, no more than normal.

When I walk, it looks like I am floating. Almost like this flowing dress is carrying me. I won't glitter in the lights like Silvi. I won't have beauty that shines like hers. But my dress certainly will. She is wearing a simple, elegant black dress. She wants to look professional, and business-like. I, on the other hand, look like I should be frolicking in the woods. Like I live in a cute cottage and talk to animals. I look *good*.

I practically dance in excitement, glancing back at myself in the mirror. I see something glittering in the box when I do, so I turn to see what else has been left for me. First, I pull out a pair of slippers that match. When I slip them on, it feels like stepping on clouds. I groan at the instant relief, amazed at the quality. My hard calluses are finally at rest. Then, at the very bottom, I see a gorgeous diamond necklace. It is fairly simple, compared to the jewelry that I see Divine wear. It's on a long silver chain, a singular, very large, teardrop diamond placed right in the middle. When I slip it on, it falls right into the dip of my chest and straight into my cleavage. I laugh lightly, knowing this, too, is intentional. Somehow, I can't find it in myself to care about the implications.

Silvi is furious. She fumes next to me, smoke practically coming out of her ears. I have to hold in my laughter, though it's obvious how giddy I am. She is jealous. She can hardly bear to look at me. It gives me this satisfying rush, one I probably shouldn't be enjoying so much.

"Where did you get it?"

"It's a gift from a…special friend." I purr as we take a step forward in line.

"A friend? Please. Only a Royal could afford to give away a dress like that to a lowly servant like you. I'm sure they just pity you since you are too poor to afford anything pretty for yourself. At least I know now they have a sense of taste for when they start gifting *me* pretty things."

"Yes, at least."

"I don't know who you think you are fooling. Whoring around with a couple of Royals doesn't make you fit in here, Celeste. You are Undivine. You may clean up nicely, but this tiny little body of yours is all you have going for you. Your personality is bland, your powers are nonexistent. And don't get me started on that hideous attitude. Get over yourself. You will never belong among our kind."

"Lashing out at me because of your jealousy? Not an attractive trait, Silvi."

"Don't—"

"Furthermore, I would like to acknowledge that you are right. Your kind is very different from mine, and I will never feel like I belong here because I don't. I may be dreadfully bland physically, but my personality is not. You, on the other hand, are very stereotypical. Most of your kind are. You are cruel out of jealousy and spite, which I expected. Too predictable, really. An awful quality in a life partner. If you were to be my wife, I would expect more creativity from you." She falls silent, bothered by my bored tone. She doesn't get under my skin like she wants. Instead, I have gotten under hers.

"If I was your wife, I think I would be much happier than I am now. Maybe, if we were in different positions, I could woo you properly and forgo this mean girl act." I turn in surprise, eyes wide. The words were barely audible, but I'm sure I heard correctly.

"What?" Did she just say she wanted to *woo* me?

"I didn't say anything." She scoffs, rolling her eyes. "Get your ears checked, little Undivine." I heard it, though. And I'm not sure how to feel about it.

We sit in silence until the girl before us steps through the black curtains, causing us to take our place as next in line. Silvi straightens, patting down her perfectly unwrinkled dress.

"Do not mess this up for me." She hisses, not daring to look down at me. I roll my eyes, unimpressed with the threatening tone.

"I will not be the one that ruins this for you. You can do that all on your own." She stiffens, making it obvious how nervous she is. I can rarely sense Silvi's emotions, but I can *feel* this one. She is unintentionally sending it out, and everyone around us feels it. I see a soldier shiver when the feeling hits him, confusion overtaking his features. I can't help but look at his eyes, relieved when I don't recognize them. Silvi quickly jerks me up, forcing me to stand straight. I want to scowl, but I also don't want to give her the satisfaction.

"Silvi Merkelly?" The soldier asks, glancing down at us.

"Yes." She replies, the one word dripping with authority. She sounds every bit like the princess she desperately wants to be.

"Go."

We both tighten our grip on each other, a reflex neither of us acknowledges. Together, we take a step forward. Then another. And another. Until we glide through the curtains and face our destiny.

The room is huge. It's a traditional theater, with rows upon rows of seats. They circle us, building up and up and up. We stand on the edge of a large circle, staring up into bright lights and unfamiliar faces. The floor is wooden, dark, and sealed. I can see a scorch mark ahead of me along with ashes piled up on the floor. Other than that, there isn't a single item lying on the ground.

My gut clenches as I stand there, feeling bare in front of

so many Divine. The whole city is present. Villagers aren't allowed to witness the Games, but any Divine can. And with just a glance at this crowd, I know they are all here tonight. It overwhelms me instantly. Somehow, it's like I can feel the power in the air. In one direction I can feel these weak strands connecting to me, in the other, it feels like strings pulling on my limbs. I begin to panic, my breathing heavy. I've never been around more than a few Divine at a time. Is this what it is like to be around the elite? The powerless feeling the power? It is intimidating, utterly terrifying. I'm not sure what, exactly, is happening. I don't want to find out. I just want this to be over with, to get out of here. Trying to pull myself together, I focus on the physical connection between Silvi and me. The touch of our linked arms is keeping me grounded, distracting me.

"Announcing Miss Silvi Merkelly of the Solar Court, occupation assistant to the Solar Advisor. And her escort, Celeste…" He looks at me pointedly, silently asking for my full name.

"I don't associate with any other name," I say, somehow keeping my voice from shaking. He nods, continuing his introductions.

"Celeste of the Lunar Court, occupation handmaiden." A collective gasp fills the air, faces flashing shock, horror, and anger. They all understand what that one little word means. I am an Undivine, standing here in an expensive dress with a High. Masquerading like I am something more when I so obviously am not. I see hands held over hearts, over mouths, gripping onto each other. What a shocker right? Silvi chose *me* as her escort, let *me* experience this magic. How lucky I should be.

We both stand with chins up, backs straight. I am trying my

best not to seem weak in front of the Divine. They like seeing Undivine squirm, and I am *not* going to let their cruel words bother me today. I am used to being sneered at. This is just in a larger capacity. Same words, different people.

I find my eyes searching the crowd, my mind looking for clarity. When I get to the center, there they are. At the bottom row, there is a large, clear box. In it sits the king and queen on their thrones, staring at me scornfully. I make eye contact, not breaking it until the queen turns away. Then my eyes find Zaeden. He winks, eyes raking over my body. I blush involuntarily, moving my gaze to Kyelin. He, too, is watching me closely. This idea of theirs is brilliant. Me, this dress, this necklace. I am taking attention away from Silvi. She is unremarkable next to me, an Undivine playing dress up. I am the spectacle here. I can only pray that playing this game doesn't end with me being injured. Or killed.

"Begin!" The announcer shouts, cheers erupting around the theater. I curtsy to the Royals, trying to slip away quietly. This is finally over. My role as an escort is done.

"No, Celeste. You aren't going anywhere. I need you for my presentation." Silvi smiles, holding tightly to my arm. I freeze, unsure. I look up to Kyelin, and he sends me a nod of encouragement. They want to see how this plays out, then. I will need to be the sacrificial lamb. But they are here, in that box only ten feet away. No harm will come to me.

"Of course." I purr, feigning confidence as I turn back to face her. I smile just as brightly as she is, trying to hide my unease. She will use any drop of fear against me, so instead I will be the picture of calm. I will show no doubts, mentally or physically. At least, that's what I am telling myself. I can already feel that warning in my head, the same one I always get when she speaks to me. But it's stronger. So strong it makes a shiver run down my spine. I curse myself for the involuntary reaction, hoping she doesn't notice.

"I am a manipulator." She announces with a gentle, perfect smile. "But do not fret. I will not manipulate you." I can practically hear the excitement tingling in the air, the tension as they wait to watch her dramatic display. "Truly, I am an Empath. My powers delve deep into the mind. I can control your emotions and your thoughts. More than that, I can send you my own emotions, my own thoughts. I can become one with you, and you one with me." She revels in the gasps from the crowds. Empaths are rare, especially ones with such unique abilities.

"I have vowed not to use my powers for evil." She tells them, embodying a goddess in every curve of those luscious, lying lips. "As most of you have seen, I have a horrific scar—a scar given to me through evil. And so, I vowed never to be like that evil. To never use my powers to harm others the way they used theirs to harm me." She just gave herself a sympathy vote. Just like that, she has the Divine in the palm of her hands. Because what better than a tragic backstory to gain their support? After a moment of silence, she begins the lies again.

"Celeste has agreed to be my helper today. A willing participant in this Game. She knows of my powers and has let me use her to train." I can see Kyelin and Zaeden's eyes fall to me, suspicious. Great. Not only has she painted herself in a better picture, but she has cast shadows upon mine. "Today, here and now, we will show you what I can do." She thinks I am going to allow her to use her powers on me again, thinks I am going to cave in front of these Divine. Because if I resist her now, all eyes will be on me. And if she thinks it is strange I can resist her, well, then what will these people think? I haven't even told Kyelin and Zaeden about being able to resist her. The thought worries me, and I have this awful feeling that it won't go over well. But I can't let her use me like that again. Can't give her the satisfaction of embarrassing me. The decision about what to do is much too easy.

I watch as Silvi curtsies to the Royals, turning towards me once she rises. I spare a glance at the twins one more time, terrified inside. But they are calm and collected. I don't get a courtesy glance in return. Now, all of the attention is on Silvi. They are no longer paying attention to me because I have already played my part. When she meets my eyes, I don't turn away. I try to focus on the glass eye, willing myself to fight. I won't become prey in front of these predators. I won't give them a taste of blood in the water.

Silvi's delicate fingers rise, flourishing in a dramatic gesture. I feel the tingle in my head that warns me, pinpointed on her. I fight hard against the feeling. For a moment, I feel a sense of giddiness rising in my throat and threatening to take over. I want to laugh at something, something that is so, so funny. Something I can't place my finger on. But I can also tell how *wrong* it is. So I growl in the back of my throat, pushing it away. I will not be controlled.

Her face crinkles up angrily, trying to pass it off as confusion. She was hoping it would work this time. Maybe she thought it had been a one-off. A fluke. Or maybe she was hoping I would defy her. To have a chance at getting rid of me. Either way, she attempts to push in my mind again. I'm not sure what, exactly, she is trying to plant into my mind or what emotion she is trying to make me feel. Now that the first one is gone, I can't feel anything. I keep my face calm, seemingly bored. No one will have the satisfaction of seeing my reaction.

"You are supposed to be swearing your allegiance to the Royals!" She cries out suddenly, feigning surprise and fear. Something flashes in her eyes, something that almost looks like...*regret*. The crowd whispers among themselves, confused and shocked. I can see the debate. Who is at fault for this: Silvi or Celeste? But while they discuss the situation she decides to attack again, pushing even harder. I feel a small amount of fear as it enters me, but I push it away, too. I am becoming too strong for her.

Then she starts screaming.

"Someone grab her!" She screeches, holding up a shaky finger. "Please, take her away! Question her this instance! No Undivine has ever been able to thwart my powers before! Do you think it is a coincidence this one became my handmaiden? She must be a spy! A rebel! Find out who she works for! Take her!" I panic, eyes wide. I let my unbothered demeanor go, true fear racing through me. I turn to the twins with begging eyes, tears stinging the corners. They *have* to do something about this. What is Silvi playing at anyhow? She practically told me she wanted to *woo* me, so why is she doing this? Why is she trying to get me killed?

"Maybe you aren't as powerful as you think you are, Miss Silvi, if an Undivine can indeed thwart you." Kyelin's voice rings out above the screaming crowd. He chuckles and part of the crowd follows suit.

"No. I am exactly as powerful as I believe myself to be. Let me demonstrate." She turns to a nearby soldier, a fierce determination in her eyes. I can see the moment she enters his mind. His face slacks and turns blank, like a canvas waiting to be painted on.

"Fall." She whispers menacingly, watching with a cruel smile. He falls to his knees, still an emotionless slate. She turns back to the Royals, arrogant. The soldier is a Low. If she can do that to him, she should have easily taken care of me. It is proof enough. A Divine's word over mine. The crowd's gasps echo across the room, some crying out for my retrieval. They scream for justice, for me to come clean now. They scream for me to be hung.

"Why?" I whisper as I let a single tear escape. Why did she do this?

"I like you, Celeste. A lot. Maybe too much. I'm sorry. But you forced my hand tonight. This wouldn't have happened if you just let me in. I couldn't let you tarnish my reputation. I had to do something to fix this. Someone needed to take the fall for this fuck up. I had to save one of us. It was either you or me. And it is always going to be me."

Two soldiers face us, each taking a step forward. I turn towards the door we entered in, running. I don't make it far. The soldiers are on me in seconds, each grabbing an arm. I scream as they drag me down, kicking back as hard as I can. I hit one in the shin, and he drops my arm with a hiss of pain. I manage to yank my other arm free, taking his surprise at his partner stumbling to my advantage. I fall to the ground, scraping my knees against the cold floor. The dress rips as I fall, one of my beautiful layers dangling on the ground. One of my sleeves has a hole from where the soldier had yanked on it, tearing the seams apart with the force. I begin to crawl away desperately, barely able to see through my tears. I'm shaking too hard to stand, and I know I will not be making it out of this situation alive. Just as that hopelessness is kicking in, I feel it. My head starts pounding, that siren screaming. I know then that magic is coming for me.

A protective creature inside me roars to life, kicking and screaming as it fights the thing inside me trying to hold it back. It circles my bones, invades my organs, and poisons my blood. Round and round and round. Every inch of my body is trembling with this vile creature's residue. An ugly monster that has reared its head. It goes up, up, up. Wraps itself around and around my neck and *pulls*. I choke, coughing and sputtering. But when I yank and pull, it doesn't come loose. It is embedded inside of me, a part of me I haven't yet met. A killer that has broken to the surface. And suddenly, I am a puppet tied to strings. I am doing something I shouldn't. I can feel how wrong it is. I should have never allowed this beast access to my body. *I didn't mean to, I didn't mean to, I didn't mean to.*

I scream when I see the ball of ice approaching, barreling towards me at top speed. All I can do is cover my head, hoping for the best. My chest screams from how hard my heart beats, panic curling through every cell in my body. I can hear the crowd screaming, but it isn't a cry of success. It is a song of panic.

Suddenly, I am somebody I was never supposed to be.

Suddenly, my world is being inexplicably and irrevocably changed.

I peer up through my arms, seeing why they a so frightened. I am surrounded by a bubble, one that wavers when I move. I can barely understand what it is. But there is no denying its presence. It is a shield. The ball hits it. Hard. And it falls to the ground limply, shattering upon impact.

I scramble back, the shield breaking. My breathing is heavy, my eyes wide. Who sent a shield over me? None of the Royals have that power. So who else would try to save me? No one. That is painfully obvious. Not a single Divine would have risked their lives for me. So does that mean...does that mean it was me? Sure, I feel this little tingling in my fingers that travels all the way up my arms. But that can be anything, right? There is no way I could have done it, and yet...that is the only logical answer. I close my eyes, the anger finally overtaking me. No one has tried to help me. It is up to me to help myself if I want to make it out of here alive.

I stand, coming to a decision. If the shield was mine, I will make another one. Soldiers start to approach again, ready to test their power against mine. I throw up my hands at a small gust of wind a soldier sends my way. Miraculously, it bounces off me and back to him. That tingling comes again, but this time the release feels *good*. It feels like a pressure lifting off my chest. I don't mean to hurt him, but the wind flings him into the closed door. I hear a crack, and he falls, limp. I don't send him a second glance. I can't stop to think about what I may have just done. How irrevocably I may have just changed my life and his.

I watch as a piece of floor is lifted, revealing the dirt underneath. The whole ground shakes, causing me to stumble. The piece is lifting high like a pillar, and the soldier controlling it turns to face me. He drops it with a finger, laughing. I hold my hands above me, praying the shield forms again. And it does. The floor piece touches my shield and it turns to ashes, floating harmlessly down like snow. I laugh in disbelief, becoming more confident. I can do this. I will survive. A Divine will not kill me.

Soldier after soldier I fight, breathless and angry. They are wearing down fast, but I am not. They are Lows, so their powers don't last long. But mine just keeps going and going. Like it has no end. And the more I use it the better I get. It's my thoughts that control it. As long as I have the intent to create, a shield will appear. It isn't about hand movements or finger-pointing, though that helps direct them. And where are the princes in all this? I was promised protection. Or is it too inconvenient to keep that promise now? I don't remember putting an inconvenience clause in our deal, but maybe I missed it. I hope I get a chance to spit on their graves once the goddesses come down to smite them.

There are a few times when I am thrown to the ground, scraping every inch of my body. But I keep standing back up, keep getting hit. My powers aren't weakening. Powers. *My powers.* I laugh at the thought, throwing my head back. Here I am, covered in dirt, my dress torn to bits, skin raw, and I am laughing in front of these Divine. All because I am no longer powerless. I actually have powers and *strong* ones. Whatever it is that Irissa has, I have too. I feel like I am on top of the moon, like nothing will ever drag me down from here. I cackle as I cause pain and take pleasure in hurting those who tried to hurt me. It's a strange feeling, to revel in such sinful desires. I've never wanted to hurt anyone as badly as I do now, never wanted to seek revenge so strongly. But I do. Oh, I do. I want to hurt them *all.* Nothing can stop me or the blind terror I have created. But—what is that?

Darkness creeps out from the stands, slithering around on the ground as it approaches. I freeze, crying out in a panic. I would recognize that inky liquid and purple smoke anywhere. I scramble back, shaking my head. No. He promised. *They* promised. My shields come up, one after the other, but it makes no difference. He is a Royal. The poison slides up my legs, goosebumps rising in their wake. I scream, clawing, kicking, flinging. Blood coats my dress, blood drawn by my own hands. The poison climbs up my body, slides into my nose, through my ears, and into my mouth. I gag, breathing in sharply on instinct. I can't taste anything, can't smell it. And worst of all, I can't fight it. It surrounds my very being, swallowing me whole. All too quickly, I am swept down into the darkness with it.

Chapter 7

All I know is the dark.

It feels like I'm wrapped in a warm blanket I never plan to leave. Is this what death feels like?

My eyes pop open, immediately closing when that blanket is gone. It's just brightness now, a never-ending light. Not death. They crack open again in a blink. Once. Twice. Three times before I can make out shapes. My heart stops when I recognize them.

I am in a cell. The cells only spies are deigned lucky enough to have. The ones where they torture you until you are nothing more than paste in their hands. I remember what Silvi said. What she told them I was. I'm not sure exactly what happens here, but I know it isn't good. Torture never is, right? Maybe I will get lucky and they will just kill me to get it over with. Send me back to that everlasting darkness.

I stand, legs shaking. I'm not sure what poison, exactly, entered my body. I remember the absolute terror that grew in me. It could have left internal damage for all I know. Whatever it was, it has left me extremely weak. So, so weak. My whole body aches, probably a side effect of the fight. I manage to stumble my way to the metal bars of the cell, leaning on them for support. There is nothing else in this bland room. Just me and the bars. And are those blood splatters? I try not to focus on those, rattling the bars instead. It wastes the little strength I have, but I do it again. Over and over and over, screaming in frustration. My movements are slow and feeble, but it's better than sitting idly while I wait to be killed. It gives me a reason to stay conscious. Finally, I became awake enough to scream more than incoherent noises.

"Let me out!" I screech despite knowing it won't help. "Let me out this instance! I'm not a spy! I'm not a spy! *I am not a spy!*" I scream until my throat is raw, becoming more and more desperate. I don't want to die here. Every one of those damn Divine have betrayed me. I should have known better than tangling myself up in Divine affairs. And what about my sister? Will the Royals go back on that promise, too? I scream and scream and scream. Maybe this is part of the torture. Or maybe it is part of the poison. Maybe my mental state is just really fragile after all that's happened.

At last, I give up, stumbling back and falling to the floor. My strength is gone. I don't try to summon my powers. What will a shield do here, anyway? I curl into myself, knees into my chest. I need to be smarter. I need to think. I don't have attacking powers. I don't have much strength or skill. So what *do* I have? Well, I guess my powers let me feel others. They let me keep their powers away. I concentrate, searching for the slightest warning in my head. I feel nothing. Absolutely *nothing*. I don't feel anyone else around. I'm not sure how far this ability reaches, though. Someone can be at the end of the hall for all I know. I don't hear anything. No sounds of breathing, no footsteps. I am on the verge of giving up when I feel it.

A Divine is close.

It doesn't take long for me to hear footsteps falling down the long hallway, the echoes bouncing from each corner. I wait for them to approach, panting as I prepare my rant. I immediately recoil, however, stumbling back as far as I can get. The Divine laughs, dark and raspy. I recognize those eyes. Brown, with a sliver of gold, and a teardrop for a pupil. I know exactly who this Low Divine is. Know exactly what he has done to me in the past. What he will do now, especially since we are completely and utterly alone. Fear is quickly rising, my body trembling underneath his stare.

"You remember me?" He seems surprised, like what he and his buddies did wasn't something I *should* remember. "I must say, I barely remembered you. When they brought you in here, I wasn't sure at first. Thought maybe I had seen you on one of your shifts or something. Then I remembered all the fun we had." I stare in shock, not believing he didn't remember beating a young girl to near death. Was he that drunk? Or did he just do this so often that one girl blends into another? He continues to speak, not bothering to let me reply.

"I remember that day very well, now. Do you? How about I come in and remind you?" He smirks at me through the bars, giddiness radiating around the entire room. I spit at him in response. He hisses as it hits his eye, swiping it away with ease. He jumps at the bars, hands reaching in to grab me. I flinch hard, pressing myself firmly against the wall. Obviously, he doesn't care much about what he says or who hears. My eyes shut tightly as I try to breathe through the fear and tell myself to just *think*. We are alone and probably will be for a while. No one will be coming to save me, something that seems to be a common occurrence today.

"No. You can't come in. I won't let you." I hiss as he dangles his keys in front of the bars, trying to sound threatening. I have powers now. Surely that means I am a little intimidating? He only laughs again, slowly pushing one of the keys into the hole on the lock. I lunge forward desperately, trying to grab them. He grabs my wrist, snapping it in one fluid motion. I scream, tears filling my eyes. I managed to knock the keys out of his hands, though, and they fell just below him. I dive, but he is faster.

"You're going to pay for that." He grinds out, quickening his movements.

"I think I already have." I breathe through the pain. "You aren't allowed in here. The-"

"Who's going to stop me? You?" His laugh invades my ears, his eyes sparkling in pure joy.

"The Royals. The Royals are going to protect me. They are going to—" I am trying to convince myself at this point, or maybe just scare him. But it doesn't matter. He doesn't think anyone will catch him or punish him if they do. He's done this so many times and has never paid for it. They will find me here, broken and maybe even dead, and never look for who did it. He is a soldier. He knows the rotations. Has friends in high places, probably. He is also strong. I know, deep down, I cannot beat him. Would I even be able to form a protective shield? I used so much power before, power I have never wielded. What if that was all I had left? All it will take is brute force. I'm too small, too weak, too Undivine. I can't dream of winning a fight against a man this giant. I can't win against a Low Divine. Logically, having hope is unrealistic. And I don't have any. But that doesn't mean I have to be an easy target.

He is on me before the door is fully open. His hand lifts,

swinging down in a sharp fist. I scream, throwing my own hands up to protect my face. The hit is so forceful it knocks me over. My shields don't come, despite my efforts to call them. I hit my knees hard, and I attempt to get back up before he can keep me pinned here. He quickly clambers over me, though, pushing my face into the hard, cold floor. I scream again, thrashing around and trying to crawl out from underneath his heavy body. My shields still won't come, and my body is still useless. I feel another crack as he pushes down onto my left leg, pain radiating up and down the length of it.

"Help!" I screech in desperation through the heavy tears threatening to escape. "Help me!" I kick my unhurt leg up, but the angle is awkward. I can't get a good hit in. I still can't muster up a hint of my shields, can't even form a drop of the power that had helped me so valiantly before.

"Shut up and sit still." He grunts, flipping me over. Before he can pin my arms down again, I swing. It's with my left hand, which isn't as strong, but it still packs a punch. I hear the satisfying sound of skin on skin, but I don't have time to relish in it. Instead, I raise my right knee as hard as I can. I miss his groin, hitting his thigh instead. It is enough to make him grunt, but not enough to stop him. He pins my hands down, pushing into my broken wrist. I scream again, crying freely now.

"Please, please, *please*! I won't tell anyone. I won't. Please leave. *Please.*" I resort to begging and it creates a boiling rage inside of my gut.

"Why would I leave? I have you right where I want you. And your screams are so delicious. How did we start last time, hmm? The fingers, right?" I scream again, fighting against his hold.

Please, anyone, please, help me. Help me. Help me.

"Get off of her." A voice growls beside us; a very familiar voice. "Or I will be starting with *your* fingers and won't stop until your skin is stripped of your body." I can't help but feel relief at seeing his dark stature. I feel the threat hit home as the soldier stiffens, still not moving off of me. I may be trading one monster for another, but I am desperate. At least I *know* this monster.

"I was told-" He tries first, surprised at Zaeden's presence.

"You were told wrong." He takes a step forward, poison leaking from every pore.

"I was just trying to help with the interrogations! My orders are from—" He leaps up, allowing me to fling myself into a sitting position. I pull on my dress, desperately trying to cover the bruises already forming on my body.

"You take orders from me, got it? Now get out of my sight. Actually, why don't you go ahead and put yourself in a cell down the next hall, hmm? Don't worry, you won't be there long." Zaeden means he won't be *alive* in there long, that much is clear. His voice sends a shiver down my spine, bringing something raging and fiery up to the surface. I wish I could watch him torture the Divine, watch *his* fingers break, and hear those cries of terror.

"Of course." He nods frantically, sending me one last sneer of disgust. "I'll leave you with the damaged goods."

"Damaged goods?" I rage, trying, and failing to stand.

"Yes, and you have been for a long time. Would we say…five years?" I spit at him again, wishing I could do *anything* else to defend myself. He turns, ready to pounce on me again. He forgets about the Royal behind him, too enraged with me to care. Zaeden has him by the throat instantly, poison slipping

117

into the Low Divine's throat and nose. He chokes and I take great pleasure in watching him fall. The sound of his head hitting the bars is one I won't forget anytime soon.

"Are you okay?" I watch hesitantly as Zaeden approaches, pace slow and steady. I don't move. Not that I can do much moving, anyway. A Low Divine has just proven to be stronger than me, so how strong is a Royal compared to that? I'm sure I don't want to know the answer.

"No," I answer truthfully, tears still falling. My body is still screaming at me, everything on fire. Will I pass out soon? Right now, I wish I would.

"You know that man." It's not a question. He reaches out to touch me, and I flinch in response. He doesn't stop, though. He puts a hand on my bad wrist, fingers prodding. I can't help but whimper.

"I don't." I lie. I don't want to talk about this. Sure, it's been five years. Sure, I should have been well on my way to healing. But I'm not. No one but Ryleigh ever found out, no one was ever punished, and I still have to walk the same halls where it happened. Talking about it isn't going to do much to help now.

"Don't lie to me, Celeste." He growls, anger flashing in those dark eyes.

"I didn't." Must we always have this same argument each time we meet?

"I don't have to protect your sister, you know? I still haven't told anyone about her. But, now that I think about it, I probably should. You are a rebel spy, after all."

"No! You swore!" I scream too loudly, too quickly. His answering smirk tells me everything I need to know.

"Tell me. Now. And while you talk, I will heal you."

"Heal me? You aren't a healer."

"Most people just know about the dark properties of my powers, but some poisons can counteract others. I won't be able to fix it completely. We will need a real healer for that. But I can take away the pain and the bruising. The healer will set the bones straight again." I shiver as the cold liquid that is his power touches me, unable to look away from his focused face. Even now, I find him unbearably attractive. Even as he demands my deepest secrets. As he threatens my sister. I should hate myself for that attraction, but I can't find it in me to care right now. For some reason, I find myself telling him the truth.

"I recognized him as soon as I saw his eyes. I never saw anything else the day they attacked me. Just their eyes. And their voices...they haunt my dreams every night. Along with Irissa's screams," I say with a shuddering breath, already feeling the burning in my body fading, "It happened my first week here. I didn't know my way around. I got lost so fast. I found myself in a quiet part of the castle, a part mostly unused. That's where they found me. I looked a little too innocent and clueless, I guess. Like easy prey. There were three of them. They surrounded me, laughing. Teasing. They had these black masks on, protecting their identities.

They pushed me into an empty room. I didn't know what to do. What could I have done? I screamed, obviously. But no one ever heard. Or, if they did, they didn't care. They took turns holding me down. One would hold my arms, the other my legs. The third would hit me. Over and over and over. Then they would move on to the next form of torture. Breaking fingers and toes, cutting me with daggers. Laughing the whole time. They treated it like a game. They started keeping count of who got the loudest scream, who made the biggest bruise, who broke the most bones. It didn't matter how much I fought, how loud I screamed, I couldn't get away. They were getting off on my pain right in front of each other, right in front of me. It was disgusting. It felt like it went on for hours and hours. I wanted to die. I thought I would. I thought maybe they would kill me afterward to keep me quiet. But they didn't. They knew I couldn't report them. They never said their names and with those masks…well, I had nothing to go off of. Besides, they couldn't just leave a dead body in the castle, could they? That would raise more questions than I was worth.

But I never forgot those eyes. Those awful eyes. Never forgot the teasing voices. They called me all sorts of names and derogatory terms. I still hear them in my sleep. Feel them on top of me. It took me a long time to be able to feel the touch of a man without flinching. Even just a brush of a hand gets me sometimes. I'm always on edge, always worried about when I might be near a Divine. Ryleigh found me and didn't ask any questions. Just said she should have protected me better. She carried me to this healer she knew, and they didn't ask any questions, either. Just fixed me up and sent me back to work. Said this happens a lot to Undivine. Apparently, there is a whole club dedicated to the subject of beating Undivine. They like to brag about their conquests. I—I never told anyone. Until now." I can see the rage burning beneath his skin, his jaw ticking. I'm not sure why he cares so much.

"I'll handle it."

"No, please. I'm in a cell. Did you see how easily he found me? I have avoided them for years. I don't want them all showing up and having a repeat of this whole situation. Why do you care, anyway? We hardly know each other. You're Royal and I'm Undivine. This is the norm for us."

"You belong to me now, Celeste. My brother and I have claimed you and sworn to protect you. We didn't do that lightly. Your enemies are mine. So that man? He has made himself an enemy to the crown."

"I don't want them locked up with or around me. Please, don't anger them. My powers...they failed me. I can't...I can't do this again." I'm powerless while sitting in this cell, just like I was powerless before. I hate that feeling, and I'm willing to do anything to avoid it.

"I wasn't going to lock them up." His jaw ticks again, his voice that deadly calm I am becoming accustomed to. "I plan on plucking his eyes straight from his head so he can never lay eyes on you again. On breaking the bones he broke in you so he will understand how you suffered. On slipping poison into every meal so he never has a moment of peace for as long as he lives. May I make you an offer?"

"I'm in no position to say no." My heart races at the violent proclamations. I have no doubts that Zaeden is a man of his word. Does it make me a bad person to wish that he does keep it?

"You can always say no." He hisses, continuing. "One day, you can do it. You can decide their fate. Whether you kill them or not is up to you. You can chop their hands off if you want to. I will let you decide."

"If it's my decision, I want them to suffer so much they still feel pain after they've been put six feet under." I don't recognize the version of myself who says those words. Goddess, I'm horrible.

"I will happily make that happen."

"Not like I will be alive long enough to watch it happen, anyways," I mutter bitterly, shutting my eyes tightly. These broken bones are likely the easiest form of torture I will endure if I stay in these dungeons much longer.

"You will be. Rest assured, we won't let you go down without a fight."

"Okay, then." I might regret it later, but they deserve it. I may be indulging this new, dark side in me, but Zaeden will help me guide it. I *want* to cut their hands off. Want to chop off each finger first, listen to them scream for hours like I did. Then I will cut it off at the wrist and move along to much more precious body parts. Maybe this is what will finally drive the nightmares away, the missing thing that will let me heal. Or maybe it won't. Either way, I am ready to demand revenge now. I don't ask how he will find the others. I know he will.

"Okay." He watches me for a moment, a curious gleam in his eyes.

"Why did you come? Not that I'm not grateful, of course."

"I came to catch you up on current events. There are a few things I think are of utmost importance that you should be aware of." I laugh, shaking my head.

"What does it matter now?"

"It matters because the whole Court is debating on what to do with you. You, my darling, are a heavy topic. One that has started a fight between both Divine and Undivine alike."

"What? Why? I thought, surely, they would believe Silvi over me. I didn't even *know* about my powers until I was in that theater, I swear! But who would believe that over her story? A supposed Undivine over a High?"

"You have been asleep for over twelve hours. The city has

been debating about you ever since I knocked you out. I apologize for that, by the way. I had to do something before more of my men were injured, or one of them killed you. I had to make it seem like we were taking the threat seriously. Kyelin, too, is sorry for his part in this. We did what we could to make sure you stayed safe as we promised. We compromised your trust to do that. To be fair, though, you did hurt many men. You were a beauty to behold. You were a raging storm and no one and nothing was going to stop you from surviving the night. You were wild and rampaging and utterly perfect. I've never been more attracted to a woman, I must admit. Confessing my love aside, I'm not supposed to be here right now. Kyelin is covering for me while we speak. I won't be able to stay much longer."

"Debating?" I avoided his apology, avoided his description of me while I was practically rabid. I don't want to talk about that, either. Don't want to know what happened to my victims. Don't want to hear him describe my rampage as something *beautiful* when it was anything but.

"It's a very delicate situation. Clearly, you aren't a spy. You're branded with our symbol. Spies never allow themselves to be branded because that means they can't slip from Court to Court undetected. So, that's a major point for you. Also, we vet our staff unbelievably well. We know everything there is to know about you. We've even spoken to your mother. She provided us with documentation of your birth and original residency information. All of that proves you originate in the Lunar Court and were birthed by Undivine parents. But it's painfully obvious you are not Undivine, and neither is your sister. So now where do we put you? What are you? How did you slip through the cracks? Those are the

123

questions we debate."

"You talked to my mother? Seriously?" I shake my head with a scoff. "I haven't talked to my mother in years. I wasn't adopted though. I can guarantee that. But I really don't want to talk about my parents."

"For now, you won't have to."

"For now?"

"You will need a story."

"A story? What do you mean?" I can't even be relieved that, from what Zaeden is saying, I won't be in a cell much longer. I am now in the eye of the public. An attraction for Divine. A thing to be flaunted and cooed at. That may be worse than being in this cell with not even a bucket to piss in.

"I am trying to get them to update your status to High Divine. Kyelin and I, together, I mean."

"What? No way! No offense, but I can't be one of you. I have a strong dislike for the Divine, and you know why, now. I will never be one of you. Never! After everything Divines have done to me, after everything they have said to me? No. Absolutely not. I won't lie about where I come from. About who I am. I'm not fabricating some story to placate the masses." No way would I ever agree to that. No way.

"You don't get a choice. After the show you put on, the decision is no longer in your hands."

"Don't you think I should get a say in it? It's my life!"

"Most Undivine would be grateful for this opportunity. And you should be, too. I know you don't want change. But you have to understand where we are coming from. Even if you aren't grateful, I suggest you pretend to be. Because you don't need enemies right now. You already have a very powerful one."

"Silvi." Of course. She's probably still fighting against me, defending her name. She told me already she is choosing herself. Well, I guess it's my turn to choose now.

"Yep. She is saying she is scared of you. You were her friend. She had no idea. Blah, blah, blah. A huge pity party, basically. She has a lot of influence here, Celeste. That influence is fighting hard to keep you in this cell. You are valuable to us, though. We want things to work out here."

I groan. "Of course. Of course, that is what this is about. I was a good little spy, was I? You wanted to know what kind of person Silvi was and I showed you loud and clear. So now I get to be trapped in the same world I was trying to get out of. I just wanted to take my sister to a safe home, to be taken care of, to live my life without worry. Is that what I get for wanting? For not being happy with what I was given? Maybe the goddesses do exist and they are punishing me for not believing for so long. It's one twisted punishment if I have to say so myself."

"You aren't being punished, Celeste. This is a blessing. Stop complaining about something that is going to increase your quality of life tenfold. I haven't even gotten to the worst of it yet. At least, what I think you will consider the worst of it. If we do declare you High Divine, things are going to be different between us, Celeste. You will be forced to compete in the Games." He is getting increasingly annoyed, upset that I dare complain about my whole life being turned upside down.

"The Games? You have to be joking! I can't do that! I won't!" Heat floods my face from the idea of it all. Yes, I found the princes attractive, and who wouldn't? But marriage? I've never really thought about marriage, but I don't think I want to get married like this. I want to find someone to love, a partner who I will never want to leave my side. I don't want to fight for someone to love me.

"Your fight was enough to get you in on a technicality. You were introduced, with an escort, and you showed us your powers. Even if you didn't know about it at the time. You may not have much family influence, but you know our people. You are a *part* of our people. You could appease this long-lasting war between us and the rebels. A peace offering. Not only that, but you are beautiful. I've already told you I thought you were too pretty to be Undivine. And your power...if we had realized how powerful you really were...well, we wouldn't be in this cell, that's for sure. Silvi said she thought it was a fluke. That you were just immune to her, a rare thing but not impossible. Obviously, that was her mistake. And you should have told us sooner. Needless to say, even without the influence of a strong family, you would make a great political match. Maybe the only girl from the Lunar Court that has a shot at the throne. But you are an anomaly, something that happens once in a blue moon. You could rally the people and inspire them. It's enough to get you in. Once the people find out what has happened here, and many have already found out, we would be fools not to give you a chance. There would be an uproar, and we don't need any more problems than we already have in that area."

How could he talk about his own marriage like this? I know why they think I should jump at this chance to be a princess, maybe become a queen. Divine are narcissistic by nature. Of course, they think if they say 'fly' then I will. They think the moon hangs over their heads. Everyone wants to be them. But to sit here and regard my life like it is nothing more than a stepping stone for their own political goals? Like I should gladly sacrifice myself to appease the Court? No way. I'm not doing this.

"Tell them to execute me, then. I'd rather die than pretend to be one of you, to be married to a Royal," I say, crossing my arms over my chest in defiance.

"Oh? And what of your sister, then? What shall we do with her?" His face twists into something I don't recognize, fear racing through me. This is the *wrongness* I detect in him sometimes.

"You won't touch my sister. You swore to me you would protect her. You won't risk the wrath of the goddesses, will you?" I hiss back. I am becoming visibly sick at this talk. Of course, it could be the broken bones causing that, too.

"The goddesses you don't even believe in, you mean? I will give her protection, Celeste. I will place guards all around her house. If one of those guards thinks he is doing something for the greater good…well…not much I can do about that, is there?"

"It doesn't matter if I believe, I know you Divine *do*. And besides, if I accept, what happens to her? Where will she go? She can't stay where she is without me. Goddess, I don't know how she is holding up without me right now. She might try to go to the village and look for me. They'll hunt her down just to feel closer to me." I can't bear to look at him any longer. He is manipulating me into accepting his offer, and I am letting him.

"She, too, will be forced into this world. I'll get her status updated as well. I knew upon meeting her that she wasn't Undivine. As for her current safety, I have discreetly placed a few guards at your home. I want you to understand that we can keep her safer if you let us bring her to Lunar City. There are many more places to hide, and more soldiers I can trust. It will be a much better situation for you both. All you have to do is participate in the Games that you don't condone, but she will be safe. A small price to pay, hmm?"

"And you aren't going to experiment on us? Try and figure out why we have these High Divine powers?"

"No, not right now. I will take some blood samples, though. Just to see if we can track down some Divine heritage. You two are an anomaly, and many Undivines will be claiming Divine heritage now. But that will come once the Games are over. The people won't be too worried about answers until then."

We sit in silence for a long time, even with his rush and my broken bones waiting. He is right. He is so painfully right. If I truly want Irissa to be safe, I have to do this. I can't be selfish. It's too late for me to have a quiet, happy life. I did this to myself. Unwittingly, sure, but I did it. And now I am facing the consequences. But Irissa? She is desperate to see the world. Desperate to have friends, to fall in love. She still has a chance at the life she wants. I have to do this for her. *I have to.*

"Okay." I breathe out. "Now what?"

"If you are approved, you are moving on to the second Game. We have eliminated seventeen candidates so far. There are twenty left, including you."

"Twenty? I have to fight twenty women over you two?" He barks out a laugh at my disbelief, throwing his head back. Yes, yes I will.

"From the second Game on, we have much more control over the choices. We typically get to choose who continues to the third. If you don't wish to continue after the second

128

Game, we will let you go willingly. I don't want to force you into marriage. That's our burden, it doesn't have to be yours. We will figure something out with the Undivines, maybe you can give a speech about how you don't want the life of a Royal and how it is just too much for you to handle. Either way, it can be done. But you do have to participate, and you will need to try. It will be demanded from the whole Court. If you choose not to continue, you and your sister will stay in the city. You will no longer be allowed to live in the villages. You will forever be a High Divine, and must live like a High Divine does."

"And the money I was promised?"

"We always keep our word. We won't be goddess-damned. We will still provide for you both. And continue to keep you safe. Kyelin and I have discussed it and agreed, so I have permission to speak on his behalf. With that being said, do you agree to these terms?" I sigh, dropping my gaze to my lap. I believed his promises before, and I believe them now. The Divine are too keen about what they do and don't promise. So, surely, everything will work out in my favor, right?

"I accept."

Chapter 8

"I want Ryleigh. Not these wannabes you keep sending my way. I've had enough. Send Ryleigh." I spit at the soldier in my doorway.

"We can't just send you the head maid." He argues back, the same argument I have heard all day. "You get who you get. You don't get to make requests."

"I don't get to make requests? Are you joking? I am being forced into this competition. I am not one of the empty-headed High Divine you are used to speaking with. I am not one of you. I'm just a maid, remember? And as a maid, I request my boss. Get me Ryleigh. Now."

"You aren't just a maid—" He starts again, but the second soldier puts a hand on his shoulder to stop him. I smirk, nodding my head in thanks.

"She's been scaring these other girls all day. Did you hear what she called the last one? I felt bad for the poor woman. Just get her the one she wants. It doesn't make a difference to us. I'm sick of hearing the girls crying and sick of this one screaming at us." This soldier is Undivine, something I can see with a quick glance. He sends me a wink when his partner isn't looking and a thumbs up behind his back. He knows this argument isn't going to be lost by me. I want someone familiar by my side, someone I trust. And it looks like being from the villages is going to help me more than I thought.

"Fine. Stay here."

"Where else would I go?" I slam the door shut behind me, beginning to pace my worn path across the room. I chew on my broken fingernails, my tattered dress swinging as I walk. They threw me in this room and kept me hostage here for hours, sending Undivine handmaidens I don't know to help me get cleaned up. But I can't have strangers in here. I don't know who wants me alive and who wants me dead. Not all of my people will take kindly to my rise in the ranks. Jealousy is truly a green monster, a lesson I've learned the hard way with Silvi. If she had just *said* something, maybe I would have...but no, it doesn't matter now. She thought she was owed something she wasn't, and now I am dealing with the repercussions.

It seems like hours before Ryleigh finally appears. And when she does, a wave of icy relief crashes into me. I want to fling myself into her arms, but I hold myself back. I want to embrace her, embrace the reality I used to have. But it doesn't exist, and she'll give me the dose of reality I need.

"Oh, Les." She coos, placing her hands on my shoulders. She looks me up and down, shaking her head sadly. She picks up a piece of tattered fabric, frowning in distaste. "That beautiful dress is ruined. How horrible. A lot of money wasted. And what they did to you..."

"What I did to them." I fire back quietly, not meeting her eyes. I had gravely injured multiple men. I remember how satisfied I felt throwing them around, remember using their powers against them. Remember the cracks of bones and the screams that rang in the air. Hopefully, no one is dead.

Zaeden hadn't told me, and I hadn't asked.

Maybe I shouldn't feel as guilty as I do. They attacked me. I was, quite literally, returning what they gave me. But that doesn't appease the wilting morality inside of me. The part of me screaming 'no more, no more' at the beast that says 'feed me'. They may have been Divines, but that didn't make them expendable. I am trying hard not to regret it, to not think about the families that have to witness broken and crippled men returning home. I did what I had to do in that moment. The guilt doesn't ease knowing that.

"Well, let's not speak of that. I'm glad I brought this with me." I watch her reach over, picking up a box I didn't notice her bring in. It is fairly simple, just a plain white box. It is what is inside that is remarkable.

She pulls out a deep burgundy dress, one I am hoping is made to my measurements. It isn't like the other dresses I've worn, though. It is small, with a deep 'v' in the chest. But it has no sleeves. No sheer fabrics. Instead, the dress is made of a sparkling material, glittering in the sunlight shining through the window. Each way it moves, each angle the light hits it at, it glows. I can see the small crystals upon closer inspection, embedded into every inch of the fabric. Expensive, no doubt. The bottom of the dress forms a long train, one I'm not completely convinced I will be able to walk with. The matching slippers lay underneath.

"You...you made this?"

"Of course I did. What do you take me for? Not that I'm entirely convinced I should give it to you. My girls keep coming back in tears, what have you been saying to them?"

"Nothing too bad." I shrug innocently. "You know I don't have a mean bone in me, Rye."

"Whatever, kid. One girl said you called her a pig-faced bitch who should have stayed in her mother's decaying womb. I think you would have been able to replace me one day, with that mouth of yours." She lets out a belly laugh, rolling her eyes.

"Can't anymore."

"Ah. This is better, anyway. Powers and a spot in society? Much better than being a head maid."

"You're right, I don't think I could live as miserable and lonely as you do." I huff playfully, turning to the washroom to run a bath. Ryleigh dashes in front of me, pushing me aside.

"Excuse you," I say incredulously. What is that about?

"You are High Divine now, Celeste. One who will no doubt be a princess, might I add. Hopefully a queen."

"Ugh. What about it?" I shift uncomfortably, not wanting to discuss the probability that I *won't* be a Royal anytime soon.

"That means no running your own baths, child. That is what your handmaiden is for. I will do it for you. Fix your hair, do your makeup, make your dresses, clean your room. I take care of you. Or did you forget how this all works already?"

"You're actually going to do it?" She hasn't been a handmaiden for a very long time, probably since the last Games. As far as I understood, she never wanted to do it again.

"For you? Yeah, I am. Besides, it's about time you let someone take care of you. You are always taking care of your sister, and what do you get in exchange? Nothing but a headache and a nice cry to sleep every night. Now, go on. Let's get you scrubbed and clean. I'm sure that cell wasn't sanitary."

We sit in silence as she gets the bath running, helping me undress while the tub fills. My whole body aches. My

133

broken skin and bones have been healed, but a large amount of soreness remains. The healer said it will be a few days before that is gone. A few days with a painful reminder of what I've endured.

When I step into the burning hot water, I can feel myself melting. I don't mind the burn. I welcome it. *I deserve it, I deserve it, I deserve it.* This is exactly what I need. When I start scrubbing the dirt covering my body, I scrape as hard as I can. I want to be raw. I want to scrub my sins clear out of my skin. But I don't account for Ryleigh, and the rag is out of my hand before I can do damage to more than an arm. I give in reluctantly, allowing her to scrub instead. I try to relax, to sink down, down, down.

"Will you still report to me?" My head snaps up, my body flinging water around and out.

"About Silvi? I'm not really sure I'm in a position—"

"No, not about Silvi."

"Well, what do you want to know?" I brush away the hand she places on my face, confused. My wet hair clings to my cheeks and neck, but I don't bother brushing it aside. The tickle keeps me on edge, punishing me with that elusive itch. *I deserve it, I deserve it, I deserve it.*

"You are on the inside now." She had been secretive before, so it is no surprise that she is being secretive now.

"Yes, I suppose so."

"We have been looking for someone on the inside. It's hard. High Divines are so pompous. But here you are, formally Undivine, converted. Who better to help us? You can obtain such good information from this position. Information that would really benefit our cause. I still need you. The Undivine need you."

"We?"

"Well, I—"

"What cause?"

"Does it matter?" She knows me too well.

"Not really," I admit quietly. What does it matter what I do? My whole life is practically forfeit, anyway. I will live and die among the Divine, now. If it means I can have a small amount of retribution against them, well, I'll take it. Even if they never knew it was me. "Will it...will it truly help people? This information? I feel like playing a spy has ruined my life. Would it be worth it to try again? Will it absolve my sins? Will the payback even matter?"

"I don't know. But you can try."

"If you plan on killing the Divine, then kill them. Kill them all. They deserve it. But I don't want to be a part of it. Not yet, anyway. Maybe not ever. The guilt that is eating away at me over those Lows...I don't even know if I actually killed anyone and yet it is all I think about." I want to tell her how I liked it, how it made me feel powerful. But I can't because I know how awful that is and I don't want to feel that way anymore. "I saw one go limp, Ryleigh. His entire body just...stopped. I did that. I don't know about the others. I was in a daze. In this fight or flight response. I don't know what I did to who. It's all a blur. But I can hear the bones cracking, the screams of fear. I don't know about the others, but him—" I can tell this has something to do with the rebels. I should have known. But I don't care. They can invade this castle, kill the Divine inside, and be on their way. I just don't want to participate. They have abused me and manipulated me. And I will eventually convince myself to kill the Lows who attacked me five years ago. But this rebellion? It's on a much more massive scale, and I am *not* ready for that. Passing on information is one thing. Killing people? That's something I'm not going to be able to recover from.

"I hope we won't need to kill anyone," she says breathlessly, a sorrowful look passing across her face.

"I will do what I can." I make no promises, and it's not like I did a very good job as her informant last time. I just told her a few things in passing, nothing that seemed of importance. Two different groups had me spying on the same person. The thought makes me snort. What has Silvi done to be so high up on everyone's radar? The rebels think she needs someone to keep an eye on her, the Royals think she's....well, I don't know what they think she is doing. Who is hiding underneath that scar?

"Thank you. This stays between us, of course."

"Mmm."

We don't speak much after that. She helps me get ready and helps me slide into the dress she brought. But not a word is uttered. There's no need, honestly. Besides, the past few days have been overwhelming. A little silence is probably good for me.

"Here to escort Miss Celeste," a booming voice says from the door, followed by a knock. Ryleigh swings it open, nodding to the soldier waiting for me. I glance at his eyes before letting him take my arm and lead me away to my new life.

When we walk into the giant room, the other nineteen participants are already there. I make twenty. They sit at a long, oval table. There are no Royals in sight. I nod to the soldier who is bowing to me, dismissing him. I turn back to the girls, awkwardly finding my seat at the other end of the room. Thirty-eight eyes follow me, silence ensuing. Well, thirty-seven if you don't include Silvi's glass eye. I want to flinch away from the fury hidden there, want to hide from the room full of Divine.

"Got something to say?" I question as I plop down, feigning confidence. No one replies as I pick up a grape and plop it into my mouth. It takes three grapes before I get annoyed.

"Fuck off. I'm tired of you freaks looking at me like I ate your firstborn child for breakfast. Find someone else to obsess over." The girl to my right laughs, lifting her cup of wine.

"Cheers to that!" She takes a long swig, sighing as she sits it back down. Finally, the others take her lead, the chattering and clinks continuing.

"I'm Dove Airess of the Light Court. It's a pleasure to meet you." I turn to face her, eyebrows raised. Is it actually a pleasure? Probably not. But at least she's trying. She, like the others, is beautiful. Auburn hair, golden eyes, delicate freckles dancing across pale skin. Her face is round, her cheeks rosy. It is painfully obvious that she is High Divine. That she belongs here. Unlike me.

"Is it? A pleasure, I mean?"

"The girls here are boring. You, my friend, are anything *but* boring. Stirring the pot at the first Game? A naughty thing to do. But I like it. So, yes, it is a pleasure."

"I wasn't trying to stir the pot. It's just how the cards fell, I suppose."

"I suppose so." She laughs, the sound loud and un-Divine-like. "I'm sorry for staring. It's just strange to see you here. An Undivine suddenly a High. A diamond in the rough. I just don't understand how they never realized. I mean, look at you! Undivine don't look the way you do. I mean, your height is odd, but not an impossibility. Your powers *must* have been sealed off. Were they?"

"I don't know. What does that mean? Sealed off?"

"Oh, well, it is a power some of the Followers are said to have. Since they are mostly made up of Undivine, it is hard to find one who can do it. Some say the goddesses give powers to the most devoted Undivine, and that's just *one* of the things they're rumored to do. They make you pay a hefty price, though. Your parents must be well-off for Undivine."

"I wouldn't know." I shrug, shifting uncomfortably. "About my powers being sealed off or my parents. My dad died when I was young. I ran away as soon as I turned 18. I can confidently say that my mother never acted like she had any money. If she did, I certainly never saw any of it. I've been in poverty my whole life. I am Undivine, after all. We shouldn't be able to live like an actual worthy-of-life being, right?"

"Well, I—I—um—"

"Change the subject. I don't feel like getting angry one more time today." I mutter bluntly, staring down at my plate. I don't want to talk about my parents, my power, my lack of wealth. Especially not with these women. They've never had to experience the things I have, and they never will. Maybe, since I'm being forced into this competition anyway, I can use my experience to my advantage. Maybe I can try to make things better for my fellow Undivine. The thought gives me a ray of hope, the air in my lungs suddenly lighter.

"Do you know much about this competition?" Dove turns away, too. I watch out of the corner of my eye as she scans the other girls, calculating.

"Pft." I scoff, accompanied by an eye roll. "Other than the fact that I supposedly qualified and somehow participated in the Game of Impressions? No."

"Oh. You didn't want to be here? You weren't trying to compete?" She seems surprised.

"Of course not. Why would I want to hang out with some snobby High Divines who watch my every move like a dog watching a bone? Why would I choose to marry for convenience and appeasement instead of love? No thanks." Dove doesn't seem to be offended. Instead, she laughs like I've told a funny joke. When she turns back to me, she has tears of joy in her eyes.

"You're so right." She manages to get out through the laughter. "Well, now that the first Game is over, the dates begin. We each get one date. I think they've decided to divide us up between princes, ten go with Kyelin and ten go with Zaeden. No one knows who we will get or when. They just show up and take us out. Personally, I hope for Zaeden. Dark and broody is my thing."

"What? Doesn't that seem a bit....I don't know...strange? That we only get to have a date with one of the people we are trying to see if we are compatible with?"

"Well, this is the first time we are competing for twins. The timeline is staying the same, so they needed to figure something out. Three months to narrow down all these women? It's a lot. So, yeah, I guess it is a little strange compared to the past Games."

"But how does it work?"

"What do you mean?"

"Well, what if you have a connection with one, but not the other? Or one likes you and the other doesn't? And during these dates, you don't get the chance to meet your actual match? And you never find out what could have been? He could be, I don't know, your Soul Divine or something. And you would never know."

"Soul Divine's aren't real. No one is truly made for each other like that. We aren't drawn to each other like magnets. That's just something Undivines tell each other to make them feel better about their sad lives. No offense. I have never met anyone with a connection like that. We marry for power and positions, not because we are fated to be together. It doesn't work like that. Sure, maybe I will like Kyelin more than I like Zaeden. But it doesn't matter. I'm here on behalf of my Court, and I will marry whoever I am told to marry for their sake." She seems so passionate, so flippant about the idea of love. It makes me wonder about her own parents, about what kind of relationship they have to make her feel this way.

"If you say so." I shrug nonchalantly. I don't feel particularly strong on the topic myself. I just know what my mother told me about her and my father's 'Divine love'. She said it was a Soul Divine connection. At the time, she hadn't fallen into the liquor bottles yet. So I can trust her with that information, at least.

"Anyways, it is actually a pretty good system. If one prince doesn't like you, but the other might, they won't write you off quite yet. Some people even get a second date with the other prince. It just depends, really. They know themselves and each other well. And compatibility is pretty important, now that our power and looks are deemed worthy. All of that will still play a part, of course, but it is in the back of their minds at the moment. Now, they get to start making choices."

"Well, sure, maybe they do know each other well, but knowing each other's sexual preferences is weird, don't you think? I mean, I don't even want to know what my sister prefers in a partner sexually. No way would I ever date someone and be like you know what? I think you and my sister are way more compatible in be-"

"My dear Celeste," a deep voice interrupts. I jump in my seat, a blush coating my cheeks. I turn my head sharply, my heart leaping.

"Zaeden." I hope he didn't hear what we were talking about. Dove seems to think the same because a deep blush covers her face, too. I can feel the others looking at us, the silence overbearing. They probably realized I didn't call him 'Your Highness' or 'Prince'. For them, that is as shocking as me jumping onto the table and kicking their plates onto the floor. Out of the corner of my eye, I see Kyelin leading Silvi out of the room.

"Are you being treated well?" He sounds polite enough, a strong hand falling onto my shoulder. I try my best not to stiffen, shrugging silently instead in response.

"I see." He chuckles darkly. Dove watches on incredulously, the confusion clear.

"Have you two already met?" She asks conversationally, addressing me more than Zaeden.

"Briefly." I lie.

"Oh." She falls silent, taking another long swig from her glass.

"Celeste, I was wondering if you had a few moments to spare. I would love to take a walk around the grounds with you."

"Like a date?" I question jokingly. I have to participate. It's part of our deal and I can't refuse. He knows that. Maybe he is trying to end my suffering quickly. At least now I won't sit around worrying about when I will get swept away.

"If you want it to be." Laughter dances in his eyes as he holds his hand out. Hesitantly, I take it. He only smiles, watching me stand. I pull a little harder than necessary on his hand, using him to balance myself out. He doesn't let me drop it back down to my side.

Lightly, I say, "I'll consider it." I let him pull me from the room, letting the whispers fade far behind us. We don't talk at first, the walk to the gardens slow and quiet. I don't mind. The silence is starting to become a welcome presence, one I embrace warmly. In this silence, I don't have to tell anyone about my past, my present, my future. I don't have to think about what it means to be a Divine, about what it's going to take to make it in this new world, about what I sacrificed to be here.

"Why do I have to do this, again?" I say it jokingly, and he throws his head back and laughs heartily. Clearly, I have amused him.

"Don't say that too loudly. We are being watched from every angle. Every whisper can be heard and reported. Maybe I can give you a real reason later, okay?" He smiles as he responds, treating me like a scared deer who is on the verge of running.

"Who cares enough to listen to us? What could they possibly be reporting on?" He squeezes my hand gently; a warning. I had forgotten his giant hand was there at all, but now it is all I can think about. My body betrays me with a shiver as he runs a thumb across my fingers.

"They report on all the dates. By tomorrow morning, a paper will be released with every detail they noticed and every detail you didn't. The people will know everything. They are going to start picking favorites, picking who they think our favorites are. Just us standing here, holding hands, will be seen as a sign of favoritism. Which is good, because I think you actually are our favorite."

I shake my head, rolling my eyes. "I'm just new and exciting. A new toy to break. That's why you think I'm your favorite. Not because I actually am. Not because you actually like me."

"Maybe so." He shrugs nonchalantly. Like what I have to say about it doesn't matter. That's one of the things that bothers me about Zaeden. He doesn't seem to care about my opinion on, well, anything.

"Do I have to fake everything, then?" I am beyond the point of frustrated. I am not meant for this. I am not meant to play the role of princess. Or as someone who wants to be a princess. Or even as someone who wants to be a High Divine, for that matter.

"I don't want you to." His fingers brush across a rose as we pass, the petals curling away from his poisonous touch. "I want you to have fun. To fit in. We don't want you to suffer. We are truly trying to get to know you. As a friend, of course."

"As a friend, hmm? Do you look at all your friends like that?" I try not to look him in the eyes, not wanting to understand what I see there.

"No. I don't."

"I'm not sure I want anything more than friendship, Zaeden. With you or your brother."

"Okay." It barely comes out as a whisper, and I worry I've offended a Royal who is used to getting anything and everything he wants.

"Okay."

"Is it okay that I hold your hand? I should have asked before doing so. I just thought it would boost your scores in the reports. I wasn't thinking about how you don't like the touch of a Divine. If you want—"

"It's okay." I breathe out, surprised. "Thank you. For trying to be considerate of my...issues."

"No need to discuss that here. But you're welcome. I was serious about having fun, you know? I don't want you cowering away from us, scared to speak up. I've seen what's inside you, Celeste, and I like it much more than the person you were pretending to be before. I genuinely want to know more about you. What's your family like?"

"My family? You already met my family."

"I've only met Irissa. I know your mother provided documentation to my parents. Where are your parents located? What's your relationship like with them?"

"My dad is dead. He died when I was seven. I hardly remember him, honestly. I ran away from my mother as soon as I turned eighteen. I took Irissa and fled. She was abusive, in every way you can abuse a person. I didn't want Irissa to have a life like that. So, we left."

"You've always protected her." His thumb runs over the top of my fingers again. I nod, ignoring it as best I can. But it's hard to ignore the feelings he leaves on top of my skin, like a breeze hovering over an ocean.

"Yes. She has always needed protection."

"I know. You've done a wonderful job. I am impressed with your bravery. Two girls, all alone. And somehow you managed to make it here, to find a job, to make a living for yourself. Very impressive indeed."

"I was determined, that's all. I didn't want her to feel the way I had. To think everything she does is wrong. To think that everything about her is a flaw. To think no one will ever love her, that she will never find happiness. I know she didn't escape all the abuse, but I forced my mother's focus on me anytime she tried to start things up with Irissa. Irissa has a beautiful soul. She does. But with her condition, it makes it so much easier for her emotions to become clogged with darkness. A majestic creature with its wings set on fire, a burning star flailing as it tries to tread air. That's why she gets so angry, you know? Because when she regresses, she remembers. I think sometimes she resents me for taking her away from her mother. She tells me all the time I'm not her mom. She knows our mother did bad things, and said bad things, but…that is her real mother. Not me. And that's not something I can easily replace or that can be easily forgiven."

"You made a difficult decision, but it was the right one. Even I, an outsider, can see that."

"I hope so," I whisper, ready to change the subject, "What about you? Are you close with your family? I know you are close to Kyelin, but what about your parents?"

"Ah, my parents. Yes, we are close. I love them both very dearly. I would have to say I am closer to my mother, though. Father works a lot and has always been very strict, so it's been hard to have a proper relationship with him. But our mother has always stood by our sides, has always had our backs. She fights for us when needed. I know she seems cruel and careless from a distance, but she is not. She loves us very much, as does our father."

"I am glad for you. That type of relationship with a parent is very rare indeed." We stop in front of a stone bench, bushes full of beautiful flowers surrounding us. I see reds, yellows, oranges. Deeper into the garden I can see blues and purples, too. And once we sit down on that bench, time begins to fly. It feels like there is nothing and no one who can interrupt this moment. It feels like we are… friends. We talk about so many pointless things. We laugh and joke so much that I find myself not hiding behind pleasantries. I'm not on guard or putting up walls. I think…I think I am enjoying his company. It's a pleasant shock, to say the least.

After what has probably been a few hours, we fall quiet. I hadn't realized how close he had gotten, how our knees were brushing up against each other. It is strange. For five years, I have avoided the touch of a man. Even just brushing against them in the streets on accident would have me on edge. The first year was the worst, when I would shut down completely and cry after those innocent touches. But now, here I am, feeling comfortable and confident next to a Divine. A *Royal* Divine.

"I've enjoyed your company today." Zaeden is the one to speak up, eyes lifting to meet mine. I watch the poison swirling inside them, gray and purple pooling together. They are hypnotizing, and I find myself leaning in to watch. Then he leans in closer, and I can't bring myself to move. Can't bring myself to think about anything other than his breath warming my lips, how his own lips are close enough to brush against mine.

"I am probably the most interesting thing to ever happen to you." My lips barely move.

"Is this okay?" His hand comes up to rest on my cheek, and my eyes flutter shut. I nod hesitantly, letting him keep it there. His touch is cold, but it is comforting.

"Yes." It comes out as a whisper. He makes me nervous in a good way. Usually. I think I like the feeling.

"I'm going to kiss you now, okay?" He barely speaks, and I barely register anything other than 'kiss'. My breathing picks up, my heart racing. As he leans forward, I panic. I have never been kissed by a man before. So, I turn my head and hope I won't regret it. His lips gently brush against my heated cheek, and I can feel the smirk stretching across his lips. He knows now how nervous he makes me. How close I am to giving in. He knows I didn't turn away because I didn't want him to touch me. I would have pushed him away and told him no. I should have done that. But I hadn't.

I hear the snap of a camera, the noise hardly audible. He pulls away after that, lingering for only a brief moment. Then he places his other hand on my opposite cheek, staring at me. He stays this way for a long moment before nodding, not taking things further or mentioning the kiss. I can only nod back. This is definitely going to be in the report tomorrow.

Chapter 9

When Ryleigh barges in, waving a piece of paper around dramatically, I can only roll my eyes and sigh. She never bothers to knock. It's not like there is any part of me she hasn't seen already, though. No chance of barging into something she doesn't want to see; not with me knee-deep in this facade of a courtship.

"What do you want now?" I try to make it obvious how utterly *not* entertained by the dramatic display I am.

"Look at this." She slaps the paper into my lap, scowling. I hold it up, reading the large, bold title:

The Lunar Court Daily Report

Of course. On the front page sits my picture, Zaeden much too close to insinuate anything less than friendliness. And here it is. The moment I knew had been caught. His lips on *my* cheek. My cheek touched *his* lips. My blush is blaring, my expression soft and vacant. I look…infatuated.

"What of it?" I know she heard the crack in my voice as I tried to sound casual.

"Read it!" She cries out, grinning. And so I read.

It seems like Miss Celeste, our Undivine mystery, has caught the eye of a certain Prince Zaeden. Our reporters overheard her telling him of her dark past, one where she was raised in poverty and without a father. Maybe her dark past is what ensnared him, luring him into her trap. Maybe it's her enchanting laughter and sweet smile. Either way, it is clear who will be the favorite player in this round of dates. I dare say, dear reader, she might be one of the few to get a second date with Prince Kyelin.

"I'm not reading more than that," I grumble. There is a whole page of information about me. I see a paragraph mentioning *a sister who she has been protecting her whole life*. I see the word *Undivine* several times. I even see the phrase *our new princess*. It's revolting.

"You didn't tell me the whole truth about your date yesterday. I didn't realize he had kissed you! And it says you held hands the whole time? Clearly, it went very well!" She is bouncing with excitement, giddy to the bone. And for what? What did it matter, anyway?

"It's no big deal." I shrug, turning away from her as I fix my dress. Today, I decided to dress simply. A long, elegant, deep blue gown. Simple, like me.

"I disagree. You have a real chance at winning here, Les! I know you don't think very highly of yourself, but you must see that. The Undivines love you. You bring them to the Royal's doors, begging for you to be one of the chosen. They have to keep you around. Don't you understand? This is a real chance for change, Celeste." She seems so excited, so hopeful. I feel guilty crushing that hope, but I must.

"I don't want a chance. I'm quitting the moment I'm allowed." I try not to think about Zaeden's lips on my cheek, about the kindness and caring nature he exposed. Try not to think about Kyelin and his easy smile, about the warmth that spreads through my whole body when he is near. I try not to feel ashamed. I want out of here. Out of this cage that I've

149

been thrown into; a cage where my captors dangle the keys and expect me to obey. Can't she see that? Understand it? She, of all people?

"Quitting? What? You can't just…quit!" I take a step away as she edges closer, her whole body radiating anger. "Don't you see how much hope this gives us? How we are all rooting for you? Supporting you? Why would you give up a life like this? A life as a princess, a life where you never have to scrub toilets again! Never have to serve under another Silvi! A life where you can have all the riches you could ever want and all of the authority to change the rules! Why pass that up?"

"Do you see this?" I ask harshly, shoving my marked leg towards her. She winces at the sight of my scar, an identical one on her right ankle. "This is the mark of an Undivine. The mark of a poor, lonely little girl who had nothing and no one to rely on. The mark of someone who was never meant for royalty. Never meant for a life that kind."

"But you *can* have it." It comes out as a whisper, her voice pleading. "You don't have to be that afraid little girl anymore. *Irissa* doesn't have to be that anymore. It's within your reach, you just have to jump up and grab it by the balls!"

"I don't want to grab anything by the balls, thank you very much. I want nothing to do with the Divine or their mind games. I will never be a Royal, not to them, not to me. I will always be the poor little maid who was rescued from the gutters. The sweet little girl who fought tooth and nail for her life in front of the whole city just to be thrown into a den of lions as a reward. I didn't ask to be here! I'm certainly not staying just to be ridiculed and looked down upon for the rest of my life. I'd rather go back to being ignored. I don't want that shame for myself, or Irissa. When people see what she is and what she does…her life is going to be much worse than mine. We are better off without that unpleasantness."

She had begun gathering pins for my hair angrily, stopping as a realization occurred. She drops the pins, rushing forward, hands clasping onto my shoulders. I stumble back, surprised. The look on her face is so panicked, so angry. Her eyes are full of disbelief, lips drawn tight. But why?

"You're scared."

"I'm not."

"You are."

"No—"

"You think everything can just go back to the way it was? Do you think you can be the girl everyone ignored again? You are Divine, now. A High. You will never be Undivine again. You will never be able to go back to your home, to your village. You will always be recognized. No matter where you go, you will always be found. Jealousy, anger, and hatred will follow you, sleep in your shadows, and dance in your dreams. You don't belong to any one world now, Celeste. You are a child of the Divine, raised with the Undivine. You have experienced things no Divines before you have. You have an experience that makes you wholly unique in this world, Celeste. And now you have influence, too. At least, you will. Use it, Celeste. You can only go as high as the goddesses wish you to, in the end. So do whatever you can to help them get you there."

"I don't know if I can do this."

"You have to continue to play in the games." She demands this of me like she has a right to do so. Maybe she does. She is Undivine, too. She knows how horrible things are. I'm sure I wasn't the first servant she found tortured and slowly dying in her halls.

151

"I just told you-"

"Forget what you just told me!" She screeches, throwing her hands up as she bares her teeth. "We have been praying for someone like you to get into the castle for a very, very long time. Someone that the Undivine can support, someone that can change things for us. You are perfect for that position. You are one of us, for goddess's sake! Who better? Who else can understand our struggles? Can change the world for us? Include us? Give us hope?"

"You keep saying 'we' like it's supposed to matter to me. I understand I relate to the Undivine, I do, but how would I ever change things? I can't demolish the monarchy, Ryleigh. And why do you think the Divine will ever accept me as Royalty? I will just be considered a Divine rider. A commoner looking for the next level. I started as nothing and managed to ride up two levels. Then what? I make it to the third? No one will ever take me seriously. No one will ever respect me. No one that matters, anyways."

"I wasn't going to talk to you about this so soon." She sighs, approaching the door. She opens it silently, glancing at the two soldiers who stand guard. She gives them both a nod, shutting the door silently as she ducks back in. "But I guess I have to, now. You are so stubborn, Celeste! You don't give me much of a choice. You have to understand how important this is. Come, sit. If I'm going to say this, I have to say it quietly. No one else needs to hear. We are blessed to have soldiers who support the cause outside right now."

"What? You are joking, right? Who would be listening in? Why would anyone care what I was saying or doing in here?"

"You are so naive, Celeste. You are in complete and total denial. You have no idea what's happening out in the world, much less within these walls. Besides, weren't you once a quiet listener for me? For the princes? Goddess knows who you can trust in this place." I gape at her, shaking my head furiously. It's not like what I did involved sitting outside of rooms with my ear to a door! I wasn't sneaking around like a creep!

"I wasn't an *actual* spy. I was just…playing at it. I barely did anything, really."

"You did enough to land yourself here, didn't you? Enough to get Silvi's credibility knocked down a notch."

"Yes," I admit reluctantly, "I did." Though I hadn't realized it at the time, my silly little listening did much more damage to my life and others than I ever realized possible. But I guess that's why Ryleigh is sitting here, telling me how naive I am, how willingly blind I have chosen to be. "But it isn't like how Silvi played it out to be. I didn't betray my Court. I'm not out telling people all of these secrets. I'm just telling you—"

"Me, who you suspected was affiliated with some type of rebel group. Me, who you have been associated with for five long years. Me, who you personally requested as your handmaiden knowing I was retired from that life. All it would take is a whisper of doubt, a hint of uncertainty, and you will be back in that cell the Divine so desperately tried to keep you in." She is harsh, hissing each word at me. I can't help but pale. I've never heard her speak like this. Not to me, anyway. It is a threat, clear as the night sky on a full moon. And she is right. It all looks so suspicious. And what does it matter what the truth is when the lies can be so damning? They will say it is treason and I will be convicted in a matter of hours. Suddenly, a truth hits me like a bag of bricks:

If Ryleigh is caught, I am going down with her. Guilty or

153

not.

"I'm listening." I manage out, sitting on the edge of the large bed. She sits down next to me, laying a gentle hand on my arm. The touch is a stark contrast to the tone of her voice.

"We are called the Undivine Army. We are a resistance, working towards freeing the Undivine. Working towards a new, better world in all Courts. We have been placing our people into and around the Divine to gather information, to plant seeds. We have some Low Divine members, ones who want change for personal reasons. You would be surprised how they treat each other, especially the ones they consider to be at the bottom of the barrel when it comes to power. We even have a few High Divine in this Court, but no Royals. You could change that."

"Really? A resistance, Ryleigh? What good have you done, huh? I haven't heard many good things about the rebels. I haven't heard of you guys doing anything but *destroying* stuff, actually." I scoff, turning away. I shouldn't be allowing this. I shouldn't be participating in this kind of conversation. It was easier when I knew nothing other than a friend was asking for help. Sure, I suspected. But I didn't *know*. Now, I will be killed in front of the whole Court. My body will dangle from the trees, on display for weeks. Every day Undivine will walk by my rotting corpse, gagging and swatting away flies. Or, maybe they will bring me to a cell to be tortured. Whip me until I am no longer able to register the pain. Break my bones until I cave. Until I no longer know my name or what the Divine are.

I have landed myself into some deep shit.

"It takes time for these things, Celeste. Our goal is to be treated equally. We aren't trying to overcome the labeling

154

systems or the Courts themselves. We just want rights. To be treated the same way they treat each other. Equality for everyone. Low Divine should not be treated as less, and we should not be treated as nothing. Things have to change. New rules need to be made. Sometimes it takes a little violence to bring it on. A little anger to spark conversations. But it takes time and resources to do these things. We have been working on this for twenty-five years, Les. Twenty-five years and this is our first big break. We have been planning on using the Games as leverage for years. We have favorites we can get through, Divine who are more likely to side with us and our cause. Some have even been told of us and will stand with the resistance once we rise. We do not want violence. We do not want to torture people or kill them. But we will fight if we have to. We will change these ridiculous laws and beliefs."

"How many?" My head spins. A true resistance. An actual army. What could they do against the Divine, though? No powers, no protection. This is hopeless. This is all utterly *hopeless*.

"Around fifteen hundred in each Court. A little more here. We are the heart of the resistance so more people work here."

"And where do you fit in all of this? A head maid that never sees the Royals? Are you just a recruiter? Do you like to spin pretty lies to all of your maids or are they just for me?"

"There are four leaders, one for each Court." She speaks calmly, ignoring my snort. "I am...an assistant to one of the leaders. I gather intelligence. You know the things we hear, the things people say around us because they don't like to acknowledge our existence. It's all too easy to get good information around here. Useful information. That's the piece of the puzzle I fill."

"What do you want from me?" My voice is barely audible. This sounds great and all, but I am just me. I'm not anything special. Until recently, anyways. And even then, I'm not sure how far my uniqueness can take me.

"We had someone else in mind, like I said before. They can be the backup plan. But now? We want you. We want you to win the Games, Celeste. Win the prize. Become the queen, eventually. We want you to help us make this change. Don't you see what I do? You will change everything."

"You keep talking about this change. Change the rules, change the games, change the world. I like the idea of change, Ryleigh, but I don't have a good feeling about this. I can't fool everyone like that. I just don't think that I, of all people, can pull it off. And I don't think I want to." I don't think I'm ready to risk my life for this, especially after what happened last time. Besides, I've already been promised a nice home and a large sum of money. Money I can use to take Irissa to the Followers if all goes well. Why would I leave that behind? It is selfish, yes, but...

"You are already so close to both of the princes." Her whispers are pleading, desperate. "They are going to keep you here because of the Undivine. They want you here enough to fight over it, as I've told you already. The Royals want the Undivine to settle. There is so much distrust in the other Courts, they don't want any more trouble inside their own borders. You will appease them. It's a wonderful solution for everyone. A convenient one. They are going to use you. Milk you of every drop you have. They will fake their feelings, and pretend to care about you. All just to keep you here and make their lives easier. You are a convenience, Celeste. You are here because they want to make a statement. Do not let them fool

156

you into believing their lies."

"That's true. But I already knew all that. Why do you think I want to go? To not be part of that?"

"Is it not only fair that you fake it, too? That you lie and use them for your own purposes, your own pleasures? They are showing you off, acting like you are a diamond that appeared right in their palms. But you aren't. We both know you aren't. You may look like one, but you will never be that shiny prize they want. You are more like a piece of glass. Molded to look like what they want you to be. But you still have your edges, sharp as daggers. And you shouldn't be afraid to cut someone with them." She is right. She is almost always right. And I have already cut them. I will continue to do so, willingly or not.

"Okay." It is on impulse I agree. I might come to regret it later. No, I most definitely will come to regret it later. But at this moment, guilt is swallowing me down into its dark, empty belly. I'm so selfish. All I have done is want for myself. I've wanted to be wealthy, to be isolated, to be free of the Divine. I've wanted Irissa to stay in the house I trapped her in, wanted her to change, wanted her to be someone she just couldn't be. How could I? What kind of person does that make me?

What else am I going to do with my life, anyway? Hideaway for however long I have left? Hide Irissa behind closed doors if I can't get enough for treatment, or worse, no treatment exists? Never let her see the world, fall in love, make friends, have kids? I know she wants a life like that. I can't give her that life safely unless I do this. Maybe it's reckless. Maybe it's plain stupid. But I can't pass it up. This is an opportunity to be a part of something bigger than I could ever be on my own. To no longer be selfish, to want and wish for new things that don't just revolve around me and my life.

"Thank the goddesses." She breathes the words out, not daring to smile. "Listen to me closely, Les. You must not ever repeat what has been said here. Not to your princes. Not to your sister. Not to anyone. Never, ever admit any affiliation with us. Do you understand? This is life or death, Les. You must promise to never tell anyone about any of this unless you are sure of their involvement."

"I promise. I won't tell anyone who isn't involved." The weight of that promise hits me hard, sweeping over my entire body. Is this what the Divines feel? Maybe this is the real reason they are so choosy about what they swear to others. Because this feeling…it makes it clear that there is no going back now.

"Good. I don't want them to conclude that you really are a spy. You would have a worse fate than the one you almost faced before." My eyes snap to hers at the subtle threat, acutely aware of what she is telling me. If I tell anyone, I will die. Very, very painfully and very, very publicly. But I already knew that before agreeing. So I nod in reply, letting her hands drift up into my hair. As she begins to braid the wild locks, she hums softly under her breath. Then, very quietly, she begins singing.

"Upon the castle we ran,
knives and bows in our hands.
Soldiers falling to the ground,
justice finally carried out.
The people cried out in waves,
done we were with being slaves.
And with no more Royals to obey,
a whole new world was made."

I shiver at the song, recognizing it immediately. All

Undivine know of it. If you visit any of the bars late at night, it is almost always being sung. The people are angry, frustrated, tired. It's a song of hope. A song of rebellion. I close my eyes, whispering the next lyrics softly under my breath.

"Though we were born as slaves,

we live to see another day."

"Together we fought with thrall,

tore them down and broke their walls," Ryleigh whispered.

"Taught them a lesson in haste,

not even Royals will be safe." We sing the last line together. There is no more speaking after that.

I sit gently at the table, placing my hands in my lap. The other girls had quieted upon my entry, staring at me with cold and judgmental eyes. "Ah. I see. Still not over the staring, are we?" I chide the girls as if talking to children. Dove giggles from my side, breaking the silence.

"Well, do you blame us? We have to know, Celeste! How was it?"

"What? My date? It was okay, I guess. I enjoyed his company." A series of giggles erupts around the room, quickly quieting.

"Oh, yes, you certainly enjoyed his company." Dove laughs, fingers tapping against my cheek.

"I don't know what you mean." I brush her hand away, willing a blush to my cheeks. It didn't take much effort.

"Oh, don't tease! You have to tell us all about it! What was it like? Was it better than any kiss you have ever had?"

"First, I would like to say it was just on the cheek. Nothing so...casual. Second, I have no clue. I—I have nothing to compare it to." I am lying, and I thought surely she would say so. But she doesn't. She just brushes the comment off, continuing.

"What? You didn't kiss? The photo looks so intimate. We were all sure..." Dove seems genuinely surprised. Most of the girls do. What am I supposed to say, though? 'Actually, I have this small problem of freaking out when men touch me, especially the Divine. I'm full of unprocessed trauma and am still learning how to cope.' Or, better yet, should I tell them how the princes are the only men I have considered myself attracted to in five years? No. Better to divert the attention from those sore spots.

"No. I think—I think he wanted to. He leaned in like he was about to, but...I turned my head so he would kiss my cheek instead. I guess it was moving a little too fast for me to wrap my head around it."

"She's obviously lying." Silvi butts in, rolling her eyes with a tiny scoff. Some of the girls nod along with her in agreement, most of whom I recognize as hailing from the Solar Court.

"Oh?" I turn towards her, tilting my head. Of course, she has no way of knowing if I am lying. And it isn't like she can force me to tell the truth anymore. Everyone here knows I can repel her mind tricks.

"The princes are keeping you around as a kindness. They pity you. Why would they want to kiss an Undivine willingly? It's all for the press."

"Is it pity or my sparkling personality that draws them in, you think?"

"The papers claim it's your dark past, do you think that's

160

true? Really, Celeste, they just want you to rally the people. A real sob story, yeah? Who would be better as our next princess, maybe even queen, with a strong background like that? Who better than someone who knows what it is like in the villages, poor and powerless? You do remember those days, don't you, Celeste?" Her voice comes out as a slow snarl, eyes baring into mine.

"Oh, yes. I remember them well." My voice cracks and squeaks and I hate myself for it. "The long, sleepless nights I endured to ensure my sister was safe in her bed while I slept on the floor. The harsh winters that kept us hungry and freezing. I remember sitting in a house that was practically caving in, one that offered no insulation. I remember the little pay and the little resources available to us. The treatment of my people as they struggled to survive. The killing, the torturing, and the enslavement of Undivine. All for the sake of luxuries your people desire. Luxuries we will never get. The unfairness, the unequal treatment because we were born different. Born insignificant. yes, I remember those struggles very well.

"I am a living, breathing product of those terrible circumstances. I am glad I rally the people. They know I understand, they know I feel their pain. And they know I can make their lives better. So, think about that, Silvi, before it is too late and I am crowned your queen."

"Oh, yes, repeat the overused sob story—"

"Who cares, either way, Silvi? Sure, I have a sob story. Do you know what else I have? More attention from both of the princes combined than most of you will ever get. I have felt their hands on my skin, their lips on *my* cheek. I think that in itself is a defeat over the likes of you."

161

"How right you are." I feel the whisper as it hits the shell of my ear, shivering at the sudden coolness. I glance to the side as Zaeden walks by, still feeling the hint of his breath on my skin. Then, I feel the heated touch of Kyelin as he slides past. His hand runs across my bare shoulders, soft fingers grazing my pale skin. He doesn't say a word, but everyone sees. They are proving my point as publicly as they can. They *are* paying more attention to me, despite the many reasons not to.

Silvi glares in my direction, fury dancing along her body. I send a smirk in return, winking playfully. She has underestimated me once already; maybe now she will have more reason to reconsider.

I can't say I understand what has changed between us in its entirety. I have my suspicions that she was jealous; not of *me* but of the *attraction* I have for others. She had been so desperate for me to like her, to be her friend, that somewhere along the way she began to want more than friendship. And yet, that too, seems to get pushed aside when it comes to her survival among the Divine. Not that I can entirely blame her for that. But why does it have to be this instead? Why must I choose between a relationship or an enemy? I want neither, but I have no other options. So, enemies it must be.

"Esra? May I ask you to take a walk with me to the stables where we can ride together for a while?" Zaeden questions a girl towards the end of the table. The Shadow Court Divine takes it instantly, letting him sweep her away.

"May I, Taryn?" Kyelin asks simply farther down the table, holding his hand out for a pretty brunette of the Lunar Court. She is also swept out of the room in a flourish. We all watch as they leave, an air of unsureness sweeping through the room. I can see the questions on their faces, plain as the full moon's light. Why were they not asked? When will they get a turn? Even I find myself wishing I had been the one to go. Anything is better than being in the presence of these snobby, evil girls. Even pretending to court a prince.

"Want to get out of here?" Dove turns towards me, a wicked gleam in her eyes.

"Definitely." I grin back in surprise, standing alongside her.

"Where are you two going?" Silvi snarls, her gaze snapping towards our end of the table.

"Away from this suffocating room." Dove waves her hand dismissively. "Celeste is the only one here who doesn't bore me to death."

"Jealous?" I send her a tight-lipped smile. I am certain of the answer, but I don't stay to hear the lies. Dove only makes it a few feet out of the door before bursting into laughter, eyes watering. I can't help but giggle at her explosion, eventually falling into the same rhythm of laughs. I lean against the wall for support, tripping over my own feet as I stumble towards it.

"I don't even know where to go. I feel so strangled in this castle, but there is no escaping." Dove finally gets out, laughter dying out quicker than a snuffed candle.

"I've felt trapped since the moment they put me in a nice dress and gave me a Divine title." I let out a small sigh, agreeing. We slowly begin to put distance between us and the Divine in the other room.

"It is a big change. But you worked in the castle before, right? As a maid? So you were here every day, even before becoming a Divine?"

"I did. I was usually here twelve hours or more a day. But I had a home to go to, a sister waiting on me. A change in scenery, I guess you can say. I live…lived in Slyvein. Village three. It is not as close as the other villages, but I often hitched rides with a merchant wagon. It was the only way I would make it on time. They offer residency here, but there isn't enough room for both me and my sister in one room. I couldn't leave her, so they assigned us that house. I wish I had the same choice now."

"So you're branded, then?" She wouldn't meet my eyes with the question.

"Yes, I am. I'm sure a Divine healer could fix some of the puffiness around the burn mark, but I've decided not to seek one out. I want to keep it as a reminder. I remember the day I got the mark. I had already been burned once, so I was sure it wouldn't hurt as much the second time around. Of course, I was young when I got the first mark. And I had to get two on the same day because I had moved to a new village.

It was excruciating, Dove. I was fifteen, I had just run away, and I had a ton of things on my plate. The Divine stuck the iron in the fire and forced me to watch it heat to the perfect temperature. And the smile on his face when he grabbed my ankle…it was vicious. Disturbing, to say the bare minimum. Cruel, even. He yanked on my leg so hard that I heard a pop. When I screamed and tried to pull away, he slapped me and pulled harder. Then, with no warning, he shoved the iron onto my skin. I screamed and screamed, Dove, but no one cared. No one came to check on me. And then he got to do it again on my shoulder. I had to wait for that one, too. He laughed the whole time. The whole ordeal is barbaric." Dove turned green, a hand coming up to cover her mouth. Her whole body shuddered before her hand lowered and an understanding passed within her eyes.

164

"If I tell you this, you won't repeat it, right?"

"Who would I tell?" I tried to joke, but she didn't take to it.

"I dated an Undivine a year ago. They told me about the mark, about how evil the process was. Your story is so similar, so terrible...something is wrong with this whole system, Celeste. They shouldn't have ever gone through that and you shouldn't have, either." Her voice is coarse, eyes slick with fresh tears.

"What happened to them?" I am sure this couldn't have ended well, not with the way Dove is breaking down right now. If Dove is an Undivine sympathizer, is she the one Ryleigh had mentioned as a backup candidate? The intensity in her eyes makes me wonder.

"One day, when they had snuck into the city to see me, their father found out. He whipped them in front of the whole village for defying him. When I realized the amount of trouble I was causing, I broke things off. I couldn't stand to keep up with the relationship knowing I was the cause of those scars. The cause of that pain. I don't know where they are now or if they are with someone else. I don't know if I *want* to know."

"Were you in love?"

"Very much so. Maybe too much. And some days I think myself a coward for just...leaving. For not fighting harder." She gives me a sad smile, that usual gleam in her eyes dissolving.

"I want to change things for the Undivine. I want things to be better."

"So do I, my friend. So do I."

Chapter 10

"I hear they are moving your sister today," Ryleigh says as she brushes my hair a few days later, grinning in the mirror.

"Truly? They have found a place for her in the city?" A mix of happiness and nerves swirl inside me. I miss my sister. But being around so many Divine…it's something neither of us are accustomed to.

"Yep. I don't know where so don't ask me. I just know they sent a dozen soldiers to retrieve her. The girls were whispering about it all morning. They couldn't believe the Royals went through so much effort to bring an Undivine to the city."

"Well, I guess they will find out soon that she isn't Undivine."

"I guess so."

My lips curl up mischievously, a million thoughts running through my head. I'm not supposed to leave this castle, but I haven't seen my sister in a couple of weeks. We have never been apart so long. Ryleigh has been staying overnight with her, and I know the toll that has taken. But now she is near and doesn't need Ryleigh to protect her. I can be there for her again. I just need to find her.

I can barely hear Ryleigh's cries of protest, her voice swallowed by the crowd. "Les! Wait! Hold on! You have to stay with us! Les!" I can tell she is on the verge of shouting my actual name and can hear the speech that includes at least three foul words about how dangerously I am behaving. But she can't.

I am not supposed to be here. It is a stupid, reckless thing to do. But the people don't seem to recognize me. They have seen my picture, sure. But those pictures had shown me in rags and covered in dirt. And then once more when my head was turned and a prince was kissing my cheek. Who was looking at me when he was there? Even now, in my fancy dress and nice jewelry, they don't see me. Somehow, I still blend in. Ryleigh knows it has to stay this way, for my safety and hers.

I keep running, ignoring her calls. I shove people as I pass, ignoring the hisses and shouts. I don't care who I make angry. I have to get there quickly before they move her. I'm not supposed to know where she is. Did they think they could keep it a secret from me? From a former servant who has easy access to everyone's secrets? From a girl hired by multiple people to be a spy? They underestimated me. Like Silvi. Like so many others before her. Soon, they will all learn from their mistakes.

Ryleigh and the soldier don't reach me in time. I am fast. I don't have long legs or ample strength, but I am small. Small enough to squeeze between people in the crowds. Small enough that they don't give a second thought to the breeze they feel as I pass. I have been running for years for work, especially on days when the Divine were all but patient. They also don't have the same determination, the same motivation that is coursing through my veins. I *will* get what I came for.

When I reach the large house on the hill, I don't bother to knock. I don't stop to gawk at the two-story beauty with its beautiful jade paint and extravagant gold accents. I just open the door, slamming it shut behind me to make sure I am heard. It comes with the bonus of delaying my entourage. I glance around frantically, eyes wide. Where is she?

"Irissa! Irissa! I'm here! Please, come out! It's me, Celeste!" I call out in a panic, becoming frightened. Did they move her already? Did someone send word ahead that I was coming?

"Celeste? What in the world do you think you are doing?" I flinch as the door behind me opens and slams shut once more. "You could have been killed in the fucking streets! You get that, don't you? Damn idiot! I have the right mind to slap you so hard that shitty attitude takes flight and leaves your body! Do you have any idea of the dangers—" I know at least five off the top of my head. And, hey, that is three foul words already! I called it.

"The soldier couldn't keep up with us?"

"He is outside waiting. Doing his job. And a damn good one at that!"

"Whatever." I huff, refusing to meet her eyes. That will be my downfall.

"Listen, Celeste, you really should know—" Ryleigh starts, but my gasp cuts her off. I squeal in glee as my sister steps out of the shadows, wings unfurling slowly at the sight of me. Then I see the shadow approaching her from behind, perfectly person-shaped. I grab her in seconds, pulling her away from the darkness approaching. I hid her behind me, glaring into the dark hall she had just arrived from. Irissa places a hand on my shoulder, in a seemingly begging way. I freeze, letting the truth reveal itself to me.

"Mother." I wish I could breathe fire. I wish I could send dark poison her way. And even though I know I can't do either of those things, a tingling within my hands begins with the thoughts. I spare them a glance, shocked to see something swirling beneath my skin. Is that...purple tendrils? The same purple tendrils Zaeden used to poison me? Is that even possible? For something like that to linger within my body? The shock I feel scares them away, slimy tendrils burrowing deep down. I can only watch as it buries itself within my body once more. I shake away the strangeness, eyes rising to meet my mother's. Maybe I am becoming a crazy person. Maybe all of the mental effort to ward off Silvi is finally getting to me. My emotions *are* running high right now, though, and probably making me imagine things. They are making me see things, messing with my mind. That's all.

"Celeste, sweetheart. How wonderful it is to see you." My mother coos, flashing me a half-smile. I scowl in return, burning with hatred at the mere sight of her. She looks just like me. Or, I guess I look just like her. Blond hair, brown eyes, thin frame, short stature. She doesn't have my freckles, though. That's why I love them so much. They make me feel separated from her, like I am somebody other than my mother's daughter.

"Don't speak to me." I use the new princess tone I have recently created. Authoritative. Decisive. Controlled.

"Please hear her out," Irissa begs behind me, tugging on my arm. Of course Irissa has fallen into her web of lies. Has given her the benefit of the doubt. Irissa is too kind. She doesn't remember enough, didn't experience enough. She is too gullible.

"Why is she here?" I spin onto Ryleigh, hissing in her direction. This is her fault. It has to be. Who else knew of my family? Who else but…no. They wouldn't do that to me. Right? I have already told Zaeden about my past, about how I ran away to get away from this monster. The report didn't even know about my mother's identity. They reported that I ran away, but they never mentioned my mother's identity or her village.

But Zaeden said they had spoken to her already.

Which was more likely? Did Zaeden, the prince, the man with poison lying underneath his skin, the man who was obligated to do what the king and queen tell him, give them sensitive information about me? Or Ryleigh, a spy and revolutionary who aches for the downfall of the Divine system? My friend and confidant for five long years? Now who is gullible?

"Who found her?" I hiss when I don't get an answer.

"Some soldiers." Vague.

"She is only here for the money and fame. Not me. Not Irissa. I don't want her near me or my sister. I don't want her in this city. Bring her back to the village she came from. Out of my sight and away from our thoughts."

"I came to make amends, sweetie." Dear mother whispers, honey sweetness slicking her tongue. "I regret how I have acted in the past. I'll admit that I have not been the best of mothers, not by a long shot. But I want to change. I regret the day I lost you both. I didn't realize things had gotten so bad. That the two of you were so upset. I want to make things better here. I just want a nice, loving relationship with you both. I am truly sorry for the pain and misfortune I have caused."

"Sorry?" I scoff, unable to stop myself. Irissa jabs me in the ribs with her elbow, hissing angrily under her breath for me to stop. I snap my head towards her, glaring. She doesn't understand what this means for her. For *us*. This is not going to be the happy reunion my mother dreamed of.

"Did you see the report?" My question is quiet as I turn away from my sister, not wanting to see the look in her eyes as she realizes the truth. At the moment, she is stable. She can understand my hurt and upset and will be able to process her feelings accordingly. Later? When she remembers this pain but can't remember why? That's when she will lose control.

"Well, honestly, yes, but—"

"But what?" I don't want to hear the pitiful excuses. I know she's been practicing this little speech in the mirror, trying to decide what words would work best. Wondering what would get us on her side. "You would have looked bad, huh? All of your little friends know about you. They would take one look at me and know exactly who you were to me. The mother whose daughters ran away. Oh, I mean were kidnapped, right? That is what you told them, isn't it? What happened when word got around? Celeste and Irissa, the lost daughters of Urona. 'Oh, Urona. How happy you must be to know your two daughters are alive and well! Oh, what's this? It says here they ran away. But didn't you say they were taken? Stolen in the night while you slept? A single mother who had no protection from the evils that lurked just outside of her door? Right under the window that led to your daughters' room? It says here that Celeste had an abusive mom! Is that true?'"

"Stop it." She growls, inching closer. I see her hand rising, shaking with fury. I grab her wrist before it can swing towards its target. I am in control now.

"Don't you dare put your hands on me. You think I don't know what you said? What lies you've spread? I have friends all over this Court. Sneaky ones that keep me in the loop when it comes to you. I didn't want you getting too close to us so I made sure you stayed in that stupid village. I know every lie you told. Every law you broke to make sure the truth didn't come out. Every married man you took home so that you could have power over *someone*, no matter whose life it ruined. I know everything, mother. And you are going to ruin *everything* I am fighting for here!

I know you do not care for either of us, not really. I know you never came looking for us. We are convenient for the money, for the attention. But we mean nothing more to you than that. Leave. Now. Before you ruin this for us. *I* managed to make it this far. *I* have fought for this life. Not for me, but for her. Irissa will be better than us both. She won't have to do the things we have had to do. Leave, and give her that chance."

"I do not know what you are talking about, you foolish girl. How dare you talk to me like that? I am your mother! I gave you a home, food, and clothes. What more could you ask for? I was good to you both, and this is my repayment? A foul attitude and hostile behavior? Disrespectful!"

"Don't spout that shit at me! I'm done with your lies! I won't ask you again. Leave." The anger in me boils. I feel the tension, and I swear I see those purple tendrils rising again.

"I am not lying, you Divine rider! I would never lie to my daughters! Never! I am a good mother! But you are not a good daughter! You disrespect me with these outrageous claims!"

"What do you know of *respect?*" I watch her take a step back, fear filling her eyes.

"Your eyes. What's wrong with your eyes?"

"You truly ask for respect? You have to earn it. Something you have not and will never do." I ignore her comment.

"They're purple. No, it's more than that. Like purple clouds. What—"

"I demand you leave. Leave and never come back. I am of higher status now. I am a High Divine. A High Divine who is very close to the Royals. I have authority over you, and I will use it. Oh, and don't forget the powers underneath my skin. I won't be too upset if I get to use them against you, I must say."

"Don't, Les. Don't be like this." Irissa begs me, tugging on my dress. Her touch soothes me, and I feel the anger flow out like water down a drain. She doesn't need to see this.

"I know her better than you, Irissa. I am doing what is right." She still doesn't understand? After hearing what I said? After being reminded of how awful our mother truly is? How can she still want her in our lives? Still want to make up for lost time? It's simply wrong and will not be allowed.

"Celeste, I'm sorry, but she can't leave." Ryleigh's voice cuts through the thick tension in the air.

"Stay out of this." This is a family matter. It is none of her concern.

"You are losing control, Celeste. Listen to me." Irissa's voice floats into my ears, so I do my best to hear her out. I admit, I *am* getting much too heated. So, I let Ryleigh speak.

"The king and queen are in control of the second Game. Part of the Games is meeting the parents of each participant. This is to be done in the week before the second Game. The actual Game is going to be a race through the villages. Each

173

village will have a hidden crown or two. The participants who find a crown and bring it back will continue. The Game will take place over two days. The parents can't leave until the Game is over. You can't force your mother to leave. The Royals have decreed it and so it shall be."

"Surely they will see reason—"

"At least three girls will be eliminated after these meetings alone." Her hand touches my shoulder. She is staring at me so intensely, like she is trying to use sheer willpower to force me to accept this. "You will have to suffer through this meeting if you want to be a Royal." When I turn to meet her eyes, I know I have no choice in the matter. If I am to carry out my promise, I have to let this go.

"Fine." I agree bitterly, spinning back to Urona. "But you have to be on your best behavior. You can stay with Irissa, but only conditionally. If I hear of any wrongdoing, any mishaps, you will leave. I will make sure of it. You know of Irissa's condition. Do not use it against her. Take care of her. Keep her condition secret. The next time I see you both, she better be exactly the way I left her." With that, I take Irissa's hand and pull her outside. The soldier moves to the side, letting us stand in the shade of the canopy above the door frame.

"Do not let her say anything harmful to you. She is not allowed to call you names or make fun of your condition. She has to take care of you like a mother is supposed to. She owes you that, and you deserve it. Lock yourself away at night. Do not let her see you at your most vulnerable point. Don't let her know how your powers truly betray you. She hasn't seen you in a long time. Pray she has forgotten." I hug my sister tightly, wishing I could convey the greatness of my love in such a simple act.

"Don't be so stubborn, Les."

"I have to protect you, Iris. No one else will."

"I know, Les. I know." She pulls away from me, giving me a sad glance before entering her new home once more.

I wipe away the few tears that slip down my face with the back of my arm. I turn away from the building, taking a deep, shuddering breath. Then, I slip back into the crowded streets. I don't look back. I can't.

Chapter 11

I find myself sitting at the same table—which I have nicknamed the table of no intelligence—again, eating lunch with High Divine once more. I've become tired of this nonstop chore, of constantly sitting here and waiting for something interesting to happen. I feel like half of my day is taken up by this table, by these people.

Today, the tension runs higher than usual. I can feel the anxiety coming off of everyone, rolling around and dancing in the air. As of yesterday, the first dates are officially over. Now, it is time for the second dates. One girl has already been asked to leave after a date. Someone from the Shadow Court, I believe. With something like that weighing on our minds, impatience tramples through us like a wild beast tramples through a forest. We wait for a prince to come barging in like they have every day the past week.

When Kyelin comes striding through the doors, I sit up straighter along with the others. We all watch his careful strides, eyes roaming from Divine to Divine. Finally, those striking eyes drift towards me. His steps echo across the room as he approaches, and I try not to listen to the frantic whispers that make their way to my ears. I feel those soft, warm hands on my shoulders, an impossibly bright smile aimed at me. He bends down, lips touching the tip of my ear. I feel envy and rage swallowing the air around me.

"Care to join me?" His voice sends a shock down my spine. I can only nod, attempting to shake off the sensation. Kyelin takes my hand, helping me into a standing position. I barely have time to send a panicked glance to Dove before he plucks me from the room. I struggle to keep up with his long strides, our large height difference once again apparent. I try to spot Zaeden, but I can't see if he, too, has swept a girl away. Is it only me, then?

"I want to take you somewhere special." I try not to compare the feeling of Kyelin's hands to Zaeden's. His just feels so… right. So warm and comforting. Not as cold or as harsh as I remember Zaeden's being.

"It won't be so special once the report sees it." I laugh, allowing him to steer me around the familiar halls.

"They aren't allowed where we are going. No cameras will be present." His grin is mischievous, laughter following my suspicious sideways glance. I hear the clicks of cameras then as if summoned by the mere mention of the contraptions. As if the Divine behind them are aware of the urgency, panicked at the realization that they will not get the exclusives they were promised. Instead, they will have a few pictures of the prince sweeping his Undivine date down a hall. Maybe they will paint it as a fairy tale to the public and put it on display as a dream come true. I can see it now! My long, flowing train flying in the air; my head turned over my shoulder, looking behind as if searching for any witnesses to this secretive date. They will paint us as a nontraditional pair of lovers, two people from very different worlds who were never meant to cross paths. Two people who found each other at the most opportune moment in their entire lives. The poor village girl and the obscenely rich prince. What a cliche.

Thinking about it makes me sick. It only complicates matters when I remember how he makes me feel, how Zaeden makes me feel. But with Zaeden it's more...like a friend. He is attractive, obviously, and so considerate and kind. I just...feel like something is off with him. Like we aren't meant to be. Like he may be trying too hard. But with Kyelin...it feels different. Like I may actually *like* him. I've barely seen him since becoming a Divine and, yet, I feel closer to him than ever. And these feelings I have...they don't matter. I am still going to be using them for my own needs. To get what I want out of this whole ordeal. How can I allow myself to fall into that deep hole of happiness knowing I hide such big secrets in my heart? Yes, a fairy tale indeed.

We fly down a set of spiral stairs, hidden in a nook at the end of a short hall. The bottom pops out into a small room, a set of double doors on the other side. Kyelin guides me to them, slipping us through and clicking the lock before anyone can follow. I should feel nervous, shouldn't I? Locked in a room with a man I barely know? A Divine, much less! I know how easily he can overpower me if he wants to. Those thoughts seem logical, probable, even. But I am past giving a shit about logic now.

I hear voices hitting the door and frantic shouts nearby. But no one dares attempt to get in. And as I look around, I realize exactly why Kyelin wants to keep this place secret. We are surrounded by animals. Most small, a few large. Glass boxes are set up all through the room, the smaller creatures moving about inside. I see rabbits bouncing in a pin across the room, and I swear one of them is glowing!

"What is this?" The room is truly astounding. But why are these animals locked up? Why do they look so strange? It frightens me, if only slightly. "Why do you have so many?"

"This is my pet sanctuary." His response is casual. "They help me and I help them. I collect them, in a way." He collects...animals?

"I don't know what all of these are." I glance between boxes, fist clenching nervously.

"Let me show you." He still has a tight hold on my other hand, pulling me away with another bright smile. We approach the first set of glass boxes, but my confusion only grows. I can tell they are reptiles, probably lizards of some kind. But they look *wrong*. As if they have been morphed into something they are not. There is a snake with two heads, tongues dancing out to taste the bitter air. There is a frog with a long tail, the tip splashing down into a bowl of water. It has bright red eyes, but they shift to orange, then yellow. I move away from the glass at the sight, disgusted. I don't want to look at these hideous creatures.

"This is a gecko." Kyelin lifts the lid off of a glass box directly in front of him. He gently plucks the animal from the box, holding it out for me to touch. It is spotted with black dots, its base color a snowy white. But it has two large, thick tails and three black eyes. All three are staring me down, sizing me up. Then it opens its mouth, showing off its teeth. They are large, pointy, and dripping with black goo. I take a shuddering breath, trying not to be scared. I gently run my hand down its spotted back, finding myself surprisingly pleased at the texture. "Her name is Gem."

"Gem." I find myself whispering as he places her back into the box. "How do you remember all of their names?"

"They mean so much to me that it isn't hard to remember. They each have such unique personalities and fun quirks. I name them based on their traits. Her eyes shine like gemstones." He shrugs, moving down the line. Most of the boxes have strange lights hanging above them, with rocks and greenery inside. This portion of the room seems to be a little humid, too. He seems so happy to introduce each one, eyes gleaming as he explains how much work was put into each rescue without going into detail. Just statements like 'this one took days to retrieve' or 'I found this one on the brink of death'. I even watch him feed a lizard a cricket, which he pulls from a large bin full of them. The small creature practically swallows it whole, eagerly waiting for more. I giggle as it runs from side to side, from one end of the box to the other. I can barely keep my eyes away from it, but Kyelin continues to pull me deeper into the strange room. As we walk farther, the reptiles disappear.

"These are my rodents." The humidity is fading away, something I am grateful for. Not that my hair is salvageable at this point.

"What is that? Why does it look like that?" I finally release the question I have been holding in, waiting for him to get angry. He only laughs, though, shaking his head. I feel his hand snaking around my shoulders, wrapping me up gently. The fluffy ball in front of us flashes its teeth, sharp and pointy like the gecko's. Its fur flashes from a muddy brown to a turquoise blue, dancing between the two colors ferociously. Its eyes don't open.

"It's sleeping. There are several burrowed down in there. They like to curl up into little balls. They have really cute faces, I promise. I don't want to wake them, though. They sleep during the day, so it isn't often they are awake at this time. Sometimes they hear my voice and come out, but not often." Why is he dodging the question? These animals are hideously malformed. Was this done to them...purposely?

"Oh, okay. What do they eat?" I try to continue along with the conversation, try to ignore the uneasiness swirling around inside of me.

"Lots of things. Seeds, some vegetables, other stuff. They need a healthy balance, of course, but I try to offer some nice treats now and then, too." I nod, eyes raking over the next box.

"Those are mice." I watch a few as they dash through some shredded paper in the box. They, too, flash between colors. Their white fur changes to a deep violet every few seconds. Their nails are long and claw-like, their tails longer and stronger than the average mouse. Then, when I catch a glimpse of their faces, I jump away. They are hideous. They have four rows of sharp teeth, mouths wide and open to accommodate. Their eyes are non-existent, only empty holes where they should have been.

"Yes. They are females, so I can keep them together like this. They are really good pets. Awful smelling piss, though." I bark out a laugh, agreeing that they smell. But as we continue on, I grow more and more uncomfortable.

Some of the larger animals snarl at me as we pass, hissing and snapping their teeth. They sling and spit goo all over the place, large, muscular bodies propelling them against the walls. They even fight each other, forcing Kyelin to pry them apart. He comes back with scratches coating his tan arms, but they don't seem to damper his spirit. I try not to look at a mutated wolf in the corner, fear rushing through my body hard enough to make me shake.

Finally, we approached the large pin of rabbits I saw upon first entering the room. Their faces and teeth are not different, but their patterns are full of unnatural colors. Teals, limes, and fuchsias dart around, fast and happy. The sight of them makes me sick, though. Everything about these animals is *unnatural*.

Kyelin leads me through a small gate, leading me to a spot to sit. We sit with our backs to the wall, arms pressed tightly against each other. I watch the rabbits approach their master, bouncing right into his lap. He strokes each one, making sure no one is left out. Without saying anything, he gently lifts one into his arms and places it into my own lap. I let my fingers run over its ears, the softness bringing a smile to my lips.

"They have heart attacks when scared, so don't make sudden movements." I only nod, unsure of how sudden he means. I let my hand drop away from the rabbit, too. Maybe it is best not to touch it anymore.

"They are beautiful." I try to choke down my disgust and fear.

"They are my comforts. All of them. I would rather be in this room than anywhere else in the world. They help me relax, to forget all of the things running around in my head. To forget the pressure I am placed under every day. If only I had been born a few minutes later, right?"

"How do you take care of them all?" I can see it when I look at him: weariness.

"I have someone who helps. A servant I trust dearly. He has worked for me a very long time. If I am being completely honest, you are the only other person I have ever shown this room. I haven't even shown Zae. I don't want him to take this from me, too. I just want one thing for myself. One thing not attached to our family name." He glances down, meeting my curious gaze.

"Thank you. For trusting me with this." I'm not trusting him with my biggest secrets right now, that's for certain. Sure, I mentioned Irissa to him. But that was out of survival. To keep us both safe and well. Plus, I didn't tell him everything. This? This is his choice. Probably the wrong one.

"I knew this was the only place we would ever be truly alone." Then, after a beat, "I want you to trust me, too."

"Okay. Do you want me to tell you a secret, too? Tit for tat?" It isn't a secret. Not really. But an opportunity is an opportunity.

"If you feel so inclined." His lips curve up at the corners, amused.

"I don't like my mother being around. Not just in this Court, but in the same home as my sister. Everything about it irks me." I try to shrug nonchalantly, to seem as if I hadn't hoped this conversation would come. As if I hadn't been planning it in my head for days.

"Oh? Why?" His body turns toward me, allowing me to capture his full attention.

"I ran away from home, remember? There was a reason. I know you read the report. I'm sure Zaeden mentioned it, too. She…she's not a good mother, Kyelin. Not by a long shot. I took Irissa away from her for good reason. I didn't want Irissa to feel the things I felt. I wanted her to be happy. Being around my mother would never allow for that."

"I just wanted you to tell me when you felt like telling me." He grows quiet, placing a hand on my leg. I let him keep it there, not bothered by the touch like I should be.

183

"I went to see her. We argued. I said some things, she said some things. Honestly, I think just being in her presence turns me into a different person. She's bad for me. Bad for Irissa. I wanted her to know we don't want her here. Well, I thought neither of us wanted her here. Turns out, Irissa is a bit more open to forgiving her than I am."

"I heard about the visit." I bite my lip, nodding. I presumed he had. That's the only reason I admitted to it. "I'd rather you not see either of them again."

I sit up straight, turning to stare at him. Does he seriously expect me to stay away from my sister? "What?"

"It's going to be better for you." His voice turns soothing, a hand running over my cheek. "You just said your mother's presence is bad for you. I know you love your sister, but she hurts you, too. I know how upset it makes you to see her in that awful state at night. I know how badly you want to take care of her. But I think you need time for yourself. Time to figure out who you are without her, and she without you. You two are constantly nipping at each other's heels, from what I hear. Maybe a little distance will do you both well, let you both relax a little. It's just for now, Celeste." He sounds so *sincere*. Like he actually thinks I will do well without them. Maybe he does truly believe it. Maybe...maybe he is right. Maybe I do need to quit worrying about Irissa for a bit. She is safe now, protected. She doesn't need me as she did before. And she *is* always saying I smother her. Now that our mother is here...does she even need me anymore?

"Okay. You may be right." It comes out as barely a whisper, despite my best efforts to fake indifference.

That brilliant smile lights up his face again. Oh, the things I would do to see that smile. "That's my girl."

My girl? I flush at the nickname, a flutter cascading down me. "Can I ask you something else?"

"Anything." Just looking at him pulls all of the air from my lungs. How does he just...look like that? So handsome, so carefree, so mature? I've never met a man like him before. Someone who draws me in so quickly, so completely. Who's very touch excites me in a way I have never felt before. I barely know him and yet part of me is being swept under his fiery current.

"What did they do to these animals? Why do they look so— so wrong?" I spit the question out as quickly as I can, trying to move past my confusing thoughts. When I had asked about the creature from earlier, he just brushed past it. He mentioned they were all rescued, but rescued from what and why?

"Ah. I wondered if you would notice their appearances."

"How could I not, Kyelin? Look at them! My sister and I eat rabbits quite often, and I've never seen one that looks like these. I *wouldn't* eat one if it looked like this. Probably would still kill it, though, to put it out of its misery."

"They're failed experiments. My father employs a few High Divine to use certain creatures for tests. New ideas and projects that they come up with. If they don't die, and the High Divines find no other use for them, I take them in." Experiments? What could they possibly be experimenting on animals for that makes them turn into these disgusting creatures? I'm not going to ask, because I know he won't be able to tell me. But the thought of the things these animals have endured...

"Why would you let them do that?" Anger and disgust flare up within me, my voice almost a whimper. How could he do that? And why wouldn't he just kill them? I think some of them would much rather be dead then spitting black ooze for the rest of their pitiful existence.

"It isn't up to me, Celeste. I may be a Royal, but I am just a prince. I'm not the king yet. I can't stop them until I am one. And I keep them because I know they can't be rehabilitated, so I want them to enjoy their lives for a little while. Their life spans are shortened. Most don't live longer than five years if that. I want the remainder of those years to make up for the ones they spent being tortured."

"Will you stop them? When you become king, I mean?" I can understand why he would want to make up for those lost years, a penitence in ways. I understand, but I don't think I would do it myself.

"I'm going to try." He lets out a heavy sigh, tilting his head back against the wall. The action exposes his long neck, and my fingers reach out to touch it on their own accord. "None of them deserve a life like this."

"Good. I don't like this, Kyelin. I don't like this at all." My fingers trail up to his sharp chin, greedy for every inch of skin.

"On the subject of not liking things, I have to admit something. I know you don't like your mother being around, but I do believe it is better than my mother's alternative idea." He tries to use a joking tone, but I can hear the sharp intake of breath each time my fingers run over a sensitive spot.

"Oh? And what was the alternative?" I make myself relax against the wall, make myself pull away without meeting his eyes. I shouldn't be so desperate for this touch. I shouldn't allow myself to feel this way. Everything with Kyelin is just so...*intense*. And I can't explain why.

"She had the bright idea of sending in everyone's ex-boyfriends." I can't hold in my laughter, doubling over. I cover my mouth, trying to hide the hideous noises escaping me. Try to keep the tears from falling.

"What? What is so funny? Your ex is that bad?" His eyes sparkle, a smirk gracing his lips.

"She's dead," I say. The laughter dies out, scared away by the memories of my past creeping up. I can pretend to be nonchalant about the subject, pretend to be over it. But I'm not. No matter how much I try to laugh it off or push it aside. She is still dead and I am still sad.

"My mother? I don't think it is that serious-"

"No. My ex. She died. I wouldn't have anyone to bring. Maybe I'm the reason they shut that idea down. Goddess, that's a depressing thought."

"Dead? And that's funny?" The confusion spreads across his face, eyebrows furrowing down.

"Not really." I fidget anxiously. "But I can't help thinking about the queen trying to hunt down my dead ex. It *is* quite a funny picture, don't you think?"

"A little." His soft smile warms my heart, melting me in all the right places.

"See? I'm not crazy. At least, not all of the time."

"Okay, okay. Are you going to tell me what happened? I know I haven't given you very many reasons to trust me yet. But that's why I brought you here. To prove that *I* trust *you*." My heart lurches, teetering on the edge of a cliff I'm not ready to dive off of. I don't understand why he trusts me or why I am about to spill my guts after those soft words.

"Well, I guess I should preface this by saying it wasn't very serious. We were just kids. We were friends first, for years. I mean, most kids in the villages grow up together. We knew each other well because of that. It just kind of turned into more, you know? One of those sudden things. Have you ever had a friend like that? When you think there may be more there?"

"Once." He pointedly looks down at me, which I promptly ignore.

"Then you understand. Naomi and I joked about being more than friends for years. Then, when I turned seventeen, I told her I had never been kissed before. I told her I wanted her to be my first kiss. She said yes. We never put a name to it, really. Never called it anything more than friendship, never made it a real relationship. Mostly just sneaked kisses and nights beneath the stars. But it felt real.

A few weeks after that first kiss, she was caught stealing. Normally, they would lash you a few times and call it a day. But Naomi had been reckless. She had stolen jewelry, but not just any jewelry. It was jewelry that had been ordered for the queen. She didn't know that. She just saw how extravagant it was and decided it would be hers. She was getting it for *me*. Her brother told me after it was all said and done. He said she wanted to make things official, that she wanted a grand gesture so I couldn't say no. If it had been a normal day, she may have been spared her life. Not a hand, but a life. But this day? This day was different. It was tax season, and the king and some soldiers came riding through. They had come to gather the jewelry and the taxes when it happened. The king was only there to make sure the quality was good, that it was exactly as he wanted for his queen. A birthday gift, or anniversary gift. I can't remember. They had hardly been there a few minutes. Bad timing, honestly. The king said it was unforgivable.

They stood her in front of the whole village, on the hanging stage. Gave a long speech about breaking the law. Told us not even women and children would be spared when it came down to it. We Undivine are all the same in their eyes. But they didn't hang her. They took a butcher's knife and just...it was a clean kill. I don't think she felt any of the pain. But I watched as the life left her eyes. And she watched me. I was the last thing she saw in this world. I think about that sometimes. What would I want to be the last thing I ever saw? I can only think that seeing me was a disappointment, compared to what it could have been. And now look at me, joking about it like it meant nothing. Like I didn't watch her blood soak into the ground at my feet. Like I didn't step in it trying to escape the sight. Like I wasn't stained with her death the way her blood stained my slippers. I feel so guilty about it. Like it was my fault she stole that jewelry. I know it wasn't. Not really. She didn't have to do that, she *knew* she didn't have to. I didn't ask her to, I didn't even *hint* at it. She made that choice. A wrong one, yes, but it was hers. But I am punished for it every day. And what if the king hadn't been there that day? What if he had been a few hours earlier, a few minutes later? Would it have changed anything at all? Would it have changed *me* at all?

It wasn't like this great, magical relationship. I mean, we were kids. She was always jealous. I was always angry. She even hit me once. I don't know. I just thought that we could get past it all. She was my friend. I didn't want to lose her. Her death shattered me in a way I never knew I could break. It was the deciding factor in my decision to leave the village."

"I don't know what to say. Other than I am so, so incredibly sorry. My father's reign has...lacked. I want to change that. What happened to Naomi...that should have never happened."

189

He pulls me into his chest, holding me tight.

I try to joke. "I have a little baggage. But at least you know my ex won't come back into the picture!"

"I can't say the same, I'm afraid. I haven't seen many girls, but they always come back to bite me in the ass. They want more than I can give them, I'm afraid. And everyone thinks they mean more to me than they do."

"Sounds like you are a heart breaker."

"Would it be egotistical of me to agree?"

"Very!" We laugh together, snuggling closer.

"This feels different, though. Different from anything I have ever felt with those girls. There is something special about you, Celeste."

"Why don't we quit talking about them, okay? I'm not sure how much more of this talk I can bear." I try to hide my blush, embarrassed. I'm not sure why everyone thinks I'm so special. I don't think I'm very pretty, and I'm definitely not very powerful. So what else is likable about me?

"Okay. You're right. Your gal is dead, I have no worries there. But for you? Well, Miss Celeste, jealousy is truly a devious, green beast."

"Oh, hush!" I shove into him lightly, burying myself in his smell. Mostly like smoke after a fire, but a hint of a flower hides in there, too. Not lavender or roses but…something sweet and delicious. Something addicting.

Maybe…maybe I can become accustomed to being in Kyelin's arms after all…

This is horrible. Absolutely horrendous. Worse than my worst nightmares, even. I wouldn't say no to jumping off the tallest mountain in the damned Divine Providence if asked. I would do *anything* to escape this blasted table. To never sit at a long table like this again. If I win, it is the first thing I will be taking care of.

This room is different from the one I usually occupy. It screams wealth, with gold dripping from every surface. Shiny gold walls, gold chandeliers, and gold frames with detailed paintings of the Royals. Even the table and chairs are golden, which makes my ass ache from the hardness. Only the dark wooden floors are not gold-encrusted, a stark contrast to everything else in this obscenely obnoxious room. Irissa is currently sitting between me and my mother, keeping us at a safe distance from each other. The king sits at the head of the table, the queen at the foot. Kyelin and Zaeden sit directly across from us. Every time I look up from my plate, Kyelin is snickering at my mother. It takes everything in me not to join and laugh aloud. Irissa keeps elbowing me under the table, but that just makes it worse. The silence is beyond loud.

"So." Urona is the first to speak, voice high and pitchy in what I guess is her 'people pleaser' tone. "What kind of life do you boys see with my daughter? What do you think your future may hold with her?"

Kyelin is the one to speak first, winking at me before meeting my mother's eyes. "Your daughter is quite a character. We get along quite well, she and I. Unlike anyone else I have ever met. I think that in itself is very telling of our future."

Zaeden smiles mischievously before he, too, responds to my mother. "I agree with my brother. There is no doubt in our minds that she will make an excellent wife to one of us. I know she will make an exceptional Royal. One the

191

likes of the Divine Providence has never seen before." They are practically announcing that I will be chosen. With the way Kyelin is looking at me…well, it is a look that sends that familiar wave of heat straight down my body. My cheeks reflect that warmth. I shouldn't be so surprised, though. We all know my *character* has nothing to do with the real reason I will be chosen. Us being attracted to one another? Well, that's just a bonus.

"Which one of you wants her more?" The silence swallows the room in one great move, nothing slow or gentle about it. It is deafening. My ears ache at the absence of movement, of sound, of speech. Even I am gawking quietly at my mother. Kyelin drops his fork, the clatter breaking the silence. Neither brother speaks. If looks could kill…

"I'm just joking." My mother laughs, throwing her head back. No one relaxes.

"Even if you were joking, the question is—" Kyelin starts.

"It doesn't really matter, obviously." Her head droops back down, a wicked gleam filling her eyes. "My Celeste isn't good enough for either of you. My Irissa, however, will be much more suited for a position like this."

"I beg—" The queen starts to speak now, face red.

"No need to beg. Just an observation. Care to comment boys?"

"You are too harsh on your daughter, miss. And know not of her great qualities." Kyelin is the first to snap back.

"Irissa is underage, Urona. How dare you—"

"Oh, hush, Celeste. The adults are talking now."

"No, the Divines are talking." My retort works. She silences, glaring in my direction. This is the first time I have pulled the Divine card, and, I must say, I like the results.

Kyelin and Zaeden both stare at me with wonder now, like they don't know who I am. And, really, they don't. Now that my mother is silenced, everyone seems to settle down. But as the conversation begins anew, my thoughts wander. Is this what things will be like for the rest of my life? Me holding authority over people I used to look up to? People I walked beside, lived beside, worked with? Can I ever learn to be okay with that? Even as the thought strikes me, I know what the answer is.

I must be.

"—and that's when she got her head dunked into the lake!" Laughter erupts around the table, Zaeden snorting so hard that water shoots out of his nose. We burst into another fit of laughter, the image of a dignified prince doing something so unflattering searing into my memory. Irissa has been so chatty all night, and knowing she can get this reaction from everyone is heartwarming. I can tell she is content. Happy, even.

"And...that time...when..." I glance at my sister, worry building. She stares blankly back, eyes drifting away into the distance. This is the first sign that she is running out of time: dissociating. Her eyes are unfocused, her speech gone. If I wave a hand in front of her right now, she won't see it. I glance at the clock, blinking as if that will make the time go backward. 11:59. She *has* to get out of here. Shit, shit, *shit.* I'm never going to get her out in time. *Fuck.* What do I do?

"I think it is time we take our leave. I think the wine is going straight to my sister's head." I try to laugh it off, try not to meet any Royal eyes. I hop to my feet, grabbing Irissa by the elbow. She is sluggish, tripping as I pull her up to stand. Then it happens. Her wings flop out, ripping holes into the fabric of her dress. Her dress slouches and I hastily pull it tighter around her chest. The folded beauties fall towards the floor, twitching at the exposure to the cold air. The tips barely graze the ground, the large muscles too heavy for her to lift in her weakened state. The queen cries out, pushing her chair back in a panic. I see Zaeden reach over to calm her, explaining that this is fine. Normal, even. By the looks of it, when he got her status updated, he didn't tell his parents why.

"Yes, let's leave." Urona agrees with me, helping me grab Irissa's other arm. We both hobble her to the door, trying to be speedy. My heart threatens to leave my chest as I struggle to pull Irissa with me. I send a worrying glance to my mother, one that is matched. She is probably worried for many different reasons, though. What will the Royals think of her now? Of her freak daughters with even freakier powers?

"Thank you for dinner! We truly enjoyed it and hope to do it again sometime." I call behind me, swallowing down my fear. We have to go before they see how hard I am shaking and before they understand that this is something more serious than we are letting on. I let a quick curtsy be our last parting gift.

I help my sister reach a soldier, directing him to rush her and my mother home. I follow them through the castle, all the way to the gates. I can't leave, but I can watch them go. And once I am alone, I am bombarded by guilt. She shouldn't have been in that situation. Zaeden knew everything and now Kyelin does too, but they are safe. They were going to take care of us. And now? Now the king and queen know that

I am not the only Divine in my bloodline. Now they have reason to look closer at us both. I have just put my sister in terrible, terrible danger. All for a crown I don't even want. Guilt encompasses me, swallowing me whole with a delightful laugh. It bounces from limb to limb, jumping inside each bone and every cell. It causes an earthquake inside of me, pushing me to my knees as the image of my mother and sister running fades away. Maybe Kyelin was right after all.

They will do much, much better without me around.

Chapter 12
The Game of Skill

I wonder if the other Divine are as nervous as I am. Sure, this type of challenge works in my favor. I shouldn't have to be nervous. But the others? They have trained their whole lives for this. They *know* they don't have to be nervous. The only benefit I have is knowing the Lunar Court better than them. I've been to several of the villages and all over the city. I can find my way around better than anyone here. Not one of them has set foot in a village before. I *lived* in one. More than one. Besides, we have two days to complete this challenge. I don't think it will take me more than one. I'm sure the others will need the time, though. If not to find a crown then to make it back.

I fidget in line, waiting. Before me is a ribbon laid across the ground, meant to act as a rendezvous point. A crowd huddles around us, banners waving in the air. Beautiful faces are painted along with names and words of encouragement. I can see the Undivine mixed in with the Divine. They hold the most banners of all. Each one is an ode to me: my name, my face, my story. I know the thought behind them is to make me feel loved and supported. Somehow, it just makes me feel guilty.

Undivine attending a Game is…strange, to say the least.

Most of us despise Divines. The ones who don't get some kind of benefit from them. I don't know if they have ever been interested in the Games in years past. My mother always talked about them like they were an annoyance, one of those things Divines do that don't make sense. When I first found out they were approaching, I only dreaded the extra work. To Undivine, Royals are Royals. It doesn't matter who marries who when everything stays the same for us. So the fact that they are here right now? Well, I suppose I shouldn't feel so guilty after all. It is clear that they see something in me. Hope, maybe.

Today is the first day I have worn pants since being told I am now considered a High Divine. Honestly, it's a relief. For the past five years, dresses have been the only thing I have worn inside that blasted castle. Only now they are heavier, itchier, and a lot more inconvenient.

I turn my attention away from the banners, listening to Silvi's silver tongue. "Hit the closest villages. Most of them are less than a couple hours away by foot if you run hard. I, of course, will take Newstall since it is the closest. You can decide yourselves about the rest."

Shit. I had planned on running straight to Newstall myself. Oh, well. I know the villages better than these girls, it won't take me as long to reach even the farthest one. I should just go straight to Silkdale. I know it just as well as I do Slyvein. Plus, I know a shorter route that diverts from the main road. It should take me three hours, tops, if I run steadily. I'm sure there will be no delivery wagons to help me out today.

"My brave warriors!" Zaeden starts his speech, the crowd quieting upon hearing his voice. And warriors? Really? Is that what he considers these frivolous Divine to be? "I thank you all for taking the time and effort to be here today. Each one of you holds a dear place in both Kyelin's and I's hearts. We hate to see even one of you go. But this is a competition. We hope to only have the best candidates in the end. We are looking for our life partner. Someone who will fight for our love and the love of our Court. So, with that being said…"

Kyelin steps forward, shooting a winning smile to the crowd. A winning one, yes, but not a real one. Together, they speak. "Begin!"

I ran.

My heart pounds in my ears, adrenaline already kicking in. I watch as Silvi shoves someone down, snickering as she passes. Great. So *this* is how the Game is going to go. If I want to win, I need to stay away from those backstabbing bitches.

I watch where everyone goes as we hit the divide in the road. Some go right, heading for the villages located the closest to the city limits. A few stay on the straight path, heading for the bridge that will get them across the small lake in front of the city. I veer off to the left, praying no one else will dare go this way. Somehow, my prayers are answered and I find myself alone very quickly. No one else wants to go so far. They would rather risk staying close to home. After a few miles, the only sound I hear is my footsteps slapping against the hard ground. I've never been light-footed. Maybe I should have practiced that particular skill, though. Because a High Divine clomping frantically through these barren lands? Easy prey for anyone with an ounce of skill. But I guess that's why Ryleigh slipped a huge dagger into my boot before pushing me out of the door. Even if I don't know how to use it, I have it. That, at least, is some comfort to my racing mind.

There are seventeen of us left since two girls were sent

home after the meeting with their parents. Those went on for about two weeks, an agonizing wait, just to find out only two Divine went home. But that means I only have to beat seven girls in this Game. Then I will officially be in the top ten and one step closer to my goals. I am estimating around ten went to those first three villages. No one else seems to want to go this far, which is good for me because I am not sure how a confrontation will go down. Will they want to kill me? Probably. I am the biggest competition, whether I want to be or not. The king and queen may be thankful for my death. At least I know Kyelin and Zaeden will mourn me.

I glance behind me as I dart into a dark alleyway, finally getting close to being out of the city. Soon I will be able to see the vast nothingness that surrounds it. The barren lands we can't even grow crops on. For now, all I see are empty streets. The city was so crowded around the line that it's no wonder no one is lying in wait at the edge of the limits. Feeling satisfied that it is safe to do so, I slow down. It has been around two months since I ran anywhere. Since I hurried up and down long halls and great amounts of stairs. I am starting to get out of shape.

I lean against a wall, swallowing hard. This is all bullshit. Am I seriously doing this right now for a *Royal*? No. No, not really. I can't forget about Irissa. About the Undivine. About the Courts. Irissa's life is already so much better. She is safe and will continue to be so. And I *will* change things in this Court and others. I have to keep going. Not just for those ridiculously handsome, charming, brilliant princes.

They are just a bonus.

I push off the wall, cracking my neck and stretching my legs. Just as I am about to start my run anew, I see a shadow.

It's silhouetted in the shape of a man. He crouches over, hobbling towards me quickly. I glance around, very aware we are alone. Very aware of the dagger snuggled up against my ankle. I attempt to make a quick pass, not wanting to stick around. It may be a fan, someone who wants to tell me they are rooting for me like so many others have today. Practically every Undivine I saw today tried to do so. But it may not be.

"What is your problem?" I bite out as he grabs my wrist, pulling me hard. I yank it away, rubbing the red skin with a glare.

"I know where a crown is." His voice is soft and gravelly. It makes the hairs on the back of my neck stick up. A bad sign, if ever given one.

"No, thanks. I am going to find one on my own. That's the rules." I step away again, frustration building as he steps into my path.

"I can lead you to it."

As firm as possible, I say, "No. Get lost." That makes him angry. Very, very angry.

He leaps, one hand aiming for my throat. I see the silver dagger in the other, sharp enough to slice me into pieces. I jump back with a squeal of surprise, his thumb barely grazing my cheek. He stumbles, and I reach for my own dagger as he recovers. I barely get it into my hand in time, struggling to pull it out of the pocket Ryleigh had sewn into my boot. The sight of it is enough to give him pause.

The man steps back, dropping his hood. I don't recognize his face, but he isn't the old hobbling man I assumed him to be. He looks no older than thirty with short, black hair clinging to his head. His face is covered in scars, a small sword tattooed on his neck. In small print on the blade are the words *Moon*

Killers. It is a ridiculous name for a band of assassins, but I suppose that's why they chose it. To seem less intimidating. Hard to do that when a man like this is who they send though, isn't it?

A weight like a thousand moons crushes me, realization dawning.

He has been hired to *kill* me.

"I don't want to do this." I try to sound casual, to make it seem like I can put up a fight and win. Like I'm not going to fall into a panic if he cuts me.

"Oh, but I do." He grins wickedly, a golden tooth winking at me. He leaps again, swinging the dagger towards my side. I jump away, stumbling to the ground and landing hard on my back. The air leaves my body, my head ringing as it bounces against the stones beneath me. I struggle to roll as he attacks again, still gasping for breath. The whole world rocks like a ship on rough waters. As he approaches again, I kick out as hard as I can. I hit him directly in the gut, just above where I was aiming. He groans as he stumbles back, hands flying to his stomach. I crawl up frantically, using the wall nearest me to lift my body. I can feel how wide my eyes are, how easily the panic is rising. What now, what now?

Shields are buzzing at my fingertips, fizzling out as soon as they appear. I am not in the right mind for this. I still don't have great control. It didn't matter how many hours I practiced in my rooms, how many nights I spent willing the stupid things to form. It was all time wasted because they *won't work.* This man is Undivine. I should easily be able to defeat him. Why have I let myself become so *weak*? So easily broken? I am High Divine. He will *not* be my end.

He swings blindly as he stumbles forward, rage making him

sloppy. I slide to the right, but I'm too slow. A small clump of golden locks falls to the ground, forever gone. But at least it's my hair he nicked and not a vital organ. I use his sloppiness to my advantage, though. I slash towards the hand holding the dagger, stomach rolling when I hear the sound of split skin and smell the heavy iron. I gag as the dagger falls to the ground, his hand still wrapped around it. What magic did Ryleigh have imbued into this dagger? No normal dagger can cut straight through *bone*. I'm shocked she gave me such an expensive weapon. More importantly, why do the Moon Killers want me dead? Or was he hired privately? That seems more likely since assassins usually don't work for free. And sure, he is sloppy, but that doesn't mean the others will be. I am lucky that it *was* such an inexperienced assassin. One who underestimated his target. And *who* had hired him? That, more than anything, will haunt me for the days to come.

I'm not sure how long it takes for me to reach Silkdale. At some point, my head stops spinning but I am so numb I can't register much of anything. I opted for the long way, scared to walk through any more dark alleyways and tunnels. I am sure it took longer than I estimated. Plus, I lost time in the fight.

Cheering erupts from the end of the road, loud applause deafening me. This is definitely a village, then. I have the common sense to hide my bloody knife, unsure if they will still be as happy to see me once setting eyes upon it. Would they, too, turn on me? I watch as they reach out their hands, trying to touch me as I approach. I see soldiers keeping them at bay, though. Pushing them away, ushering me forward. No, no. I don't want to speed through this crowd. I may not know these people personally, but I used to be one of them. They will help me. They have to.

I glance from face to face as I walk slowly, looking for a sign. Anything. I notice some of these Undivines aren't even from Silkdale. Were they placed here or did they come on their own? I watch for expressions, but not one stands out.

I am near the end of the long line when I see him, striking copper hair catching my eye. The butcher's son, around ten years old. I used to play with his older brother when I lived here.

When our eyes meet, I know. He winks and turns around, stuffing his hands down into his pockets. I froze upon hearing his whistling. I can hardly hear the sound above the crowd, but it puts every inch of my body on edge. He is whistling the rebellion song Ryleigh had sung to me weeks ago. He *has* to know. I fasten my pace, making sure my eyes stay glued to his figure. We quickly leave the crowd behind us, soldiers holding back waves of people. We walk for miles before he stops, now far from prying eyes. Halfway through I had begun whistling back, letting him know I was still there. Letting him know I got the message.

His whistling is gone now, replaced by the sound of splashing water. We are next to a large fountain, a recent installment. I don't remember there ever being a fountain here. And it's loud. So, so loud. Even the distant cries of the crowd have stilled.

I watch the boy turn back towards me, smiling. Goddess, I wish I remembered his name. Silently, he takes a gold coin from deep within his pockets. He flips it haphazardly behind his shoulder, laughing at my surprised expression. It spins a few times before falling, the small 'plop' hardly audible over the roaring water. He winks again. Then, without ever saying a word, he walks away.

I approach the fountain cautiously, scanning the area. I peer into the shallow waters, breath catching in the back of my throat. There is no crown. The crown isn't in the middle or top tiers, either. Just coins, coins, and more coins. What are these coins doing here anyway? No Undivine would leave this amount of money just sitting here, most certainly not a whole village of them. I desperately run my hands along the sides, the tops, anywhere I can reach. There has to be something here, right? Maybe some kind of mechanism or button? But if there is, I can't find it. So maybe the coins *are* the clue. Desperately, recklessly, I jump in. I wade through the water, eventually falling to my hands and knees. I crawl through the coins, searching and searching. Moving every coin. Touching every surface. I am quickly becoming too cold, the iciness wrapping around my bones like a blanket. A tear of frustration slips down my cheek as my hand slips over *another* large, useless pile of coins. I should check…there! A purple glimmer mocks me below the surface, the odd coin hiding among the others in a pile to my far right. I run my hand over the coin, attempting to clasp my fingers around the edges. That's when I hear the 'click'.

I scramble up, water dripping from every inch of my body. I stumble out of the fountain, slower than usual since I am so weighed down. I strip my jacket off, flinging it to the ground. It leaves me in a tight camisole, but at least I shed a few pounds of that heavy, all-too-tight feeling the water left behind. I gape at the fountain, watching it cave into itself. The water begins to drain, disappearing somewhere far below. I can't help but hope it is going back to the Undivine, though I doubt it goes anywhere but to waste.

The top two layers have folded in like an umbrella in

the wind. Just enough to leave everything visible, nothing untouched by the light. When all of the water is gone, I can see the outline of a door. I crawl back into the fountain, digging my fingers into the seams. I flinch as my nails begin snapping off. But the pain is worth seeing the door ripped open, revealing a small alcove.

It holds the crown.

Relief washes over me as I reach for the simple beauty. It's mostly silver, a single dark thread twisting throughout. It's littered with sapphires, each shining brightly with the last rays of the sun. My hands clasp around it tenderly, lifting it from its bed. I am so distracted by the crown itself that I almost miss the note underneath it. I lift the small piece of paper, hands shaking.

I am coming.

Who?

"Ah ha!" The screech reaches my ear the second I feel the tug on my crown. I jerk my hand away, shoving the note into my pocket. I step back and pull the dagger from my boot simultaneously. Blood has dried on it, speckled and crackling. I thrust it in front of me, almost laughing at the sight of the Divine at its tip. It is another High Divine, one from the Light Court. I think her name is Amaya, but I can't be certain. I never bother talking to anyone but Dove.

"Stay back!" I wave the dagger around flimsily in her direction. I've taken care of an assassin already, I can certainly handle her.

"I've already seen what you can do with that dagger." She snaps meanly, stepping closer. "I saw you cut that man's hand off. Wouldn't it be a shame if someone found out about that? And about your special dagger, too? Because I dare say someone might put up a fight about you cheating. But we can prevent that, can't we?"

"Oh. My crown for your secrecy? No, thanks. Go ahead, tell everyone. The only rule for this Game was to find the crown without any help from other Divine, which I did. Besides, maybe they will respect me a little more after hearing I'm a killer. Fear me. Everyone does think I'm still a weak Undivine for some reason. They think my powers are no good in a real fight. You all mutter about it every meal. Did you think I couldn't hear? Those Divine think I'm not strong because I haven't tamed my powers yet. They're wrong. Want to find out how wrong they actually are?"

"I tried to do this the easy way. The diplomatic way." She shrugs, squinting her eyes. Then she throws her hand out, a bright blast emitting from it. Lightning. I throw a shield up, beyond grateful they work this time. Why do they only show up when other powers are involved? I raise my eyebrow as the bolt deflects out of harm's way. She screeches, throwing more lightning my way. Bolt after bolt after bolt. None weaken the shields, but the shields weaken me. It takes a lot of energy to release large amounts of power and I'm not sure how long I will last. The first Game I felt like I was standing on the top of the tallest mountain; like I had the world at my fingertips. Now I feel like I have been running and fighting all day and I don't have the time or energy for a fight.

Finally, I made a hard decision. One that doesn't come lightly. I send a bolt back her way. I don't have time for this. I have to end the fight. So, I aim the shield just right. Allow it to deflect straight into her body. She flies back, screaming in agony. Part of me rejoices in it. I shouldn't. I feel horrible about it. But it's the same as it was in the first Game. This darkness in me has been fed and, oh, is it ravenous for more.

She falls to the ground and doesn't rise. Slowly, so slowly, I approach. She still doesn't move, so I bend down to check her pulse. She still breathes, thank the goddesses. I glance up at the sky, realizing the time. The day has turned to night. I need to find somewhere to stay. The path is full of assassins and lunatic Divine during the day, so what will happen to me at night?

It's a short walk to my old home. The same one I ran away from all those years ago. I push the door open, locking it behind me. Not that it will do much good. I check all of the windows, ensuring they, too, are locked. I know better than to check for food since my mother has been gone for weeks, but I do anyway. I find a small pitcher of water and greedily swallow every drop. No food, though. My stomach rumbles at the thought of the meals I have been privileged to have every day. What I would give to be at the damn table I hate so much right now.

I drag my aching feet into Irissa's old room, sighing as I sit on the bed. She would have never let me sleep in it. Part of me wants to go to my old spot on the beaten couch so she never finds out. But I am sore and tired, and the extremely uncomfortable couch won't help prepare my body for tomorrow's journey. So, I lay back on the thin mattress and pushed my worries away. I am asleep in minutes.

I wake up well into the morning. My whole body is sore and I can barely bring myself into a sitting position. I flex my fingers, wincing at the cuts. I have been squeezing on the crown all night, dreaming of thieves and assassins who wanted it for themselves. I sigh, placing it on my head. Might as well wear it, right?

As I had guessed, no supply wagons are running through town for me to hitch a ride on. Instead, I have to walk the long path back to the city. I run some, of course, but my body hurts. It's barely manageable. I don't make the mistake of using any alleyways again, either. I keep my dagger out, clutching it tightly as I make my way through the quiet city. I stay on high alert, eyes and ears on the lookout. Somehow, I don't run into any trouble the whole way back. A blessing considering the state I am in. It's past nightfall by the time I reach the rendezvous line. A crowd stands there, but much smaller than before. They cheer for me, though, crying out as I take the final step. I practically collapse onto the poor maid who has fetched me a cup of water.

"Congratulations, Celeste," Zaeden announces. I try to smile but flinch instead. I try to wave off healers, too, but they refuse to leave my side. Soon, my hands are covered in bandages that have been soaked in oils. I try to insist that they are just small cuts and won't scar, but my words are abandoned. They also pour a tonic down my throat, the taste similar to that of grass. Despite how disgusting it is, it makes my achy bones not so…well, achy.

"Celeste is our last winner!" Kyelin calls out now, glancing at me slyly. "We are officially down to our final ten candidates. We have one final Game to get through before announcing your new princess and future queen. Seeing as we are so close to the end, we have a big announcement to make. Per tradition, we have graciously accepted the Solar prince and princess into our Court. Prince Edge Zorander and princess

Valaine Zorander." My eyes snap over to the Divine I hadn't noticed yet, panic seizing me. More Royals?

The prince is handsome, maybe more so than Kyelin and Zaeden themselves. His skin is dark, but not like the color of Silvi's. A hint of gold lies underneath, shining in the light like a beacon. His black hair is cropped, a few lines shaved on the sides. His face is square, his nose large. He is fit, of course, but not in the same slim way as the twins. Much…thicker. He is shorter than the others by at least a foot. It surprises me that a Royal can be so short, but, well, so am I for a High. His left eye is steel blue; the right is covered by a black patch. It looks like the top of an 'x' is poking out above it, a scar no doubt. The tips just reach bushy eyebrows, the bottoms hitting round cheekbones. Dark rings adore his fingers, glistening every time he taps them against his legs. His arms are covered in tattoos that inch up to his neck, though I can't see what they are from here.

Valaine is gorgeous, too. Of course she is. She has the same black hair, cut short like a man's but somehow still in a feminine way. A few blue highlights are thrown in, too. Her skin is a couple of shades lighter than Edges with the same golden glow. She has blue eyes, too, but they are much deeper. Tiny nose, oval face. She is taller than Edge, but still on the short side for a Royal. She wears a tight dress that shows off her petite frame. It's so similar to my own, so different from the other Divine. Divine are curvy and plump, meant to be another divide between the Undivine. Only the wealthy can afford to eat enough to maintain their voluptuous forms. Valaine's body…well, if it wasn't for her outrageously good looks, I would have assumed she was Undivine. It is a shock and one that I can't seem to get over. That someone here looks like *me*. That I can fit in, after all. They can make fun of me, but who can make fun of *her*?

It's like my stare calls to Edge, his gaze turning to me. Very subtly, he winks. I watch the smirk lift his thick lips afterward. I roll my eyes, looking away. Already, we are off to a bad start. I just have this feeling that we will not get along. There haven't been many Solar Court Divine I have liked, anyway.

"In celebration, our friends will be joining us for dinner tonight along with our beautiful contestants. As for everyone else, thank you for coming to support us in this journey." It is a dismissal at its finest. The crowd tries to swarm to the Royals but they are efficiently escorted away. I decide they have the right idea. Quietly, I slip out of the crowd and make my way to my room. All I want right now is a warm bath, food, and my soft bed.

When I arrive, Ryleigh awaits. I practically attack her with affection when I see the bath already drawn up, little bubbles overflowing the tub, and a food tray lying to the side. She only laughs, pushing me away. I can't strip fast enough, sinking into the tub with a groan. My sore body drinks in the warmth, muscles relaxing if only slightly.

"Oh, Ryleigh. This is exactly what I needed. You are amazing. More than amazing. Absolutely astounding. The best friend I could ever ask for. You need a raise. I should get you a raise." My eyes are closed as I ramble, ears sunken beneath the water. I bite into a piece of bread, moaning much too loudly.

"We can discuss that." I jump at the deep voice. That isn't Ryleigh. Even with my ears underwater, I recognize it.

"K-Kyelin!" I sputter out, bringing my head back out of the water. My eyes shoot open, granting me access to the view

210

of him leaning against the doorway with hands shoved into pockets. "What are you doing here?" I try to push the bubbles around to hide my body, my cheeks blazing.

He laughs. "I wanted to congratulate you. But I see I have interrupted. Would you like me to come back another time?"

"No! I mean, no, that's okay. Just—just give me a minute, okay?"

"Okay." He sends one last, lingering look before entering the main room. I scramble to scrub myself down, scraping against my skin harshly. I stumble out of the tub, water dripping everywhere. I wrap myself in the fluffy robe Ryleigh left to make sure I am completely covered. And, oh, where is she anyway? I use a small towel to dry my legs and face before running a brush through my messy hair.

"I'm going to kill her!" I whisper to myself, taking a deep breath. I had just been complimenting her, too! Alright. It is what it is. I can do this. I just need to go out there and speak to him. How hard is it to talk to a prince wearing just a robe?

"I'm sorry," I say. I step out of the bathing room hesitantly. "I wasn't expecting company." Maybe he is the one who left the note for me? It did say someone was coming. But surely he would have left a signature for me? Even just a 'K'? And how would he have known that is where I would go? It was a last-minute decision! I didn't even know!

"I should be the one apologizing. I was the one who barged in here uninvited."

I laugh, taking a seat next to him on the bed. "You didn't barge. I know Ryleigh let you in."

"Ah, that is true. Maybe she does deserve a raise." We laugh together, my head bobbing in agreement.

"I'm glad you made it through the Game of Skill. I'm glad

211

you decided to stay. I was worried when you took so long. I thought…maybe…" The tips of his fingers run down my arm, leaving small bumps in their wake. I try not to shake beneath his touch, try not to flinch away. I do like him. I like his touch and the carefulness with which he shows me. But my mind and body are at war with each other and I am not sure who will win.

You aren't there. I remind myself. *He isn't hurting you.*

"I'm glad, too." My voice is barely a whisper.

"Am I making you uncomfortable? Being here? Touching you like this?" His fingers stop their trail, his worried eyes watching me wearily.

"It's okay. I just have to get used to it. That's all." He nods but still pulls his hand away. He quickly changes the subject, asking about my journey. I lie and say there were no issues, pushing away the image of a bloody hand falling to the ground. Pushing away the fear that there will be more assassination attempts to come.

Our conversation seems to go on forever. I'm not sure how long we sit here, not that I care. I find myself genuinely enjoying his company once more. I know he is a Royal. I know he might be using me. Might be using my feelings against me. But that's okay because I am using him, too. If we are to marry, I will whisper in his ear about changing policies. Whisper about my plans to help the Undivine. And he will be so in love with me that he will listen. It sounds like an awful marriage, but I know it will be worth it. Even if he does come to hate me after he figures it out.

"Celeste." Ryleigh pushes open the door. "It is time to change." Oh. Is it already time for dinner? My stomach rumbles in answer, remembering the forgotten food tray.

"Oh. Okay." I stand, glancing at Kyelin over my shoulder. He doesn't move, awaiting my instructions. "Will you help me choose? Ryleigh usually does this, but we do choose them for you. I don't know what you like, after all." I try to seem shy, turning my head away as if embarrassed. My robe slides slightly, exposing my shoulder. I know it has worked when he comes behind me, a gentle hand laying on bare skin.

"I would love to help." He whispers in my ear. He takes a step towards my wardrobe, a thoughtful look crossing his features. I watch as his long fingers dance across fabrics, eyes wandering. Finally, his fingers stop. He plucks the dress out, gracefully swinging it in front of me. He holds it up to my neck, looking me up and down. He nods in approval. "This one will do."

It's dark blue, like most of my gowns. Silver dances beneath the sheer fabric. The neckline dips down just to my chest in the shape of a heart. I haven't worn this dress before, but I know it is form-fitting. Ryleigh has a preference for form-fitting dresses. It's practically the only thing she creates for me. The fabric bunches at the sides, meant to cling to my waist and hips. Its length seems to be just enough to fall to the middle of my thighs, leaving a majority of my legs on display. The sleeves are small straps. The material is much more risque than anything I typically wear.

"You like dark colors?"

"I do." He smiles as I take the dress, fingers brushing against each other. "I think you look best in the colors of our Court."

"Noted." I wink playfully. He chuckles, hands clasping behind his back. I shift from one leg to another, suddenly nervous.

"Well, I guess that is my signal to go. I will see you at dinner, okay?"

"No, stay!" I blurt, grabbing his wrist as he turns around. "It will only be a moment."

"If you are comfortable with me being here, I will stay." He nods. I don't look him in the eyes as I speak once more.

"Will you...turn away? Just for a moment?"

"Of course." His voice turns raspy, rough.

"Thank you." He turns his back, allowing Ryleigh to whisk me away from his side. She snatches the dress from my hands, allowing me to slip off the robe. I step into the new dress, the soft fabric sliding up my body. She quickly zips it, adjusting the area around my breasts accordingly. I tug on the hemline, hoping my ass is covered, too. She steps away with a nod of approval. Quickly, she powders my face and blushes my cheeks. She makes an annoyed gesture at my partially dried hair but says nothing. Then, she winks.

"You can turn around now." Ryleigh ushers me into a chair. Her hands move fast as she starts pinning my hair back, pulling half of it up into a beautiful, flowery design.

"Your hair." Kyelin reaches up, touching the small section that is shorter than the rest. "What happened? Did someone cut it?"

"Oh, it isn't a big deal. Just a little accident I had. I needed to cut it anyways." I laugh casually. My hair is the only thing I lost during the fight at the Game of Skill, and I won't forget to be grateful. He steps closer, hand brushing against the back of my neck.

"I must say I prefer it long. You look beautiful with long hair. Don't cut it if you don't have to. But I am sure you would look good with short hair, too. I'm not sure there is anything that would make me think you less beautiful." He says finally, fingering the shorter locks.

"You think? I've never considered short hair before." Ryleigh slips out of the room unnoticed.

"Most certainly."

"Maybe I won't cut it then. I quite like how it feels when you play with it." I swallow hard, eyes fluttering close at the feeling of his breath fanning against my face.

"Like this?" He whispers, twirling a few more strands around. "What about when I touch you? Do you like that, too?"

Kyelin's hand moves to rest against my cheek, the other grabbing the base of the chair. His nose touches mine, lips frozen an inch away from my own. He is giving me a chance to back away, letting me decide if we continue or not. But I don't back away. I'm not sure how much of me truly wants this and how much of me knows it is what will help me win. After a few impossibly long seconds, he closes the small gap and I know exactly which it is.

I have been kissed before. Never by someone who looked like Kyelin. Never by a Royal, either. The heat from his body seers into mine, spreading inside of me. He is gentle and unmoving at first, allowing me time to adjust. But I don't need to adjust. My hands move to his head, fingers curling into crimson hair. With a response like that, he groans and deepens our kiss. His soft lips move against mine, leading me into something much more passionate. Something that leaves me gasping for air. It is very intimate. More intimate than any kiss I have ever experienced before. We go on like this for a few minutes, his touch melting my entire body into this chair. I am breathless in his wake. My stomach flips and churns, my heart on fire. Is this how it feels to kiss a Royal?

215

Or is it Kyelin himself making me feel this way?

Kyelin nibbles my bottom lip as he pulls away, smirking as he stands back to his full height. His hands leave my cheeks, falling back down to his sides. I gaze up at him, trying to hide my embarrassment. But I can feel the heat in my cheeks, deeper than the blush Ryleigh had already given me. There isn't much I can do to hide it.

"Can I escort you to dinner?" His question is quiet, pleading.

"Of course." I struggle to stand on straight legs. He holds out his arm, though, graciously giving me support. Without another word, without discussing what just happened, he leads me away from the crime scene.

Chapter 13

It would be a lie to say I don't enjoy the eyes watching us right now. Yes, I am being escorted by the future king. Yes, he is holding my hand. Yes, he wants *me*. As much as I usually dread these dinners, I am happy to be here today. Excited, even. Not only for the delicious envy that soaks the air but also for the feast I can't wait to dive into. I'm not sure what, exactly, I like so much about the eyes following us. Maybe I like knowing that they think he will be mine. Maybe I like the idea of him actually *being* mine.

Kyelin leads me to my seat, pulling the chair out with a flourish and a bow. I laugh lightly, smiling up at him as I sit. To my surprise, he sits down in the empty seat beside me. Glancing around, I realize we are the last arrivals. It brings a blush to my cheeks thinking about *why* we were so late. Ever so subtly, his hand comes to rest on my shoulder. I glance at him under my lashes, spotting the possessive glare he sends to the other end of the table. To the spot Prince Edge sits. Is he being possessive over that dickhead? Does he think a Solar Court prince has any chance with me? I've barely accepted that a *Lunar Court prince* has a chance, especially after our kiss today. It will take a lot more than a sultry wink to tear me away from my Court. From the man I may be able to fall in love with.

It doesn't take long for conversations to start between the girls and the new prince. I try to ignore the blatant flirting surrounding him. Three princes, ten girls. Plus a princess to flirt with if someone is brave enough to try. Some of them seem furious with me, glaring at me from the side. Others purposely avoid looking at me altogether. At the end of the table, I can hear Silvi chatting away with Princess Valaine. She laughs loudly, little bells tingling in the air. Ugh. It gives me a headache to listen to the sound I used to adore. She is purposely loud, drawing attention to her familiarity with the Solar Royals. Well, two can play that game.

"Have I told you how handsome you look tonight?" I force out an embarrassed giggle, my voice slightly higher than normal. I don't flirt often, but it also doesn't take much to catch a man's attention.

Kyelin startles, chuckling after a second. "You haven't. But I must say, I should have already been praising your beauty. That dress is perfect. Stunning, if I might add. Whoever chose it has wonderful taste." His eyes rake over my body, a smirk gracing his lips. I can't help but laugh, covering my mouth to hide the awful snorts threatening to escape me.

"Oh? You think? I wasn't so sure about it myself. Not quite my style, you know?" I let my hand brush against his thigh, leaning forward to show a hint of cleavage.

"Hmm. How interesting. Well, then, I see why it took so long to be promoted to handmaiden! You have no taste whatsoever!" The room falls silent at the mention of my past, eyes following my face.

"You're probably right!" I erupt into laughter again, my head falling back. Once his laughter starts up, the room lights up once more.

"Will I get to see you again tonight? I was having a wonderful time earlier."

"If I so wish." He purrs in response, placing a hand over mine.

"Then I hope you will honor me with your presence, Your Highness." He shakes his head, grinning. My mind wanders now, replaying the image of our kiss. I enjoyed it far too much. The feeling of his lips on mine, my hand tangled in his hair. I shiver when I think of it happening again. Not only at that but at the thought of him standing so close while I undressed. That he saw me in the tub in such a vulnerable state. That he didn't try to sneak a peek at any point, not even as I slipped into the dress *he* chose. I can imagine myself back in my room with him, letting him watch as I slip it back off.

I snap my head up at an unusual noise: Prince Edge snickering. He quickly covers it with a cough, hiding his face underneath his hand. But his eyes gleam as he watches me, almost as if he knows exactly what I am thinking about. Quickly, I imagine a shield around my mind. I'm not sure if it will work, especially against a Royal, but I am going to try. How stupid can I be? I am letting my guard down around Divine! I don't know what his powers are, but I just *know* he saw my thoughts. His powers will involve more than that, of course. Mind reading is the power of a Low Divine. I will need to be more careful around him. I try to listen now, try to figure out more about him and his powers. But despite the constant, annoying noises that escape his mouth, the prince doesn't utter a word over dinner.

I am one of the last Divine to leave the table. I want to stay with Kyelin as long as possible. I am quite enjoying his company, and I can't picture this happiness ever ending. But I do have to leave. So, before I can second-guess it, I kiss his cheek in farewell. A blush blooms over his cheeks, surprise warming my heart. I feel good as I walk out, practically bouncing away. At least, until Silvi grabs me from behind. Her hand goes over my mouth, arm around my waist. Before I can do anything to fight back, she is whispering in my ear.

"Don't fight, just listen. Got it?" I nod, her hands slipping away.

I spin to face her, glaring. "What do you want?"

"I want to tell you that we aren't blind. You can't just sleep around to work your way to the top. You haven't lived in this world. You haven't fought tooth and nail to make it here. You haven't proven yourself worthy. This world is so much more than you know it to be. You will ruin *everything* if you are allowed to be queen. You are such a waste of power. To think that a prince would ever want to associate with the likes of you. It's ridiculous. Quite a turn-off, really." I will not deny her accusations. Let her think what she wants to think. Let her destroy herself with doubts.

"You stopped me just to insult me? Really? Are you really that jealous? I'm sorry I didn't return your affection—"

"Oh, stop. Not everyone is in love with you, Celeste. Don't be so conceited." Despite her anger, a blush still rises to her cheeks and I know I am right.

"You are a beautiful Divine, Silvi. You will find someone who appreciates that and more."

"I don't want your pity. I just wanted to warn you, that's all."

"Oh?"

"Watch your back, Celeste. Or should I say Cerina? Now that the Solar Court has Royals here, you can bet your ass you won't be with us much longer." I freeze, breath catching. With us as in at the Lunar City, or with us as in...dead?

"What did you just call me?"

"What? Did you think I wouldn't find out? Cerina Celeste, the runaway maid. So determined to stay hidden you started going by your middle name. I had some friends do some digging after you told everyone you don't go by a last name. Is there a reason for that? Maybe because of a certain dead father?"

"Don't talk about him. And don't threaten *me*. Your Royals can't put a finger on me. Do you know what kind of war they would start between our Courts? I'm much more valuable than you think." I hope.

"I just wanted you to be aware of the...potential issue." She shrugs, sweeping her long silver hair over a shoulder. "I don't want anything bad to happen to you. Someone *will* come for you." *I am coming.* The words ring through my head.

Silvi watches my internal panic with interest. She can't feel it or get into my mind to see it, but she knows it is there. It isn't hard to see. I feel my face quiver, and my smile drop. My mental shields are still up, and they are strong, but I can't hide the fear racing through me the way a rabbit races away from a wolf. Then, she does the unthinkable. *She kisses me.*

It's not slow and gentle, not easy and loving. It's harsh and rushed, desperation seeping through every spot our skin touches. I'm slammed against the wall, my lips moving on their own. Her hands are digging into my hair, mine finding her chest. I need to push her away. I need to stop this. So I do. I push into her weakly, whimpering underneath her. It is enough to break the spell. Silvi jumps away from me, eyes wide as she swipes at her lips with the back of her hand.

"I'm sorry. I—I shouldn't have done that. Goddess, I need to get over you. But how can I when you are so close to me all the time? When every thought of mine is occupied by you? You are the only person I have ever met who can match me in power. Everyone else is so weak. So incapable. But you, Celeste...you are so different from other Divine. I couldn't stop myself this time, after seeing your fear...but I will from now on. I'm sorry."

"I don't understand." I breathe out, not entirely sure what just happened. I thought she was over her attraction to me. That's why she has been so mean to me, isn't it? Silvi turns to flee, taking a few steps before looking over her shoulder at me.

"And Celeste? I meant every bit of my warning. I *will* get you out of my head. Even if I have to destroy you to do it."

This is a problem. A really, really, *really* bad one.

"Thank the goddesses you are here." I can barely breathe as I barge into my room, relief hitting me harder than a fallen star hits the ground.

"What's happened? Are you hurt?" Ryleigh swallows me in her arms, alarmed.

"I think I am going to have a panic attack."

"Sit, Les. Sit. What has happened?" She pushes me onto the bed, plopping down beside me. I bury my head into my hands, shaking all over.

"What do you know about the Solar Royals? Tell me everything."

"Oh. That's what the fuss is about? The Solar Royals?

Really?"

"Yes, really, Ryleigh. I was just *threatened* by Silvi. Told me now that they are here she has reinforcements. They're going to kill me for this alliance. I think…I think Kyelin likes me. And I him. And I made it so obvious tonight. I'm such an *idiot*. I shouldn't have paraded him in front of everyone like that! I just wanted them to be jealous. Everyone listened to us the whole night. Watched us.

Everyone knew before I was a *good* choice, but we have made it increasingly obvious that I *will* be chosen. I practically put a target on my head! I don't know how to fight a Royal, Ryleigh. My powers…they came on so fast. I just—I just *did* it. It was so natural, so easy. And now…now things aren't so easy. They come and go like the breeze. And I have limits. Royals are one of them. I couldn't fight off Zaeden on that stage. And I know Edge was in my mind tonight, hearing all my thoughts. I don't know exactly what it is he can do, but I don't think I can block him out. Shit, Ryleigh. Shit, shit, shit. I can't die. There's so much work to be done. And who will care for Irissa? I am such an impulsive, self-indulging fuck up. I fucked us all over." Her rough hands cover mine, arms wrapping around me once more.

"Calm down, Celeste. Breathe. Things aren't as bad as they seem."

"Yeah? Because from my view things are much worse than they seem." I can't forget the kiss either, not that I'm going to mention it to Ryleigh. I don't want anyone to know I just kissed my biggest enemy and didn't necessarily hate it. I still don't like her, but…she is a good kisser.

"Listen to me, okay? Let's make a plan. I don't want you going anywhere alone anymore. I will be close by from now on, so let me know if you plan on going somewhere."

"Okay, but—"

"Sit there and take deep breaths and I will tell you about those Royals, okay? I don't want you walking into things blind."

"Tell me. Anything and everything you know." I'm not sure this will make me feel better, but at least I won't be thinking about Silvi's lips anymore.

"Edge's father is known for his cruelty. The Solar Court takes punishments very seriously, much like we do here. They throw people in jail for the smallest of things. Thieves are jailed for life. Doesn't matter what they stole. It can be an apple or a horse, the difference matters not. Children get off with only lashings. Parents will send them out to do the dirty work, typically. If they don't pay their monthly taxes, they are taken away until they have worked off the debt. The issue is, they never really pay it off. The debt increases with time and so does the amount of work. People are beheaded every day, some for no reason other than perceived crimes. *I* can whisper of *your* unfaithfulness and you will die, whether it is true or not. Someone can claim to hear you denounce the Solar Court. Maybe you trespassed on your walk to work. At least the children get light beatings. The adults...well, they don't get that luxury.

In the city though? Well, Solar City is a much different story. They fight in the streets, use their powers against each other, and cause downright chaos. There is no control, no order. It's known as the City of Rot. This is due to the amount of blood and gore lying about in the streets. They say it smells horrifically. Their Royals do nothing to change this.

I've heard all kinds of rumors about Edge. They say he takes some prisoners to torture himself. That he likes to perform the lashings himself. That he uses his powers to dig out the unfaithful and the rebellious. That he gets too excited and kills the prisoners too quickly. All I have heard is cruel, untoward remarks about him. The Undivine there are much worse off than they are here. And though the Divines have been making things out as friendly between our two Courts, it is anything but. That's the real reason they want the alliance with Silvi so badly."

"What happened to his face? Silvi has a similar scar. Is that...do they do that to their own?"

"I think it is common, yes. Scars, especially facial ones, are prevalent among the Solar Court. They are symbolic among their people. They fight to prove their worth. High and Royal Divine alike want their children to fight for their place in life. They don't care if they lose. It proves a point. Their child is willing to fight in a battle they know they can't win. Their child will do whatever their Court demands of them. The scars represent that. The more prominent the scar, the better. I'm sure that's what happened. It is not talked about much outside of their Court. When they fight, they don't aim to kill. But severe injuries like theirs are more than enough proof for the Divine. There is a man who many of the more connected Divine use for these fights. A man with a preference for eyes. He has never lost." She pauses, letting that sink in. They send their children to beat the unbeatable? To a man they know will permanently damage their children? Who will take away something so precious? I bend over, hand over mouth. It's *unfathomable* that a parent could ever do that to a child.

"Continue." I barely manage the word. It feels odd coming out of my mouth, almost like it isn't me saying it. Because I don't want her to continue. I don't want to hear about the torture of children, even if they are Divine. If someone had done something so cruel to Irissa? They would not be able to hide anywhere on this damn planet where I wouldn't find them.

"Solars send their children to him when they are overconfident. They think their child will be the one to finally beat him. It's a joke among them all. They place bets on which eye will be gone, on what injuries will occur, and on who will win. It's as barbaric as it sounds.

Valaine...she is quiet. If she ever fought, her scars aren't visible. She stays out of the way and doesn't put up a fuss. I don't know much about her behavior. I don't know if she is similar to her brother or not. No one does, really. Which probably means she isn't cruel. But that doesn't mean she is good, either."

"Great. A psychopath and his possibly empathetic sister. No need to worry, right?"

"I don't know, Celeste. I don't know. Our mutual friends will watch out for you. They will try to be nearby. This room is safe, but the rest of the castle may not be. Just...try not to be alone, okay?"

"I won't. I—" A loud knock interrupts me, the noise ringing in my ear. Ryleigh hurries to answer the door, glare in place.

"Your Highness!" She glances back at me in regret, sighing in defeat as she slips away.

"Zaeden." I breathe, surprised. I thought Kyelin might be the one to come see me. I guess not.

"Celeste." He smiles, casually sitting beside me. His presence takes up the whole space, a discomfort floating in the air. "Are you well? You look pale."

I clear my throat, attempting a kind smile. "I'm fine. What brings you here?"

"I wanted to speak to you about Kyelin."

"Oh?" Why would he want to speak of his brother? Has something happened?

"I noticed tonight how close you two have gotten, how you look at him. It is…discouraging, to say the least."

"Yes, I suppose that is true. About our closeness, I mean. Though, I won't pretend to know how he feels about the matter." I tilt my head, unsure of where this is going.

"I know. I can tell he cares for you deeply. So deeply that I believe he wants to choose you at the end of this."

"Oh. I see." My heart races, heat flooding my face. Damn. I *was* obvious tonight, wasn't I?

"No, you don't."

"I—"

"It's unfair, Celeste. I care for you, too. I want you, too. But you haven't given me a chance. None at all."

"What?" I squint at him, unsure of where this conversation is heading. I thought maybe I was going to get a 'Be good to my brother' speech. But this?

"I have done so much for you. I obtained a place for you here, a place in the Games and among the Highs. I have kept your secret, for goddess's sake! At least, until your blasted sister ruined it all. Luckily for her, my parents only cared about her powers and didn't notice anything else strange about the situation. I managed to persuade them the wine had gotten to her head and made her lose control. And yet, despite these things, my brother is getting your time and devotion. I don't want you to be tricked by him or his status. I'm sure he seems like a better option because he will be the next king and I will not. I know you were Undivine and still think like one. It's only logical to work your way up the ladder. But I think we should try things out between us before you make that decision. I want you to know that I am still vying for your attention. For your heart." My face heats in anger and embarrassment. I think like an Undivine? Is he seriously calling me a Divine climber? Is he trying to manipulate me into his arms?

"I thought I was supposed to be vying for *your* attention," I say, looking away. I won't say what I want to. I have to be careful. Zaeden is a Royal. I don't need another one of those as an enemy.

He laughs. "Yes, but you seem to have done that and more." I can tell the kindness is forced. Something here is wrong. He isn't being honest. I prepare myself to ask him to leave, but his hand on my thigh gives me pause. It inches up higher, higher. He squeezes tightly, painfully, when I try to inch away. I cry out, feeling the nails digging into my skin. I hate this feeling of being helpless, being weak, and being scared when it comes to Divine men. I can't let it control me any longer. I have to get myself out of this.

"Zaeden, I'm sorry you feel this way. I just…don't see you like that. Not anymore. At first, I wasn't sure if I could imagine myself with either of you. Now, it's only you I don't see myself with. I'm sorry. I think we can be great friends. I enjoy our conversations. I just don't have romantic feelings for you. It has nothing to do with the crown. Only love and who I think I may have it with."

"Oh? Is that because of the kiss?" He leans closer, scowling.

"We did kiss," I confirm, "But I don't think that was the deciding factor. I had great feelings long before that. Ones I denied myself but have decided to do no longer. You know how physical touch makes me feel. It was a big step and one I don't take lightly."

"Yes. So you remind me. Kyelin and I share everything, you know? We have no secrets. That's why I told him about how you let those men use you. But we are very understanding about that situation, aren't we? You were young, exploring things a little too complex for you. I got the real story out of them. They say you begged them to hurt you. That it pleased you. But that is beside the point. What I have been trying to say is that it is unfair. Unfair you love him and not me. Unfair he gets to taste you and I don't. I can't bear the thought that he has something that I don't. He always gets everything he wants. He is everyone's favorite. They always choose him. Always! And I have been so *nice* to you. And what has it gotten me? Don't I deserve more, too? Don't I get a happy ending? I want you, Celeste. And I always get what I want. I told you before that you are mine and I meant it. I didn't do all of this work just for you to fuck my brother." Does he think I wanted to be attacked? That I *liked* the pain? There's a difference between having some sexual fun and being brought to your deathbed! He defended me before and told me he was on my side. Made me promises about what we would do to those men. So where did this Zaeden come from? Is it just the jealousy talking or something more? Either way, something major has changed within him. He is not the man I know. This man has lost control and is desperate to get it back. Was everything between us fake? All because he wanted to *own* me?

I try to speak slowly and deliberately. Try not to shake in fear. "Forget what those evil men said. They lie and we both know it. Again, I just don't have romantic feelings for you. There is attraction, of course. But I like you as my friend. Nothing more. We have a great friendship. I just don't want to take it further. Kyelin and I...well, I think we can be good together. You understand, right?" I am starting to reconsider anything I have ever felt for this Divine. Does Kyelin know about this side of his brother? Maybe there is a reason he was born with poison inside of him.

Zaeden doesn't respond with words. Instead, his hands snake up to the back of my head and tangle into my hair. He pulls me to his lips, forcing them upon mine. He doesn't wait for permission as Kyelin did. I try to pull away, but he is strong. The kiss is forceful and harsh, but not in a good way. I know it will leave bruised and swollen lips on both of us. It's nothing like kissing Silvi. Definitely not like kissing Kyelin. A hand slides down, moving to cup my breast. That's the final straw for me.

"Stop!" I yank away, panting. A large smile is plastered on his face. Satisfied, proud. I, on the other hand, want to cry. I am alone. Utterly, utterly alone. The one thing I had just promised Ryleigh I would not be. Yet she left me here. So maybe she is at fault, too. It's not just on me.

I can't do anything to retaliate. Not only will I be killed, but I will never be allowed to be with Kyelin. Not if I act out against his brother. His other half. And then I circle back to the same issues I can't run away from. What happens to Irissa? The Undivine? Our Court? I'm not allowed to think for myself anymore, to act for myself. I am a weapon for my people and I will endure.

"Remember this, Celeste. Whatever you grant to Kyelin, you grant to me, too. I loved you first. I will love you last."

Then, he sweeps out of the room like he was never here. I break down the moment he is gone, tears pooling into my lap. How can I have let this happen? What has my life turned into? Is it worth it? A chance at Undivine freedom for my dignity? My body? My mind? Is it worth every bit of myself being violated? In the end, I'm not sure it matters. I'm stuck in this situation, worth it or not. I made promises and I *will* keep them.

Even if I am destroyed in the process.

Chapter 14

Ryleigh doesn't question me when I ask if I can keep the dagger she loaned me. She only begins sewing all of my dresses with a secret pocket, an unseen hole buried at the bottom. I can strap the dagger to my thigh and have the handle easily accessible from said hidden hole. I've become diligent about sharpening the dagger every day. About making sure it is always with me. We don't talk much about why I do it, we don't need to. She sees what a mess I have become. She and I both know the danger I am in.

In the past week, it has become rare to leave my room. I come out for lunch and dinner with everyone else, but I try not to speak. Dove has given up on trying to make me. It drives a wedge between me and my only friend. She knows something is wrong but doesn't push me. I don't deserve a friend like her.

Silvi is always smirking at me. Her devious smile haunts my dreams, which makes it easy to dismiss our kiss. I avoid the princes at all costs. It pains me to see Kyelin look at me with such *wanting*, but I can't bear to have Zaeden touch me again. And I don't want the Solar Royals to see them fawning over me anymore.

I have become so overly aware of my surroundings. I count

the tiles on the floor, the cracks in the walls. I know how many seats are at the tables and how many guards stand outside the doors. I know their faces and their postures and their breaths. Soldiers escort me everywhere now, ones Ryleigh says she trusts. A mix of Undivine and Lows. When Kyelin asked about it one day, I admitted I had been attacked during the Games by a fellow competitor and Ryleigh ordered the extras just in case. That is the story Ryleigh coached me on, so that's the one I told. The worry that passed over him cracked my heart in half. He didn't even seem mad that Ryleigh hadn't asked before ordering more. Just said that he was going to look into a raise for her since she is doing a better job at protecting me than he is.

I don't know much about fighting, but I have decided to learn. I practice in my room. I don't know if what I'm doing is proper etiquette, but I'm getting faster at this whole 'slicing and dicing' thing. I can swing for hours, cutting pillows over and over again. I have Ryleigh throw punches, ducking and rolling away. Kicking out or throwing my own swings. I practice slipping my dagger out in the brief seconds between my dodging and her recovery. Over and over and over. I must do this, I must do this, *I must do this.* The burning of my muscles is a relief, a reward. I know I am progressing. Part of me likes to remind myself that I still deserve that pain. That I have not been forgiven for my crimes yet.

Today has been just as painful as all the others. I avoid Kyelin and he does his best to see to it that I don't. He tried to talk to me all through lunch, sitting at my side and whispering everything and nothing at all into my ear. I only turned away, heart breaking over and over and over. I refused to look at Zaeden, especially when I overheard him speaking to Silvi. I don't want to look at her, either. I'm crashing and burning and dying inside. I can't yell at Silvi. I can't speak out against Zaeden. I can't tell Kyelin anything. I can't be alone. I can't take on a Royal. I won't be murdered. Fear has become a part of me, sitting on my shoulder and hissing into my ear. It tells me of all the things I know and everything I don't *want* to know.

When I left lunch, a soldier immediately followed. He has escorted me only twice before, but I know him well enough. Everyone who is assigned to me knows there are some… unusual circumstances that may involve increased danger. No one asks for specifics.

It is now that I walk with him, glued to his side. We round a corner, the same one I round every day, but something is different. There's a presence here. I can feel it all around me. The soldier can't. Or, if he does, he doesn't let me know. A single footstep is the only warning I get.

"You can leave now." The cold, drawling voice speaks from behind us. The soldier doesn't need to be told twice. He leaves. He doesn't even *look* at me. Bastard!

I freeze, mind spinning. My dagger. I need the dagger. Slowly, imperceptibly, I let my hand drift down into the secret pocket. I feel the cool handle of the dagger and am instantly reassured. My magic may not be able to hurt him, but this can.

Suddenly, strong, inked arms are wrapped around my waist. I'm dragged into an empty guest room to the left. I don't fight at first. I let him think I am being complacent. When the door shuts, he discovers I am not.

I swipe out with the dagger blindly, praying I hit *something*. The damn goddesses don't care about my prayers, though.

Prince Edge slides away easily, fury gleaming in his uncovered eye. I dart forward again, slicing downwards. He dodges once more, making it seem all too easy.

"Stop this nonsense." He drawls, seemingly bored already. But I leap again, determination rising high over the panic threatening to cloud my brain. A Divine will not kill me. A Divine will not kill me. *A Divine will not kill me.*

"I'll stop when I'm dead. Unfortunately, you won't have the pleasure of seeing my dead body today." I watch him spin to the side dramatically, his cloak flying behind him. He throws it to the ground, the fabric fluttering violently. I didn't even see him undo it! That's how fast he is, how dangerous. I'm so fucked.

"This will be quick, then." He doesn't pull out a weapon. He doesn't need to. He moves so, so fast. Much faster than I ever will be, despite being at least twice my weight. He grabs the hand holding the dagger, glaring. He squeezes, tight, tight, tighter. I cry out, tears stinging my eyes as my only defense clatters to the ground. It lands mere feet away. The prince chuckles, eye following the descent. He thinks this is easy. It will not be.

I throw my elbow up, swinging it into his perfect jawline. He hisses, loosening his grip in surprise. It's enough. My hand slips out and I dive. Shield, shield, shield. I land hard on my stomach, fingers curling around the hilt. I spin, baring my teeth and panting. The shield is there but it doesn't hold. He taps the large bubble and it shatters, my hope crashing with it. He comes to stand over me, clearly annoyed. He looks at me like I'm an inconvenience, or an annoying task he needs to take care of. He reaches down but I refuse to let him touch me willingly. I swing; praying, praying, praying. This time, it works. I hit skin and bone, slicing the smallest finger of his left hand clear off. I try not to gag at the smell of blood, at the chunk of meat that hits the ground. The ring adorning his finger rolls off, disappearing under the bed. I try not to compare this finger to the hand of an assassin.

Prince Edge holds up his hand in disbelief. That's the only reaction he has, though. He turns back to me before I can even *try* to get up. "You damn fool!" The dagger is kicked from my hand. I scream in a panic as I flip back around. I need it, I need it, *I need it*. I try to crawl, screaming at the top of my lungs. Begging for help. My powers are useless, just as I feared. Pure force is all he needs and he has plenty of that. He demonstrates it as he climbs on top of me, pinning me to the ground. He barely puts any pressure on me, though. It's like...like he doesn't *want* to hurt me. Using only one hand, he grabs a fistful of my hair at the top of my skull. The blood from his finger drips into my hair and down my cheek, the disgusting iron scent filling my nose. A Divine will not kill me. A Divine will not kill me. *A Divine will not kill me.*

"Calm down, little star. Stand up and speak to me. Stop this nonsense." He pulls me up with him slow and gentle, and all I can do is scream, scream, scream. That dagger is my only hope. I do the only thing I can think to do. Something desperate. I force up a shield. We both stumble from the sudden impact, his mouth dropping at the visible barrier I placed between us. I trip over his cloak as I stumble away, falling back to the ground. I hit my head hard and the room begins to spin. I see the shield flickering, weakened by my lack of focus. Not that it matters. I still force myself back up, using the wall for support.

"Useless." He drawls, shock gone. He taps on the shield,

chuckling darkly. It shatters once more, invisible shards disappearing under his touch. I scream again, begging anyone, anyone.

"Someone please help me! Guards! Please! Anyone! I need help! Please! Please! Please!" My pleading voice pierces the thin air, the cries echoing in the small room. But he only chuckles again, shaking his head to confirm my suspicions. No one will be coming to help me.

Prince Edge is on me faster than I can blink. His hand wraps around my throat, shoving me into the wall and forgoing the gentleness from before. My head slams back again, ears ringing. I can barely see now, my world hazy. I can't scream, can't force out anything more than sputtering sounds. My body is trapped under his and I hate it, I hate it, I hate it. He's so strong. I can feel every one of the hard muscles in his chest tensing up and can see the ones flexing in his arms as they trap me. He hasn't even broken a sweat over my antics. He barely had to make an effort to incapacitate me. The look of pity across his face is almost insulting.

"I warned you I was coming and you couldn't do better than that? I tried to give you time. You have some work to do if you truly aren't seeking out death."

He doesn't seem angry about it. Just disappointed. Like he expected more out of me. But how could he? He doesn't even know me!

A Divine will not kill me. A Divine will not kill me. *A Divine will not kill me.*

"A Divine will not kill me," I whisper to myself, barely audible. Then, with great effort, I spit in his face. I can't help but smirk through my labored breaths. But Prince Edge doesn't flinch. Doesn't move to wipe it away. Instead, he stares into my eyes, looking for something.

"I'm not going to kill you, little star. Relax. I could have already been inside your mind, forcing images of death into your pretty little head. Could have sent little whispers about taking that dagger into your own heart. You would have done it without a second thought, too. But I didn't and I won't. And I let you have your worthless fight. I would say it was fun, but it wasn't. You are weak. I barely made an effort. You need to gain a lot more strength and gain control over those powers. If you truly want to live, you have to start training." His grip loosens just enough to allow me fresh air.

"At least I got a souvenir." My deep, gasping breaths ruined the dramatic effect I was going for. If he can do all that, why let me take a finger? Something so permanent?

He exclaims, "Because I didn't *expect* you to cut off my finger! You didn't even know you were doing it! And don't pretend you enjoyed it! We both know how disgusted with yourself you are. I saw it all over your face then and I see it now. You're better than that." Shithead mind reader. You can go and stick that finger straight up your—

"Enough of that." His hand tightens once more, still more gently than I can comprehend. "I'm tired of the chit-chat. Drop out of the competition. Walk out of this room and tell your beloved prince that you are done. If you want to survive, quit. It's for your own safety." What? He attacked me, almost killed me, and lost a finger to tell me to drop out of the competition? To run away with my tail tucked between my legs? No way. I've come this far. I've put up with far too much and sacrificed too much of myself.

"No. I don't think I will. I will continue. There are more lives at stake than my own." He makes a noise in the back of his throat, one I can't quite decipher. That pitying look makes a reappearance.

"You will die! Don't you care for your life, girl?"

"I will gladly die for my sister. For the people of this Court. No matter the cost to myself." My mind flashes to Zaeden forcing his lips on mine, threatening me with more.

"I can see that quite clearly." He whispers, disgusted. Shit. I forgot he can see straight into my mind. Slowly, he releases his hold on me. My hands fly up to my throat, my mouth gaping like a fish as I gasp for air. He had put just enough pressure to scare me, but I don't think it will bruise. His hold wasn't tight enough. It's strange because one glance at this man tells me he knows exactly how to crush a windpipe. I look up to his face as he steps back, making sure he isn't watching my lower half.

Slowly, I move my foot over. I wedge it underneath the hilt of my dagger. I try not to think about what I am doing. I fill my thoughts with insults, calling him any and every name I can think of. Tell him how idiotic this all was. I guess he will feel that way in a few moments. I kick the dagger upwards in the blink of an eye. I have practiced this a maximum of two times in my room, missing both times before giving up. I can only hope I do not miss now.

The blade flies in the air, gleaming as it rises. I shoot my hand out, capturing it in my fist. It nicks me but I pay no mind to that.

My arm is pulled back over my shoulder and I am prepared to do what I must. I aim for his heart, ready to fling the blade in a long arch. Once again, he defeats me. All it takes is another grab of my wrist. He pries it away, *again*, and holds it away from his body and mine. I scowl, swinging my knee upwards. My aim is true. My knee slams into his groin, hard. His pained moans are satisfying, a reward for all my efforts. I turn, ready to flee. This will be my only chance.

Prince Edge grabs the ends of my long hair, yanking me back towards him. I cry out in pain, stumbling back into his chest. He takes a step back, raising my own dagger against me.

"I'm sorry." The words are quiet, sure. I flinch, expecting the death blow. Instead, I hear the distinct noise of cutting hair. He had swung the knife behind my head, removing over half of my hair. I scream out in anger, shaking hands reaching to touch the choppy curls. They barely touch my shoulder now, the luxurious length gone. Kyelin said he liked my hair long. Kyelin won't like it short, I just *know*. And how will I fit in with the other Divine now? Everyone has long hair. *Everyone.* Short hair is for the Undivine. I'm a High, I can't look like an Undivine anymore!

"How dare you?" I don't have weapons, I don't have strength, I don't have usable powers. But I *do* have a remarkable gift for impulsivity. I slam my fists into his chest over and over and over. I have this urge to hurt him. As if his pain will make my hair reappear. I'm sure my pain won't regrow his finger.

He bats my hands away, looking away from my face. Away from the anger he created. I scream profanities at him, cursing him in every way I know how. He doesn't care. Doesn't do anything other than look away. I watch as he slides the chunks into his pocket.

"You creep! You kidnap me, fight me, threaten my life, then cut my hair and pocket it like gold? Astonishing. Truly astonishing!" The silence engulfs us both.

"I tried to warn you. You were foolish not to listen." Then, as quick as he came, he was gone.

A Divine will not kill me. A Divine will not kill me. *A Divine will not kill me.*

Today.

Chapter 15

The thought of leaving the safety of my room is terrifying. To leave this place and look in the eyes of a Divine...it's too much to think about, much less live through. That's why Ryleigh fetches my food now. It's always cold leftovers but I prefer that over death who lingers around me like a buzzing fly.

I haven't been out in a week, so it isn't surprising when a Divine comes knocking. As long as it isn't Zaeden, Silvi, Prince Edge, or anyone else who wants to hurt me, it might be okay. By the sounds of the hushed whispers at the door, it must be a prince. Maybe I can pretend to be ill. If Zaeden stands at the other side I can say it is contagious.

"Prince Kyelin is here to see you," Ryleigh announces bitterly, widening the door. She looks to me, waiting. I nod, allowing her to leave.

"Kyelin."

"I like your hair," he says after a brief pause, "You look stunning." Lies, lies, lies. That whisper in my brain tells me so and I know it is right. I can feel the disappointment somehow.

"Thank you." Maybe if I don't engage, he will go away.

"I wanted to check on you. You've been absent from our meals. And quite frankly...I miss you." Goddess I miss him, too. It's been physically *painful* to be away from him. His being near intensifies everything I feel.

"Kye…if we are going to have this conversation, I need you to do something for me."

"Anything." He breathes, stepping closer. "I will do anything for you if it means you will stop being angry with me."

"I'm not angry with *you*, Kyelin."

"What do you need, Les?" It comes out breathless, almost a moan. He looks at me like I've hung the moon and it *hurts*.

"You cannot tell anyone you were here," I say fiercely, glancing towards the door. I pray no one saw him enter this room

"That's a strange request. But very doable." He nods along furiously, desperate.

"Not even Prince Zaeden. Especially not Prince Zaeden. That's all I ask of you. Promise me. Promise me!" I know this is a risk. Promises are so strong here, they hold so much more than empty words. He's made promises to me before and has kept them all. But this is different. We both know it. Hiding something from his other half…

"May I ask why? Zaeden isn't like everyone else. He's my *twin*. We don't usually keep secrets from one another. Except when it comes to you, it seems."

"Don't tell anyone," I whisper, eyes pleading. "Please, Kye. If you will truly do anything for me, do this."

"I…okay. Yes. I promise not to tell anyone, especially Zae, that I visited you today. And I won't tell anyone of our discussion or what happens behind this closed door." I sag in relief, finally relaxing. Maybe I *can* be with him again. Surely we can figure something out?

"I've missed you, too," I admit after a moment of silence,

"I've just been hiding. That's all. I'm not angry with you. I could never be angry with you."

"Hiding? From who? Is someone threatening you? I don't want you to worry about your safety here, Celeste. We will take care of any threats. Isn't that why Ryleigh increased your guards? Are you still having problems with the other girls?" He puts an arm around me, pulling me into his warm chest. I let him hold me, scrambling for a lie.

"No, no, nothing like that. I think I'm just nervous about the Solar presence here. I've heard some nasty rumors and I think Prince Edge was in my head a few times. I don't know much about politics or their Court. I just don't want to make things difficult between you all. I saw the way you two glared at each other. I don't want to be in the middle of things. That's all. And, well, maybe it's about some of the girls, too." It's a pitiful excuse for a lie, but it is all I have.

"Silly girl, all you need to do is ask." His grip loosens as I pull back shyly.

"Are they here to make sure you choose Silvi? I know she is my biggest competitor. I'm sure they want her to win just as badly as she *wants* to win. She told me as much herself." Right before she kissed me and told me she was going to destroy me. Maybe if I play jealous, I can understand these dynamics a little more. Understand my options, if I have any.

"Of course not." He denies it, but I see the flames light up behind his eyes.

"You're lying." I hiss, shoving him away. "I have no use for liars in my life." I regret it as soon as I see the look on his face. The pain.

"I'm not," he says just as harshly. The flames wiggle higher. His skin practically glows now as fire flows through him, anger rising. Apparently, he is easily angered. I must remember that.

"I'm sorry. I'm just worried for you. For us." I choke out the words, tears falling. That, at least, is true. I *am* worried about us. About what we may lose. "I've never been in a situation like this before. I barely had time for relationships between my sister and work. I don't know what they look like, or how they work. I just...these overwhelming feelings make me nervous. They came quick and easily and I don't know what to do with them."

"No, I'm sorry. I will be the first to admit I am quick to anger. My flames should never rise against you, Celeste. This is new to us both. We can learn together." He presses a hand to my face, flames gone. But the heat remains. I take a sharp breath, nodding. I need to quit being this scared, whimpering fool. I am going to be the next queen and I need to act like one.

"So? What is their purpose if not to threaten?"

"Their purpose is to remind us of the real reason for the Games. We started them early because of unease between and within our Courts. *Of course* it would be ideal to have the Solar Court united with us. Politically speaking, I am sure they are here in part to engage in that. It's also tradition for them to be here for at least one of the Games. It is up to them which Game that is. This time, they have chosen to stay for a longer period."

"I will accept that answer for now. I need you to understand how I feel, though. I fear there is worse to come. I don't think they are here for peaceful politics." He has to understand. He *has* to. Prince Edge has already threatened me, attacked me. They aren't here to *discuss* the Games. They are here to *change*

245

them.

"And are you a politician now? An advisor, perhaps? Did my father appoint you to his Court and forget to mention it to me?" He chuckles at the joke, shaking his head. I don't find it so funny.

"Have you forgotten what I was? What I am at heart? Divine are all the same. You think we are dumb, that we don't understand what is happening around us. But I know about the tension between the Lunar and Solar Courts. I know about the horrific crimes that happen daily at their Court. I know how they *kill* Undivine for no reason at all. About the scars they give to their Divine. They do that to their own people, Kyelin. What do you think they will do to yours?"

"Of course. Your worries are valid, Celeste. I apologize, my jokes were in poor taste. I will look into it." He shifts uncomfortably, gaze drifting away. Good. I hope he feels guilty and that he realizes what he stands to lose if he refuses to listen to reason.

"Thank you." I don't have to tell him what happened to me for him to trust me. To trust my opinions on subject matters I definitely have no business poking around in. My heart flutters knowing he values me so greatly. That he holds me in such high regard.

"I don't need to remind you that they are staying through the third Game. But I will tell you that they will most likely stay for the Choosing. I was informed two days ago. We are allowing them to stay so our Courts can work towards a better alliance. If you truly fear them, I will make sure they can't get you alone." This is the second time I have been told that, but it does nothing to reassure me. I know how flimsy loyalty is around here. I grit my teeth and nod my head, deciding not to bring that sore subject up.

"What—um—what is the third Game?" I ask shyly, changing the subject. His advice sucks, but I can't tell him that.

"It's a fight," Kyelin admits as he presses back into me unwittingly, fingers dancing across my skin. It's like we are magnets, destined to be together and hard to pull apart. "There are ten of you left. You will be put into pairs, ones that will be a fair match. Then, you will fight for the crown. Only five of you will succeed. The next day you will stand before our Court and we will choose our brides."

"Assuming I win." I let my own hands drift up his chest absently, desperate for some kind of contact after weeks without any.

"I have no doubts. You are strong, Celeste. Powerful. You just need to believe in yourself." His answering smile is pleasant and faithful.

"Knowing you believe in me will help, I think. But I don't know how to fight. Would you be willing to teach me?" I don't mention my dagger practice sessions. Or the workouts I have been doing to gain body strength. Or that Prince Edge *told* me I should train.

"Teach you?" He seems surprised. I guess not many Divine have to learn that skill at this point in their lives.

"Yes. I know we only have a few days, but I think it will be beneficial to know a few proper techniques." Especially from a prince who trains with his soldiers.

"On one condition," he says happily.

"Hmm?" My fingers dance lower, down to the hem of his shirt. He swallows hard as they slip under, grazing across smooth skin.

"You will be my date for the full moon ceremony. It is

the night before the last Game. I guarantee you will have a wonderful time." His voice is tight, eyes closed.

"You guarantee?" I trace the lines of his muscles, distracted.

"Yes. And there will be dancing."

"What kind of dancing? Because I'm not much of a slow dancer. I like to have a...faster pace."

"It won't be slow," he promises, running his nose along my neck, "I'll make sure the music stays nice and fast, that your feet are so sore you won't be able to walk the next morning."

"Count me in." I breathe, eyes fluttering close.

"Then we have a deal. I have to say, I am quite looking forward to it. The dancing, the ritual, *you*. And the training, of course."

"The training needs to be a secret, too. Can you promise?" I add hastily.

"I promise. What's with you and all these promises?" He chuckles lightly against my neck, biting down softly. I shiver, releasing the breath I had been holding.

"I just don't want Prince Zaeden to get jealous of us hanging out so much. I don't want him to be mad at you because of how we feel for each other. I feel as if I am taking his other half away." More like I don't want him coming to my room to demand his half of the attention.

"Silly girl. Zae isn't the jealous type. Besides, he and I have had long discussions about the Games. We both know how they are going to end if the fights play out the way we expect them to."

"I'm glad this is almost over. This competition business is hard. But I'm sure it is hard to pick one Divine out of so many, too!" I don't want to talk about Zaeden anymore. It's spoiling our moment alone.

"Oh? You know, you haven't asked who I would pick. Don't you want to?"

"I didn't want to be so bold," I say, shocked that he had been. We both know it is between me and Silvi. Dove might have a fighting chance, but there isn't much of a real competition there. As much as I love my friend, her Court isn't enough. It will just be Silvi and I fighting all over again.

"It's an easy choice. When you are in love with someone, it always is."

"Love?" I choke out, leaping back. Suddenly the distance between us is not great enough. He can't mean that?

"I am in love with you, Celeste. The first moment I laid eyes on you, I knew you were special. I knew you were Undivine and I still thought about you constantly. To find out you weren't? It was a dream come true. I thought the goddesses were casting their blessings on me. And they have. The days without you have been empty. My heart has ached to be near yours. The only good thing this time apart has done is made me realize how crazy I am about you. So, yes. I love you." Fire dances in his eyes once more, but not in the fiery blaze from before. It's soft and glowing, not angry and ferocious.

"I—um—well—" I'm not sure what to say. Do I feel the same way? Sure, I have had thoughts before about maybe *falling* in love but am I *in* love? I am very attracted to him. I like his personality. He has some traits that I can do without, but he does seem to genuinely care for me. He will give me a good life and will probably make me very happy. And I want to see him happy, too. He's been a good friend to me, something I haven't had in a long time. These feelings started suddenly and strongly, and they seemed to be increasing. Is that what love is?

When he touches me I feel that drop in my stomach, the goosebumps on my skin. Sometimes he takes my breath away. When he kisses me it feels so different than anything I have ever experienced before. Better. Maybe that is the effect Royals have on people below them, or maybe it is how I feel. To think I can love a man I hardly know is scary, but I know that there is a strong possibility my little crush has grown to be just that. I'm not sure that we are Soul Divine, but that can come later. I have never been in love, but our relationship checks the boxes. So I must be in love. Right?

"I love you, too, Kyelin." I blurt out, turning away so he can't see I lack the same passion in his eyes. He laughs loudly and happily, sweeping me into his arms and lifting me above the ground. He swings me around in a full circle before planting me back on my feet. His happiness radiates through him and leaks into me. I laugh out of surprise, holding on to his biceps tightly. The heat that radiates through him sinks into me, dancing down my fingers. The feeling is...strange. It doesn't feel like he is making me warm like it usually does. It feels like that heat is being shoved into my own body. So I let go, unsure of this sensation. Whatever happened, Kyelin doesn't seem to notice.

"I'm so glad to hear you say that!"

"I think it would be an easy choice for me, too." I laugh, cheering up at his delight. Him being happy makes me happy. That's what love is, right?

"I want to kiss you." He murmurs, suddenly serious.

"Then kiss me." He guides me to the wall, lifting me and pushing me against it. It's so much easier to reach his lips this way, easier than trying to climb up him. He leans forward, crimson hair tickling my cheeks. In the back of my head, I think of Prince Zaeden. I don't want him to come back to my room, demanding his kisses. Demanding he, too, be told he is loved. But when Kyelin's lips meet mine, I shake the thoughts away. I don't want Kyelin to think I'm not enjoying this. I am. Oh, I am. My mind is just a little preoccupied with his evil brother.

His movements quicken, hands roaming down my body and back up. They leave a fiery trail in their wake that is excruciating and thrilling all at the same moment. I try not to flinch when those soft hands run over sensitive areas. It's easy to remind myself he won't hurt me, though. He will never hurt me. He *loves* me. I try to return the intense passion he is desperate to give me, but he is so enthusiastic that it is hard to keep up. His hands curl into my hair, body flush against mine. Part of me wants to stay this way forever, to never be apart again. The other part is desperate to get away. When I open my eyes, though, I am only comforted by the soft orange hues within his eyes.

"I love you, I love you, I love you." Each word is more desperate, more breathy than I have ever heard. He grabs my hands, placing my thin fingers on the top button of his shirt. My fingers shake as I stumble over the button, popping it free with great struggle. I manage to make my way down, my heart pounding right out of my chest. When I push the shirt off of his shoulders, I know I am dying. Divine goddesses! I have never seen a man who looks like this. Who makes me feel this way just by showing a little skin. I try to take in the smooth expanse of muscles, to feast on the amazing view. My hands wander on their own, exploring.

Suddenly he is moving, walking away with me in his arms. I am tossed on the bed, weightless for a few precious seconds.

I yelp, eyes widening as he crawls over my body. I close my eyes as his breath hits my face, kisses trailing down my neck. I try not to think about Prince Edge pushing against me like this. About how his body felt so similarly imposing and so, so different. Kyelin's hands travel up, up, up. Fingers graze against the bottom of my breasts, teasing. But now that I have reminded myself of Prince Edge my mind wanders to Prince Zaeden. My mind spins images of *his* hands groping me, of him kissing my neck. I can't, I can't, I can't.

I push Kyelin away as hard as I can, scrambling backward. No. I can't do this. It's too much. Too far.

"I'm sorry." Kyelin sighs, running a hand through his hair in distress. He sits up, crossing his legs at the ankles and leaning back onto his hands casually.

"I don't think I can do this." I shake my head rapidly, wrapping myself into a ball. "I just...certain things make me remember. And my mind tricks me. I'm sorry. I thought I could do it. Be...intimate. But I can't."

"Don't apologize. I understand your turmoil. Well, maybe not understand, but empathize. Thank you for trusting me enough to try." His smile is genuine. He isn't mad?

"I'm sorry." I can't help it. I feel so, so guilty. My throat dries up, mouth tightening.

"We will work to overcome this together, okay? Like a husband and wife should. Don't worry about me, baby." He stands and grabs his shirt, taking a few steps toward the door.

"I will see you for lessons?" I'm not sure he will want to give them to me anymore. Not with how fast he is fleeing this room.

"Of course. In two days, at sunrise. Ryleigh will know where to go. Goodbye, Celeste." That leaves time for only *one* lesson.

I will need to do a lot of work on my own.

"Goodbye." I bristle, watching him go.

I hardly have to recollect myself before another knock sounds at the door. It's soft and delicate, hardly a sound at all. I glance at the door, knowing I shouldn't answer. Ryleigh has yet to find her way back to my room, so she is unable to check it for me. Despite knowing better, I stand to my feet. I tiptoe to the door, cracking it open just a hair. But I recognize the woman standing in front of me. I definitely, definitely should not have opened this door. My hand slips into my pocket, searching until I feel the familiar cold steel of my dagger. My fingers wrap around the hilt, tightening with every breath.

"Princess Valaine. What a...pleasure to see you here." The guards glance over at the hostile tone, unwavering in their defensive positions. But they aren't worried about me, not in the slightest. Their eyes are glued to her. The beautiful Solar Court princess. *Men.*

"May I come in?" She smiles, tilting her head to the right inquisitively.

"I probably shouldn't let you. You know, considering what your brother did to me." I won't say much more for fear of the guards overhearing.

"Probably isn't the same as won't." I want to deny her, but I don't. I glance at the two guards wearily. They are still watching her like a prize to be won. They will be of no use to me. None of these guards are. So, I step back and allow her to enter my room.

"Everyone just sits on the edge of my bed." I gesture vaguely towards it, shutting the door behind her. I don't move my hand away from the dagger, watching every move she makes.

"You haven't left this room all day," Valaine says softly, eyes sparkling.

"No. I'm sure you can understand why." I don't get any closer to her, sure she will be able to feel the fear pumping through my veins.

"Yes. I do. That is why I came here. I was waiting for you at lunch, but you never came. I want to apologize on behalf of my idiotic brother. He is too prideful to admit his wrongdoings, but I am not. What he did was wrong. And he deserved what you did to him in return. I want you to know I hold no ill will against you. I wish no harm to you. I know Silvi has been telling you otherwise but it isn't true. That is not why we have come. Between her and my brother, they seem to be leaving a very bad impression."

"Yes, he did deserve it." That's all I can muster out. How does she know what Silvi told me? Unless Silvi admitted so herself...

"Please. Take your hand off that dagger. Come, sit with me. I will not harm you in this room. I swear it." Just like that, she has wrapped me in a false sense of security. They are powerful words, ones I can't ignore. So, I let go of my dagger as she suggests. I won't hurt her if she truly doesn't wish to hurt me. I sit near her, leaving ample room between us. As long as I stay in this room, she will not harm me. She can't.

"I have been threatened multiple times. Most of which are by the people of your Court. What I am, what I was...no one likes it. No one likes the power I hold or the sway I have over the Royals. I expected him to attack me. I did not expect him to take my hair and run. To not even kill me. I was certain I would die that day."

"My brother has duties as the prince. One of those duties is to make sure we obtain an alliance here in this Court. It is a different kind of game that I have chosen to stay out of. That I am lucky to have a choice in. He does not. When he does extreme things, it is because he thinks he is doing what needs to be done. He never planned on killing you. That would be unjust. You have done no wrong to our Court. I am sorry for the hurt he has caused, even if he may not be." She is genuine. I don't know *how* I know, but I do. That voice in my head tells me so and it is always right. It was right about Silvi, wasn't it?

I watch a single tear trail down her face, but she turns quickly to hide it. "I see. Well, I must ask another question. I have to. Why did he cut my hair? Why did he take it with him?"

"I cannot say. That is beyond my knowledge."

"Beyond your knowledge?" I fume. He gets to just cut my hair and get away with it?

"Yes. You will have to ask him yourself. He never told me and I never asked. He told me what he did and I came here immediately. I don't know his reasoning. Please, speak to him so he can apologize himself."

"I have no intentions of speaking to *him*. And I have high doubts that he will be apologizing to me anytime soon. He tried to afterward, not like it mattered. He wouldn't have attacked me in the first place if he was truly sorry."

"Of course. I understand."

"Good. If that is all…"

"No, actually. I wanted to come here to offer my friendship. I know how the other Divines treat you. I find it distasteful. I don't hold your past against you, and they shouldn't either."

"Your friendship? Are you joking? Why would I agree to be friends with you?"

"Yes. We both know the outcome of the Games. You *will*

win. Our Courts will be interacting much more frequently if Silvi wins, too. We will see each other often. I would like to offer friendship so these meetings will be tolerable for us both."

"We are in love. It is more than just winning." I wrinkle my nose, daring her to disagree.

"Oh? In love? Isn't it a bit…too soon for that? It has only been a couple of months. Surely you don't mean that?" She seems genuinely surprised, maybe even a bit worried.

"It is a little shocking. I know because I can hardly believe it myself. Kyelin feels the same. Our situation is so unique, so strange, that I think maybe we were meant to meet. Fated, if you will. I wasn't sure at first, but now I am. It must be love."

"Your mind cannot be swayed?" She breaths out, inching forward. I squint at her, jumping in surprise as her small hand touches my leg. It inches up swiftly, fingers brushing against my thigh. I jerk away from her touch, not realizing how close I had let her get to me on this giant bed. It takes a minute for me to process what she was about to do.

She speaks before I can. "There is a place for you at the Solar Court. It is obvious that you are unsure about this supposed love you have for Prince Kyelin. I can see it plain as the sun, even if he can't. If it is power or money you want, you can find that elsewhere. You don't have to stay here if you choose not to. You can come to my Court. We will take care of you and make sure you lead the life you want. The one you deserve. Maybe not as a queen or a princess, but as someone held dear to the Royals. Someone who will be protected, and not with guards who have flimsy loyalty like the ones you have been presented with. You don't have to be here with the Court who mistreated you your whole life. Who let you believe you were

Undivine. You don't have to work for a better life. I will give you one." Her body inches forward again, eyes desperate and pleading. I can feel it as much as I can feel the air down my throat.

"I think we can be a better match. Don't you?" Her hand reaches out, caressing my face. I jerk away again, scrambling to my feet. Is she serious right now? Is she attempting to gain my trust so she can seduce me? Offering friendship to get a chance at more? Not that she wants it. This is all a ploy, one I don't need a magnifying glass to see. They must be desperate for Silvi to be on the throne, then. But why go this far? Why not kill me? Not that I *want* to be killed. It's just obvious what the easiest option is.

Unless they can't kill me. For some reason, they will not do it. Prince Edge has had so many chances and I have had none. I don't know why, but they need me alive. Something is going on. I don't understand it. What could possibly be the reason they are trying this hard to get Silvi on the throne and me on their side? It's suspicious, and I don't like not knowing what their plans for me are.

"Get out." My face hardens, anger rising like Kyelin's flames. I hope she doesn't notice the trembling in my hands. I shove one down into my pocket to hide it, grasping onto my dagger like a lifeline. Even if it amounts to nothing.

Princess Valaine stands, emotionless. Her steps are slow and purposeful, delaying the inevitable. She is giving me a chance to stop her. I'm not going to. One hand on the door, she stops to glance back.

I don't say a word as she slips away

Chapter 16

I try not to shake as Ryleigh opens a set of double doors, guiding me into a large arena. I have been telling myself this is an awful idea for two nights, my mind warning me of the many dangers that lie behind this choice. What if Zaeden finds out? What if he shows up? How can I fight after just one lesson? Not just one lesson, my *only* lesson. But then I remind myself of Kyelin. Of how it won't just be my heart hurting. And after that kiss…I don't think I can stay away anymore. Not if it means I will never get to taste him again. Never get to feel his presence searing into my very own. Never get to feel the comfort of knowing he is by my side. To know I am not alone anymore and never will be again.

"Quit worrying, Celeste. Nothing is going to happen to you here. I have guaranteed it." She has said that many times and, yet, it has never been quite so guaranteed. I am not sure I can trust Ryleigh's word anymore. Her tone is thick with annoyance, though, and I can hear the eye roll as she shoves me forward.

"Have you really, though?" My eyes snap to hers in desperation.

"I will be outside, within hearing distance." She mutters in response, not bothering to answer my question. She sends a brief glare toward Kyelin in warning before slipping out of the doors and away from my reach.

"Do I want to know what you have told her about me to deserve a look like that?" Kyelin laughs as he approaches, taking my hand into his own. He lays a gentle kiss on top of it, letting it fall back down to my side after a long pause. Our eyes meet briefly but it is enough to fill my cheeks with heat.

"Only bad things." I purr. Those bright eyes trail down my body, taking in my very tight attire. I shift, still unused to such tightness. It is custom-tailored to me, clinging to every inch of skin it touches. It feels strange not to be wearing shoes yet have my feet enclosed, to have my fingers covered but not be wearing gloves. The fabric is meant for this, or so I was told. Soldiers wear similar suits when they begin their training. The material softens blows and weakens physical powers. It's a simple, black jumper, but I don't mind. I'm grateful that the time and money were spent on it when it didn't have to be. Plus, it's a huge upgrade to the extravagant dresses I am usually shoved into.

"Wonderful." He winks as I straighten. I watch as he lifts an object, a circular cushion of some kind. He holds it between us, tapping it with his knuckles.

"What is that?" I glance at it wearily.

"This is what we will be using in our first training exercise. You must learn how to throw a punch. That is a necessary skill in a physical fight. I want you to punch this over and over and over. Do it until I tell you to stop. I want you to practice the power and aim of your hits. This will be your biggest offensive move as you fight for our love." My stomach sinks. Yes. For our love. *That* is what I need to remember to fight for.

"Okay." I lift my fists in front of my chest, feet planted apart. I know this much, at least.

"Good, you already know what to do. Feet a little wider. Fists higher. Tighter. Angle yourself a little to the right. Stand straighter. Perfect. Now, I am going to show you a few defensive moves." His smile lights up the room. It makes me happy to see him so proud of me and encourages me to do more just to see that smile remain. I watch as he pulls a white ribbon from his pocket, hands twisting into his hair effortlessly. Something about this look makes me breathless.

"I won't hurt you, will I?" I cock my head, unsure if this is okay. He is a prince who is to be crowned king. My future husband. Should I be hitting him?

"No, you could never hurt me." He laughs, shaking his head.

I frown and say in a harsh warning, "Good because I won't hold back."

"I don't want you to." He takes a few steps back, preparing. Quickly, I throw the first punch in hopes of taking him by surprise. It does. He stumbles back a bit, not expecting the strength. His eyes widen ever so slightly. There is an echoing 'thud', the sound like music in my ears. I retreat, waiting for his signal.

After a few seconds, he nods for me to continue. So I do. I throw punch after punch, slamming fists towards his chest over and over and over just like he said to. I am out of breath, sweating profusely, sore. But I keep going. If I start feeling tired, I think of Irissa. I think of Silvi. Prince Zaeden. Prince Edge. I imagine taking Irissa to a safe place, protected as the queen's sister. I imagine taking down each of my enemies and watching them fall from injuries made by my own hands. I can *see* their blood spilled onto the ground. I think those thoughts came across my face, warning Kyelin that I was starting to drift away into a different world. He lifts his free hand, signaling me silently. With that single motion, I stop. His eyes drift down to mine, concerned. I huff out an 'I'm okay' and glare at my bruised fingers.

"Let me show you how to dodge now." I wipe my brow with the back of my hand, watching him approach. He dances around me for a minute, a predator following prey. His body practically floats around me. He never blinks, but I do. That's when he pounces.

He throws his leg out, aiming for my chest. I yelp and jump back, barely dodging his foot. Just as quickly, his fist comes flying towards my cheek. He has the speed of a Royal, the strength of one. I fall trying to duck away, panicking as I try to just *think*. I throw myself back up, balanced low on my feet. While I squat, I throw my leg out and sweep his out from underneath him. Kyelin falls hard, laughing as he goes down.

He stands easily, unperturbed. "Good. You have a lot of potential. Now, let me show you something." He puts his hands on my shoulders then my arms, whispering to me about where to watch and how to effectively dart away. He tells me not to look away even for a second, to keep my eye out for any weakness like I had with him. Every move counts. I can barely focus, though, with his hands all over me. Moving my arms into proper movements and pushing me against him. By the end, I am barely breathing, and it isn't because of the physical strain on my body.

"Okay, but what if they do grab me? What do I do then?" I asked after he had explained how to avoid being grabbed. Suddenly, his arms are around me, pinning mine down. He is whispering into my ear about using elbows and feet to my advantage, to use my small size to help me escape. To not forget that I am powerful and can put that power behind every hit. That I am Divine now and have the strength of one. Says that my shields should work against other Highs and that I can use them, too. So, I do as he says. I twist unexpectedly while he is whispering, ramming my elbow down into his thigh. His grip loosens and I spin out of his arms, back into a fighting position. He grabs me easily enough and I am falling. Within seconds I am on my back, growling as he pins me down.

"See? Always be alert. You did well in escaping, but you weren't staying focused. You thought you had won already. Never think that unless your competitor is incapacitated or dead." I can only nod, too worked up to speak. Kyelin sits on top of me, unmoving, eyes roaming my face. Searching for something I am not ready to give.

I scramble up and back to get out of his reach. He doesn't say anything or resist, just sighs under his breath. "What about my power? How do I do this and use it? It was so natural when I fought the first time, but it slipped from my control quickly. It didn't take much after that for me to lose. And it turned me into someone I didn't recognize. Still don't. How do I control it? That beast that's ready to take over?"

"Your power is the most important thing in a fight, Celeste. You have to keep it in a cage. They have a mind of their own. You are going to have to practice balancing the two. Your powers are so new that you haven't found that balance, but you will. It is something you will have to do on your own. Only you know your limitations. But if you will it under control, under control it will be. Once you accept that, it will do your bidding without you needing to ask anything of it. Do you understand?"

"I understand."

"Good. Something I have always been taught is to keep it at your fingertips. Make sure you can always feel it there, ready to attack at your command. That's how you know it will be reliable, that it will listen to you and work with you. If you release that feeling, it shrivels up inside you and hides. Then you have to coax it back out and beg it to play again. You can't risk that in a fight. You have to urge it out when you want it to be out. Then you have to keep it there. It will be a mental struggle at times. I know you don't have a large amount of time to practice. Don't let fear control you, Celeste." Kyelin takes my hand in his, clasping our fingers together. A shiver runs down my spine as he leans down, lips touching my ear. "Run a few laps, Celeste, and we will be done here."

"Are we still on for tonight?" My eyes close as I relish this closeness. Soon, I can have this whenever I want. One more day and one more fight. That's all.

"Of course. I will be at your room an hour before midnight. Wear something nice. Tell Ryleigh what event you are attending. She will know what to do. Until then, Celeste." His lips barely touch mine before he is gone, not bothering to stay and watch me run laps.

There is a stranger in the mirror. I do not know her and she does not know me.

Ryleigh says this outfit is appropriate for the ceremony, but I am unsure. She says that I need to stand out, that I need to look like the future queen. She knows best, though, so here I am. There is a reason she has been the head maid for so long, after all.

The silver material is beautiful, sparkling in the lights brighter than any star. The top is short, falling just above my belly button. It has loose sleeves that fall off my shoulders, unrestricted. It hugs my chest tightly, showing off every single line and bend I have. The pants are the opposite, loose and flowing like the sleeves. I wear dark blue slippers since I don't want the embarrassment stilettos will bring my way. Ryleigh insists I wear a silver headband across my head, stars dancing along to an unknown rhythm. The whole outfit is a homage to my Court.

My hair is down and free, curling up in crazy formation like the wildlings they are. I, too, wish to be a wildling sometimes. They dance through the trees at night, twirling each other around and around. Sing to the sleeping creatures and bless every surface they touch. The tiny, ugly creatures party all night long and sleep all day. But they can go wherever they want. Do whatever they wish. They aren't held down by a Court or allegiances or a home. They do as they please for the pleasure of doing it. Oh, to be a wildling.

Looking at myself now, I feel the most beautiful I have ever been. The most desirable. Dark lined eyes, ruby red lips. It's bold and daring and more Divine than I could have ever imagined. I not only look High Divine, but I finally *feel* like one, too.

When Kyelin shows up and his eyes rake over me, darkening the more he sees, it brings deep satisfaction. His flames reach up to meet me, dancing at the sight before them. They don't burn me in agony but in a gentle touch, roaming my skin in a way I wish Kyelin's hands would. But his lips are what meets my skin, touching flushed cheeks in a soft greeting. He lingers, pressing one more kiss to the corner of my lips. If I had flames, they would have completely engulfed us by now.

"You are beautiful," he says into my neck, the words practically melting into my skin.

"Thank you. I feel beautiful." I feel his smile before I see it.

"As you should. I'm so grateful you agreed to come." His voice sounds strained, almost as if it is painful to look at me.

"As am I," I smirk, a teasing hand roaming his chest. Maybe Ryleigh was right. This outfit is already doing wonders. I should have known better than to question her. And as we leave I take another piece of her advice: I leave my worries behind the door.

"We have to cross the lake?" Our walk has been long and silent until now, but not uncomfortable. I only speak because I can see the lake ahead, a small boat tied to the dock.

"Yes." He clears his throat, not meeting my eyes. I swear I can feel guilt radiating off of his body, but what would he have to feel guilty about?

"I have never been on a boat," I admit, trying to bring conversation as I glance at the boat wearily. It seems small, almost too small for the two of us.

"Oh? Don't worry, I'm an excellent captain." When we reach the wooden boat, he holds my hand and helps me step inside. It rocks underneath me and I briefly lose my balance. But Kyelin holds me tightly, uttering sweet reassurances into my ear before joining me. His long legs take up so much space, crowding over onto my side of the boat. He unties us from the dock and pushes off, picking up two paddles. His arms move efficiently, swiftly guiding us towards the other side.

"I've never brought anyone to this ceremony before," Kyelin admits into the calm air.

"Oh? No pressure then, huh? Well, I must say I feel very lucky to be your *first*." He chuckles, shaking his head. It's an attempt at nonchalance, but I see the facade.

"Zae always brings someone. But I'm glad you are my first. It is a wonderful ceremony to share with someone. There is nothing in the entire world like it. I plan on sharing many more with you." We are nearing the halfway point now, and his rowing is slowing down. He leans closer, the paddles coming to a full stop.

"I'm grateful to be your guest. If I truly have a good time, as I was guaranteed, I may consider sharing a few more with you." I watch him curiously as I speak.

He says rapidly, nervously, "Will you dance with us tonight? For good luck?" Is this why he has felt so guilty? Because he wants me to dance with his brother?

"Both of you?" My voice shakes as I speak.

"Yes. Both of us. It will bring good luck to our Court. So they say, anyways." He adds an insincere chuckle in an attempt to convince me. I hastily nod, not daring to say no. How bad can one dance be, anyway?

"Wonderful!" He kisses me gently, pulling away with a smile before continuing to row on. I try to smile back, but I know it isn't a true one. Probably not even a believable one. No matter how I feel about Zaeden, this night isn't about me. It is about tradition, restoring power, and celebrating the Lunar Court. I will do what needs to be done.

It doesn't take long for us to hit the other dock. He skillfully ties us to the post, hopping out with ease. He has to practically pull me out, an arm wrapped around my waist protectively. He doesn't let me go as we walk, fingers digging into my skin. When we enter the field, Kyelin's arm drops and his hand

266

entraps mine. The quiet night doesn't stay that way. Drums begin to bang, louder and louder and louder as we approach.

The music becomes overbearing so fast. It swallows every noise in its wake, like a hungry beast feasting. My heart thumps along to the beat as Kyelin leads us forward, pushing past soldier upon soldier. Each one cheers as we walk by, hands clapping onto Kyelin's back. He grins sheepishly, waving and shaking hands. Finally, we enter a clearing. No more tall, dead crops. Just clean, chopped grass in the shape of a circle. The soldiers crowd around the circle, leaving us in its center. Then, the singing begins. I can't understand a single word of it. Everything is muffled and sounds like pure gibberish.

Kyelin whispers into my ear, "It's an ancient language. It's a dead language, honestly. No one uses it except the soldiers for this very reason. Most only know the words to the chant and they don't know what it means. It helps keep the ceremony as secret as possible so no one can hinder it." He pulls me in tightly, nodding into the crowd.

That's when I see Prince Zaeden and know the inevitable is coming my way.

He pushes out of the group, nodding to me in greeting as well. He walks slowly to my other side, offering his hand. Reluctantly, I take it. I look between the two princes expectantly, unsure of what is about to happen or *why* I am the only female present.

"May we have this dance, my lady?" Kyelin pulls me away from Prince Zaeden, spinning me into his arms.

We swirl around over and over, our bodies dancing around the circle's edge. I feel like I am floating, like I am dancing through the stars. I am joyful, laughing and stepping along to a high only we feel. It came on so suddenly that I am unsure if it is the ritual or Kyelin himself, but I don't want the feeling to leave. Even if it isn't real. We dance and dance, giddy and excited. The music pushes us on and on and on, the clapping of hands and the stomping of feet following us around. And then I am swept into Prince Zaeden's arms. He takes me happily, laughing at my surprised expression before beginning the same sweeping motions of his brother. Around, around, around. I find myself uncaring that he is touching me, dancing with me. It is all too much fun and my bubbling laughter comes again. We laugh together, having the time of our lives. I bounce between the two men, my head light and my heart full. The more we dance the more careless I am. I can barely feel my body. All I know is how good I feel, how free. But then the music is gone and so is the singing. I try to object when Prince Zaeden slows us down, his arms pulling me to a halt. He bends down to whisper in my ear.

"Now it is time for the fun to begin."

Then I am being yanked out of his arms. A soldier is pulling me away, my shouts of protest dying down when I look to Kyelin. He mouths 'It's okay', his gentle smile calming me. The high I am on probably helps with that, too. The soldier pulls me to the edge of the circle, nodding when we are a good distance away. Then, Kyelin reaches down and undoes the first button of his shirt. I gape at him, turning my head to find Prince Zaeden following suit. I open my mouth to ask what they are doing, but the soldier clamps his hand over it with a shushing noise. I watch with wide eyes as their hands continue down, shirts falling to the soft ground. Their pants follow soon after. I can't look away, though. No one else does, either. Of course, these men are used to it. They do this every month. They have no reason to be as embarrassed as I am. Even if I am keeping my eyes on their chests. Well, I am trying to, anyway. Suddenly, hands are pushing me forward. A bucket is shoved into my hands, the creamy liquid inside sloshing around.

"This is your part." A gruff voice says, pushing me again. I want to ask what I am meant to do, but I am shushed before a word can escape from my mouth. As I approach, the princes fall to their knees. They bow their heads before me, hair falling forward like curtains to cover their faces.

"The time has come for the goddess's representative to present our Royals with their blessings." A man announces from behind me as someone else gestures for me to move forward. I do as I am told, finding myself between the two. I turn to face the same direction after someone makes another motion for me to do so. I try not to think about their naked bodies. Instead, I look towards the man making a pouring gesture. I nod to let him know I understand. Can they not just tell me what to do here? Does it all have to be so quiet and confusing? My head is already spinning so fast, how am I supposed to understand?

"Each prince will now be doused with lake water that has been blessed by the goddesses. The blessed water will mix with Royal blood. This holy mixture will allow our Royals and every one of the Lunar Court citizens to prosper and remain more powerful than ever." I glance down at my bucket, unsure about it being lake water. There has to be something else mixed in, something that makes it worthy of the ceremony. The creamy liquid definitely doesn't look like the mucky water I saw in the lake.

"Cut my hand with your blade, Celeste. I know you have

one." Kyelin's voice is barely audible, head unmoving. I take a deep breath, watching as they simultaneously hold out their hands to me. I gently lower the bucket, letting it sit idle between us. I slowly pull the dagger from my pants, the blade shining in the light of the full moon. I look between the two princes quietly, my heart stopping when a soldier nods for me to continue.

I reach forward, taking Kyelin's hand into my own. I allow the blade to kiss his palm, pressing deeply. I am quick to cut across his skin, trying not to worry as the blood pools. He brings his hand down after I pull away, pulling them into a cupping position in front of his head. I move on to Prince Zaeden, taking his hand into mine. I'm not as gentle with him, my cut much harsher. I can tell he wants to say something, but the moment is much too serious for anything more than a scoff. As I pull away, I drop the dagger to the ground. I hate seeing their blood dripping down its blade, bile rising in my throat at the sight. The blood is sobering me up quickly. Then I see the darkness from before rising to the surface of my own hands, pooling up defensively.

Quickly, I grab the bucket of blessed water, bringing it over Kyelin's head to distract myself. I don't have time for hallucinations right now. Slowly, I tip the bucket and allow the liquid to flow freely. After half is gone, I turn to Prince Zaeden and pour. I watch as the lake water mixes with their blood in cupped hands, deep red swirling around and around that creamy white. It's mesmerizing. I watch as it sinks into their skin, their wounds vanishing. Without warning, the three of us are surrounded by a powerful, heated wind. I feel it push back my hair, slamming against our bodies. When I blink, it's gone. Kyelin and Zaeden are on their feet, completely dry and blood-free. They bow to the soldiers, causing an eruption of cheers. The drums begin anew, their deep thrums entering us all. Then the soldiers begin to disperse, their reactions as mild as if nothing happened at all.

"I quite enjoyed this night." Zaeden whispers on one side, the realization I am trapped between them still hitting hard.

"I'm sorry I couldn't tell you about this before," Kyelin whispers on my other side. I choose to face him instead of Prince Zaeden, searching his eyes for answers. This is what the guilt was about, the nervousness. I feel him moving, seeking out his pants. He slips them back up without breaking our eye contact. He glances over at Prince Zaeden, nodding to his brother. Then he is pulling me away without bothering to retrieve his belt or shirt.

"Does this happen every time? Who else has done this?" I ask as we slip away, the beat of the drums dying out. I don't ask where we are going. I don't care. The strange feeling from before has come back, freeing my thoughts and lightening my mind. I find myself dying to be in Kyelin's arms, desperate for his touch. The need for contact grows, heat building inside me. Part of me longs for Prince Zaeden, too, but I know that is the high talking. Though I'm still not sure exactly what I am high *from*. I still don't think I care.

"Zaeden always has a new girl picked out. I don't always know them. That part of the ceremony calls for a female. But I did not lie before. I have never brought anyone with me to the ceremony. It is a tradition that one of us does, so I have always asked him to do it."

"Tradition? Why is everything always about tradition around here?" My head swims. I feel so light and ecstatic. I feel like I can do anything. I laugh at the idea, stumbling as

271

Kyelin continues to lead me on.

We stop at a small cottage at the edge of the lake. He opens the door fast, yanking me inside. I fall into his arms, still laughing. His breathing is so heavy and I wonder if he, too, feels that overwhelming urgency to be near me, to touch me.

"Wow!" I gape as I glance around. There is a giant tree in the middle of the room, a blue pool surrounding it. Branches hang over the pool, beautiful white flowers blooming down their arms. There is a bed at the end of the room and a door that I assume leads to a washroom. I turn back to look at Kyelin, not sure where, exactly, we are.

"Isn't it beautiful?"

"What is it?"

"A special place meant for the Divine couple who is celebrating the ceremony." He practically pants, stepping away from me.

"Oh." He had planned this? To be alone with me?

"Don't worry. You don't have to do anything you don't want to do. I just thought we would want to be alone for a little while. The ceremony—it—well, it affects us differently. The soldiers feel a little bit of lust and have a little bit of a high, which is why they are now gathering their dates to continue celebrating at the party. But since I am the one who brought you here, it is you and I that feel this the strongest. It is you I crave like I have never craved another. Looking at you right now is killing me, Celeste. I can't bear it. I've never wanted someone the way I want you right now." He steps towards the pool, slipping out of his pants. I squeak, turning my head away. He only chuckles, his feet splashing the water as he enters the pool. "You've already seen everything I have to offer, Celeste. Besides, I'm just going for a dip. I feel like I am on fire right now and I need to cool off." His voice is husky, despite his efforts for it not to be.

"I feel so...so..."

"I know. I'm sorry. I've never felt this way before, I didn't know to warn you. Zaeden never said it feels like this. But we don't have to do anything, Celeste. I will stay over here and won't put a hand on you if that is what you wish. I just didn't want this feeling to overwhelm you in front of everyone else. I know *I* needed a little privacy away from their prying eyes."

The lightness in my mind is encouraging me to step forwards, consequences be damned. I don't care if Prince Zaeden finds out. Kyelin won't let him touch me. That voice is telling me to follow him, to take everything he is offering. So, quietly, I listen. I let the stunning silver outfit drop right to the ground.

I hesitate at the edge of the pool, wrapping my arms around my body. Shaking, I step forward. The water splashes as I enter the cool pool, my body drifting towards him. I press myself against his hard back, wrapping my arms around his waist. My fingers dance dangerously below his waistline, my heart racing. Slowly, with a great amount of self-control, he turns to face me. He hardly ripples the water as he turns, giving me a chance to change my mind. And then he is facing me and all doubts are gone, if they were ever there. Something strong overcomes me and I practically climb up him, clasping his face in my hands. I pull him to me harshly, kissing him fiercely. Our lips dance with a passion I never knew existed, flames rising even through the water. Everything turns smoky and I can barely see, barely think, and I am drowning, drowning, drowning in his touch. My shields are exploding haphazardly around us, but our powers don't hurt one another. They merely play together, bouncing off each other's energy.

His hands slide down my sides as mine slip behind his head, tangling into the silky crimson hair I have come to love. I gasp as his fingers graze my hips, tugging lightly on his hair. He groans and bites my lower lip, both hands going to my lower back to push me flush against him. Everything is so intense, every touch like a lightning strike. It's thrilling and terrifying all in the same breath.

"Is it normal to feel like this?" My breathing is wild and harsh, the words barely escaping my lips.

"To feel like what?" Lips trail down my neck. His teeth graze a sensitive area near my collarbone, a low moan relinquishing itself from my mouth.

"To feel like you are irresistible. Like I won't live unless I have you. Like you are the only thing that matters in this life. Like I would murder someone if they walked through that door right now just so I could make love to you." My head is so, so cloudy. My whole body is somehow hot in the chilly water, every inch of me feverish.

"The ceremony is like a drug. You would feel that way about Zaeden, too, if he were here."

"I don't think I would," I whisper, hissing as he bites the base of my neck.

"You can still say no." He murmurs against my skin, but I can tell he doesn't want to stop. And I don't either.

"I'm not saying no, Kyelin. Keep going."

"As you request, Your Highness." He purrs.

"Is this part of the ritual." I shake as his hands begin drifting lower.

He grins. "No. It's for good luck. Just like the dance."

"I love you, Kyelin." I groan as he pushes me against the side of the pool, hands going exactly where I need them to.

"I love you, Celeste." He breathes back, kissing me again.

His touch is addicting. I can't get enough of it. And everything feels so *good*. I'm practically melting into his arms as his fingers stroke me, noises I never knew I could make escaping my lips. I moan out his name as one finger enters me, then two. He pumps them slow and sensually, teasingly. I can hear myself begging for more, but he seems to not hear it. He just continues that torturous pace, not picking up speed. I begin to grind against him, my eyes rolling into the back of my head as I feel my release approaching. I might have been embarrassed about how fast I was coming if I wasn't so high. That high causes my clouded thoughts to cave, though, and every doubt or care is banished into the deepest corners of my mind.

"Oh, goddess, Kyelin." I moan right before I explode onto his fingers, my world spinning. It goes on and on and on until I can't breathe anymore, can't see. I can only feel, and goddess, it feels *great*.

"Turn around, Celeste. Put your hands on the edge." Kyelin growls into my ear, pumping his impressive length below the water. I'm quick to obey, breath hitching in anticipation.

"Good girl," he murmurs, slowly pushing the head of his cock inside of me. I groan, clenching hard around him. He curses, pushing in one inch at a time. I shove my ass back, forcing him to go deeper. He grabs my breasts roughly, punishingly, but I don't care. I rock back, begging for more. Pleading for it. Finally, he decides to give it to me.

His movements are soft and thoughtful, not as frantic as I want them to be. But we have all night for that. I know he is just trying not to hurt me. So, I let him go slow and steady. Let him control the pace. Each pump is a moment of complete and total ecstasy. Our moans dance around in the air, my name leaving his lips over and over and over.

"Harder, please," I whimper, nearing another orgasm. I glance over my shoulder at Kyelin and let him see my pleading eyes. He groans, throwing his head back.

"Look at me like that and I will give you anything you want, baby." His hands clench onto my hips, his thrusts hurrying. I moan louder the harder he pumps, clenching around him. He begins to get sloppier and more frantic, chasing his release. My own comes to me fast and hard, and stars begin to form again. I can barely register Kyelin's seed spilling inside of me, can barely think about anything other than this feeling I could chase forever. Just like that, I am dissolving in his touch and drifting away in his bliss.

Chapter 17
The Game of Power

Goddess am I sore.

Kyelin kept me busy all night, not that I was complaining at the time. But now? Now when I stand among my competition waiting for the trial to come and can't stop thinking about that pleasant soreness? Yeah...no, I still don't regret it.

I stand, still as stone, eyes wondering to said competition. My armor is heavy, my helmet suffocating. When they put my chest piece on, it looked thin and flimsy. I didn't even *think* about the weight being an issue. But standing here, waiting for the inevitable, I know my muscles aren't prepared. Or maybe I'm not mentally prepared and my mind is failing my body. Either way, it doesn't matter what part of me is failing. The failure itself will deem everything I have endured here to be pointless. I can't let that happen.

I can hardly see through the helmet, the slit made for my eyes falling much too low. It is the smallest size they have, but it is still too big. They are used to the tall, perfect Divine who are born to compete. Used to the same sizes fitting each participant every time the Games roll around. They don't have accommodations for someone like me.

We are in a room just outside of the arena, a large doorway

allowing us to enter and exit. I can see the dirt floor outside, the tall, cement walls rising around in a perfect circle. The crowd is above those walls that enclose us, their cries and cheers echoing around the hollow building. The sun shines brightly through a glass dome up above, lighting up our soon-to-be stage. We are all pacing in this hidden space, our eyes focused on the world beyond.

"Oh, Les." Ryleigh fusses, dusting off my tight sleeves. The jumper I have on underneath my armor is meant to withhold no matter what, similar to the one I wore when training with Kyelin. If I fall, it won't tear. If a knife is pressed to my ribs, it won't cut through. I'm not sure why I still have to wear this chest piece if those claims are true. The helmet covers my face and a portion of my neck, but there is still a sliver of skin shining through. A weakness.

"I look fine," I mutter angrily, eyes darting towards her. She continues to dust me anyway, beginning to tug and smooth out wrinkles that don't exist.

"Fine, sure. *Perfect?* Not yet." Her fingers dance across the back of my neck, pulling curls from my jumper. I hiss as she yanks my hair a little too harshly, rolling my eyes. She has braided a crown across my head, leaving the rest to hang loosely in the back. I'm not sure why she even bothered. She should have known the helmet would only ruin her work. According to her, the crown of hair is meant to give me confidence and make me feel like a 'true princess'. At the moment, I can't say it makes me feel that way at all.

"Welcome to the final Game! The Game of Power!" An announcer roars in the distance. My heart drops, but it is enough to get me moving. I shift uncomfortably, sweat pooling in my palms. "I am pleased to announce that our first contestant will be the lovely Silvi Merkelly of the Solar Court! Come on out, Silvi!" My hand goes up to my mouth as I wait for the second name to be called. She will no doubt win against any competitor. There is no true competition with her. I know it and so do the others. Our silent pleas fill the tense air: *please not me, please not me, please not me.*

I barely hear the name, Dola something or another from the Shadow Court, because I am too busy feeling relieved it isn't me. Of course, logically, they wouldn't put us up against one another. They want both of us in the finals. I can't help but pace now, mind drifting into a different realm. Ryleigh tugs on my arms, begging me silently to stop being so antsy. But I can't. This fight means everything. *Everything.*

Why can't Kyelin just tell them he is in love with me? He is our king-to-be. He should get to make the decisions. I shouldn't have to participate in a ridiculous fight for their pleasure. And to think Prince Zaeden will be here, watching my every move. Waiting for me to succeed so I can be his new plaything. No. That will be the first thing I tell my husband-to-be. I will not allow his brother to touch me. If he lays a single finger on me ever again he will regret it. I will hold the power from now on.

The thought of Prince Zaeden begging on his knees for me to spare him is a motivating one and it makes me feel better. No matter how ridiculous this whole ordeal is, I will do it for my love. I will win and everyone will regret the things they have done to me and the Undivine. I will change everything.

With a jolt, I look up. Silvi and Dola have entered the arena, already in their fighting positions. I glance at the women around me, realizing I am the last of the Lunar Court representatives. I am alone in that aspect and many more.

The confidence I just built up crumbles, the doubt sneaking in through the back door. My nerves reappeared and the pacing renewed. To my relief, even the most composed women seem nervous, too.

"You will win." Ryleigh smiles, grasping my hands in her own. I glance at her once more, shaking my head lightly. She adjusts my helmet so she can stare directly into my eyes.

"Will I?" My lips quiver at the question. I'm sure she can feel my body shaking from there.

"You won't be facing your strongest opponent. They want you *and* Silvi. You have a strong chance. They put you in separate pairs for a reason. Whoever you get will be an equal or lesser match. They need you. The people need you." I know she is right, that they are playing this to their liking. The thought isn't comforting because I am horrible at combat. My powers are meant for protection and I can barely use them. The odds are stacking higher and higher against me as we speak.

"I know," I reply, glancing into the crowd. I see Kyelin there, watching intently as the fight begins. I will do it for him, for my sister, and for my people.

"And it begins." Ryleigh whispers, finally looking away from me. Her body turns towards the arena, mine following. I focus my eyes on the two Divine, watching as Dola strikes first. Her fists fly forward, aiming for Silvi's face. Silvi bats her hand away easily, jabbing her fist into Dola's side instead. Dola stumbles backward, temporarily stunned. I can see her struggling to breathe from here, her face turning alarmingly red. I swear I hear cracks, even from my distant position.

The rest happens so quickly that it feels as if no time passed at all. Dola grabs her head, her screams piercing the air. The whole arena falls silent, our breathing shallow and labored as we wait. It is painful to listen to, painful to watch as Dola is tortured right in front of me. She begins throwing out weak streams of water in an attempt to defend herself, those terrified screams still echoing across the arena. I whimper along with her, covering my ears to dampen the horrific noise. Silvi steps closer to Dola with a grin, clearly enjoying manipulating the poor Divine's mind. The screams only grow louder, even soldiers grimacing at the noise. And she wonders why everyone from the Solar Court is terrified of her!

Silvi is the one to finally break the intense silence by saying, "Let your greatest, deepest fear enter your mind. Let it fill your entire being. It is inescapable. You are trapped in it, unable to free yourself. Fall under its weight." She commands. Then, just as quickly as it started, the screaming comes to an abrupt end. Dola collapses in a puddle of piss, body twitching as she lay unconscious on the ground. The match is quick work. It took a total of three minutes, according to the booming voice of the announcer. The crowd claps politely, a little intimidated and a lot impressed. Healers come forward and take Silvi's victim away in a rush. Silvi bows, turning her gaze to Kyelin. I watch their eyes meet, an understanding passing through their eyes. My blood boils at the sight.

"I'm going to puke."

"Calm down." Ryleigh hisses, grabbing me again. "You can do this. You have to do this. You are strong, you are capable, you are beautiful. Remember that."

"There is more to it than just *believing* I can do it. I'm in love with Kyelin. I *can't* mess this up. He has assured me that he will choose me to be his wife, but I'm worried. I don't know if I can make it far enough to get to the Choosing. Fighting isn't my specialty. My powers are geared towards protection. I don't have the skills necessary to win a fight, especially if it is going to be as brutal as this one just was. I trained for one day. One day, Ryleigh! Sure, I've been practicing amateur moves in my room, but I didn't know what I was doing. I was just trying to build up strength and swinging at random. But more than that, I am scared of what this life can mean. I don't want Prince Zaeden anywhere near me. But I want everything Kyelin has to offer. The love that I don't deserve, the life that I didn't earn. And I keep telling myself that this life will put me in control. That I can make sure Prince Zaeden never touches me again. But that doubt is still lingering, waiting to attack. I don't know if I should even be here. This whole thing is insane."

"Celeste, there is more on the line than you will ever know. You have to win. Do you understand? You have to win. I wish I could tell you everything is going to be okay and that there is no reason for you to have these concerns. But I can't because it wouldn't be true. Right now you need to get out of your head and get ready to fight. There are no more options. So wake up and fight for what's right." Before I can object, a stinging feeling spreads across my cheek. I never saw it coming. My head flies to the side, my silence a response to the shock. Slowly, I gather my thoughts and turn back to her in a rage. "It isn't just about you anymore, Celeste. It is about the Lunar Court and all of its citizens. Soon, it will be about the other Courts, too. If you don't win, we have other plans in place. But you are the best option. You have to do this now and you have to at least try, dammit!" I watch Ryleigh wearily, a single tear slipping down my cheek. Fuck, that hurt.

"You're right. Why are you always right about everything?"

I rub my sore cheek with a sigh. I let the anger deflate before swallowing it back down deep inside, hesitantly glancing over just to realize the fourth fight had ended. I have been far too distracted and lost precious time because of it. Without much warning, fate approaches.

"Celeste of the Lunar Court! Now, this is the fight we have all been looking forward to! The newcomer is ready to show off her powers, I'm sure. Come on out, Celeste, and show us what you've got! What do you think folks? Does she have what it takes to be a Royal?" The announcer booms, a symphony of noises erupting from the crowd. Some are excited and boastful, others disgruntled and angry. I close my eyes, wishing I was anywhere that didn't involve so many screaming Divine.

Ryleigh gives me a light shove, urging me forward when I don't move. I feel robotic as I step into the sunlight, my legs taking me to the center of the arena on their own.

"And her lovely opponent, Dove Airess of the Solar Court! Wow, what a pair! Am I right, folks? These are two very different kinds of powers, here. Well, who's ready to find out how those powers are going to clash?" The applause builds again. No, no, no. My eyes are wide as I watch my friend approach. I can't do this. I can see the look in her eyes, the sorrow and regret brimming there. Time slows, our gazes locked until she finally stands before me.

"I'm sorry," Dove whispers to me as if it matters.

"As am I." This is not what either of us wants. I spare a final glance at Kyelin, dropping my head when he doesn't meet my eyes. Prince Zaeden, on the other hand, is watching me with an amused gleam in those dark eyes. Before I can process what that may mean for me, a horn is blaring. The battle has

283

officially begun.

Dove is immediately on the offense, blowing out a spiral gust of wind straight for me. She is an Elementalist. I should be relieved that it is a manageable power, but I don't have the strength or time to be relieved. I throw my hands up, pushing it away sloppily. I swallow hard, struggling to focus. I have to win. *I have to.* I wiggle my fingers, calling for my powers. I let them settle at the tips of my fingers, let them build inside me the way Kyelin taught me. I manage to lift my hands, taking a deep breath before Dove starts throwing wind at me again. She has taken the brief seconds to concentrate on building up her own power, throwing sharp cones of wind over and over. Each one is stronger than the last, making them harder and harder to block as I slowly inch forward. Finally, I let out a cry and swung my foot up, managing to land a kick into her side. She yelps in surprise, jumping back much too late. The wind stops briefly, allowing me to advance. I throw my fist the way I was taught, hitting her square in the jaw. I feel guilty immediately, my conscious screaming that this is so, so *wrong.* But if hitting my friend is the only way I can win...well, then, I'm going to hit my friend.

I duck as her fists reach out for me, breathing heavily. I can't stop thinking about how hard I swung at her, even if I had to do it. She is the only friend I have made my entire time at the castle as a Divine. And I just *hit her.* The thoughts cost me. In those brief seconds, I stumble. I shout profanities as I fall, back hitting the ground hard. My helmet tumbles away, the large size making it all too easy. My head is now exposed and so is my entire neck.

Dove takes the opportunity to jump on top of me in a hurry, pinning me between her legs. I thrash against her but I have little physical strength compared to her. She has trained her whole life for this. Her fist slams into my cheek, her other hand lifting immediately after. She hits me over and over, giving me no mercy. No break between blows. And I can't stop her because my powers aren't exactly useful in physical combat. I still try, throwing up shield after shield after shield. Sometimes they ease the blow, but they never stop her entirely. Goddess, why did I feel bad about hitting her earlier?

I can hear the crowd screaming, most angry. The other battles had been quick and efficient. This is anything but. They scream out in my defense, my name being chanted across the arena. It only fuels Dove's rage. I swear the hits are getting harder, my face tingling in an icy numbness. I can barely see through my swollen eyes, but I search for Kyelin. When I finally find him, he is standing up and shouting. His hands are balled up tightly, the panic clear on his face. His lips are forming my name over and over and over. I feel every ounce of fear radiating from his body, the emotion crashing into me so hard that tears are wrenched from my eyes.

Once again, my foolishness costs me. It's during that small glance that I feel the cold blade of a dagger against my exposed neck. I don't dare turn to look at her, shock sweeping through me. The one rule for this Game is that weapons aren't allowed. But Dove has one and is preparing to use it to end my life.

"I'm sorry," Dove says again, pressing it deeper into my skin. "I'm doing what must be done. If I don't win, I'm as good as dead when I get home. I'm sorry. You were a good friend. I pray the goddesses watch over your lost soul." I close my eyes, feeling the blood trickle down my neck. I scream, crying out for help. The movement pushes my neck against the blade, digging deeper into my skin with each passing second. No one realizes she has a weapon, something that would disqualify her if they ever found out. Some people laugh, still unknowing. The panic and rage build as I realize no one will be coming to my aid. If there is one thing I am beginning to understand about living in the world of the Divine, it's that no one can help me but myself. Because by the time they realize what has happened, it will be too late. I will be dead.

A Divine will not kill me.

Something explodes inside of me. It's like a bomb in my chest, like a crystal shattering into a thousand pieces. I feel the power rising, and the power that I held at my fingertips is no longer the power I am familiar with. It is something dark and twisted, something that seeks revenge for everything that has been done to me. I howl out in anguish, writhing underneath Dove's body. It's so cold, like ice traveling through my veins. I manage to grab her face in an attempt to push her away, to warn her of the terrible thing rising within me to take her away.

The dagger digs deeper but I hold tightly. I feel an unfamiliar power within me, and I just *know* something is very, very wrong. Deep purple poison begins dripping from my hands and out of my fingertips. I can't stop it, despite my best efforts to will it away. I watch the familiar poison seeping out, washing over Dove's helmet. It snakes through the exposed holes, drifting into her eyes, her nose, her mouth. I see the panic flick across her eyes as she realizes what it is. It's the same poison Zaeden has, the poison that he doesn't typically make deadly. But now it is in me, belongs to me, and I have no control.

She screams, the terror piercing my heart. It's worse than listening to Dola. I can feel it in every bone, my own screams escaping my lips. I feel every bit of pain and every bit of fear as she approaches death. Bloody tears fall down her face as the poison works its way through her system. Her eyes are covered in it and I am certain she has gone blind because I feel blind, too. Her nose begins dripping that awful red, a few tendrils seeping out of her mouth. My own tears spill out, our screams echoing around the arena. Until the curdling cries stop abruptly and her body falls limp on top of me. Until I no longer feel any of her pain, my cries halting alongside hers.

The dagger falls from her hand, creating a soft 'thud' as it hits the dirt. The horror overcomes me when I realize what just happened, what I just did. The screams of Dola, the screams of Dove, the screams of *me* bounce around in my head on an endless loop. I have to get rid of them. I don't hesitate to release the last tendrils of poison, my shrieks crueler than anything I have ever heard before. I am gagging, choking, vomiting. Anything to expel this evil from within me.

I try to get out from underneath her body, but she is too heavy and I am too weak. My mind is lost. I can't focus on anything that isn't her face, that isn't the blood that covers us both. Her eyes aren't eyes anymore. All that is left is black holes, like they were never there to begin with. I continue to scream and shake until I see the healers come running. The crowd has gone deathly silent, listening to my cries of anguish.

Someone pulls her body off of mine, granting me the opportunity to scramble up to my knees. Someone else squats next to her painfully still body, too shocked to move. I stop screaming abruptly, crawling forward and ignoring the healer trying to stop me. I grab her body, shakily reaching up to her neck to feel a pulse. There isn't one. I shake her as hard as I can, frantic whimpers escaping my lips. I tear her helmet from her head, looking into the deep abysses I created.

"Wake up!" I beg, shaking her again and again. "Wake up, Dove. Wake up, damn it!" My hands are covered in her blood, my face is covered in my own. Both my neck and face throb painfully and I grab at my neck, realizing it is still gushing blood. Someone grabs my shoulders, yanking me away from my friend. I continue to scream at her, my heart hurting. She has to wake up. *She has to.*

"I didn't mean to." I cry, tears falling freely as I allow the pain to sink in. "She is my friend! I didn't know what I was doing! I didn't mean to! Please! She had a dagger! I got scared and something just exploded in me. It hurt so bad. It hurt me. I tried to push her, I tried to warn her. She had it so deep in my neck. She was going to kill me. You see that, don't you? I didn't mean to! I didn't mean to! She's my friend! Save her, save her, *save her*!" I am hysterical, my words chopped and frantic as I barely convey what truly happened. I don't even know who I am talking to, or if I am talking to anyone. I am being pulled back but no one answers my rambles. I dig my fingers into their arms, screaming for my friend. Where are they taking her? Why aren't they doing anything to help her?

"Calm down, Celeste! You need to hold still, you're losing a lot of blood!" Ryleigh screams over me as they drag me into the waiting room. I don't listen, thrashing around as the healer tries to hold me down. I don't care that I am bruised and losing too much blood. I don't want to be healed. They need to save Dove first and they need to take me to her.

"No! I have to see her! They have to fix her! I didn't mean it! I didn't mean it!" I cry as they bind my hands and feet, restricting me. "I don't know what happened, Ryleigh. Something came out of me. Something I can't control. I don't know what it was. It hurt so bad, Ryleigh. It was like pure ice in my veins. It just forced its way out! I couldn't stop it! It was an accident! You have to listen! You all do! I didn't mean it! It was an accident! It was an accident! I didn't mean it! She was my friend!" A rag is shoved into my mouth, silencing me. I try to scream but hardly any noise comes out. A healer begins sealing my wounds as Ryleigh holds me.

"I understand, Les. I understand." She soothes me, hands sliding over my hair as my wounds become nothing but small scars and yellow skin. "This isn't the first accidental death in the Games. You won't be punished if that's what you are concerned about. No one understands the depth of your powers or how they work. They can't punish you for not having control when you have only had these powers for a few months. They blame themselves for putting you in this situation. There's nothing to punish you for. The guilt will be enough punishment, I can promise you that. Now you have to compose yourself. Quickly. They are choosing within the next two hours. They want to distract the people from Dove's death. You have to be prepared." No one saw what I did or the dagger Dove held. They didn't see the *thing* that had infested me.

They unbound me once I had been still long enough, removing the rag from my mouth hesitantly. I breathe hard, trying to compose myself as Ryleigh instructed me to. But my mind still races, the only image in my head of Dove lying limply next to me. I can feel that heaviness, can smell the blood all over again. Though, that's probably because I'm still covered in it. They begin to escort me away, realizing I am calm enough to walk. They make sure no one sees my blood-soaked body, several guards circling me. I cry the whole way.

"Please let me drop out," I beg Ryleigh once we have entered my room, "I don't deserve this anymore. I have hurt so many people already and now? Now someone is dead because of me. I killed someone. My friend. One of my only friends. I don't deserve a crown."

"It was self-defense. Just like the other times." She tries to explain it away. Like the reason makes it any better. Like murder is justifiable in any circumstances.

"It isn't fair. The other women haven't *murdered* someone to win!" I argue.

"Suck it up and move along." Ryleigh hisses harshly, glaring at me. "Stop feeling sorry for yourself. I understand the severity of the situation. I do. But you are about to be crowned queen. Act like one. Get yourself together and get ready to fight again, just like you fought for your life in that arena. You are about to fight for Undivine lives now." I fall quiet, argument dying on my tongue. I let Ryleigh undress me in silence, shoving me into a tub of warm water. I sink underneath it, my whole body shaking as I prepare for the event I no longer want to be part of anymore. An event that will change my life and the lives that reside in the Lunar Court forevermore.

Chapter 18
The Choosing

"Welcome Celeste of the Lunar Court!" The crowd cheers, drowning out everything else the man is trying to say. I thought there would be less cheers, that they would see me for what I have become: a murderer. Instead, they cheer for Dove's death, praising me. It makes me sick.

I'm trying not to shake as I step forward, trying to hide the guilt and shame rolling through me in tidal waves. No one knows what happened because Dove's body had completely blocked mine. No one saw the dagger, no one saw how she died. The theory is that my shields reflected Dove's power, causing them to crash back into her own body. The force caused head trauma, along with the eye problem. That's the story being told and it's the story I have to stick with. So, as I step into this arena once more, I try not to think of the murder that just took place here. Try not to think about the screams that haunt this room like a ghost. I focus my thoughts on Kyelin, on the new life we will have together. I will get through this for him.

I put on my brightest smile as I look at the crowd of Divine, hoping it looks even remotely real. I coached myself for the full two hours before this. It took an hour and a half just to stop crying. I am still terrified, still ashamed. But what I feel doesn't matter right now. I have to put all that aside and do what is demanded of me.

The crowd roars even louder, calling my name over and over. My hair drifts in the wind, my dress gently swaying. They have opened the glass dome, allowing fresh air to come in. Allowing the breeze to take the smell of blood and death with it. My dress fits in perfectly, created for this dramatic and distracting entrance. They can't think about my victim if they are thinking about how beautiful I look, how queen-like. That's what Ryleigh said, anyway.

The dress is a deep purple, practically the color of the poison that escaped from within me mere hours ago. It's a harsh reminder of what I have done. It's giant, the thickest ballgown I have worn yet. It's soft on my newly bruised skin. The bruises that remain, anyway. The neckline is low, a perfect 'V' to show off what little cleavage I have. There are no sleeves, so the dress is only held by tape and luck. Sparkling jewels dance across the top, slowly fading down into the giant lower half. It makes me look like a princess and everyone here knows it.

I catch Kyelin's eye, winking in an attempt to show more confidence than I feel. Truly, I feel like an impostor standing before him. I am not the woman he knows. I'm not the woman *I* know. That stranger I saw in the mirror before? She has become so warped and twisted that I don't think 'stranger' can define her any longer. Is there a word for someone beyond that? Monster, maybe? Beast in Divine form? That is what I am now. He just doesn't know it yet.

I step onto the platform that now sits in the arena, taking my spot next to Silvi. I don't look at her as the crowd dies down, don't speak as I wait for the next announcement.

"Celeste. *Celeste*. Look at me, Celeste." Silvi hisses at me quietly. I ignore her, trying to block her out. I don't need to hear her tell me how horrible I am. I already know. I just need to get through this. I need to make it to the final announcement. Kyelin will call my name and everything will be okay. "I'm serious, Celeste. I need to tell you something."

"What do you want, Silvi? I'm not in the mood for your craziness today."

"I'm sorry."

"For what?" I scoff quietly. "There are a lot of things you should be sorry for. You are going to need to be a little more specific than that."

"For how I behaved. For what's about to happen."

"Oh? Are you going to throw me under the wagon again? How did that work out for you last time? Considering how I am standing next to you now, about to be crowned queen, I'm going to say *not well*."

"Celeste—"

"I'm done with this conversation, Silvi." Honestly, I don't have the energy to argue.

"Fine. I tried to warn you." I ignore this, too.

All five winners are lined up now. We face the crowd, watching as Prince Edge steps out from the Royal box. He approaches the wall of the box, rings glistening in the sun. I watch his gaze rake over us all, falling on me as he opens that wicked mouth.

"I'm glad to be able to witness such a tremendous occasion. I am very fortunate to receive advice from not one, but two kind gentlemen on how to navigate the Games. We have seen some horrible things today. Regrettable things. A precious life has been lost. But I'm sure we can all agree that the outcome will be worth the sacrifice. We fall upon hard times. The people have called for action, a call Kyelin and Zaeden took upon themselves to answer. I applaud them for their bravery and their sacrifice. The future of our Courts relies on these competitions and they don't always end well. We can't expect them to. We can't always have the happy ending we think we will get." I can barely breathe with the way Edge is looking at me now, like he is speaking to me personally. *Something's wrong, something's wrong, something's wrong.* "I'm glad to say that two special women will get their happy endings today, despite the horrors they have seen and endured. With that being said, I would like to turn things over to the future king of the Lunar Court. Kyelin?" The crowd cheers and applauds as the two men shake hands and switch positions. Kyelin smiles brightly to the crowd when he approaches and it takes a while for the noise to settle. My heart skips a beat as I watch him, begging him to look at me. To reassure me that this was worth it all.

He doesn't.

"I am overjoyed with our finalists. These are beautiful, talented, courageous women who have come from all corners of our lands to fight for a chance at love. These women are more than capable of being Royals and have proven so time and time again. Some of these ladies were born into this life and trained from birth. Others stumbled into our world, only to become one of the elite. That is the point of the Games, I think. To find an equal among such diversity. I am proud to stand before you all and announce the name of my future wife, your future queen. As well as the name of my brother's future wife, your future princess. We have gone through so much to get here, but it has been worth the heartache. As

Prince Edge stated before, there have been great tragedies on this day. But I can also agree that the outcome will be worth it all. I am honored to have him here and to be able to give him advice for his future competition. To receive his kind words and support in return. Just as I have received my people's support. You are all an essential part of this process, whether you realize it or not.

I am happy that this day has finally come, a day I have dreamed of for a very long time. My brother and I have fallen in love. We have found the women we are meant to spend the rest of our lives with. There is nothing more we could ever ask for, to cherish and be cherished. With that being said, it is time to announce our winners." My heart flutters and I smile brightly, knowing he will soon say my name. He will call for me and everyone will know about us. This will all be over.

"Silvi, Celeste. Please rise." We glance at each other, her face unreadable. I stand, knowing what is plastered on mine: joy, excitement, smugness. This is it. This is what I have fought so long and hard for the past three months. I can't stop grinning as Kyelin begins to speak again. Finally, *finally*.

"I tried to tell you." Silvi whispers, voice cracking in an almost sorrowful way.

"I proclaim Silvi Merkelly of the Solar Court the winner of this competition. Rise for the next queen of the Lunar Court!" My smile drops and my fluttering heart crashes to my stomach with the weight of a large stone. I stumble, clutching onto my chest like I can drag my aching heart back up. Like I can change what just happened. I will not be the next queen. I will be the next princess. I will be marrying Prince Zaeden.

Everything drowns out, screams and shouts from the happy crowd fading away. The banging drums disappear. Kyelin still won't look at me. Instead, he beams down at Silvi, her smile radiating. I don't understand. He told me he would pick me. We are in love. He had to have announced the wrong name. Surely, he must realize?

A tug on my shoulder awakens me, pulling me away. My eyes don't leave Kyelin. I know the crowd is still roaring, cheering for their soon-to-be Royals. But I can't hear them. I can hardly see Kyelin anymore, his face fading in and out of focus. He doesn't even look to see the betrayal I feel, the hurt in my eyes. I hardly breathe as I am dragged away, my powers bubbling under my skin. I'm such a fool.

I'm led back to my room, a prison I am never able to escape from. Ryleigh waits on me there, her arms pulling me into her chest. I drop to my knees in front of her, unable to shed any more tears. I had been crying for hours before the Choosing. There is nothing left inside me. Ryleigh drops next to me, keeping me wrapped in her comforting arms.

"It has to be a misunderstanding," I mutter, shaking my head, "He told me he would pick me. We are in love. We did the full moon ritual together last night. He told me he had never done that with anyone else before, that I was his first. We are bonded, him and I. He loves me. He would never pick her in his own volition. Never! And the plan! I was going to change everything! You trusted me to do that and I failed you. I'm so stupid! A damn fool!" I bury my face into her shoulder, shielding myself from her disappointment.

"It's okay." She shushes me, running her fingers through my hair comfortingly. "Don't worry about the plan. The backup plan worked. Now we have two people on the inside. You needn't worry about that." I freeze under her touch, understanding far too slowly what she means. Silvi was the backup plan? Silvi? Before I can think of how to respond, there is a loud knock on the door and Silvi herself is barging in as if summoned by her name. I scramble away from Ryleigh, looking between them in disgust. How could she do this to me?

"What happens now?" Silvi breathes, frantic.

"You leave." I snap, standing. "This is my room. I want you out. Now."

"This is more important than your hurt feelings." Silvi rolls her eyes, waving at me dismissively.

"He isn't in love with you. He told me he would pick me, you know? It wasn't supposed to be you. It was never you. This is all a big mistake."

"Please. I don't care about who he loves and you shouldn't either. It's not my fault you fell into the Royals trap. Things are serious now, so stay out of it. Let the adults talk, yeah?" She turns to Ryleigh, all hints of sarcasm evaporating. "I plan on marrying him as soon as possible. Hopefully in a few days. We can begin plans then."

"What? No way!" I screech. A few days? She can't seriously be planning to marry him that quickly?

"Stay out of this," Ryleigh repeats Silvi's words in a harsh growl, "I understand that you have been through far too much heartbreak and pain today, but this discussion does not involve you."

"Like hell it doesn't," I growl, but they ignore me.

"Marry him as soon as they let you, Silvi. We don't have time to make any errors. We will talk more about the specifics when we have more time. It will take time and patience to get plans started, but it will be done."

"This is why you made me watch her and report back to

you." It all clicks together like puzzle pieces. "To make sure she wasn't going to betray you. She acted like the other snobby High Divine, just like I expected her to. Like everyone did. All for what? Why would she care about the Undivine? Do you know, Silvi? Do you know how I spied on you for Ryleigh? That she didn't trust you?" I round on her, furious. I thought it was Dove. I thought she was the backup plan. But she wasn't anywhere near the plans. She was a sympathizer, but that was all she was. I have been so very wrong about *everything*.

"Yes, I did send you to spy on her. I was worried at first. She knows and we have talked about it. She has played her part well."

"As for my intentions." Silvi interrupts, glaring. "Look at my face. This is what happens when you are born into the Divine. How you are treated. We are brainwashed into thinking this is okay, that it is how things are and will always be. The Divine system is fucked up. We shouldn't be split up or at each other's throats for being born different from one another. The system needs to be destroyed." For a second, I plan on arguing. But I can see it in her eyes: passion. I can *feel* the truth.

"I'm going to speak to Kyelin," I state, pushing past them. I need to be anywhere but here. I need Kyelin. They try to protest, to grab me, but I am too fast. I am out of the door and past the awaiting soldiers in seconds.

It doesn't take long to reach his chambers. I know the shortcuts, know ways to avoid the soldiers. There are a few at his door that try to stop me, but I don't let them. I pound on the door, ignoring the hands nervously grabbing at me. Then I start screaming at the top of my lungs.

"Open this door right now, Kyelin! Open this door and face me you coward!"

Prince Zaeden is the one who answers my calls. He pulls me into the room with a scowl, glancing towards the soldiers. "Take a hike." They do as they are told.

"Don't look at your future wife that way. It's unbecoming." I snap. He doesn't laugh.

"Why are you here?"

"To speak to my future king. The man who is *supposed* to be my future husband. He has obviously made a mistake. Tell him to come out and face me. Don't be a coward, Kyelin!"

"There is no mistake, Celeste." Kyelin's voice is grave and harsh. It is like nothing I have ever heard from him before. I turn sharply, meeting his eyes. They are cold, tired, and weary. There is no hint of the flames I am accustomed to.

"What do you mean? You told me—"

"I told you it would be an easy choice, Celeste. And it is. But it isn't my choice to make. This competition was meant to gain the support of the Solar Court. If you had been born there, this whole situation would be much easier. But you weren't. The people love you. I love you. But this isn't about love and it never has been. When I found out you were Divine, I knew immediately what an asset you could be to us. Zaeden understood, too. So we used our Royal powers on you to help get you to this point. It took a lot of effort on our part to make this happen. Unfortunately, my duties as the future king overrule my duties as a lover. I'm so, so sorry I have to hurt you like this. But I can't marry you, Celeste."

"Royal powers? What does that mean? What powers have you been using on me?" I barely get out the words, my body practically frozen. He...he's been using *powers* on me this whole time?

"Shit. I thought you knew! I thought everyone knew...but

299

you wouldn't, would you? It's hard for me to remember that you weren't always Divine. I—"

"What powers," I scream hoarsely, tired of beating around the bush.

"Royals have the power of attraction. It...It's kind of like this little knob that we can turn up. The higher we turn it up, the more attracted to us you will be. So—well, we used it on you. To gain your trust and to help you adjust." My mind spins, my heart twisting painfully. This is why I was drawn to them so fast, why I fell in love so quickly. I thought it was strange, but I've never been in love. I didn't know how it felt. I thought that, maybe, it was meant to be fast and furious. I guess I was wrong about that.

"You used me," I whisper, "And you didn't even pick me after all of that work?"

"We can still be together, Celeste. Zaeden has agreed to let us be together in private. I have a plan! Can't you see? This is the only way for us to be together."

"I'm not being passed between the two of you like a ball." I hiss out in surprise, taken aback by his pleading tone. He expects me to be in *both* of their beds?

"You said you understood what comes with this position." He argues, becoming desperate.

"That was before I realized how in love with you I was!" I scream angrily, taking a step forward. "Why would I ever want to be with anyone other than you? Touch anyone other than you? And why would you let anyone else be with me? Do I mean so little to you? You are my world. At least, you were. Now I don't even know which of these feelings are mine and which ones you manufactured. Did last night mean nothing? You told me I was special. Told me that it was an easy decision to choose me. Are you a liar now?" My anger builds higher and higher and higher. There's a band inside me stretching farther and farther and it is about to *snap*.

"I never lied about that! It *would* have been an easy choice to pick you, Celeste. You are amazing, everything I could have asked for and more wrapped into one beautiful package. But I had to make a hard decision. I had to do what was right for our Court. Why can't you understand that we will still be together? That our love lives on? This isn't over. Zae said—"

"Zaeden doesn't own me!" I screech, band snapping. I slam my hands onto his chest, no longer fighting this anger within me. I have a right to be angry, after all. "I don't care what he says! What permission slip he gave you. I was supposed to be your *wife*! I was supposed to be yours and yours only! You don't love me. Or maybe you just don't love me enough. We will not be continuing this relationship. This will be the end of us, Kyelin. I love you, but I will never come second. I deserve more than that. And I'm not sure I can trust you anymore. I'm not sure if any of this was *real*." I want to strangle the stupidity out of him, to suck the life out of his body for hurting me in this way. I regret the thought immediately, but it doesn't matter. I had the thought. That is all it took.

The band that snapped in me is much more than anger. It unlocks something I did not know existed. I feel the rush as power soars into my hands, up my arms, and into my body. It hits me hard and I cry out in surprise. I try to take my hands off Kyelin, but I can't. It's like they are glued to his body, stuck against his chest. He looks down at them in a panic, trying to pry me off of him. He can't remove them, either. He tries to send his flames at me, but they die as soon as they are formed. That's what makes me understand. *His* power is the thing soaring inside of me. I am taking it. I am literally sucking the life out of him.

I try so hard to make it stop. Everything is so slow and so, so painful to watch. To feel. Prince Zaeden is screaming behind us, his poison reaching out for me. But I have unwittingly placed a shield up. Nothing is reaching us. No matter how hard they try, or I try, it isn't stopping. I scream at myself, fighting against it. I am going to kill him. I know I am. I can see the light leaving his eyes, the flames evaporating from his body. Our powers are our source. They are intertwined with our lives. If the power leaves, so do you.

Kyelin's whole body seems to decay in front of me. Everything is in slow motion, his death agonizing. I can feel that terror and pain the same way I felt Dove's. It breaks another part of me and twists my heart until it bleeds. One second he is there, begging me to stop. The next he is crumbling to ashes before me. I watched those ashes form, starting with the point of contact. His chest turned black and chalky first, spreading like a disease until every inch of his skin was covered. Even his clothes were changing, crackling like logs in a fireplace. That darkness began slowly fading into gray as it cracked, turning white in its final stages. His chest is what falls first, a large and gaping hole where my hands had just been. The rest of him follows soon after, floating around like dust on the wind. His eyes are the last thing I see, the fire that I am so familiar with gone forever. Instead, it is replaced with fear as he watches his body incinerate. He looked at me in those last moments, his regret and fear washing over me. And then he was nothing but a pile of ashes.

I scream at the sight as I stumble back, disgusted by the pile. Disgusted with myself. Prince Zaeden leaps forward, falling to his knees by the ashes. He gathers them in his hands, weeping. He screams in agony, and I know the sound is another thing that will haunt my dreams. Another memory from this day that I will never be able to atone for. Soldiers rush in now, confused. Only two stay near us, the other two searching the room for a threat. They don't realize that the threat is *me*. When Prince Zaeden looks up, hatred pooling in his eyes, I know what is truly lurking inside of him.

Death is finally coming for me, but it no longer wants me alone; it wants my pain, my suffering, my very *soul* torn to shreds. And maybe I deserve it.

In the beginning-

No.

I can't say 'in the beginning' because this is not the beginning. I can't say 'in the end' because, miraculously, it will not be my end. I can't say 'in the middle' because I do not believe I am anywhere near that place. So where am I?

This I do not know.

I know what just happened. I know it has not always been this way. I know I saw death, that I *caused* death. But why was it summoned? Did *I* do that?

Death inhabits Prince Zaeden because a piece of him lies in ashes on the floor. A small noise leaves my mouth and I try to smother it with my hand, trying to make it die, too. But that hopeless, desperate gaze is on me and I feel the change in the air. Watch the vulnerability wither and die right in front of my eyes. I feel the anger boiling to the surface, that torturous venom burning underneath his skin as it rises to the surface.

I shake my head, stumbling away from the ashes before me. How? How? *How?* I guess that doesn't matter though, does it? Because Prince Zaeden doesn't *care* that I am shocked, too.

That what just happened couldn't have been *me*. And I can not only see that, but I can *feel* it, too. So, I do the only thing I can think to do.

I run.

Chapter 19

The soldiers around here are *useless*.

That's what you get for hiring the very people you despise as protectors, I suppose.

I slip out of the room much too easily. The soldiers rushing in never glance at me and Prince Zaeden doesn't even look like he is *able* to speak. I am to be their princess, after all. Couldn't we have just had some kind of lovers quarrel?

I bolt down the hall, my panic rising into a crescendo. I can't think straight, my thoughts muddling together. I just killed a Royal. The future king. My lover. The weight of my guilt slams against my heart, screaming to be let in. I almost fall over at the intensity of it all, slipping into a hidden alcove to recover. I pant as I lean my back against the wall, clenching my eyes shut. With a growl, I bang my fists against it and lean back up. I can't stop. I have to keep going. I'll die if I don't figure out what to do and *fast*.

I pick up my pace again, darting down the steps. The farther I go, the more I begin to lose control. It slips from my grasp so easily, like the stars slipping away from the moon when they decide to come crashing down. It takes control, limb by limb. I can feel the warmth rising, the heat, the pressure, the *need* to be released. The power won't listen to me because I am not its master.

As I reach the bottom of the steps, I relinquish everything to that power within me. I scream, tumbling over as the heat burns me from the inside out. Then, I erupt in flames.

I try to crawl up, to throw shields around myself. But the shields trap me with the heat, the flames suffocating. I scream again, my panic over the fire greater than the panic of being caught. I can't lift myself to a standing position, can't even get to my knees. Everything within me is lost to the flames, to the power I was never supposed to have. The power I *stole*. It has a mind of its own and it seems all too aware of what I did to its master. It will not bow to me.

"Celeste." I hear the voice distantly. "Celeste, can you hear me?" I try to answer the calls but nothing comes out. My flames rise higher, acknowledging the person approaching. Warning them.

"Get Edge! Now! He knows where to meet us." A different voice, now. More authoritative. I am sure if I can gather a single thought I will recognize it. I will know who has come to witness my downfall. But everything is so, so muddled.

"Can you handle her? You don't know her as well as I do—"

"I told you to go. Don't question me. Ever." There is no reply but I can faintly hear footsteps echoing speedily away. "This might hurt." That is the only warning I am given.

Cold water hits me fast and hard, cooling my heated skin. I cry out as my flames are extinguished, the pain horrific. This power isn't meant to be put out by another. It is meant to be controlled by me, to obey me. The fact that another is taking control is what causes the excruciating pain and I try to retrieve the flames so I can stop *hurting*. They still won't listen. This is a power meant for a Royal. It knows I am not its master, that I am a new Divine. It knows and it is *angry*.

"Please," I beg, tears falling hard and fast. I spit out the water as it slams into me, desperate for relief. I'm not sure if the word escapes my lips or not. Maybe it lives on inside my head. Not that it matters. The water doesn't stop and the person in front of me never replies. I can't see through the thick flames, through the smoke surrounding us.

"Control this, Celeste! Control it!" I cry in response, my hands coming up to my face. I can't, I can't, I can't. This isn't my power to control. It's Kyelin's. I remember the way these same flames danced behind his eyes, the heat that lingered underneath his skin. I close my eyes, picturing the beautiful face I will never see again.

The flames finally dim, retreating into my body. I'm not sure if it understands that I mourn for him, too. Maybe the images of him calmed it. The water continues to slap against my skin, the excruciating pain dying out to a dull sting. I breathe out hard, wiping my tears angrily. I look up, wanting to thank my savior, but the words die on my lips. I knew it was a Divine, but it is a Divine I do not want to be around right now.

Princess Valaine Zorander.

A Royal.

"Get up." She commands, holding out her hand.

"Why are you here?" I breathe through the last bit of lingering pain, slipping her hand into mine. She pulls me up slowly, watching me wince.

"Did you hurt yourself when you fell? Are you able to walk?" She ignores my question.

"Just sore. Those flames...they aren't meant for me. They never were. But they *are* meant to be controlled by me, put

307

out by me. Water powers were not a great solution." I spit, even though I am secretly grateful.

"It was a quick one." She shrugs, turning to leave.

"It was a painful one." I hiss, following her lead. "Where are you going?"

"I'm getting you out of here. I don't know what happened, but the whole castle is in an uproar. I'm assuming it has something to do with you having fire powers all of a sudden?" She glances down at me, her heavy gaze unwavering.

"You assume correctly." I don't want her to know what I have done. The evil I have become.

"What did you do?" I suck in a breath, shaking my head. I'm not telling a *Royal* how I killed one of her own.

"Does it matter?"

"It will." She gives me a harsh look, eyes trailing over my freshly burnt and bruised body.

"I did something bad. Something very, very bad. They are going to kill me, princess. If I don't get out of this castle and away from this Court, they will kill me." I don't look at her face to see her reaction. I don't want to know what she thinks.

"Then we will get you out," she says simply. I'm not sure how to respond, so I don't. Would she still do this if she found out what I did? What I am capable of? I'm not sure what happened or how I was able to steal someone's powers. But I am scared of how easily it happened, of how easily I lost control. With one thought, his life had been mine to take and his powers mine to own.

"Val? Val, where are you?" I stop at the cold, drawling voice. He will know by now what happened. Now that I have become too much trouble, he will kill me.

Prince Edge rounds the corner, stepping out of the shadows.

I balk at the sight of him, fear racing through my twisted, broken heart. He seems relieved when he lays his eye on his sister and I see how quickly the expression leaves at the sight of *me*.

"Edge. Thank the goddesses you made it." Princess Valaine greets him, glancing back at me. "We have a problem."

"Yeah, we do. Do you know what she has done? The whole castle is locked down. I could hardly get away from the soldiers guarding my room. We have to get her out of here."

"You know what I've done and you still want to help me?" My voice cracks when I speak to him, my mind sifting through the memories of our violent encounter.

"You are much more valuable than you realize." Princess Valaine is the one to answer. "So, no matter what you have done, we will help."

"Do you want to tell her what you did?" Prince Edge growls, stepping closer. "The stupid, irresponsible, reckless thing you did?"

"I didn't mean to! I was supposed to marry him. I loved him. I *love* him. I would never—"

"But you did. And aren't you tired of that 'I didn't mean to' excuse? It's getting repetitive."

"But I did." I agree, ignoring the rest.

"What did you do?" She asks, spinning to me again. I close my eyes, wrapping my arms around myself in an attempt to hide my shaking body.

"I killed him," I whisper, the words barely leaving my lips. It's hard to admit to myself, much less to the two Royals in front of me. I killed him and he is gone and there is nothing I can do. Gone, gone, gone. It's a crack in my heart, in my body, in my soul. Why did I do it? Why did I do it? *Why,*

why, why? Nothing changes the outcome but the outcome changes everything. I am no longer Celeste, the soon-to-be Lunar Court princess. I am now Celeste the traitor, the thief, the murderer. None of those titles have the same ring to them. "I killed Kyelin."

"Shit."

"Yeah, shit. And now she has dragged us into this mess." Prince Edge's glare cuts me into a thousand tiny pieces.

"I have done no such thing! I don't even know why you are here. You owe me nothing." I scowl, confused. I am a traitor to the Lunar Court now, a traitor to all Royals. Are their lives worth mine? The answer is easy: no, no they are not.

"No, but you owe me." He waves around his hand, indicating the missing finger. I wince at the nub I left behind.

"You deserved that. You attacked me and took my hair, which I still don't know what you did with or why."

"Yeah? Does my finger grow back like your hair will? Ever think I had good reason to do that?" He steps forward, grabbing me by the arm.

"I don't want to go with you," I say stiffly, tugging away from his grip. He holds on tight, unwilling to let me go.

"What other choice do you have right now?"

"I've heard things about you. About your Court. I don't want any part of it."

"Do you want to know the things I have heard about you?" He grins, leaning down until I can feel his breath hitting my face. "I heard that I am not the first man you mutilated. Of course, he is missing a little more than I am. I've heard that you planned on getting a crown no matter what, even if it meant being the wife to one prince and the lover to the other. Do you want me to continue?" The words are cruel and bitter,

310

enticing me to bite back.

"Oh? Do you know what I have heard about you? About the people you torture, the Undivine you toy with? About how much of a sadist you are? I don't want to go to your Court. I know that's where you are going to send me. Being together on the same *planet* is already painful enough. Being in the same Court will be torturous. I don't want to be in a Court that takes lives so easily."

"Says the girl with multiple kills under her belt." He barks out a laugh, almost disbelieving.

"Those—"

"Let me guess, you didn't mean them? Yeah, so you've said."

"I'm not going."

"You are. Now come on and stop arguing with me before you get us killed. You are lucky you know these hidden halls so well." He pulls me along and I follow begrudgingly. He is right. What choice do I have? I hate this man and I have taken something valuable from him as proof. I am sure he feels the same hatred for me. Yet, here I am, following him out of the familiarity of the castle and the comfort of my Court. With another crash in my heart, I realize what else I am leaving behind.

"Where is my sister?" I tug on his arm to get his attention.

"We are taking care of your sister. Well, Ryleigh is, anyways. They are meeting us at the drop-off point." Princess Valaine glances at me, nodding. The knot in my stomach relaxes if only slightly.

"Drop off point? Are you two not coming?"

"No, we can't just leave. We are Royals, Celeste. We can't be associated with you or what you did. We are taking a huge risk bringing you to our Court. A monumental risk. To be

311

honest, I'm not sure what we are going to do with you once we get you there." We have reached the hidden exit at the back of the castle, the streets of the city within reach. Prince Edge is suddenly thrusting something into my hands, the soft fabric surprising me.

"What is this?"

"A cloak. Put it on." I watch as he flings his own cloak over his body, his face covered by the darkness it brings. I swiftly sweep mine on, drawing the hood tightly over my head.

"This is where I leave you," Princess Valaine speaks, opening the door just a smidgen. She pokes her head out to look left and right, nodding before slipping out. I hear her shouting, claiming she saw a blond girl heading to the north.

"That's our signal." Prince Edge mutters bitterly, grabbing my hand once more and pulling me into the open. We run in the opposite direction, finding ourselves under the cover of the city fairly quickly. I hear whispers as we pass, the Divine questioning one another. They are everywhere. There are even some Undivine present, drawn out by the Divine crowding the castle. We slip by them as quietly as we can, not trying to draw any unwanted attention.

"I heard someone was murdered." A hushed voice speaks as we pass.

"Not just someone! A prince!" Another hisses back.

I squeeze my eyes shut tightly, drowning out the voices. Just the simple whispers of the murder make my skin warm. Maybe the power is showing sorrow for its previous owner. Maybe it is trying to hurt me for what I did. I deserve it, if that's the case. *I deserve it, I deserve it, I deserve it.*

"Calm down." The prince snaps, fingers tightening around my own. "We don't need you flaming up in the middle of the streets." My eyes snap open and I realize how hot my skin has become. Little embers spark along my skin, prickling us both. Surely this is hurting him?

"I'm sorry," I reply, truly meaning it, "I can't control it."

"Obviously."

"I need you to lose the attitude, okay? You chose to help me. I don't even know what you get out of this. What use could I possibly be to you?"

"You don't know what you are, do you?" He chuckles, pulling me past a Divine couple making out in the alley.

"What do you mean? I've been told already I am High Divine. I know what I am. As hard as it is to accept that, I do acknowledge it. I've been trying to embrace it."

"I'm not talking about being High Divine." He doesn't clarify what he means.

"Then what are you talking about? I'm so sick of all the secrets." I snap back, annoyed.

"You, my dear, are on Absorbid."

"A what? What does that even mean? You definitely just made that word up."

"It is very rare, but not made up. Think about the primary word in there—*absorb*—and think back to your little murder fest earlier to put two and two together. You are something incredibly unique and special. And they let you fall right through the cracks. These imbecile Lunars have no idea the power they let slip right through their hands." He cackles, chest heaving.

"I don't under—"

"We are here." He interrupts, glancing around. We walk a full circle around the small building we have approached, his eye scanning for any signs that we have been followed.

Once we made the full loop, he seemed satisfied there was no danger. He knocks on the back door three times, glancing down at me in disdain before adding a fourth knock. The door swings open and I am yanked into darkness.

A flame appears before us, lighting the room. And there is my sister, fear and worry written all over her face. Ryleigh stands next to her, a fierceness in her eyes. My own eyes tear up as I take in Irissa's state. She is controlling the wings and talons, both hidden underneath her skin. There is a scratch on her cheek but it isn't deep. She is okay. She is really, truly okay.

I sigh in relief, pulling her to me. "Irissa."

"Celeste." A tear hits my shoulder, then another. I shush her, pulling away to wipe the tears.

"No time. There's no time." I whisper.

"I know. But there will be." Her smile lifts my spirits, encouraging me. I nod, turning to Ryleigh.

"What's the plan?" I try not to think about the lies Ryleigh has been feeding me for months, about how the two Royals she warned me of are now saving me. She must have known they weren't as bad as everyone makes them out to be. And she lied to me anyway. I'm not sure I can handle falling down this rabbit hole. Not that it matters right now. I have been trusting her for years before this and I have no choice but to continue in that trust.

"There is a wagon outside heading for the Solar Court. It is full of food and all the other supplies you will need. You will hide inside until you reach the Solar Court. It will take you directly to their castle. I have someone on the inside who will take you to a hidden location within their castle. All three of us will be there within a month of your arrival."

"A month? We have to hide for a month all on our own? Without anyone we know?"

"It's nothing we can't handle," Irissa whispers, a hand reaching out to touch my cheek. I glance at her, unsure.

"Whatever we have to do." I sigh eventually.

"Good. Because you don't have a choice." Prince Edge spits out, looking toward the door and listening.

"They're here," Ryleigh says.

"Draw your hood, Iris," I tell my sister with a sigh. She follows my instructions, covering her face with the dark fabric. He opens the door, glancing around before leading us out. We approach the wagon cautiously, Prince Edge taking the lead.

"Ho, Celeste." The driver says cheerfully. It's my old friend Darius!

"Ho, Darius!" I grin, happier than I should be in this situation.

"Get in." The prince snaps impatiently, flexing his fingers. I wince at the purposeful reminder. Irissa and I carefully climb in, sitting as close together as possible.

"Cover yourself with those sheets until you are out of this Court. Here. I have two sleeping droughts. You will sleep like the dead if you take one of these. You will need the break from your mind tonight." Ryleigh tells us. I gulp, nodding as I lift a hand to grab the droughts.

"I will see you soon." Prince Edge mutters, looking into my eyes. "You will be safe in my Court. I swear it." I'm not sure what to say, so I don't reply. The wagon begins moving, horses slowly trotting away. I watch him for a long moment, unable to break contact. He finally turns away, breaking it for me.

"Les?" Irissa is holding up a sheet, asking me to cover myself.

315

I nod, ducking underneath. We lay down next to each other, hands curling together.

"I'm sorry. I'm so sorry." I whisper in despair. This is all my fault. My fault, my fault, my fault. I close my eyes as the wagon rattles along, holding my sister's hand tightly.

When I open them again, I have decided who I will become for her. What has to be done. I will do whatever it takes to ensure she is safe and gets the happy life she deserves, even if it means playing a part in a game I don't understand.

"I'm ready for a drought," I say.

"Me too."

"Alright, then. Here you go. To death." I clink my vial against hers and swallow in one gulp.

And so I die.

The darkness is comforting. I like the warm embrace, like an old friend or a lost lover come to claim me at last. It is better than any feeling I have ever had. Calms me like nothing else ever will.

I think I want to stay in this dark place as long as I can.

Because as long as I am here I don't have to acknowledge what I am about to become: a cruel Divine seeking refuge in an even crueler Court.

Side Note

First and foremost I would like to thank you for making it this far! I have had this book sitting in my drafts for three years before deciding to pick it back up. I tried to publish Royally Divine immediately after finishing (a rookie mistake) and quickly realized that I was no where near done. It took me a little while but I am finally happy with the outcome and I hope you are too! And don't worry, there's another book on the way.

About the Author

M.N. Lash, despite having a bachelors degree in biology and minors in chemistry/psychology, is a stay-at-home mom from Alabama. When she isn't reading or writing you can find her crocheting or attending to her many pets. Royally Divine is her first book. You can find her on Instagram for updates on future works @m.n._lash